The Eye
of the Mirror

by
Liana Badr

translated by
Samira Kawar

THE EYE OF THE MIRROR
A Modern Arabic Novel from Palestine

Published by
Garnet Publishing Limited
8 Southern Court
South Street
Reading
RG1 4QS
UK
www.garnetpublishing.co.uk

Second English Edition.
First published in Arabic as *'Ain al-Mir'ah* by
Tubqal Publishing House, Morocco.

ISBN-13: 978-1-85964-201-6

British Library Cataloguing-in-Publication Data
A catalogue record for this book is available from the British Library.

Typeset by Sarah Golden.
Edited by Anna Watson.
Jacket design by Cooper-Wilson.
Cover illustration by Peter Hay.

Printed by Edwards Brothers, USA.

Introduction

❧⊙⊙⊱

The Eye of the Mirror is an epic novel set during the 1975–6 siege and subsequent massacre at the Tal el-Zaatar Palestinian refugee camp in Lebanon. The siege of the camp, in the area of Beirut controlled by the Christian militias, drew the Palestinians into the battle. This was one of the bloodiest incidents of the civil war, and has given great symbolic importance to Tal el-Zaater (or Tal Ezza'tar, in the Palestinian pronunciation). In 1976 this 'Stalingrad' of the Palestinian refugees fell, 'there were about 4,000 casualties and some 12,000 Palestinians fled to other parts of Lebanon. What remained of the camp was razed.'[1]

Faced with mass destruction and systematic annihilation Liana Badr, a Palestinian writer, has held on to the threads of a narrative weaving through the chaos. As a journalist in Beirut she witnessed how Tal el-Zaatar stood firm for a year despite being completely cut off from supplies, ammunition, water and food. After witnessing the destruction of other Palestinian camps in Lebanon, including Sabra and Shatila in 1984, she returned to document Tal el-Zaatar. She spent seven years collecting documents on the daily lives of the camp's inhabitants and interviewing survivors for eye-witness testimonies. The historical accuracy of the novel's setting is a powerful force in driving the story to its conclusions. What is left to her and other women writers is to create narratives and write an alternative history. The writer feels strongly about documenting and preserving this part of Palestinian history in the collective memory of the Arabs and the wider world. Liana Badr records this chapter of her people's struggle in order to possess it, preserve it and exorcise it.

Right from the beginning Liana Badr allies herself with Scheherezade. She tells stories not to save her own life but to ward off evil and death from her people. In an attempt to defy death and forgetfulness she re-creates history through the lives of her imaginary characters. But unlike Scheherezade she cannot hop from one story to another, from one country to another. She distances herself further from the fairy tales of *A Thousand and One Nights*, saying to herself "Yet you know that I am not Scheherezade, and that one of the world's greatest wonders is that I am unable to enter my country."

Liana Badr can be considered a Beirut Decentrist,[2] who writes of the dailiness of war. Women of the camp, and the camp itself, come out of the novel triumphant and defiant. Despite the continuous bombardment of shells they knead the dough and bake bread, under threat of sniper fire they fetch water, they feed their children, nurse the wounded and try to keep their families together. These simple and apolitical acts sustain the besieged camp for an entire year. They have no say in the political decisions made by men, but they dutifully pick up the pieces and try to normalize their lives. Survival becomes the ability to brew some tea and drink it with your friends and neighbours.

Aisha, the beleaguered central character, represents many Palestinians in Lebanon at that time. She works as a maid in a convent school, where her cleaning is exchanged for an education. She is acceptable to the Lebanese as long as she remains in her designated position, does not step out of her class and adopts their culture and religion. This tension in the Palestinians' position could not be avoided indefinitely and the trigger to the start of the conflict is generally agreed to have been the killing of a bus-load of Palestinians by Christian militiamen in April 1975. After that massacre it was no longer possible to live in a grey area between Christian and Muslim.

Aisha is taken out of the convent in complete silence. She walks with her family back to the camp in silence. Taking her away from the convent marks the end of the state of artificial tolerance – the silence which preceded the civil war in Lebanon. Arriving back at her home in Tal el-Zaatar, Aisha's father takes away the crucifix given to her by the nuns and forces her to re-embrace her Muslim identity.

Aisha's father, Assayed, has strong ideas about what Aisha's life and behaviour should be, but he himself is defeated in other areas of his life. Since leaving Palestine in 1948 he has moved from one refugee camp to the next. Defeated at a military and political level, he has nowhere to exert his authority except in the domestic sphere, where he tries to keep the women under tight control. This alcoholic father, who tries to live peacefully with his Christian friends, is claimed by the very civil war which he neither supports nor acknowledges.

As she grows from a girl to a woman Aisha's conflict with her father intensifies and the threat of physical violence from him increases. Despite his domination of Aisha, it is her consciousness which remains the focus of the novel. Her weakness, fear, confusion and the semi-imprisoned life she leads reflect the double alienation she suffers. She is marginalized as a young girl in a society with very fixed definitions of what womanhood entails, and also as a Palestinian who is homeless and whose entire nation has been displaced.[3] Together with most of the other women, Aisha lives in a state of confinement in the private space within the male-dominated camp.

Within the poverty and desolation of the refugee camp, hope is born when Aisha falls in love with one of the guerilla fighters. His *nom de guerre* is George but his real name is Ahmad – another reference to the confusion of religious identities. Aisha suffers her passionate love in silence and is even drawn into the arrangements for George's impending marriage to Hana, a radio operator in the camp. Hana is the exception to every rule, the antithesis of Aisha. She is loud and outspoken, works in the resistance and even exchanges obscene insults with her enemies over the radio. Through the fictional stories of Aisha and Hana, and their families and colleagues, the real history of Tal el-Zaatar is brought to life.

When the siege of the camp begins, the writer temporarily sets aside the narrative lines to focus on the realism in the setting of this novel. For a disconcerting moment the author, as a journalist working in Beirut, enters the camp and the book itself. Before going on to describe the horrors of the evacuation and the massacre, she throws us this vivid reminder that although her characters may be fictional, their fates typify those of the inhabitants of the camp. Some of the scenes are so horrific that the reader is left wondering how the inhabitants survived. And in some cases we are left uncertain as to the fate of characters we have come to care about, an uncertainty which reflects reality for many Palestinian families who for years after this massacre searched for loved ones who may have been killed or abducted or simply off fighting elsewhere. Liana Badr comments on the resourcefulness of her people in these atrocious conditions by saying that, "I hoped to recreate some of what violence and death had destroyed, just as raindrops gather in a well, just as the thyme plant, Zaatar, sprouts from rocky crevices to grow over barren hillsides." [4]

To describe the lives of the people in the camp, Badr draws on the rich oral tradition of Arab culture. The voices of women, which frequently cannot be distinguished from one another, are written in colloquial Palestinian. Badr's awareness of the literary heritage of the Arabian Nights, the Quran and numerous folk tales is evident through-out the novel. In the past Arab women writers have used the formal style of Arabic, Fusha, to prove their linguistic credentials to the literary establishment. The writers in this series have made a clear departure from this previous pattern in order to be true to women's social, religious and sexual experiences. From oral testimonies, newspaper accounts, folk tales, songs and radio broadcasts Badr has brought the camp back to life. "From girls to women to old men to fighters, in whose imaginations the beginning of the tale survived . . . the words flew; images were formed; songs were recited and proverbs remembered. Then the horror flooded in." [5]

Despite the defeat, horror and destruction, the setting of this novel emerges triumphant like a tragic hero immortalized through narrative. "We shall not forget," is written between each and every line. Aisha, who remains silent throughout the bombardment and fighting, survives to see another day for the Palestinian people. Through her suffering she gains self-esteem and awareness; she literally finds her voice. She slowly takes control of her life, confirming that freedom for women is an essential precondition for social and political freedom in Arab countries.

Arab women are generally treated as a minority in most Arab countries. They feel invisible, misrepresented and reduced. Perceived as second-rate natives, they are subjected to a peculiar kind of internal orientalism. Native men assume a superior position to women, misrepresent them and in most cases fail to see them. This parallels the orientalist attitudes with which westerners have treated the Arab world for so long. To most westerners Arab women are effectively hidden behind a double veil of gender and culture.

To redress the lack of interaction with Arab culture, the Arab Women Writers series was started. This series hopes to open a window on the walled garden where Arab women's alternative stories are being told. Out of this private space Arab women sing their tales from countries which still, to a great extent, treat them as second-class citizens. Women writers in this series create a different language where the patriarch is lampooned and ridiculed, and where women's daily experiences and oral culture are placed at the centre of the discourse. Rejecting the standard perceptions about masculine and feminine language these women writers have created a third space within the language from which they can question a culture which has been based on exclusion, division and misrepresentation of women's experiences.

Translation is an act of negotiation. "A translator's job is like buying a carpet in an oriental bazaar. The merchant asks 100, you offer 10, and eventually you agree on 50." [6] This delicate balancing act entails being faithful to the spirit of the Arabic text while presenting a fluid text for the English-language readers. The translator becomes a kind of double agent with divided loyalties, and this task is further complicated by the consciously colloquial language used by Liana Badr. In English, where colloquial language is more commonly used in novels, the impact of the informal language does not have same implications. This translation is both idiomatic in English and also faithful to the full power of the original text. Samira Kawar has a great personal understanding of the situation in the Palestinian refugee camps, stemming from her own experiences as a journalist in Beirut during the period in which this novel is set. Reporting for radio, television and newspapers such as the Washington Post, in 1983 she also interviewed survivors of the Sabra and Shatila camps whose experiences were very similar to the Tal el-Zaatar siege and massacre.

I now invite you to open the pages of this novel and to the experiences of Arab women. This book is part of a secular project, challenging the assumptions of a patriarchal and often violent culture and also setting out to counter westerners' stereotypical images of Arab women's lives, thoughts and feelings. As you lift this double veil you will see the colourful and resilient writings of Arab women, and hear their clear voices singing their survival.

Fadia Faqir
Durham, 1995

1   David C. Gordon, *The Republic of Lebanon: A Nation in Jeopardy*, p. 92, Westview Press, Boulder, Colorado, 1983.
2   Miriam Cooke, *War's other Voices: Women Writers on the Lebanese Civil War*, Cambridge Universtiy Press, Cambridge, 1988.
3   Rashida Ben Masaud, 'Riwayat Ain al-Mir'ah aw Sirat Schahrazad al-Zaman al-Filastini', *Al-Jadid* magazine, April 1993.
4   This and other quotations from the author are taken from *In the House of Silence: Conditions of Arab Women's Narratives*, Fadia Faqir, ed., a forthcoming collection of testimonies to be published by Garnet Publishing to complement this series.
5   Ibid.
6   Umberto Eco, 'A Rose by Any Other Name', in *Guardian Weekly*, 16 January 1994.

Glossary

❦

Abu Ammar: Yasser Arafat's *nom de guerre* and the name by which he was most commonly known in the Arab world.

Ahrar: a rightist Christian group founded by Camille Chamoun. Together with the Phalangists and the Guardians of the Cedars, they formed a coalition of Christian militias which fought the Joint Forces during the first part of the civil war. The Christian militias were also known as the Isolationists. The Phalangists later turned on the Ahrar and annihilated them.

Al-Barq Al-Arabi: a fictional group made up by the author as a reference to several actual groups which had been created by Arab regimes and were active within the PLO to further the interests of those regimes and sabotage the PLO from within.

Al-Rajfa cup: a special cup which people who tremble because they are afflicted with evil spirits drink from in order to be cured.

Ala Dal'ouna: a refrain with which several popular ballads and folk songs begin to set the rhyme.

Amti: a title meaning aunt, used to address the sister of one's father.

Arab Deterrent Forces: a contingent of about 40,000 soldiers, mostly Syrian, who entered Lebanon in 1976 mandated by an Arab summit conference with the declared aim of keeping the warring sides apart.

arak: an alcoholic drink made out of Anise.

Arghoul: musical wind instrument related to the clarinet, consisting of two pipes of equal length.

Bint Jbeil: a coastal town in southern Lebanon.

Culpac: a circular fur hat.

Dastour: an exclamation equivalent to bless you, which is said to soothe someone who is badly startled.

Deir Yassin: on 10 April 1948, members of the Zionist Irgun and Stern gangs massacred 254 Palestinian civilians in their village of Deir Yassin.

Deuxième Bureau: the Lebanese internal secret service depatment.

Feda'ee (sing.) *Fedayeen* (pl.): Palestinian resistance fighters who were members of the various PLO factions were called *Fedayeen*, Arabic for 'those who give their lives for others'.

Haganah: a Jewish militia in pre-1948 Palestine, later giving rise to the Israeli army.

Hajjeh: a Muslim lady, usually elderly, who has been on pilgrimage to Mecca. The title is often used when addressing elderly women, irrespective of whether they have actually done the pilgrimage.

Inqath Army: a joint force from Egypt, Jordan and Syria which entered Palestine in 1948 to try to save it from falling.

Jemayel, Pierre: the late founder and leader of the Lebanese Phalangist party, mostly made up of Maronite Christians.

Joint Forces: a coalition which fought the Phalange-led Christian forces during the Lebanese civil war. It was made up of the various PLO militias and leftist, nationalist Lebanese militias such as the one belonging to the Progressive Socialist Party of the late Druze leader Kamal Jumblatt. The Joint Forces are also referred to as the Nationalists.

Khalti: a title meaning aunt, used to address the sister of one's mother.

Khawajah: a title usually used to address or refer to westerners or westernized Christian Arabs.

Knafeh: a sweet dish made with unsalted white cheese, very thin brown or orange-coloured dough noodles and syrup.

Kubbeh discs: Fried oval disks of meat and cracked wheat stuffed with pre-cooked spiced minced meat, onions and pine kernels.

Labaneh: strained yoghurt, usually made from goat's milk. It is more solid than yoghurt and is popular in the levant as a sandwich spread.

Mamoul cakes: semolina cakes stuffed with ground walnuts, spices and sugar, then sprinkled with fine sugar after they are oven-baked.

Mezza: a collection of appetizers to be consumed with alcoholic drinks, usually arak.

Mijwez: musical wind instrument with a double pipe.

Mujaddarah: a dish made of lentils and rice with olive oil, cumin and onions.

Muloukhiyah: a leafy vegetable resembling spinach, also known as Jew's mallow.

Safarbarlek: a Turkish word referring to the way in which the ruling Turks conscripted Palestinian, Lebanese and Syrian men, mostly against their wills, to fight for them abroad during the First World War.

Sha'rawiya and *Shamaliya* dances: traditional Palestinian folk dances performed by groups of young men or young women or both, usually to rhythmic folk songs.

The Organization: the PLO itself, which was made up of three major political factions and their armed militias: Fatah, the Popular Front for the Liberation of Palestine and the Democratic Front for the Liberation of Palestine, as well as several smaller, minor factions. The factions themselves are also referred to as organizations.

UNRWA: United Nations Relief and Works Agency for Palestinian Refugees.

Ustath: a title meaning teacher, lawyer or someone who is learned.

Ya Ein Ya Leil: a refrain from a song. Referring to someone singing it can also signify that the person is blissfully indifferent to the surrounding dire circumstances and not lifting a finger to change them.

Yaba: a colloquial Palestinian word used for addressing one's father.

Yamma: a colloquial Palestinian word for addressing one's mother. Sometimes, mothers use it to address their children. It is also used by older women when addressing youngsters who are young enough to be their children.

Dedication

To those who have offered me their words and voices.
And those who spent hours telling me what befell them.
And to him, who never knew how the tale began.

The same old longing will make its claim on me, will it not?

And I will go back to sleep, pulling the quilt over my body and wrapping myself in the covers. I will hide so that you won't see me any more, disappearing beneath a tent of drowsiness . . . far away from the springs of consciousness.

I run away from you, falling asleep again, although the morning is crystalline and the sun shines radiantly outside. If only you had asked for something else less burdensome and not as wearying. Something light, charming, amusing and transient like drinking tea in a café, or a joke or an anecdote.

You are insistent, calling again. You want me to tell you the story of Scheherazade, who rocks the sad king on her knees as she sings him tales from wonderland. Yet you know that I am not Scheherazade, and that one of the world's greatest wonders is that I am unable to enter my country or pass through the regions around it. Do not be surprised. Let us count them country by country.

Strange, is it not?

As strange as your request to me and my promise to you. I made that promise, to tell you a love story, without realizing what it would cost me.

A deep, profound love; joyous; filled with laughter, dancing and weeping; rational; crazy; impulsive; balanced; beautiful; endearing, realistic, and also mythical.

A love story made of golden miniatures, silver etchings and the clay of tales. Made of letters and words.

I collect my thoughts and rummage through the corners of my memory for the remains of tales, for the ends of words and scraps of stories. You may like them, or you may not. They might stream forth, flow, pour down and multiply, sweeping away anything in their path like a flood, hatching like yeast into thousands of beings.

I begin with the tale of a girl or a woman. I tell perhaps of you and I, or of women and men whom I have never met. I tell of an alley, a street, a neighbourhood or a city. Or perhaps of a camp, of a camp, of a Tal! Tal Ezza'tar for example . . . Now you shake your head reproachfully again, fearful that the story will turn into political rhetoric like the slogans we've become weary of. Your eyelids bat mockingly in my face, hinting it is necessary to reassure you that what you fear will not happen. But I am compelled to begin with Ezza'tar, Tal Ezza'tar in particular, not only because of its poetic name, but for many reasons which I am under no obligation to reveal now.

I must begin my words exactly from there, although the heroine will not win your admiration because of a flaw in her basic attributes. For she is human – we are all human in the end. The flaw causes her qualities to be either excessive, or below the normally required average. She is educated yet ignorant, common yet possessing aristocratic pride, more imaginative than necessary, unbearably idealistic and indescribably stupid. She believes herself to be better than others, yet she is besotted by confused mystical thoughts which have sensuous emotional roots. And she is . . .

But here I am enjoying the narrative for you . . . so why allow my conversation to drag on?

1

꧁꧂

The three of them walked, with short rhythmic footsteps along the dirt track leading up to the school. The engine of the Mercedes taxi rumbled in the background, and the chirping of the birds hiding in the willows and palm trees near the wall assailed their ears.

The three of them walked up to the black iron door, and the mother raised her right hand towards the doorbell and pressed it for a long time. The mother – a short, plump figure in a synthetic navy blue dress, its pleats gathered untidily at the waist betraying the cheapness of its fabric, her hair, tied back with a scarf running down her back in two folds. The little girl, holding her mother's left hand, stepped forward. She cut a slender figure in wide, purple slacks, an old red t-shirt and plastic shoes. The boy with closely-cropped hair, wearing a khaki suit at variance with his slightly-built body and his seven years of age, stepped forward with her.

The three of them.

The mother pressed, and the bell rang, letting out a weak, remote ring as though it were inside a huge mountain. A silence of suppressed reverberations descended on everything. The leaves stopped rustling, and the protrusions on the high wall stood out like the ruins of a mythical castle deserted by humans many ages ago. The long quiet, insistent ringing came to a sudden end, and was followed by a resounding emptiness. It seemed that everything had stopped murmuring and moving, no longer emitting hidden sounds like invisible radiation. Even the birds buried in the rustling leaves on the old trees stopped chirping, or so it seemed at that moment.

A small square window in the black iron gate opened. Through its crossed bars appeared the face of a nun, a pink mass emerging from black folds. Without making an effort to speak, she raised her palm and lowered her fingers as though drawing down a thread, signalling them to wait.

The three of them froze as if someone had poured a magic glue over them: the mother with her heavy-moving limbs which reflected ill-health and malnutrition; the girl with a trace of mischief etched into her black eyes; and the boy, with his close-shaven head and his expression of sad dignity – an expression that resembled a man's and was in stark contrast to his alertness and agility.

The three of them stood still.

Or time stood still as they waited.

Five minutes or more.

Half an hour or less.

The pink mass of flesh emerged again, without expression or words. The leaf of the door swung silently back without so much as a squeak, its easy movement belying its massive weight. A young girl stepped out onto the road. She was wearing a pink dress and carrying a bag. The door returned to its former position, and the young girl froze. The other three moved towards her as a fresh breeze carries a ship towards the shore. The girl in the pink dress held on tighter to her bag, and her dark pigtails stretched down her shoulders, twitching nervously like the widened pupils of her dark eyes. The mother stretched out her thick hands and pulled the young girl towards her, wrapping her arms around her and embracing her. She kissed her on both cheeks with great affection, and the girl shivered involuntarily as though the plump woman's perspiration had increased her apprehensiveness.

The mother said, "Let's go."

The younger girl jumped up and pinched her older sister in the waist. The pain sank deep into her flesh, but Aisha did not shout, biting her lower lip instead. The boy sprang forward, jumping and uttering sudden wailing yells as though he were receiving violent unexpected slaps to his face. The boy ran and yelled. The girl jumped and stretched out her hand as she pursued the boy and tried to catch him. The mother enclosed Aisha's hand in hers and surveyed her with admiration until her emotions turned into a light, watery ghost that glistened in her eyes, catching the last rays of the sun setting over East Beirut.

The woman repeated her phrase in a voice thickened by chronic hyperthyroidism and oversmoking the cheap cigarettes that were burning out her lungs: "Let's go."

The noise of the cars in the adjacent street became audible once more. The hubbub of human beings and the clamour of their movement in their homes and shops could be heard; and the sharp chirping of birds bloomed anew amongst the branches of the palms and willows.

They walked, the four of them this time.

From that day on, Aisha longed for the classrooms and their worn-out wooden benches, for the girls, for the garden, and for the kitchen. She missed the fragrance of ambergris soap which permeated the school and its long corridors. She even missed the icy, delicate voices of women singing hymns on feast days. She would rush to her bag, hidden under the only bed in the house, open it and take out the veil she used to drape over her head to visit the church. She would sniff the rough piece of cloth as though it were a fragrant patch of violets slowly wilting before her very eyes.

Over there, games would stretch across the red arc of the aurora at sunset, running with the sound of the girls' laughter in the playground. There, she would do her chores. Once she had finished them and her lessons, no one would keep her from the skipping rope or flying in the swing to the farthest possible limit in the transparent air. She would skip over the rope and chant: "*shabara, qamara, shams, injoom*; hairband, moon, sun, stars." Skipping would take her upwards to become a velvet hairband or a moon floating in the heavens, or maybe even a sun or a star. As she jumped, her heart would jerk with the excitement of the slow, musical movement as it coursed through her blood. The cypress trees surrounding the playground would sway, jumping with her upwards and downwards. The shining blue sky would swing, first to the right, then to the left. The wooden benches planted in the playground would move, walking amongst the flower and cactus beds. The ground on which the girls stood would sway, going up and down like scales sliding to either side of her. And Aisha was fond of her classmates.

She would forget everything that bothered her about them. Things would be very different when she would wake up before them. She would rise in the calm dawn, put on her clothes, wash her face and comb her hair. She would drop by a side room beneath the stairs leading to the first floor, pushing open its wooden door to reveal brooms, mops and metal buckets. She would take the cleaning implements and roam the rooms and corners. The girls would go to the washrooms and bathrooms, leaving a hellish chaos in their wake. Aisha would enter the rooms one by one. She would throw open the windows and the shutters, and make the beds, tidying the blankets left in piles on the sheets. She would smooth out the pillows and beat them rhythmically to even out the cotton inside them. Then she would put away in the cupboards the clothes left lying everywhere. The girls would return to their rooms and not find Aisha, but they would detect her trace. They would call her and joke with her, playfully slapping her shoulder or the back of her neck when she passed them: "Aisha, ma cheri." They would talk to her with noticeable tenderness, the way they would address their nannies at home, or the way they would praise a creature whom they all agreed was quite unique. They would admire her ability to put up with hard work, and with tidying up static, depressing things. They would wonder how she could sweep lightly and daintily without twisting the discs in her back as she bent. Oh! How could she touch the ice-cold water that could cut glass like a saw without shivering?

They would ask her, but she would not respond because the nuns had taught her that it was best for her not to talk and not to try to mix with the daughters of influential families. Names that the girls would rattle off all the time. Names that would come up in the nuns' conversations and gossip as they had breakfast at their round table. The news of the families. Their marriages, their divorces and their feuds would turn into something akin to the pieces of cake which the mother superior dipped in her tea as news rolled off their white lips in quick mutters. And for the one thousandth and tenth or twentieth time, the nuns would say to her whenever they noticed she was lurking close to them: "Aisha, you work here and you also learn here. Do not talk to the girls. Do not repeat what you have heard."

Aisha did not talk. She would turn her back, carrying her wet cloth to a remote spot in the tiled dining-room, automatically distancing herself as she had done for seven years, during which she had become used to her surroundings. The school. The occasional scolding of the nuns. The mysterious anxiety of being present with the girls. The reassuring peal of bells. Everything. Everything. Even her absence from her family, since being left by her mother in the care of the nuns after being admitted to hospital for surgery on a card from the United Nations Relief and Works Agency. It was as though she had become a partner to those meditative women. The grudges of every-day life would creep into their hearts, but they would make sure that they hid them behind a mask of silence and purity. Women who moved as lightly as white doves on noiseless heels. The only sound they made came from the rustling of the long rosaries dangling from their belts. Sister Mary gave her a collection box into which she dropped coins every now and then, and she taught her to pray exactly like the nuns. She would wash herself, dress up, then go to church to kneel before the icons.

"I beseech you, Oh Prophet," Aisha would say.

Sister Mary would be amazed, and say to her with a mysterious smile, "Not Oh Prophet. Say I beseech you, Oh Christ, Oh Jesus."

I beseech you, Oh Christ. She would contemplate him with exuberance, the pale-skinned handsome young man with the sad expression. The thorns around his head would take on colours like a bouquet of flowers. He would remain hanging on the cross. No hand would stretch out to bring him down and allow him to rest. He would stare out to infinity with an unchanging gaze as though he could see nothing but himself and the tragedy. I beseech you, Oh Christ. All these women pray to you. They play the organ and make supplications to you, kneeling on the cold white marble tiles, but you remain unmoved. It is as though you could not see the sad Virgin as she shifts her gaze from the ceiling to the women. Sometimes, the Virgin would be unable to hold back the sadness in her heart, and her tears would turn into drops of olive oil on the cheeks of her icon. Once, her gaze met Aisha's in a trance of hymns, and the girl shivered, her eyes filling with tears of sadness for the holy woman who had suffered so greatly. Our Lady Mary. The rosary beads rustled between Aisha's fingers as she said her prayers before the altar. I beseech you, Lady Mary, I beseech you, take pity on us.

As Aisha would fold her scarf, careful that no other member of the household would notice her, she would recall the smell of stagnant air in the church vestibule, mixed with the smell of wax from the slender candles burning at the alter.

The bus. Perhaps if that massacre hadn't happened, they would not have taken her out of school. Her mother used to say, "The bus," wincing as though she were being struck on the forehead by a ray of very strong sunlight. She would lick her oval-shaped lips with her cracked tongue, panting as she moved the fingers of her right hand over her chest as though she were shaking imaginary dust from her wide dress.

"The bus. Woe is me. What a catastrophe! What a shame! What had the young men and the boys done to get killed in this way? Twenty of them, my dear. Twenty. That's what your father said. They attacked them, bang, bang."

The mother clucked her tongue and pressed her teeth, her arms gesticulating right and left as though she were carrying an imaginary machine-gun. Her expression reflected her panic as she added, "We have become refugees, without a country, without dignity, without a home. Our honour was lost long ago and now our children are dying. The bus. The bus. The bus. Woe is me. We have such ill-fortune."

She would only visit home three times a year. Then she would return to school, her nose blocked by mucus tinged with soot from the fumes exuded by the kerosene stove. At home, she would have the vision of yellow sulphur whenever she combed her hair. She would tilt her head and her loosely falling hair would touch her cheek, flowing down her neck towards her shoulder. As she moved the comb's teeth along her scalp, the vision would occur. She would stop combing her hair, and clean the comb's edges of little cotton lumps and the dust of blankets, of earth and of the smoke storms caused by the machines in the factories around the camp. The dream! The dream of yellow sulphur assaults her, attacking her in her sleep and burying her in murky whirlwinds. She sees its blackened splinters on the tin houses, the cement rooms and the rusty metal rooves. She is surrounded by ruins. Alone, she shakes the burning matter from her skin. She is alone. The whirlwind takes her far away, pushing her to a precipice of emptiness. The quicksands form circles which pull her downwards. Sulphurous sands block her nose, mouth and eyes. Her hair falls to the ground around her feet. The vision brought back to her the spectacle of the fire at the sulphur factory after the army attacked the camp in May. In 1973, the factory had burnt down following clashes between the army and the camp. For unknown reasons, the authorities had made no effort to put out the fire. No one knew why the factory had burnt down or why the fire brigade had not come. Yellow ashes had covered the ground, shining like frantic glow-worms on the roofs at night. During the day, it settled in people's chests, giving them all sorts of ailments. Aisha saw the factory with thick columns of smoke rising from it. She saw its ruined facade and its dilapidated structure, and she smelt its hellish odour. For a long time afterwards, burning bits of sulphur covered everything: the sky, faces, lips and hair, hands, roads, feet, corners, chicken's feathers, radios, taps, the down on young bodies, plants, sewers and the road to the clinic. It covered heaven and earth and everything between them, even her dreams.

The bus, the bus.

Woe is me, what bad fortune I have.

This time, Aisha had not known. She did not know until she saw the black flags of mourning on the roofs of many houses in the camp. She heard the moaning of women and the crying of children as she walked along the roads. She saw the faces of women who had not caught her attention before, struggling under the burden of a heavy blow which had changed their features and mutilated their bones. Their misshapen faces overflowed with grief and anger.

"My goodness! What's it all about?" The neighbours stood in the doorways and on the roofs carrying their children or hanging out their washing. Their faces carried expressions of dumbfounded sadness. Even their fast clucking tones as they bounced from one to the other collapsed into a kind of low echo.

Since her return, her mother had told her time and again: "Did you know, my dear, that the clashes were going on before you came? Yes, by God, hell broke loose for days on end."

And Aisha would comb her hair, picking the flowers of nasty dust off her head with her fingertips. She would plait her hair, comforting herself by thinking that she would go back to school. She would comb her hair, directing her rapt gaze towards the concrete floor, making her way to the school playground where the girls would come out of class to laugh and play.

Oh God. At least before, on previous vacations, she used to think, wait, expect to complete her studies and become a teacher, someone of whom the whole world would take notice. She would work at the school's kindergarten and earn a salary. She hoped to be able to come to an understanding with the nuns about boarding with them. She doesn't like it here, to live or to stay. She is disgusted and frightened of every whisper between her father and her mother. It's as though everyone were conniving against her. It's as though she and the nuns were responsible for the bus incident. So they were keeping her at home, turning her into a corpse of constrained misery, while the girls in the playground still chased their dreams that floated in the air like white butterflies and pursued their games behind the tree of secrets, which shed its silver leaves on their shoulders.

The girls had many secrets. Some they would mention in front of her, others they would only whisper, excluding her from them. Many a time she had listened to them in amazed fascination, disguising her wonder beneath a shield of silence and presumed ignorance. They spoke of things beyond the imagination. Things that one could scarcely believe. Trips to every part of the world which turned distances into a straw bag that one could just pack, sling across one's back and go. Islands where the birds of heaven fluttered over the trees. Huge ships like floating land sailing the seas. Magicians swallowing glass and sharp metal pieces as though they were cherries and pears. Train stations with thousands of people coming out of their underground interiors. Volcanoes and lava enveloping whole cities in ashes and oblivion. A goat with a bull's tail. Precious perfumes taken out of the bellies of whales and gazelles. And coloured bubbles poured into crystal glasses only to be emptied out again. All this was above imagination. It was there and not there to her. She didn't care if she saw anything like it or not, came across any of it or not. The important thing was that it amused her, and filled her with pleasure. She would go over the memory of it over and over again like a "sour-sweet" bonbon which one slowly sucks for as long as possible so that it doesn't melt all at once.

There were stories, tales and reports which they enticed her into hearing and mysterious faces of charming heroes which they were reluctant to describe or hint at. And there were things which they never mentioned, but she knew about them of her own accord. Her body told, and she listened. Her body spoke, and she heard the words it was saying to her.

2

❧❧❧

And Aisha would pass the comb repeatedly through her hair with a desperate monotony, trying to remove the particles of dust tucked amongst the roots of her hair. She would raise the wide comb and remove smoke-coloured clumps from its edges, clusters of camp dust that would hardly disappear before condensing again. A dark earth that never stopped floating in the narrow sky, spreading like whirlpools with fiery arms above the houses. In her dreams . . . the rooves would disappear before her terror, and she would be left there all alone. But when she would wake up and open her eyes, she would see the wilderness in which the miserable houses were planted like sails fixed to the edge of a desert gulf, causing the camp, which rested against the mountains, to resemble a hunchback who had been forced to squat at the edge of Beirut. There, he had grown, casting his trunk downwards, his feet sinking into Dekwaneh and Sinn El-Feel, which was crammed with luxurious villas and beautiful houses that had shining wooden balconies.

Her body spoke, and she became agitated. She shivered before her mother's inquisitive gaze as it searched her body inch by inch, and the intrusive stare of her father, who would never stop gaping at her. She was forced to hunch her back when she walked to hide her growing bosom, ignoring her mother's cheap hints. At first, her bosom sprouted out into two small buds. A brownish-pink circle spread over a small protrusion that formed a small hill on each breast. It spread and turned into a chocolate-coloured halo with a little nipple in the middle. Inside her bosom, the centre of the swelling became excruciatingly painful, pressing against her, if she collided with something hard while running or walking. There, two pebbles grew. They took their time, protruding gradually. They rounded up and turned into eye-catching breasts. Sister Mary noticed and said: "You've grown up, child."

And she gave her a bra to wear. A bra made out of firm cotton material. It was machine stitched with circular threads on each side, and it contained her bosom which bounced, its roundness protruding whenever she bent down. A new useless organ, giving rise to embarrassment and a deep sense of its superfluity and meaninglessness.

Sister Mary. If only. If only *she* had been her family and spared her all this suffering. Her own mother could never stop talking about the awaited bridegroom. She would boast of her to the neighbours. My daughter, my educated daughter, she would never tire of saying.

Every now and then, she would pounce on her and kiss her, enveloping her in the odour of her putrefying perspiration and a cloud of smoke from her cheap cigarettes. Her mischievous sister Ibtissam, who seemed as though she didn't know the way home, spent most of her time in the camp alleys. Pebbles in hand, vulgar language was never absent from her speech. Water never found its way to her face, nor a comb to her matted hair. She was always barefoot, carelessly wading through the mud in the middle of winter as though her legs were the soles of rubber shoes. As for the naughty little boy, my goodness. He would never be still. Carrying his slingshot, he would wander through the forest or the fields, keeping up with the boys' problems and rows. As for the strange man! Assayed! Her father. My goodness me. She couldn't understand what coincidence had made him her father and made her his daughter. She wasn't surprised that he could be the husband of this slow-moving, stolid woman. It was possible to imagine him as the father of his children. But! But her.

Her hatred of him grew in her heart. She would stick to the walls of her disgusted self like black soot. Every morning, at first light, everyone in the house would wake to his loud curses as he demanded money for his transport and his café excursions from her mother.

"Give it to me."

The mother would open her swollen eyelids. No sooner would she rub them to see around her, than she would be attacked by another loud call: "Give it to me, woman."

She would cough and hurriedly light a cigarette, which she would smoke on an empty stomach. She would hold the cigarette in one hand as she inhaled her first drag, and silently give him the money with the other hand. Every day, Aisha would ask her: "All the time, he says give me, give me. Why do you give him the money you earn by the sweat of your brow, while he does nothing but sit around?"

Her mother would answer her impassively. In a a very ordinary tone, she would say: "To avoid an unholy row, my child. What else can I do. It's a choice between him beating me up and me giving him the money. Giving it to him is better."

Assayed would turn his back and go down to Dekwaneh without a care in this world or the next. He would go out, cutting a strong, squarely-built figure. He had the beginnings of a beard, which he grew without allowing it to get long. It was as though he were trying to create the impression that the short white hairs of his beard, which seemed as thick as cactus thorns, had deliberately been left unshaven out of respect for his dignity and age. Assayed, with his big mouth and dangling lips, had a savage laugh which only bellowed at the most unexpected of times. Assayed would put his hands in the pockets of his light-coloured jacket in summer, and inside the folds of his worn-out coat in winter, when he would wear a woollen beret, adding a tidiness and gentility to his scruffy appearance beyond the limits of his modest elegance. Assayed would turn his back and go without so much as a thought for the household. Nothing would move him even if the world turned upside down. Nor was he interested in his oldest son, the ever-absent son, either in the Beirut offices or attending military training courses in the south.

Assayed! Oh how she detested Assayed; and her brother and sister;

all of them. It all made her feel dizzy, ground something bitter in her stomach, rising like an acid fire into her throat.

The pain within her would remind her of that ill-fated day, when she was taken unawares by a looseness and weakness all over her body. She woke up at school with nausea and cramps in her tummy. It felt like a hot nail piercing her organs, pushing its sharp end amongst them. In the mirror above the sink, her face seemed unusually pale. It was a whitish-yellow. Under her eyes were two dark blotches which had a different colour to the rest of her complexion. In the bathroom, her amazement increased, and turned into violent trembling, causing her knees to bang together. A spot! A piece of coagulated blood as black as coffee dregs. A pungent, disgusting smell. A black spot. It terrified her. It grew larger and started to soil its surroundings. Whenever she removed it, another one would appear. She thought, Whom? Whom could she tell just to get reassurance that she was alright? Sister Mary? The bra scandal was enough. She wouldn't dare say a word in front of her.

Aisha ran to an elderly cook with whom she was friendly. There, in a corner of the kitchen, she told her. As the singe of the hot fire scalded her pale face and the smell of tomato sauce with its sour aroma rose, mixed with the warm smell of frying onions, she told the cook, almost bursting with embarrassment. Her head was bent towards the floor as though she awaited the final verdict for a transgression or crime she had committed. The cook laughed, revealing her big teeth, and winked at her with her narrow eyes. Patting her shoulder, she said: "This is normal, Aisha. It happens to all women. God willing, we will have the pleasure of marrying you off."

Aisha continued to shake, her teeth chattering as though she were in a yard full of ice despite the fire in the oven which would normally cause perspiration. She weakly asked herself: What had marriage to do with what was happening to her? What was it that happened to all women? For a moment, the terror drying up her saliva was blunted, and a faint echo of hidden secret pride moved within her. All women? That means I am no longer a little girl, rather "women". Then. Oh what a catastrophe. Impossible. Happening to her. She herself. Something she did not want. Women put up with things. As for her, what was her sin?

She began to be able to recognize the mysterious smell that evaporated from the cloth napkins given to her by the cook. The napkins. And the smell of coagulated blood, looking like grains of crushed wheat as they were rinsed away under the stream of cold water. Freezing water which only she and the cooks used in the back yard of the school. The reddish black odour resembled the vapour of melting iron with organic acids. The odour of hidden rottenness which her stomach would sense and convulsively reject as she was overcome by nausea. Then she began to watch the girls using the disposable napkins, which they bought with their parents' money. The lightness of their cotton fabric as they pulled them out of their drawers. That used to revive the sense of debilitating heaviness that overcame her every time she carried those pieces of cloth, soaked with the remains of blood like lumps of flesh that had forcibly fallen from her body and stuck between her legs.

But on that day they had come to take her away, it had never crossed her mind that they would keep her with them and not allow her to go back to school. On the day that they came, Aisha had finished cleaning the dormitory and gone down to the kitchen to have breakfast. She entered it quickly as though compulsively following a vague smell of warmth, the glow of the blue fire and the fluffy bread. The cooks had already beaten her to the table, shaded by the metal fan extractor. She had a *labaneh* sandwich for breakfast with tea. The hotness of the liquid, into which the taste of the plastic glass had melted, stung her. The tip of her tongue was burnt as she eagerly took her first sip of the day from the glass that shook in her hands. The thin cook whose voice sounded like the bleat of a lamb said, "They asked for you. Go and see the Big Sister."

"Why?"

A look of confusion came over her face. Now or after I've cleared up the plates? Another cook, who seemed to have read her mind, sharply responded, "Clear them up now, before you go."

Every day, she would clear up the empty plates and glasses. She would go round the empty tables, cluttered with glasses and spoons. She would pile what she was carrying onto a large tray, then empty it onto the ledge, swollen like an idiot's tongue, of the window between the dining room and the kitchen. Every single day, she would walk with a calmly balanced gait, knowing how to step lightly amongst the seats and spaces between the tables. But on that day, she tripped. Her feet hit the legs of the chairs, the tray jumped in her hands, and her heart beat with apprehension. She could hear its slow low pounding in her ears. Why did the Mother Superior want her? Had she done something wrong? Had someone reported her? I beg you Jesus, what have I done to them, what do they want with me?

Tables. Tables, and tens of chairs around them, and she wondered whether she had made a mistake with her work. If not, why was the Mother Superior summoning her? She finished off wiping the tables one by one, trying to shut out the remaining rancid smell from the bits of fried egg stuck to their surfaces. She struggled to control the anxiety that suddenly sprang up from deep inside her, shattering the peace that drew her body to the warmth of the kitchen.

To the Mother Superior. She walks and hears her heart beating as though it were pumping into her ears. The long corridors, the narrow yards stretching like the skeleton of a snake whose tail leads to the Mother Superior's office. The floating smell left by the Lysol antiseptic and the water in the buckets of the cleaning ladies. The slight pressure she applies to the door knob as she opens it. The same movement as she closes it, then turns her back to the other side of the school to pack her few things.

The Mother Superior. Something different emanates from her clerical gown like an unbearably cold smell rising from the heart of time as it passes over the room's heavy furniture. The clock's pendulum swings with a metallic infinity. The cross on the wall and the saviour hanging on it with thick nails provokes overbearing violence. And that terror one feels before the tranquillity and submissiveness of the statue despite the savagery of the crucifixion. The Mother Superior's wax-like hands in the ray of light spilling from the high window in a conical beam. The sliminess of the weak light despite the spring outside. The hat on her old head like a broken ship stuck on a deserted shore. Through her white teeth, at variance with her worn out gums, with the ridged wrinkles around her jaw forming her mask of cold seclusion, the Mother Superior said, "Go and pack your clothes, Aisha, and wait for your family to come and pick you up. But don't forget us, or the Virgin, who let you be raised with us."

Aisha did not dare ask anything or utter a word.

Later, Aisha's mother told her.

It was the bus incident, and the mother had been too frightened to tell the Mother Superior that that was the reason. She rang her up.

"My daughter. My daughter. I want my daughter."

"Why do you want your daughter, madam?"

"I want her to come home."

"Why, what's wrong, madam?"

"Nothing's wrong at all. Her father wants her to stay at home, and that's all there is to it."

"And you madam? Is that your opinion as well?"

"Well, that's just the way things are. Her father wants it that way. She's a young woman now, and we have to think about her future."

And the three of them . . . the four of them walked with short rhythmic steps along the dirt track outside the school.

Life still goes on as usual. Aisha rarely leaves the house. Her heavy, slow steps don't go beyond the end of the alley, where the shop from which they buy handfuls of tea and some sugar is situated. No one has asked her to go further than that. Assayed goes out to see his friends. The mother goes to the flats where she works in Dekwaneh, Boushrieh and Ashrafieh, and her brother and sister go to the UNRWA schools or the camp streets. How wonderful is the sense of security that returns to her during their absence. How beautiful the peace and quiet that envelope her within a delicate cocoon of isolation when their voices and gestures disappear. It's as though a joyous shower of spring rain washes away her tiredness and loosens her body from the burdens of tension created by their severe scoldings over things she knows and others she doesn't know. It straightens out her arching backbone, and she becomes active again, springing up, jumping and running inside the small room. She dances if she catches songs she likes on the radio. She rubs the button, moving the needle quickly and eagerly in search of light, cheerful songs because she hates heavy oriental music and everything that reminds her of them. Um Kalthoum, the best-known Arabic singer, resembles a fat woman who cannot stop complaining and moaning. Assayed is transported by every moan she makes. She hates all these singers, except

Feirouz. She searches for her and listens to her with a feeling that resembles the fresh coolness of white marble. A coolness that soothes her veins as she stands before the church alter absorbed in the hymns addressed to the meek child in his mother's lap. She likes that singer, and imagines her to be a young girl the same age as herself. A lonely girl, standing at a crossroads every day, asking passers-by about her love, who has disappeared without giving her a thought. A secret lover who has no definite features, but he inspires her songs and fills her life with memories. Her voice resembles the yellow genista flowers when they climb the fence and their delicate discs spread in every direction. The flowers fall off whenever she tries to pick them, their soft powder sticking to her fingers as though they were the remains of a star continuing to burn as it descends from the sky onto the ground.

Their absence turns her into a silkworm slowly spinning the threads of its cocoon. She weaves her solitude with a slow pleasure. The silk thread of her dreams unravels, taking her to a spacious place. Its dimensions change, but it is always close to the sea. A place, rather many places. She does not know where they are or how she will reach them, but she is sure that one day she will get there. She stays at home alone, listening to the songs she likes on the radio, but not to political news items, which are of no interest to her. She works slowly, enjoying her aloneness as though she were tasting a unique flavour whose secret is unattainable to others. She washes the floor with water and kerosene, and once again shines the broken glass of the cabinet, careful not to touch the electrical tape which keeps it from disintegrating. She wrings the cloth and tries to rub away the remains of an old black mark from the wood of the double-door cupboard. She flattens her soft hand against the cloth and uses all her strength to scour the spot, moving her hand to the right, then to the left. She only awakens from her reverie to the shine of the light assailing her eyes through the window. She suddenly discovers her accumulated craving for the light and the sun, and leaves what she is doing and goes to the roof. She spreads the lentils on an iron tray, and enjoys the light bursting forth from the sun as it fills her and surrounds her. The warmth begins to penetrate her pores, and the parts of her body that are sick of the shade. Warmth makes its way to her across the air, and through the rough concrete that rubs against her bottom and thighs whenever she moves as she sits cross-legged on the ground. In that solitariness of hers, everything she did gave her enjoyment and invigorated her spirit. She would pick out the little stones from amongst the crushed lentils with the joyous care of one picking flowers in a garden. And she would water the vine climbing along the roof and the tins of Arabian jasmine and speedwell like one offering water to green birds that had descended from heaven.

But Assayed soon comes home, and a huge heaviness descends onto her chest like an immovable stone. He steps onto the mat with his shoes on, not removing them as is the habit, and sits facing the rest of the room on the ottoman, resting his left elbow on the cushion, taking long thorough sideways looks at her as he inhales his cigarettes with a languid greed, feigning inattention and absent-mindedness. She avoids him, turning her back to him, paying attention to anything that might serve to divert his evil looks away from her. She sweeps, makes dark tea and serves it, cleans the dishes and rubs the aluminium saucepans until they shine like a mirror, while he follows her with his eyes, casting an invisible chord that traces her movements between the kitchen, the room and the roof. He throws incomprehensible looks at her, emitting sparks which burn her whenever she is hit by them. If by chance she comes face to face with him, embers stir within her bosom, creating violent currents of resentment. God help her if he is taken by an urge to speak to her, because she will not know how to talk to him. The words disappear into the top of her throat, sinking deep down, unable to spring forth. If she forces herself to speak and succeeds in saying a few sentences or phrases, her voice is pushed out like balloons hanging in the air. Talking to him was a heavy burden. Her voice would thicken, turning into a hoarse, dissonant rumble.

On that day in May, the sky was clear and the sun shone warmly, making her wish that she were able to go out somewhere where she could see people, any people. Her wish was an overwhelming desire. Her mother knew most of the people in the neighbourhood, but her own haughtiness and aloofness prevented her from getting to know any of them. She doesn't want them, is afraid of what they are, or, more precisely, has a mysterious instinctive fear of belonging to them. She would become one of them if . . . that day, she was overcome by her first urge to visit an acquaintance or a neighbour. Even at that moment, Assayed did not hesitate to make her life miserable by coming home unusually early. He sat in his favourite place commanding the whole room and brought out his small stack of cigarette papers. He opened his tin tobacco box, and stretched his fingers to fill the white square piece of paper with ottoman tobacco. He uttered a word she was unable to catch, as though he had remembered something. He said, "Girl."

"Why are you always wearing that pink dress?"

"That's my dress, Yaba . . . I haven't got another one."

"Why d'you say Yaba the way spoilt kids do?"

" . . . "

"You think you're one of the nuns' girls, don't you?"

" . . . "

"What a catastrophe this is. What am I to do with you in future?"

He sighed as he finished smoking his cigarette, continuing sarcastically, "D'you want to go to Paris, Yaba?"

She made no answer. But she felt all her blood rushing up to her head. She used her hands to fold the laundry piled up next to her. She distracted herself by pulling the ends of the washed clothes, pretending to smooth them out so that he would stop interfering with her. She prayed to God that this man would forget her, that he would go out again to his friends at the café. That he would do anything. Just that his attention would be diverted from her. His eagle-like eyes stare around the room, then land on her as he inhales the tobacco in his cigarette with obvious pleasure. His glances follow her, clutching onto the edges of her dress like a fire that lights up whenever it comes her way. For goodness' sake, Yaba! What's up? She said it to herself, without uttering a sound. He spoke to her again: "You! Aisha"

"What is it?"

"You, girl. Say yes Yaba."

"Yes"

She swallowed as she said it.

"That's it. That's what you should have said in the first place. I thought you were going to say Papi like those pampered foreign girls."

He burst out laughing, the sound bouncing around the house. Aisha lowered her head, burying her terrified glances amongst the pieces of clothing spread out on the floor next to her bent over body. Her hands traversed the shrunken clothes, trying to impart some kind of order to them. She got to the wooden clothes pegs scattered around them, picked them up and carried them off like someone who had found a priceless treasure. She made a rush for the roof, careful to give the impression that her trip was nothing to do with running away from him, but purely to do with her household chores. She walked dejectedly and hurriedly, feeling that the heaviness of her pink dress was hindering her movement, weighing down the flexibility of her body, which had been free before.

She fled him so that he would not repeat the anecdote he would never tire of telling to ridicule her. He had called her once with his customary bluster, startling her. Unconsciously, without meaning to, she had said it: What is it, Papi?

She never knew how her tongue had gone out of control, and how that word had broken loose from her. Her sister laughed so hard, she twisted her waist; and the boy somersaulted on the floor with excitement. As for Assayed, he had roared a scolding in her face, before indulging in a sharp sarcastic fit of laughter: "You, shame on you. We're Palestinians."

If she had not fled towards the kitchen at that moment, he might have pulled off his belt and started beating her the way he had when she had come home happily with a cross. The nuns had all pitched in to buy her a golden cross as a gift on one of their feasts. A small shining chain with a small cross on it. It had caused her enough kicks and slaps from her father to last her a lifetime. She never saw the chain again. Her mother told her as she treated her with cold water compresses that he had probably sold it and used the money to buy more bottles of *arak*, of which he couldn't drink enough. "We're Palestinians," he had said, as though he were continuously searching the heavens and earth for excuses to humiliate her.

Recently, he had started coming home always surrounded by an aniseed-smelling cloud of *arak*, belching nauseatingly. Her mother had removed her scarf, reclining on the mat in her striped pyjama pants beneath her flannel house dress. Aisha fled to the kitchen, waiting for her father to finish his supper, so that she could spread the mattress and make up beds for her sister and brother, who had fallen asleep on the side cushions. She went to the tap and turned it, pouring water over her wrist. This gave her some relief from an accumulated tension for which she knew no other remedy. As she stood at the sink, her attention was drawn to Assayed's hand as it held the bread over the edge of the dish that had contained the spring greens. He passed it several times over the empty plate. He sensed that she was watching him, and stopped whispering to her mother, who was sitting next to him. After he had gone out on his usual nightly excursion, Aisha went up to her mother and asked: "Yamma, what were you saying about me?"

"What would we be saying about you? My dear! You've grown up and have turned into a lovely young girl. God protect you from the evil eye. Go on my dear, go to bed. Stop prattling. May God bring you a decent young man."

"A decent young man. A decent young man," Aisha said to herself. "That's the only thing that they can't stop thinking about." She keeps her infuriation to herself. She wants to sleep to forget. Everything will come right in the morning. Everything around her tortures her. She wants to sleep. To forget. To erase the misery from the page of nightmares ahead of her. I beseech you, Jesus. No, I mean, I beseech you, Oh Prophet. For the sake of your eternal sadness, Oh Virgin. Just a spot of calm sleep.

3

Once upon a time.

There was Aisha, there were the father and mother, brother and sister, Tal Ezza'tar and Beirut . . . and the whole world. The June weather was fine, except for an occasional dusty seasonal wind and the clashes, which had broken out again between the camp and the Phalangist forces.

The clashes continued for several days, making Aisha experience war for the first time in her life. Missiles, mortars and machine-gun fire poured down on the camp. Fiery rain. The crackling of weapons, the friction of their firing and the heavy quakes sickened her with fear. The concrete walls of the house, surrounded by thousands like it, shook and the corrugated metal roof creaked. A thick darkness descended on the room in which the family cowered. Outside, the world stopped its usual cycle for several days. Time crumbled like the glue peeling off the cupboard. It seemed to Aisha that the days had turned into signals of death. She adopted a suffocating silence, refusing food despite her mother scolding and insisting that she swallow a bite or two. She took

up a position in a corner near the cupboard and surrendered to the
overwhelming illusion that any missile fired from anywhere would
penetrate the door and head straight for her. It crossed her terrified
mind that the mortars would succeed in finding her as they circled the
sky. She became firmly convinced that her tongue would stick to her
palate because of the concentrated body odours of people confined
next to one another, and their putrid panting through dry mouths.
The sour air, mixed with the smell of gunpowder smoke assailing the
camp, pressed down on her chest. She froze in her place and did not
leave it, despite the spreading numbness in her squatting legs. Pain
flashed up the spine of her back, which stuck to the wall. She turned
into a cold wax statue. Over and over again she wrung the fabric of her
pink dress, gathering the tips of her fingers at its edges, crushing the
threads inside her palms, reweaving them between her sweaty palms,
unresponsive to her mother's voice, which rose scoldingly every now
and then. Her mother rocked herself backwards and forwards repeatedly, touching her upper body to the ground. She repeated her soft
prayer in a beseeching whisper:

"Crisis intensifies, then is relieved.

Intensify, bring relief, intensify."

The mother said it in a low voice as though repeating the charm
incessantly would silence the tremendous haphazard noise outside. As
though anyone out there would hear her and answer the fervour of her
wish. As for Assayed, he would go into long dazes, his hand to his
cheek, his face bearing the expression of one fighting off an unexpected
nightmare. Aisha was buried beneath the weight of her fear of the
camp, which had become a hell inhabited by monsters. From time to
time, she would direct her gaze towards the reflections of phosphoric
fires shining in the darkness of the closed room. Assayed would sometimes tremble, stretch as though he were waking up and begin cursing
God, the Arabs, the bastards and Palestine itself. Had it not been for
Palestine "we would not be in this terrible fix" in this strange land. He
would roll his short cigarettes, addressing himself gravely to an
imagined audience: "Those who have no luck need not bother to exert
themselves. The day the Jews threw us out of Jaffa is enough. I have a
nervous breakdown whenever I talk about it. My old man said to me:
Son, escape if you have no arms to fight with. He said: In the end, you

will return. I said, No Yaba, how can I leave you alone in this big house? My father had buried his brother, my uncle, with his own two hands. He dug a grave amongst the rocks and buried him after he was killed in the English raid on the orchard. What could I do? Shelling and raids going on, and God alone knew what we were going through. I said: I put my trust in God. Morning came and people swarmed at the port like worms."

It was as though an ugly dream or hateful prophecy were beginning to shatter his remaining sanity. He went on like this for days on end. Aisha forgot to comb her hair. No. She didn't forget. Actually, between her and herself, she mocked her own horror of combing her hair in days gone by. The sulphurous smell of fear evaporated and entered the realm of imagination. The heavy powder that covered everything as she had combed her hair alone, removing the sticky bits that upset her whenever she was able to, no longer frightened her. That was all over, and there was now something crazier than dreams or visions. The clashes robbed her of the taste for food, drink and breathing, sprinkling her bad dreams with their reagent salt. Something that helped to reveal a whole new range of discoveries.

The clashes pass. They are over. But the echo of the crackling weapons continues in her ears with the stinging rhythm of the bullets, whose din has not stopped inside her brain.

But she.

Once upon a time, you who listen, shall I tell, or shall we go to sleep?

All of the years away from home had not made Aisha forget the bedtime stories her mother used to treat her with a long time ago.

"My green mare, bring forth a small blue foal so I can ride with the soldiers."

True to the tale, it was as though the ground had opened, revealing that good-looking young man who started visiting their home after the clashes. The boy. The young man . . . the man whom her mother had recently begun to treat like a brother because he had helped her to get free medical treatment at a nearby hospital. If it had not been for him – her mother makes a negative gesture with her index fingers in front of her bosom – we would not have been able to get documented proof of our difficult conditions from the popular committee in the camp.

"Yes, by God. If it hadn't been for him, what would have become of me. He left the Sobiet Union after completing a military course. Thank God that he came and helped this wretched woman who had never before found anyone to help her."

Aisha would comment, "Yamma, I told you, it's not the Sobiet Union. It's the Soviet. Don't scandalize us."

God have mercy on the Prophet. If only words could describe his wonderfully good looks. It's as though the beauty of the whole world is concentrated in his face and body, which are surrounded by a halo like the prophets. Her mother says: "No dear, he's older than your older brother, Jalal, but he has a young-looking face."

The young man was better looking than imagination itself. The eye had not seen and the ear had not heard the like of his attraction. Magic appeared wherever his piercing hazel eyes looked. Enchantment accompanied his dignified captivating step.

Assayed used to invite him and bring him home whenever he met him on the street or near the office of the organization at the beginning of the alley leading to their house. He would bring him with a hospitality he had never shown towards any of his other acquaintances: "Make way. Tidy up the room. I've brought him with me."

He would stay close to him after seating him. While sweet lightly-roasted coffee or mint tea was being served, he would compliment him: "Welcome to our guest. Greetings. A warm welcome. The world has lit up. Welcome George. A thousand welcomes to my son's friend."

Assayed always insisted that he was his son's friend although George had only met Jalal once or twice through sheer coincidence.

His presence would release a secret thread of the invisible tenderness that Assayed harboured for his son Jalal. He would burst into the house, followed by George in his khaki uniform, his hair unkempt beneath his military beret, his young beard sprouting and growing despite his obvious attempts to shave it every day.

The old man's joy, which he reserved for his loyal night-time friends, would overflow. For Assayed was usually haughty towards his neighbours and acquaintances because his family in Jaffa had been rich – a fact that never left his memory. But things were different with George, inspiring his affection and admiration for that boy and all his contemporaries, who had not hesitated before taking up arms. The actions of these young men obliterated his internal humiliation, the misery buried deep within him and all the deprivations of his present life. In God's name, God be praised, as his wife, Um Jalal would say: "Look at them, like honey to the taste. Yamma, my darling, may God keep and protect you lads, you Fedayeen."

Assayed would accept her words good naturedly, although such affectionate phrases did not become her. They highlighted the deep wrinkles at the corners of her eyes, revealing even more the blackness on her teeth, and bringing out the veins in her neck. Assayed tolerated her attachment to George, attributing it to a kind of craving for her absent son, who was in West Beirut, and comparing it to a kind of insanity and stupidity peculiar to women. His wife would not stop acting as an intermediary for George's engagement. He would ask her to be more reserved: "Woman, enough of that. Is he your long-lost son? I pamper him, but within limits, not the way you do."

It seemed that such talk only made Um Jalal prouder of him, because she considered herself to be the most responsible person for anything that might happen to the young man, to a point that exceeded Assayed's tolerance. She argued with George, trying to convince him to protect himself and hide well whenever the clashes broke out. If it had not been for the sense of formality necessitated by the presence of the dear guest, Assayed would not have hesitated to beat her and punch her mouth to teach her not to interfere in men's affairs.

And Aisha sees him. The young man. The boy. The Feda'ee. She looks at him. Forgets herself. Stops feeling everything around her. The sounds of the camp retreat from her ears, and its sights recede from her vision, so that she sees nothing but him. She hears him only, and feels him alone. She draws a chalk circle that brings them together so that she can stare at him to her heart's content, and takes him in slowly slowly despite the loud pounding of her heart. She observes the freshness of youth in his upright, firm figure, the calmness of manhood in his face, the overwhelming liveliness of his features when he speaks, the harmony of his movements when he sits down or gets up. And the world ends, comes to a stop. Nothing remains except him.

The eyes draw her to stare secretly at them. She sees the reflection of their light like a sun casting its rays along a river bed. And she is the fish of darkness receiving the light that filters down to the bottom, basking in it, uniting with its crystal flashes. There, beneath the water, where no one can find her, she tries to draw her body to him, to the sun outside, to the transparent halo of light, to him and no one but her. All she wanted was to continue to stare and look at his eyes, as though she were drawn to them by the secret pull of submission to their strange power. She hopes that no one notices her obsession, not even she herself. My God, she has never seen eyes like those before. The man could almost be nothing more than a pair of eyes to her. His moon-coloured complexion, dark chestnut hair and uniformed figure, upright as a spear, have become a frame for those eyes.

She used to await the opportunity to offer him coffee second by second so that she could raise her gaze towards him as he took the cup with his left hand in his usual manner. At that moment, she would look at his eyes. A second. A minute. The whole of time. She would squat in the corner, the edges of her dress touching the floor, to follow his chuckle, which floated up in a pure melody, penetrating the invisible depression around her. He laughs, and the eyes laugh as though she has never in her life seen mirth shining in two heavenly windows. It's as if those eyes don't acknowledge her except during a moment of laughter, when the two pupils dance in a watery sheen, speaking to her and going to her in a specially intimate movement. . . .

"How handsome he is, how good looking," she says to herself. She is frightened. Because such words were not created by God for her. And because if she dared to say them, they would turn into a hard steel blade that would cut her neck. She walks its narrow edge, and the world splits into two parts. Her body falls cold and stiff into one of them because she is without a tongue, or she has swallowed her tongue into her throat, as her mother says, noting the sudden pallor of her face whenever she announces the coming of the man. The young man. The boy. The Feda'ee.

The mother runs panting from the kitchen to the roof and from the door into the room, and from the roof down to the yard looking for a sprig of green peppermint or basil leaves to mix in with the tea. She calls out to her: "Aisha, George has come."

She mutters: "He's come . . . he's come. . . . "

He comes. And she comes.

And a pinkish-hazel twilight spreads across the horizon.

And he arrives.

Aisha trembles with the plants in their pots when she hears the sound of his happy arrival at the doorstep. The whole world turns into a fountain sprinkling light wherever he comes or moves. Aisha drops anything that may be in her hands at that moment and runs down to him. Downstairs. But she always freezes on the last stair, fixing her feet firmly onto the concrete ground, her features impassive, swallowing her breathless excitement, trying hard to extinguish the light kindling in her eyes. My God! He's here. He who is different to all of them. He is not afraid, is not shaken, says whatever he wants, and fights what he hates. She, on the other hand, is afraid of herself and of looking at him. He talks to everybody, but there are no words between her and him. No, no. no. She does not dream, does not expect anything of the sort. Because she is fully aware that she is Aisha. She will not utter a single word in front of him, although she is charmed, captivated by him. She is the poor one, to quote her mother. He arrives, and her anticipation soars through a lavender space. He comes. And a lump rises in her chest up to her throat, causing her to almost suffocate with gloom as she watches George listening to the details of the mediation with her mother. And her mother is trying to get Hana to marry him.

She used to wonder why a perfect man like him could not find it enough to enjoy his own distinct existence, and why he would try so hard to pursue a girl from the camp who tramped the alleys and streets all the time with the girls from the women's organization. A girl with nothing special about her except that she worked as a radio operator at the Signals Department. She would become oblivious to her surroundings as she became absorbed in her daydreams of his impending nightmarish marriage. Lost and unable to understand those special people who would concede their elevated station, descending from the heights of their heavenly light to the low cheapness of others.

In the evening, she would go to the roof and watch the ebbing away of the last fragments of purple light from the world. There, over there. Far away in the sky, a woman whose body is casting away her luminescent robe. She enters step by step into the transparent dark waters. A sea and a sea. It retreats and shrinks, leaving behind a complete darkness in which the moon shines, looking like a golden coin. The sky lights itself with thousands of candles, turning into an altar that beams out strong flashing rays. Aisha puts her right hand on her left wrist and feels the throbbing flow beneath her skin, thinking that she will catch the rush of blood within her body whenever she craves the presence of her love. But her yearning soon turns into another candle that dissipates in the sky like a shooting star. Feeling her pulse was a habit that took her to infinity whenever she cast her longing to faraway space. Beneath the clear heavenly dome, all the stories she had read or heard would burst forth like bubbles in fizzy mineral water. Stories of love, insanity and obsession. Thousands of them dangling like stars, merging with the sea of the surrounding sky, attacking it in waves that crashed onto the sands of its bosom. And she did not know what all that feverish recollection had to do with her. The nuns' moving stories about our Lord Jesus were not the only source of knowledge. Because there she had learned to read everything, even what the girls had brought with them from their homes in absolute secrecy. Many people moved through the pages of the books. She would look at their features, their moods and their behaviour closely. She would share in their difficulties and complicated lives. No sooner had she grown to like them and become attached to them than they would disappear through the last pages. Men and women from different times. She would be preoccupied by them, hoping that they would return any minute. They had airy bodies woven from special emotions. They overflowed with goodness and nobleness. Others dripped with malice and spite, making it one's only wish to be saved from them. But her increasing depression caused her to fall victim to strange ideas about his imminent marriage. Her resentment was not directed at the fiancée-to-be because she despised her and held her beneath consideration even before seeing her. However, she was jealous of the man's future family because it would threaten his relationship with hers.

Burning, penetrating steam would break loose inside her, their fires incinerating the world, when she imagined his lucky son in his father's arms, hanging around his neck, sleeping and waking. She used to imagine the look that George would give the child as he cried or played, completely oblivious to all creatures he had known before the child. The look! The eyes! It fired her indignation, tore her apart, sapped her health, increasing her pallor and darkening her imaginings. She got so carried away with her fantasies that she gave the baby a name which occurred to her without any clear reason. She imagined that the baby's name was Sameeh.

The baby completely resembled his father. Actually, he was the same person, but smaller in size. She, Aisha, would work as a nanny in their home free of charge. Their home, next to her family's, would give her the opportunity to care for the child and see to his needs, especially since his mother worked outside the home, and was there for short periods only. If it were not for her, Aisha, what would become of the child? She would sing to him, carry him, call him all sorts of affectionate nicknames, play with him, gurgle at him, and steal him from his bed whenever his father paid him any attention. She would buy him cleanly wrapped chocolates and sweets whenever she got any money. And when the baby would grow up, she would not let him go out onto the dirty road, and she would prevent him from wallowing in the piles of rubbish and near the open sewers. If need be, she would spank his hands if he cried and tried to follow her brother and sister and the other children in the neighbourhood.

Aisha began to carefully scan various radio broadcasts, searching for women's programmes to get advice and directions on how to raise children. She no longer listened to Feirouz and her songs, because the voice filled with blossoms only made her feel sorrier for herself. She only looked for programmes offering advice which no prospective mother hoping to bring forth a child into this world could do without.

4

❧❧❧

"Ezza'tar! My God, how things have changed," thought Assayed as he walked down the road without knowing exactly where his footsteps would take him. The hot weather had activated his headache, and a languidness spread through his limbs. He belched, bringing back the taste of alcohol. He wavered, hesitated, unable to decide if he would walk on to Khawajah Yacoub's café. Down there. In Dekwaneh. Anxiety surged forward like an agitated hornet in his face. He continued walking, slowly recalling the increasing list of names of people kidnapped in mysterious incidents. He did not want to return to the camp's café because he did not want to encounter once again the depressing atmosphere which the worried men were exhaling with the smoke of their water pipes. Their groups had been growing smaller every night until the café had almost lost all its customers. Most of them had been prompted by their invisible fear into joining the militia as night-time guards working shifts organized by the resistance. What had seemed like a storm in a teacup presaged an approaching tragedy. No one could predict what would happen or whether he himself would become the next victim, especially those working in Beirut, or in the workshops near the river or in Boushrieh. But he, Assayed, was under no compulsion to go that far or expose himself to the mobile kidnap road-blocks which the Phalangist forces threw up on an almost daily basis. Should he go down to Dekwaneh then? There had been no problem up till then, especially since Khawajah Yacoub's café faced the sandbags behind which the resistance fighters were holed up. And then, Khawajah Yacoub Abu Nimr was his friend, knowing only too well that his lifelong pal, Assayed Abu Jalal, was not to be underestimated. The issue at hand was Assayed's need to ascertain that Khawajah Yacoub was in his café, that he had not closed it as he had following the last clashes.

He stopped to light a cigarette, but walked on after slapping his jacket and discovering that he had no cigarettes. The bitch, Um Jalal. She had not given him any money that morning. He stifled a heavy sigh and re-inhaled the remaining air before any of his acquaintances could pass him in the alley and notice his gloom. For Assayed was not accustomed to confiding his worries and preoccupations to anyone. He was careful to hide them beneath a cloud of bitter sarcasm and stone-like harshness. He behaved as it behoved a man to do.

In days gone by when things had been calm, he used to go down to Khawajah Yacoub's café. He had become used to mixing with him for twenty years, although the Khawajah was Christian and had a son who was a member of the Phalangist Party. But the word Christian had been a normal word back then, and most of the Khawajahs and factory owners were Christians who smiled at everybody and gave people jobs if they agreed to reduced wages because they did not have legal work permits. There were never any problems about raising wages. Those who did not like to work under such conditions and without the right to compensation or health insurance could go to hell. The people of Ezza'tar used to accept that sort of work without objecting because it was impossible for them to get work permits from the government. Ultimately, most of them believed that God provided. There had been no serious problems in the past, except for a few strikes. Assayed, who had never participated in any of them, thought that a few people had been foolishly misled into joining in because they had been carried away. He still remembers the strike at the Usseily fabric plant and the Ghandour biscuit factory. That strike which no one can ever forget.

The threats of the factory owners, and the unyielding workers whose minds were like stone. Then the demonstrations, the police, the shooting and the victims. Assayed recalls something about a girl shot dead by them. Her name was Fatimah or Suheilah or something like that.

He had met Khawajah Yacoub during his first year in Ezza'tar, and had regularly frequented his café, even after many other cafés in the camp and around it had opened. He never abandoned that old habit of his. On regular week days, he would go down to the café in the late morning and have a game of backgammon with the Khawajah. The Khawajah would offer him the first glass of *arak* on the house. In those days, they used to indulge in a well-established habit of teasing one another inside the large dilapidated café, which comprised a large hall at the corner of the pavement near the taxi station and a group of car repair shops, which were the source of disturbing metallic clangings. Amid the clouds of fatty sausage odours emanating from the neighbouring café, they used to begin their antagonistic sparring. They would start their conversation with a kind of complicity by having a glass of his best *arak*. The Khawajah would stealthily go to his table, covered by a cloth saturated with the penetrating smell of aniseed, and out of the sight of the other customers, would pull out a bottle of home-made *arak*: "Have this, Sayyed. What better could you ask for? Original, unadulterated lion's milk. If you were to come to my village, you would see the *mezza* that Um Nimr can prepare. Nothing beats sitting on the balcony in the afternoon and the wonderful breeze. It's as though you were at the top of the Empire State, where my father emigrated long ago."

The songs of Feirouz blare out around them from an old tape-recorder with large reels. The Khawajah automatically mentions Um Nimr, his wife, and the demands she repeats every day: "Eh, by God. Today's women have no shame. She thinks she's still a bride when her head is full of white hair. One day she asks for new fashionable curtains, the next for an automatic washing machine because she sees it on television commercials. A washing machine that rinses and wrings the washing all by itself, if you please. I say, we're growing old, woman, let's take things easy. She just can't understand that the children have grown up and are ripe for marriage. Nimr is wonderful. He's a man now, but she yells at him as though he were a little boy."

Assayed relaxes on the wooden chair lined with plaited straw. He avoids the subject of his own wife so that the Khawajah will not find out that she works as a cleaner in other people's homes. He remains silent. Because if the Khawajah finds out, he will despise him. He changes the subject of wives by throwing his hand over his shoulder to signal the boy to give him a live ember to rekindle the dead flame of his water pipe. He comes into his own and starts to talk about his son, Jalal. After all, the Khawajah is no better than himself. If Nimr is at university, and works at the Phalangist headquarters and is considered by his father to be an impressive official, so is Jalal. He misses out Jalal's escape from school and his leaving home. He begins his reminiscences with the moment he came back to them after that military operation. As he makes the yellowish water of his pipe bubble, he tells him how Jalal got lost during a military training course in the south. His companions had gone on a mission and he was with them. Assayed pretends to clear his throat as he goes over the details of the tale in his own mind. The Feda'ee who had been supposed to give the group a compass was slow about it. He forgot to give it to them until they were on the other side of the border. The members of the group called to the guide after they had crossed the electrified wires, requesting the vital instrument. He threw it hurriedly and agitatedly towards them. The compass flew in the air, then disappeared in the earth amongst the rocks. In the precious following minutes that followed, they were unable to find it. Then, they had no choice but to move away before being discovered by Israeli patrols as they passed the barbed wire. The map they had with them did not help them to get to the Zionist settlement. They got lost and came face to face with an enemy patrol. After clashing with it, they got separated. Helicopter planes attacked, spraying the woods and rocks with napalm. The combing operation continued with machine guns and incendiary materials for three days, leaving several fires burning in the rough pine woods.

Assayed continues telling the Khawajah the tale of the mission. How they had confronted the Israelis like lions, opening fire on them with their machine guns. But then, where was Jalal? No one knew where he was. God almighty, he had melted away like a lump of salt. His comrades were upset and didn't tell us that he was missing. They waited for a week, then had to officially declare that he had become a martyr. But goodness me, only hours after the news of his death was announced, he arrived. He had slipped into a ditch amongst the rocks while withdrawing. His leg was twisted and he was unable to run. He hid for several days. The patrols and the sniffer dogs were unable to find him. Imagine his suffering, his hunger, his thirst. He told me that he had eaten grass, ignoring the pain in his stomach. But he made it. Like a bird, he took care of himself and returned.

Khawajah Yacoub would turn towards him with his light thin moustache, his well-worn Turkish *culpac* and his narrow hazel eyes: "Better late than never. A sad thing, by God. You left your country without lifting a finger, and now you're using our country to make up for it. Why? Don't you know that your actions in the south are harming our produce? The apples are going bad in their crates because no one is trucking them. Military operations all the time. Have some shame and leave people alone. Such talk doesn't even impress a child."

Assayed gets involved in explaining. No. It's not our fault. The Arab regimes. "Tfoo!" He fills his mouth with saliva and spits it angrily out onto the floor.

"Khawajah, if you had been with us and seen what happened. . . . "

What happened. He tries to tell him, but does not succeed. Only the sea knows what happened. That moment when it had grown and raged to swallow up people to punish them for leaving. The vegetable shop he had left without even closing its iron door bursts into his brain. And the smoke. The smoke spreading across the port of Jaffa. The ship whistling coarsely. Then the small boats swaying and lurching, almost throwing their passengers overboard. He does not want to remember what happened. Perhaps he drinks to forget the life that followed his departure from Jaffa in the Huy boat to Sidon, and then to hell. He must not reopen that subject, the subject of misery and gloom. The Khawajah stirs up his memory with a fire-hot ladle, without a thought to the bitter taste which stings his mouth until he is intoxicated.

"You left your country on your own legs. What's that got to do with the Arab regimes, Sayyed?"

Assayed would spare no arguments that came to mind, even if that meant repeating them over and over again. He would come again when the sun was high in the sky the next day as though he had been assigned an important mission, and he would try again until the sun reached the middle of the sky, but he would not succeed in convincing the Khawajah. Assayed would ask for another glass, two, three or more. His tongue would grow heavy and little water droplets would trickle from the corner of his eyes. He would put that down to the strong sun and the spring conjunctivitis, of which he was never free. But on the cold days, he was sure they were caused by grief. Those drops would immediately dry up if he won the game, and would become clearer when they welled up as he cleared his throat after losing the game. He would pay his bill sometimes, but ignore it most of the time, promising himself to return to the Khawajah to pay it the next morning.

During the period following the bus incident when the atmosphere between the two sides had become heated, Assayed reduced his visits to the Khawajah's café. The arguments there had become harsher, becoming closer to quarrels. They would meet, and the Khawajah would offer him the usual drink on the house, then press down on him with his questions: "Why do you take up arms against us? You're all armed now from the baby to the old man. You've forgotten that we took you into our country. You came naked, thirsty and dusty. If it hadn't been for us, you'd have starved. We gave you work, but when you became human beings again, you rose up against us. Where will you stop? No, the bus was your fault. Every other day, a bus coming and a bus going. Every time a different excuse. One day it's celebrations, the next it's strikes. As though the world were your playground. So the bus! It's just an incident that happened. Why did you have to raise hell over it and attack like maniacs?"

During the calm period that had preceded last month's clashes, Assayed had ignored him. It was as though he were blaming him personally for every incident that occurred. As though Assayed were responsible for the brigades of the Turks and the Persians, and the important people across the Arab world. How many times had he tried to make his friend understand that he had nothing to do with what was going on? But one of his ears was made of mud, and the other of dough. The Khawajah ignored him with a silent rejection, avoiding his banter, shunting him on to others at the café, whose customers had grown fewer. He began to send the boy to wait on Assayed instead of doing it himself as he used to. But he would never lose the opportunity of getting across to him what he wanted to say: "What news of Jalal,

God keep him. Where is he?"

"He's on the western side. He's not here."

"I want to know, Sayyed, what has happened to you people? You used to keep yourselves to yourselves and mind your own business. Why do you spread all over our country like ants? The country is ours, but you behave like a bunch of demanding beggars. When will you stop? Disarm yourselves and kick out the armed men amongst you and things will be alright between us. Let the police into the camp like before and there won't be any trouble between you and ourselves."

"In another three years, we will have been here for thirty years, Khawajah. How do you want us to return to Palestine without those young Fedayeen? Just as you have your Phalangist forces on top of your army, we should have one too. Why not? D'you want us to be patient and stay quiet and wait for God's mercy? Okay! We've waited for twenty years and more and no one has given a damn about us. Everybody crushes us. If we were to spend another twenty years like that, the way things are, we'd get nothing."

"Why, haven't I told you what the Inqath Army did when it came to Palestine to liberate it and ended up liberating it from us? We've become homeless, evicted and languishing like the fool who went to Jericho for a holiday in the heat of summer and so neither enjoyed winter nor summer. What can happen to us more than has already happened? Once God has reduced you to being a monkey, you can't go any lower. We can't do without the Fedayeen and we won't allow the police into the camp come what may. Why should we? So that they can go back to harassing us and throwing us into prison whether we've done anything wrong or not?

The last time, Assayed had completely given up trying to explain. It occurred to him with a painful sharpness that the Khawajah belonged to a different race, remote and strange, unaware of the humiliation people were experiencing. "Disarm, says he," thought Assayed to himself as he neared the area overlooking the Dekwaneh Square. "That means they want to scalp us at the road-blocks, and even take away our arms." He slapped the pocket of his jacket again, pulling it away irritably, missing his cigarettes once more. Um Jalal had been telling him for two days: "I haven't got any money, Sayyed. I don't dare enter the houses to which I used to go. If it weren't for the home of Sister

Mary's family, no one would want to see us. The Christians can't stand anyone any more. Where d'you expect me to get any money from, Sayyed?"

Assayed wondered whether he would find the café open or empty! After last month, the Khawajah had put a table out on the pavement and sat leaning his elbow against it. The café had been completely empty, except of its owner. That was the first time that Assayed had noticed the colour of the yellowing tiles at the entrance. There had been silence; no songs or chatter or radio stations. Assayed had pretended to be passing by without a specific reason. The Khawajah had called out to him.

"No thanks, I'm in a hurry. I just thought I'd pass by and see how you were."

How empty and desolate the café had seemed then. Like his first day in the camp. As though it had been time's sudden blow since the exodus. He had not wanted to sit down. He had not wanted to. The Khawajah had strongly insisted, but he had repeated his excuses. New feelings had formed like snowflakes along the line connecting their glances. Something that starts out being light and fragile, then becomes thick and hard like white steel. Had he sat down, perhaps old, accumulated buried grievances would have surfaced. Perhaps they would have had a punch-up or spat at one another. Assayed had not wanted to risk what had remained of a life-long friendship with that Khawajah who had preferred to, or been forced to, join the ranks of his enemies. His insides had ached with wanting to sit down for a game of backgammon. But he too had felt compelled to destroy the trappings of the old friendship.

"Please don't get up. Remain where you are. I'm in a hurry. The high esteem in which I hold you prompted me to pass by and say good morning before going back home. I've got an important engagement, and I must go immediately."

Now he came to a spot where he was facing the café, still fighting a mysterious urge that brought him there every day despite his full knowledge that Khawajah Abu Nimr was not there, and that – a fact that increased his melancholy – he might never return. But never mind. He would perform that daily little duty without which he would be unable to bear the rest of the day. He raised his eyes from the small pebbles bouncing ahead of his shoes. His gaze hit the wide iron door that was shutting the café. The empty pavement was unwelcoming, and his heart sank with fear. He was sure that the café's continued closure meant that "the others" did not have good intentions. After all, Khawajah Yacoub had a son in the Phalangist Party, and he would doubtless inform his father of their future intentions. Assayed muttered a prayer for protection against Satan, spitting his premonition of imminent clashes onto the ground. He gritted his teeth angrily after a wave of craving for tobacco welled up in his blood. He was confused about the situation. The whole month had gone calmly by so why would the Khawajah not be so good as to reopen his café?

He cast an empty glance around the closed shops in the square. The stiff doors hanging in a vacuum. A grey colour dominates the square, covering everything with desolation. The corners empty of pedestrians or itinerant vendors. The stalls empty of customers. The dryness of the place which used to be filled with the smell of grilled meat rising behind the feathery fans carried by the errand boys. The silence of the car parks in the main station. The disappearance of sesame seed bread sold with green thyme. That was the one thing which had reminded him of the home country, since the taste of other foods had been lost and become meaningless in this wasteland. Nothing but the sandbags along the sides of the square around the positions that face each other. Even the fighters themselves have disappeared and not one of them is to be seen. He directed his trembling gaze from the ground to the sky, and was blinded by the bright sunlight mixed with the stifling summer humidity. He looked carefully to make absolutely sure of what he was seeing before he left. Deep in his heart, he wished that Abu Nimr had just returned and begun bringing out the tables onto the pavement and put tablecloths on them. But he could see nothing other than the closed iron shutter, which put the finishing touch on the ruin of the square. The place seemed as though it had been abandoned for a very long time.

Aisha heard her father whispering to her mother after her brother and sister had fallen asleep and she feigned slumber.

"Khadijeh"

He rarely called her by her first name, only doing so when he wanted to talk about an important matter.

43

"Khadijeh, we haven't seen your jinxed son, Jalal, since he went to live on the western side. I hear that he is responsible for supplies with the big organization. It seems he likes it over there. Hasn't the fellow got any days off on which he could pass by and ask after us? George is a Feda'ee and has no family, yet he comes to check on us every day. What is your pant-wetting son so stuck up about? He could at least visit us between one truce and the next. Or is he only good at being 'Abu so and so's' bodyguard and sitting prettily in the car next to the driver?"

"My dear, let him stay on the western side, it's safer for him that way. I spoke to him on the phone yesterday and told him not to come because there's kidnapping going on at the road-blocks."

"Curse you and your son, whose face we never see. He doesn't give a damn about anyone. By God, I crave a packet of cigarettes and can't get my hands on one except by begging or borrowing. Curse the hour that made him my son."

"For shame man. Leave the boy be."

"You've always been that way, not caring about anyone except yourself and your children."

"Me, Sayyed?"

They entered into a whispered argument which aroused Aisha's interest, who had thought they were engaged in nothing more than a fight. Their whispering turned into a fit of panting that clutched around her father's throat, sounding like the quick running of a lost animal. After that, moans of tiredness and exhaustion rose from her mother, together with the rustle of the bedcover, under which they did not stop moving. The shadows of their movements appeared to her like an octopus moving its tentacles in the darkness of the night. Only the talk of George filtered down into the depths of her consciousness. A Feda'ee, her father had told her mother. A Feda'ee, and she loved him because he was the hero of her heart. She did not know how to describe the taste of that love. Something like Christ. Like the young Virgin holding the child to her bosom, where the deepest feelings of the heart are, inside.

"Oh Virgin, where are you? For God's sake. What is this love?" she would say to herself when she would see him. She would look at him and feel that it was enough to slowly take in his form into the depths

of her imagination. She feels that if she were to touch his skin, holy oil
would come out onto her hands. She thinks that staring at him to the
full will make the wine from the holy cluster of grapes run forth over
her lips. She shakes her face, opens her eyes, and discovers that she was
passing through a day-dream, and that her tongue is still touching her
lips. It's almost as though real drops of wine are dripping, shining,
sweet and matured, across her lips.

She only knew the days of the week by his comings and goings. She
wants him to come every day so that she may understand the secret of
that strange happiness and soaring joy like the bells on a feast day. He
enters. The children's jubilant voices rise, and Assayed utters phrases of
warm welcome although he hardly ever smiles. She hears the pattering
of her mother's feet summoning her. She leaves everything she is doing
and goes to make coffee, or she slips into the corner, where no one will
notice her. She stares, watches. Her glances drink up his eyes. Slowly.
Slowly. Husam comes to show him the marbles he has won or the birds
he has hunted with his slingshot in the Thabet Woods. George warns
him: "It's best that you stay away from the Thabet Woods these days.
There are lots of snipers there."

He advises Assayed to keep the boy in the camp.

"The Thabet Woods have become a flash point between us and
them."

Assayed makes a relaxed, unconcerned gesture: "Let him go, there's
nothing to worry about. There are only one or two bullets around. A
clever fellow can escape them. It'll teach him to be a man."

With her dirty hands, Ibtissam would run to George, jumping all
over him, throwing herself into his lap without thinking of the rancid
smell sticking to her hair. He would bend over her tenderly, paying no
attention to her shabby appearance and the vulgarity of her movements. Aisha would be surprised, and would scold her, trying to
encourage her to comb her hair, at least in the presence of guests. But
the naughty little Ibtissam, who has stopped growing two years ago
and remains short, ignores the call, pinching George, who is engrossed
in a new conversation with the head of the household. When she loses
hope of drawing his attention, she asks him: "Hey, George, are you
Muslim or Christian?"

Um Jalal scolds her:"You, have some shame, girl. Say Uncle George."

And Uncle George laughs in the face of the rude little girl and says: "Guess."

"Your name sounds Christian."

"I'm not Christian because that is my *nom de guerre*. Can you guess my real name?"

"You're George . . . only."

Assayed has his say, feigning a dignity associated with the elderly: "Shut up you! Religion is not important. What are you asking him that question for?"

Um Jalal smiles and her eyes shine because she is the only one to whom he has entrusted his real name so that she can convince his fiancée's family to allow him to marry her.

And Assayed does not stop spitting mucus into a tin box he keeps beside him.

George goes on: "It's exactly as your father says. What difference would it make if I were Muslim or Christian? In Palestine, we don't ask or care . . . Your neighbour, down to the seventh house away, is important. Isn't that so?"

"But here the Christians shoot at us?"

"Not the Christians. The Phalangists and the Ahrar and the Guardians of the Cedars."

At that moment, Assayed blurts out with an indignation that only he can understand: "By God, they've always been our friends, if it weren't for their crazy leaders. Where did that Monkey's Party come from . . . I haven't got the slightest idea. . . . "

The quiet Um Jalal jumps into the conversation to uphold what George has said, unmindful that she has just interrupted Assayed at the height of his diatribe. Ignoring her husband's glare, she says: "Actually, most of the Fedayeen are Christian."

Husam puts down the slingshot, which he has tied tightly, and asks with interest: "Really? George? Does that mean that you're not the only Christian one amongst them?"

George replies: "Of course my boy, of course. Christ himself was a Palestinian. The people of the Dabyah Camp are Christians from Palestine. If you like, the whole of the Jisr El-Basha Camp and Qal'ah are Christian. They've always been compatriots and nationalists."

Ibtissam interferes in her sharp, thin voice: "Why are you from Palestine George?" She asks, adding, "Does that mean you've come from there? Were you born there?"

"Yes. But if you're clever, you'll know the name of the town I've come from. Look dear: I'm from a town that is full of green vines. It is so large and green, it has been called Toulkarem, which means the long vine."

A thought crosses Aisha's mind like a bolt of lightning as she remembers his impending engagement. Oh Virgin Mary! There is no one here she can talk to. Her mother is out of the house most of the day looking for work. When she returns, her only concern is to get the evening meal ready before Assayed comes home and throws a fit. Her father is busy as usual with his drunken friends, whom he only parts with at the end of the evening. As for Ibtissam and Husam, they are like lost children roaming the streets. When there are no clashes and no school, they only come home at bed time. Anyway, there is absolutely no way that she could ever tell her parents any of this! And that engagement is like a fateful rug being pulled from beneath her feet. When she hears anything that reminds her of it, things float up into the air, swim about around her, and she can find nothing to hold on to, nor discover a way of handling that which is so wounding to her. If she thinks of his engagement as she is walking, the pain moves from her heels to her spine, and she is unable to lift her body, as though her joints are being pulverized by stone weights. If she stares at anything, it floats up into space and disappears. Sounds enter her ears like echoes. Any laughter she hears hits her head like stones being thrown at her.

Everything has changed. Changed. Everything. Her mother shouts at her to get her to help with the housework, but she is distracted as though the scolding were not directed at her. She calls her, hoping to take her out with her on visits to the neighbours. But she is evasive, using the headache that is eating away at her head as an excuse. She manoeuvres her mother secretly into talking about him, and revealing news of him. The mother mutters something about the difficulties facing his engagement, slapping one palm against the other, and saying: "Poor one! Esh-Shalabi!"

Esh-Shalabi, the good looking, was the new name the mother was using as a nickname for him.

"How can the poor man get married? He hasn't got any money. He's simply got nothing. How will the family agree to let him have their daughter?"

If Assayed happens to hear her, he rebukes her: "Enough of that, woman. You're such a bad omen. People don't marry off their daughters for money; they do it for the sake of propriety. It would be better for them to marry her off instead of allowing her to go all over the place, running loose with the Fedayeen without any control. If I were them, I would pay to see to it that she would be contained and kept at home."

Days went by and he did not come. The terror that he would not come again drove her to the edge of a dark abyss. Nothing would move her or awaken her consciousness, except for the creak of the wooden door, which was made out of the wood of crates, or the sound of steps at the door. George was absent for a whole week. She trembled with fear lest they discover the reason for her illness. She was in a panic. When would he come? His presence was a magic balsam with which she would rub her body and all her pains would disappear. It was June, and the Beirut heat was stifling. The nausea. The vomiting. The cramps. The doctor at the Red Crescent clinic diagnosed her illness as a fever caused by pollution. What pollution? She did not know. They all ate and drank the same food and were exposed to the same causes of her supposed illness, yet only she . . . ? She would only awaken from her high fever to take a sip of water, which her intestines would reject. Then, once again. The crackle of gunfire in the room. The rattle of machine guns gathering like a storm above the ceiling. Missiles shaking the insides of the earth. An earthquake overturning the world, the room, the house, the camp, the alley. Ezza'tar. Assayed began to shout threats of doom directed at Arabs, Europeans and Persians. The Christian positions opened fire with increasing intensity. The Phalangists were saying they were determined to uproot the camp, which they considered a thorn in their side.

The headache, the fever, and Aisha in the delirium of her heavy brain could only hear the radio repeating: Israel is showing an increasing interest in events in Lebanon. Assad announces that Lebanon's security is linked to Syria's. Shooting in the green line area and sniping in the capital and the surrounding areas as the clashes intensify in Ein-Arummaneh and Shiyyah and Ashrafieh and Karantina and Ghobeiri and Ras En-Nabe causing . . . people to be killed.

Assayed refused to move to a nearby shelter when the shelling intensified. The shelter was nothing more than a three-storey building. He mocked Um Jalal: "The shelter, what for? I swear, no shelter, or any such thing. It's all a silly panic. No. We're staying here."

As for Um Jalal, she would plead every now and then, her teeth chattering as she whispered a verse from the Quran. Assayed did not know how it had occurred to her to seek protection in that particular verse: "One sin shall not carry the responsibility of another." Then she would say with full conviction: "Why won't they leave us alone? What have we done to them? What have we to do with international communism of which they accuse us?"

Aisha only talks to herself: "Where is George?" That was the question buzzing through her mind like a savage bee stinging her eyes. The noose of terror dangled around her shoulders. The rope tightens around her neck. The land is a wilderness, desolate. Nothing but a sulphurous yellow powder pouring down on her hair, her cheeks, her feet. Her flesh melts away, disappears, evaporates. Sulphur enters through the mouth, the nose, the ears. And she begins to disintegrate, turning into a skeleton with hollow eye sockets. A premonition tells her that the skeleton is George, not her own body. George! George. Where is he? She shouts, uttering unintelligble words. Her mother ties a red ribbon across her forehead to absorb the headache and dry up her pain. She cradles the head of her sick daughter in her lap, massaging her forehead in olive oil and saying her prayers. She rubs the veins in her temples with moist warm palms, sprinkling her face with water laden with pleadings to the Almighty God and the glory of the Blessed Prophet Mohammad.

Then the clashes die down.

Everything stops, and silence spreads its grey cover over the embers of the camp.

At last, Aisha recovered. With the fever, she lost her talent for counting the days. The illness removed the rebelliousness of burning longing from her. As her strength melted away, the intensity of her expectation, of monitoring the sounds of comings and goings between the house and the street, was spent. All she had left was the longing alone, manifesting itself in long, mute waiting. The waiting remained the same, although it was masked by muteness, silence, paralysis. Silence is the only possible form of waiting.

At last. At last Aisha accepted that he should do anything. Get married, become engaged, have children, or even devils if he wanted them. It was then that she was able to control the image of the future child, whom she imagined as not resembling his father at all, although she had not met the prospective mother yet. She also became able to remove the child from her imagination, banish it, and destroy the image of him with his arms around his father as he carried him. No. No. She didn't want it. Although she had accepted the unfair verdict of fate, which had ruled that George should not care about her. Nevertheless, she began to struggle against her imaginings. All for the sake of his survival. He, the like of whom did not exist. All she wanted was that he should survive the battles he was fighting. So she began to fight time by wiping out all the images that occurred to her. The important thing was that he should live. The boy! His child! No, it would not be, although she was capable of imagining what he looked like. Nothing in the world except him. He, whom no other was like. Praise be to God for his most glorious creation.

5

❦

One dove, two doves, three doves.
   One that prays, another that fasts
   And a third that worships God and the Prophet.
   It was met by Aisha, daughter of light,
   Carrying her lantern, off to visit.
   She said to Aisha: Why do you weep?
   With incense wipe away your tears.
   And once upon a time, the beloved returned. He had not been
injured or harmed. Although the camp experienced a period of com-
parative calm, interspersed with limited clashes at its edges, most
people could not relax. They remained under the influence of a bad
dream, unable to distinguish between it and reality upon first waking
up. Everybody would relate their dreams to everybody else with an
interest in themselves they had not shown before.
   We return to the man for whose survival Aisha forsook everything
else in the world. George returned with a long beard which he was
never again to shave. Ibtissam attacked in her usual way, climbing his

back and searching the pockets of his khaki jacket. Her mother noticed and thundered at her in her hoarse voice: "You, girl. Have some shame and stop that."

But George brought out the gold-coloured one pound coin which he usually gave her, and handed it to her.

"No Um Jalal, let her have it, because she's like my sister."

My sister. My sister . . . Aisha repeated the same phrase. If Ibtissam is like his sister, that means that I am too. She felt comforted that she was as close to him as a sister. A comfort mixed with a hidden agitation which she could not explain.

Ibtissam jumped up, breaking loose from his lap, and before running off to the nearby shop, she stared at him and said: "But your hair is so very long. And the beard. What's up? Aren't you going to shave it?

"No, I don't want to."

"You look frightening. Will you leave it like that for good?"

He answered jokingly: "Till Palestine is liberated."

Ibtissam clapped, and ran for the door, ululating. Assayed raised his side, which was leaning on his elbow on the ottoman. He grabbed one of the slippers nearest to him and threw it at her. It hit the wall near the door.

"Dry up, you impudent thing. All we need is ululating and filthy behaviour."

Then he turned to George: "Just look at those mindless girls. All you have to do is utter one word, and they are ecstatic."

"But she is young, Sayyed."

"They're all alike, both young and old."

Aisha was peeved by the insult he was directing at her, and she pulled her limbs closer around her body as she squatted like a porcupine sheltering within its prickly framework. Her father continued his dialogue with the guest as though nothing had happened: "Till Palestine is free? That means you are optimistic."

"Optimistic. Of course. Why not?"

"You are hopeful that Palestine will be restored, while the Arab nation doesn't give a damn about us? And while those Khawajahs are giving us hell?"

"And why not, Sayyed? If it were not for that hope, I would not have become a Feda'ee. Would I fight for death alone? No, by God. I want a state that will be democratic and against oppression."

Assayed's features showed a clear distaste.

"I trust, son, that you don't want that thing. What's it called? Communism!"

George answered with his customary courtesy: "What of it, uncle? They too fought colonialism in their countries like all the peoples of the world who struggled to become free."

He expanded on the subject as he stretched out, his eyes fixed in space as though he were surveying several models and choosing from them: "And why not? No one is better than anybody else. One of these days, we must have a state like everybody else in the world. And what is wrong with it being a socialist state?"

Assayed answered him with sweeping conviction: "No, anything but that. We've had enough of catastrophes and poverty. All the countries you talk about are poor. What a bad omen, man. We don't need more poverty do we?"

Assayed began to eloquently repeat the gist of a conversation he had had with Khawajah Yacoub, who was an expert on foreign affairs. He had so often imparted to him information from all over the world and the world of business and interests. George interrupted him as though he were responding to a personal insult: "If only you could see, Sayyed. I saw it with my own eyes when I was on my military course. Everybody is equal, and there isn't a beggar or a pauper."

"No son, no. What have you seen compared to others? Even if, as you describe them, they are respectable people and not like us."

Assayed went on with a gloom that he was unable to hide: "We're the only ones who will never be like other people. We've had fifty years of continuous revolutions and we haven't got anything. My father and his brother, my uncle, took part in the 1936 uprising. After that, we saw all the mess that followed for twenty years after that until 1948, and all we got was misery and hard times."

"You have a point, uncle. First we were ruled by the Turks. They left and the English came. The English departed and installed the Zionists in their place. Each gives the next one a power of attorney before leaving. The only solution is to fight until we have our own independent state."

"D'you think so? Will we get a state in the end?"

George answered: "Of course. Do you think we're playing or amusing ourselves, losing all those martyrs just so that everybody can continue to step on us?"

Um Jalal took advantage of what she thought was the end of the conversation to reassure herself: "How will this situation end? I beg you, tell me, when will the clashes stop so that we can go to work?"

But Assayed, who was full of resentment towards her because she had recently stopped bringing in money, snapped at her, pretending to be irritated by the triviality of her question: "Stop it, woman. Stop asking him what's going on. D'you think he's the head of the truce committee? Work? Work? You make it sound as though that's all you were doing. Blast work and its creator."

His boisterous laugh burst out, and little tears trickled out of the sides of his red eyes. He stopped, and turned to George, who seemed startled by his thundering laughter. The mother called on God and looked at her husband with disapproval, like one who fully understood the signal he was giving out. Assayed said with a crafty smile that slowly grew bigger and bigger: "Now, shall I tell you the dream I had a couple of days ago?"

Um Jalal began saying in a rapid, mechanical tone: "Your forgiveness, Oh God, Your forgiveness, Oh God."

Assayed said: "The story, my friend, is that I dreamed that I died and went to God on the Day of Judgement. Yes, I did. First the angels of torture, Naker and Nakeer, climbed onto my shoulders and said: Confess your sins and trespasses on earth, or we will strangle you. I said: whatever you do, I won't talk unless I am before God Almighty. They would not agree. But after a while, they got fed up with me. They dragged me off to Moses, that is, the Prophet Moses. I saw Moses as an old man with white hair wearing a robe made of lamb's wool. He was grazing his sheep in a valley. I wouldn't confess to him. I said: It's enough that your people have taken away our country, Palestine, and are making our lives a misery. By God, I shan't tell you. Naker and Nakeer tried to force me to talk, but I swore that I wouldn't obey them. I said I would only talk to God Almighty. They forced me to go to Our Master, Jesus. He was milking a ewe on a hill. I wouldn't speak to him. I said: The holy places are held by the Jews who crucified you, and you want me to talk? No, by God, I shan't utter a word. Naker and Nakeer were angry, but would not agree to take me before God. They took me to see Prophet Mohammad, blessed be his name, and he was wearing a robe made of camel hair. I said: It's true that you are our Prophet Mohammad, but if you are sorry for me, will you intercede for me to go before God? In the end, he allowed me to go before God Almighty. Naker and Nakeer took me to a vast valley. Clouds covered the mountain peak. I shouted upwards, saying: Oh God, why are you making it so difficult for me to make a living? Suddenly, an angel in the form of a bedouin appeared, a halo shining around his headdress and robe. The angel said: God has sent me to answer your question. He looked ahead of him and stretched out his hand, touching a large copper cauldron, which had so many holes in it that it looked like a sieve. He said, this is livelihood as you can see. Every human being has a hole. A big hole signifies a large livelihood. He who has a small hole should thank God for what he has been given. I said: Okay, where is my hole? He pointed his finger at a minute hole, no bigger than the eye of a needle. Even a tear would not have got through it. I suddenly found myself behaving like an excited bull. I threw myself at the man, I mean the angel, shouting: what is this injustice? Injustice on earth and injustice in heaven. I opened my eyes and found that I was holding the pillow and punching it like mad. What a sight."

George was doubled up with laughter. Assayed calmed down, his tense features relaxing after telling the story, which he had taken to relating to everyone in sight. Um Jalal's features contorted as she watched Aisha carry the coffee tray and draw closer to George with shaky steps and trembling fingers as though she were about to trip and fall. She wished she knew what had happened to the girl after the bout of fever she had suffered. She had the faintest suspicion that there was a strange connection between her daughter's fits of depression and George's absences or visits. When he would come, her daughter's steps would get smaller, she would be mesmerized in the far corner, not moving unless called. Um Jalal attributed her daughter's behaviour to the confused modesty displayed by young women. But shyness surely did not have such an effect. She wished that she could explain the aura of strangeness that surrounded her daughter whenever George came to the house. Her hearing would become more accurate and keen. Her eyes would shine like silk threads. Her pale face would blossom like a rose bed. But Um Jalal quickly put those thoughts out of her mind. It must be that Aisha was still upset at being taken away from school. She thought back on her row with Assayed a short while ago, as George had arrived at the top of the road. She ran to Assayed, who sat smoking his cigarettes in the front of the room: "Abu Jalal. Abu Jalal. He's come. I saw him from the roof. He's at the top of the road."

Encouraged by his calm temper, she was carried away by her joy: "If I had work and was earning money, By God I would have slaughtered a sheep at the doorstep as thanksgiving for his safe return."

"What!" he had thundered, jumping up towards her as though he would kill her. Her eyes bulged as she stepped backwards. He said: "Don't you dare repeat the Jalal episode. You can see that we're almost starving. We can't even find a donkey to slaughter and eat."

Um Jalal whispered in unexpected panic: "Shshsh! Lower your voice. Don't scandalize us with the stranger. He might walk in and hear you."

"I thought you were about to do what you did before!"

He was harping on about her behaviour the day she had received Jalal upon his return from the guerilla operation in which he had almost been killed. On that day, Assayed had asked her for money, banking on her happiness that her son had survived: "The office said that the boy would come at noon. Give me some money."

Um Jalal pulled back her heavy body, leaning her hips on the bed, turning away her swollen face in a pout. Assayed bent his knees, kneeling on the bed and directing his fiery gaze at her: "I said give me money, and I meant give me money."

The grinding of his teeth emphasized his threat. She moved, touching the purse she had kept between her breasts during the night. She pulled it out and gave him the amount he was used to getting every day. He shook his head, laced with white hair, batting his diseased eyelids, and said: "No more than that?"

She remained silent, staring at the quilt in front of her as though she had not heard. He cleared his throat, leaning forward as he got up to leave to wherever it was that he went every day.

That day when he came back, he was taken aback by the threads of red blood dripping over the doorstep, staining the lime wall over-looking the alley. He saw the remains of a slaughtered animal that had just been skinned, and he burst into the house in a rage, demanding to know what was going on. No sooner had he embraced his son, congratulated him and kissed him, than he looked at Um Jalal, who said: "Well, Sayyed, it is a slaughtered offering to fulfil a vow for the safety of our son."

"Thank God for his safety, but where's the need for an offering? D'you think you're sitting on a fortune?"

"Never mind, Sayyed. Is there an occasion nicer than this in the whole world?"

He fell silent with the submission of someone waiting for the right moment to retaliate. When Jalal went out into the yard, he immediately went to the kitchen. All he could see was the ladle in a sieve on the floor. Suspiciously, he asked:

"Where's the meat?"

Um Jalal wanted to speak, but she was too frightened, and remained silent. Jalal walked into the kitchen, and at a glance, realized what was going on. So he answered: "We distributed it amongst the neighbours."

Assayed thought about this, forcing himself not to attack one of them.

"A whole lamb! And you gave it away for the spirit of the Prophet? Are you out of your minds?"

But the storm of his fury receded before his son's intervention. The mother was possessed by an unusual courage, placing her hand on her waist, she said firmly: "But of course. Why else is it called a vow? One doesn't eat an offering made to honour a vow. It must be given away to the poor."

Assayed shook his head right and left, shouting: "And what about us, aren't we poor?"

He added: "I vow here and now that if you do this again, even if the Prophet himself were to come, I will bring a wild donkey and slaughter it across the doorstep. That'll show you and your neighbours what a proper vow is."

Um Jalal put her hand over her heart as though she were pushing off such a spectacle: a slaughtered donkey, its blood trickling and foaming at the doorstep. The neighbours looking on. Passers-by staring. Everybody pointing. She forced the image from her mind dismissing it with her hand as one does a blue fly. She remembered the need to tell George the news she was burning to impart as soon as he came in. She stretched her thick neck forward and proclaimed: "George. George. I have news that should make you happy. If only you knew what happened while you were away."

The mother added: "I will accompany him to meet her family, because I'm like his sister."

Ibtissam, who could never be still, jumped up and encircled her mother's neck: "Yamma, I'm like his sister. You're like his mother."

Um Jalal laughed with satisfaction, her front teeth showing.

"His mother or his sister! It's all the same. He's one of us. Nothing is as tender to a walnut as its shell."

Ibtissam jumped about near George, tucking herself under his left arm: "The wedding! The wedding! When's the wedding?"

Um Jalal told her off, then addressed herself to George: "You're such a pain, you really are. Is a wedding an easy matter? It's a good thing that the bride's family have even agreed to talk to us. Shalabi, thank God that they turned out to be nice people and didn't snub us!"

Ibtissam found a way of getting back at her mother for her indifference towards her: "George, my mother said that they're afraid to let their daughter marry you because you are a Feda'ee and they don't know the first thing about you, and they don't know your family in the West Bank."

George answered without changing the expression on his face: "A Feda'ee, and I have no one. You're my family!"

His calm response seemed to disappoint her, prompting her to challenge him further. Speaking to him again, she said: "Why d'you pronounce the 'ka' as a 'cha' when you speak? Aren't you worried that your fiancé's family will think that you're a peasant?"

"I *am* a peasant."

She jumped with joy at the strange news, which aroused her interest: "A real live peasant? Does that mean that you plant and harvest the land?"

"I'm a peasant and the son of peasants. But I've no longer got any land to plant and harvest."

"So how d'you make a living?"

"We're just like everybody else. My brothers and sisters and I, each of us is homeless in a different country."

"Have you got a mother and a father?"

"My father's still alive, but my mother died a long time ago. My older sister took care of us."

"What about your brothers and sisters?"

"My older brother is in Saudi Arabia, working. . . . "

Um Jalal had had enough of her impudent little daughter playing smart. She picked up the coarse broom leaning against the wall, raising it as she aimed deep-felt curses at her: "Begone, you. Leave us alone, you urchin. You're still a child, you dwarf, and yet you're winding us up? I'll twist that mouth of yours."

Apologetically, she tried to make it up to George: "Have a seat, Shalabi, until Assayed comes. I'll make you a nice cup of tea."

From her usual place in the corner, Aisha followed the conversation, heavy with emotions that were savaging her like the teeth of an iron monster and a pain that turned over like hot coals in her stomach. It boils over, its froth rising as a tiredness that saps all her strength. She looks at him as though she is seeing him for the first time. She comes out of the circle of his eyes, shining with light, and her eyes begin to traverse his body as a real man, not an image in an icon. Distress will scald her and sadness will kill her before she is free of her obsession with him, despite all her wishes that she consider him as nothing other than a brother. However, she is afraid of a new thing that is spreading through her soul, and she cannot shake it off. She's no longer only attracted to his laughter and his eyes, nor only to the halo that goes before him. She's now captivated by all of his form. His appearance. The tender moustache, some of its hairs touching the upper lip when he speaks. The strong, fine hair outlining the chin. The thick eyebrows meeting over the nose in an arch resembling a light tattoo. The rough, balanced voice coming forth with the familiar movement of the Adam's apple – a thing she had previously considered to be one of the ugly aspects of manhood. Everything that had been hateful about them had become nice because it pertained to him. She became aware of a few hairs climbing the top of the chest to the neck. She found them intriguing and very interesting. Once, she had considered that what men and monkeys had in common was that they both had hair on their bodies. Even the bottom of his trousers, gathered at the ankles and tucked into the military boots had a unique beauty that she had not known before.

She was shy to admit to herself that she was in love with his shadow. She would stand on the roof, awaiting his arrival, so that she could see his shadow entering the house with him. If only she could be his shadow, she would find rest and be healed.

Um Jalal could not believe her ears when her daughter asked her to accompany her to the home of George's fiancé. She had never understood why her daughter had resisted visiting their neighbours and acquaintances in the first place. So how could she now understand her eagerness, especially since she was so weak and lacking in stamina?

"Okay, my dear, perhaps it will give you something to do. All your illnesses are caused by being by yourself."

And she took her with her on the visit during which an agreement would be concluded regarding the objects necessary for the marriage to take place.

In the parlour at Hana's house, wide couches lined the four walls, their sides sticking to each other because they had been crammed together despite their large sizes. A brown vase decorated with sea shells painted a dark brown colour stood on a shelf against the wall. The feathers of a coloured peacock protruded from it. Through the narrowly opened door, Hana entered and welcomed the guests keeping company with her mother. Hana was not much different to the image that Aisha had drawn up in her mind's eye. She was an ordinary girl. A camp girl. Her relative affluence had not changed the ordinariness of her appearance and her indistinctness. The scene was familiar to the point of banality. Couches with carved woodwork, lined with velvet in the French style in a cramped room. Small formica tables wedged between the legs of the seated guests. Aisha was amazed because Hana did not deserve such insistence on George's part to get consent to marry her. At that moment, she felt her incomprehension of George's behaviour and her bedazzlement with his actions were trapping her in a web of bewildered wonder. Why was he determined to pursue such an ordinary girl, while he was such a unique man? At the beginning, Aisha studied Hana's mother. Heavily powdered cheeks, Arabic kohl smudging the edges of her eyelids, and a flowered silk dress deliberately emphasizing the roundness of her bosom and buttocks. She noticed how large, how full of male-like hair her nostrils were. Um Hana had bedecked her wrists and arms with shining golden bracelets. Except for her dark complexion, Hana did not resemble her mother. Her green eyes tilted upwards and were shielded by thick lashes, although they were narrow eyes with sharp corners. The ends of her hair were longish and winding, suggesting that they ought to be trimmed. She had a small mole on her left cheek matching her deep black hair. The most noticeable thing about her was her expression of self-confidence, which was clearly worn on her face. One couldn't make out whether it came from being a pampered only child, or from being a member of an organization.

The bride's mother brought in bowls of nuts, roasted melon seeds, dried chick peas and pistachio nuts. Hana offered Pepsi Cola in coloured glasses. The mother's closest relative brought in a water pipe with Persian tobacco, which Um Jalal received with eagerness, remarking on the disappearance of the good tobacco brands during those days. The two women alternated in taking drags from the pipe through the narrow chord with obvious pleasure. Um Jalal praised the hospitality with which she was being received: "I usually smoke cigarettes. I only enjoy a water pipe when the company is good, although a water pipe tastes better than cigarettes."

Um Hana told her: "I learned to smoke a water pipe from the wives of Abu Hana's business partners who live along Al-Jadida Road. Gosh, what a good time I used to have with them before the way to the western side was cut off. They are Sunni Muslims and originally from Basta. The women always used to have morning coffees."

Another relative brought in bowls of blancmange topped with blanched almonds. Um Jalal sucked her lips in preparation for broaching the main subject she had come to raise. She made ready to speak after noticing Hana's restlessness, and she feared that the girl might leave the room. Hana's movement, however, was due to her agitation, brought on by the intrusiveness of Aisha's stares, which were cast at her like a spider's threads. The girl, with her searching looks and conservative posture, sitting transfixed on the sofa, resembled the women who used to visit her mother with proposals of marriage from their male relatives. Her appearance was disturbing as she closely examined the fiancée, looking distracted as though she were in a trance. However, the argument – the first and most important round in the process of forging a marriage agreement – soon began. The bride's mother demanded an account of the bridegroom morals. Um Jalal waxed lyrical as she praised him and extolled his behaviour. Then, without further argument, the conversation moved to the practical aspects after everyone understood the gist of the implicit consent given by Hana's mother. It became necessary to discuss the details of the agreement, before the subject could be referred to the men for completion.

The bride's mother asked for the customary list of clothes. Dresses, silk nightgowns in seven colours. A pampered young girl like Hana must change into several different dresses during the wedding. She said that the wedding jewellery must be comprised of several gold ornaments as was the custom. She repeatedly emphasized the need for a black evening suit "habillé", stressing the "é" at the end of the word to draw attention to the fact that she had picked up French-Arabic words through her friendships. Um Jalal sensed that the atmosphere had become suitable for manoeuvring: "Listen dear. The esteem in which you are held is unmatched. The bridegroom is a fine man, God bless him. His family will soon send him some money, but you know the problems of crossing the bridge these days. No one can leave the West Bank without going through a hard time. The Israelis interrogate people thoroughly before they allow them to come. Soon things will calm down and they will send more than anyone has ever seen. Just think of the huge tins of olive oil which we'll all get lots of . . . Let's get the marriage contract signed and set a date for the wedding. We'll do everything you ask for, Madame Um Hana."

Um Hana retreated before her guest's assurances: "At least a complete bedroom suite. And a diamond ring with two pairs of thick golden bracelets."

Unexpectedly, Hana's voice piped up: "And who said that I want any gold?"

Her mother's embarrassed looks did nothing to quieten her down, so she spoke to her pleadingly: "Hana, hush. That's my business, not yours. D'you think your father would just accept things to happen casually? What will people say about us?"

"People or not, that's not my concern. I'm saying no to gold."

Um Jalal gave her a look of open admiration because her objections to her parents' conditions would make her mission easier.

Hana said: "I've got all sorts of clothes that I never wear. Why the waste? Seven colours indeed!"

The mother turned pale before her daughter's insistence and she scolded her: "God help us handle you and your generation. You've made our hair turn white"

Continuing her conversation, she said to Um Jalal: "I can tell you, from the day my daughter began working at the Signals Department, I've had sleepless nights. If only that were enough for her. What would she have done if she were repressed and ill-treated like the girls who work at the factories?"

Using what she considered to be an irrefutable argument, she silenced her daughter:

"It's enough that your father only agreed to this match after giving us a very hard time indeed. Now you want to create problems all over again?"

After give and take, the two women agreed that the couple's home would be equipped with the bare necessities, and that the preparation of the clothes would get underway as they waited for financial help to arrive from the bridegroom's family in the West Bank, and that the wedding would be celebrated in September.

Before Aisha and her mother went home, Hana looked closely at Aisha, then said to Um Jalal: "What does your daughter do?"

"She stays at home."

"You said that she had been to a nun's school. Why doesn't she help us out with our literacy courses for adults?"

Um Jalal beat upon her chest and gasped, saying: "Assayed is very strict and jealous over his daughters. He barely accepts that she should walk on the street! I wish that Aisha worked."

"Well then, you prevail on him to allow her to help us with the course."

"D'you think anyone can talk to him? . . . One can't go near anything he disapproves of . . . Just think of it . . . he wouldn't even let her stay at school!"

The conversation excited Aisha and moved something deep inside her. On their way home, she asked her mother: "Why didn't the girl talk to me? Does she think I'm too young?"

"Perhaps it's because she doesn't know you."

"No . . . She thinks she's better than I am."

"May Hana, the electrician's daughter, swagger in vain. Why should she patronize you? Why dear, what is it that she's got that you haven't?"

"Alright Yamma. Why won't you let me work?"

"No, my dear. All our other problems would seem like nothing if this became an issue. D'you think we need more of your father's rages? I'm the only one who works and it makes him throw scenes."

"But I used to work at school. Why can't I work over here?"

"That was considered part of going to school. But here, it's different. How could we allow you to, when you're just a naïve young girl? No, my dear. Everything but this. On top of it all, the clothes factories aren't taking workers from the camp any more. Where would we send you?"

"Let me go and help them with the literacy course."

"Leave us be and close the subject. Your father won't agree."

"Won't agree? Won't agree? For God's sake – what misfortune is this?"

Aisha walked through the narrow alleys in the waning evening light. On both sides, women washed their doorsteps or threw the remaining laundry water into the open sewers. Barefoot children, half naked or wearing torn clothes, jostled and scampered about oblivious to the cattle dung, metal bottle stoppers and faded pieces of fabric littering the ground. She walked beside her mother clenching her teeth, her jaw creaking, and said: "If I only went for a couple of hours a week, what would happen?"

But the mother walked on without answering because the experience of her long life had taught her to avoid the man and his cruel nature. She dealt with him like a stream of water, going around the rock, but never penetrating it.

As soon as they walked in, Assayed swooped down on his daughter, who was choking with unhappiness. He stared at her and asked her with intense sarcasm: "Why are you distracted, Yaba? Are you upset because you haven't been to Paris?"

6

⮞⮜

The light of a new lantern shone in the house. Everyone joined in the argument about his engagement and marriage except for Aisha. During the intermittent days when there was no fighting, Um Jalal was able to get to the New Market on the pavement of Ar-Rawsheh. The shop-owners whose shops downtown had been burnt down, had set up shop there, spreading their wares on the street, or selling them in tents. Um Jalal convinced Assayed that it was necessary for her to go to the western side during the temporary periods of peace on the pretext of getting some money from her son. But she never brought any money back with her. She would always use the excuse that she had not been able to get hold of him because he was so busy. But Assayed remained convinced that she had definitely met up with him, and that she was holding on to the money he had given her for a rainy day. He interrogated her several times, but she swore on the Holy Quran that she had not met her son because she had been in a hurry to get back for fear that the return route would get blocked. So Assayed would have to set her free every time, despite his overriding eagerness to get a small amount of money. This dumpy woman would always return with a few purchases for the anticipated wedding, as she did the day she brought back a white linen jacket for George to wear on the wedding day. She would never tire of telling those around her of the horrors she had borne with great courage, such as crossing the dangerous flashpoints, within aim of the sniper's guns and their deadly bullets. She would get carried away with excitement, and perspiration would cover her forehead and trickle down her temples, forming big drops. She told him in her tremulous voice as she lit a cigarette, her phrases punctuated by thick panting: "Look at this nightgown and matching dressing gown. Just the thing for a bride. It's full of lace. The vendor swore that if it hadn't been for the situation, he wouldn't have let me have it for a hundred-and-fifty liras, which is half-price. They're original Valisere."

She would shuttle between the roof and the entrance, talking to her neighbours. She would shake the fabric of her wide dress over her bosom and say: "Things aren't bad this month, and there are only a few clashes, although it's burning August. Perhaps the folk on the western side have had enough of making trouble, and gone up to the mountains on summer holiday. If only they'd leave us be. May God and the Prophet go with them. May God keep them happy and far away. They've given us such a horrible time. I can't wait till we've married off Shalabi. I gather his mother may be coming from the West Bank to attend the wedding."

And Aisha would turn into a soulless statue as she listened, seeing and hearing and only able to feign coldness and indifference. Her mother even scolded her for her negligence and for not asking after George. She became thinner by the day, as she imagined the wedding candles. She would rush to a private oasis of tears to bathe her woes. She would savour the dulling relief of secret weeping that would drug her when she locked herself into the bathroom pretending she was busy washing the laundry. She would spread out the dirty clothes beneath the water flowing from the tap and begin to rub and wring them, crying as she did so, out of everybody's sight. The basin would fill up with water, but she would not turn off the tap. Instead, she would stand inside the heavy copper basin, stepping on the clothes and imagining them to be her jailers. People with no definite features. They were a cross between her mother and her father, the neighbours and everyone on earth. She would stamp her feet on them, passing her heels over them and rubbing them in the overflowing water and the soap bubbles. Once she had exhausted herself with the rubbing, paddling and stepping over the wet corpses, and with silent weeping, drinking in its moans and pains like a dose of poison trickling down to her heart, she would emerge with swollen eyes and a red nose, slinking up to the roof to hang out the washing up there in the fresh air, far from the din of the cooker and the hiss of kerosene. She would regain her panting breath, and become engrossed in studying the colours of the plants and their degrees of greenness. She would water the acacia bush with its outstretched, rounded branches, full of water, and its infinitely soft white flowers. She would moisten the trellis on which the morning glory climbed, its petals closing at sunset, refusing to be roused until the very first light of morning. She would stretch her gaze through the leaves of the vine, planted in a large barrel to the horizon and the buildings of Qal'ah and Jisr El-Basha. She would turn and look to the north east, but her view would be blocked by the high buildings of Ashrafieh, topped by forests of black television aerials. She would scour the horizon for an empty patch, knowing that she would not find the island of which she dreamed, because the camp was besieged from every direction. A very few people could enter and leave it. What would rescue her from the trap in which she was imprisoned? The camp itself had become an inmate condemned to a long sentence that could last a lifetime. Aisha began to think of the need to get a job. At least if she were to have a job, she could move around a little. If the situation had been normal, she would have tried to convince her parents to let her get one, but now she daren't say a word to her father, especially since the factories were closing down and sacking their workers. If the original workers were losing their jobs, what would it be like for her, being so green and inexperienced in the ways of the world, as her mother said?

As she moved around on the roof, the radio broadcasts to which everyone in the camp would listen in a manner resembling a collective act of prayer floated up to her. The sounds of transistor radios would get mixed up. The voices of the various radio announcers spreading into every corner, alley and crossroads would only be drowned out by the announcer giving directions on the safe roads and those that were open and free of kidnap road-blocks and sniping. Sprinkled amongst all that were strange phrases with which even little children became familiar. Words like: isolationists; political sectarianism; reforming the electoral system; the Phalangist leader Pierre Jemayel's accusation that the resistance is an agent of international socialism. And from day to day, Israeli attacks on the camps and villages in the south increased. Continuous air raids on Ein El-Hilweh, Sidon, Tyre, Nabatiyyeh and several other names. No sooner had one learned those names than one would be surprised by the need to learn new ones. Assayed still continued his daily habit of going down to the Dekwaneh Square, still hoping that the situation would improve, and that the days would go back to normal. But he would only find barricades, their number growing by the day, surrounded by an increasing number of sandbags and cement-filled barrels. Delusions would tempt him to go down there despite the ever-present danger of sniping. He descends on the square, hastening his steps, imaging that the man over there with the culpac standing at a corner is Abu Nimr. But when he gets close to him, he discovers that he is someone else. He takes two steps forward and raises his palms to his forehead, lowering his lids as he looks to- wards the café, but he sees no one. He leaves wracked with depression, considering several possibilities, then trying to push them out of his mind. But a cursed premonition assails him as he raises his heavy feet, climbing the hill – a feeling that Abu Nimr's failure to return means that the war will be resumed and go on indefinitely. He grits his teeth and talks to himself: "I know the bastards. They won't be satisfied until they have dragged us through the dust and made us homeless all over again."

A black despair rises within him whenever he turns his back to re- turn home. An inner conviction assures him that he will never see Abu Nimr again. His experience as a former guard at a factory has taught him that the Khawajahs never go back on what they decide, and that now, they will use all they have to smash the camp and uproot it. The siege will continue to ring the camp, and its rhythms will become more savage and destructive. Assayed even began to secretly hold the young men responsible. Why had they not kept quiet and stopped fighting a war which they had no hope of winning? Then he would begin to remember the oppression to which the Lebanese police had subjected the camp. Sergeant Abu Abboud who used to eavesdrop on the camp dwellers through their windows to pick up conversations to which he could attach political interpretations so that he could drag them off to prison, where they would languish. God spare us the Deuxième Bureau and its days. Who would agree to the return of its authority? People would be prevented from rebuilding a collapsing roof without the permission of the police and the censors. Now everyone, especially the poorest of the poor, had taken advantage of their departure to replace their old shacks with concrete-built ones. At least now they were free of the water leaking through the holes in their rooves. People would no longer agree to tear down their houses and live in huts made out of cartons and empty milk tins. They were now used to the role played by the "Popular Committee" and "The Armed Struggle" and no one was willing to put up with the swagger of the police any more, and the unfair fines and prison sentences they had been imposing.

"Curse that time. They think they're the children of the lady, and we're the children of the slave."

Assayed spat and walked on, talking aloud to himself, recalling the twenty-five lira fine that Um Jalal had paid Sergeant Abboud for pouring the laundry water outside her doorstep.

And he, what would he do now? Penury had taken him to the brink of torture. How would he be able to save enough money to pay for a bottle of *arak*? He would wait for his wife to leave the house so that he could rummage through the clothes and search the saucepans and dishes in the kitchen. He would pass his hands over every crack in the wall searching for folded notes of money. When he failed to find what he was looking for, which always happened, a stream of curses would fly out of his mouth with droplets of the saliva gathered at the corners of his mouth: "The bitch, she cleans other people's homes, but doesn't give a damn about her own, I'll. . . . "

It seemed that the latest events had diminished all his previous strength. He would rage and foam at the mouth without achieving any results. Most of the enjoyment had gone out of his life once he stopped entertaining his loyal friends and acquaintances.

When his friends used to visit, he would feel that life, which was worth less than an old shoe, would regain its brightness. He would be transported back to the beach in Jaffa, when he had been in the prime of youth. Those where the days when he was the son of a family that did not fear its tomorrows because it owned tens of *dunums* of orange groves each a thousand square metres. He would finish working at the vegetable market in the evenings, turn the shop over to an employee, and rush home to change. He would put on a western suit and a red fez with a black silk tassel, and go off to the promenade with his friends. They would walk through the Ajami, and have meat grilled with onions and tomatoes for supper. On Thursdays, they would go to the cinema, or to a nightclub to listen to the latest songs and shows. After he was married, he had wanted to take his wife to the cinema on Thursdays, but his mother had prevented him from taking her, warning him that she would become like those immoral Jewish women if he did. The Jews. His friend Khawajah Dori, had been his closest friend. He used to speak Arabic and lived exactly the way he and his family did. He used to meet up with him and their other friends at the weekend. He would only buy clothes for his wife, Wahiba, from the Khawajah's shop in Tel Aviv. Those Jewish Khawajahs. Who would have thought them capable of doing what they did? They would be your neighbours for ages, and suddenly, one would discover that they had joined the enemy ranks of the Haganah and Stern Gangs. Curse that time. Friends had been parted, and there was no news of Khawajah Dori. But the atrocities of his Jewish relatives since their blighted emigration from Europe was more than enough. Oh, how cruel time was! Wahiba's death, which still stung his heart. He used to bring her necklaces made of narcissus flowers, which she would weave through her hair in the evenings before he came home. She would quarrel with his mother and sister-in-law and wait for him on the doorstep so that she could report them. Her voice was like music to his ears despite his mother's censure and continued nagging. She would wear a brown lipstick, the colour of jujube, and paint her nails a bright red. They would stay in their room beneath the warmth of the quilt and the mesh curtain around the copper bed. His mother would shout outside the door so that they would hear her: "What's this woman, who paints and pampers herself instead of getting up and cleaning the house! It seems that no one enjoys life except for the riff-raff!"

His mother would nag all day. They would only be free of her interference when they took refuge in their room, which they wouldn't leave till the next morning. Those were the days. How he loved her, and how his heart still jumped when he remembered her. She died of septi-caemia during pregnancy. How different the two wives were. God had replaced a palm tree with a goat. How different the two countries were. Since then the drinking had started, and it would continue that way until the end because he wanted to forget. Oh, how nice it was to drink with friends. If it hadn't been for that, he would have died long ago.

Assayed's angry outbursts continued whether there was a clear reason or not. The only new thing was his audible talking to himself. Then suddenly, he would go into a daze, forgetting the excuse for his anger. Aisha was the only one who felt that his new distraction endowed the house with peace. The absence of her father's night-time companions made the house quieter. They had been in the habit of coming every Saturday night. They would spread a nauseating cloud of aniseed odour. They would distribute the milky white liquid to one another, and Assayed would belch between one laugh and the next. He would clap, demanding more tomatoes and olives. They would sit cross-legged on the floor, their worn-out shoes piled at the doorstep. One of them would pull out an old lute, tune its chords, check that the ivory pick was in good order, then start playing simple tunes, that would turn into long songs in which they would all take different roles. Assayed would refine his voice as though he were chanting holy verses. The names of Sayyed Darwish and Saleh Abdel Hayy would turn into jems imparting a blessing to those mentioning or touching them. Their singing of "Why Oh Violet" and "Oh Zaghlouli Dates" and "I Fell in Love and Expired" would ring out as though during those moments they were avenging their wasted lives. The music and reminiscing would go round inside the magic circle created by the dancing tunes in the smoky, stuffy air in the corridor topped with a metal roof. Aisha would yawn on the blanket spread next to her mother, who had fallen into a deep sleep, her head leaning against the wall and lolling to the right and to the left.

Towards the end of the night, when the owner of the lute would weary and stop playing, their collapsing voices would fall. Political discussions would begin, punctuated with sighs, shouts and repeated oaths that they had known then exactly what would happen. . . . Their voices would clash as each assured the others of his early detection of the signs of the tragedy and the signals foretelling their fated and bloody

71

exodus from Palestine. Sorrows and woes would arise, scattering amongst the empty bottles and little rows that would mingle with their tales. Every now and then, her mother would wake up, bending her head towards the crack of the door to see whether they were still there, vaguely muttering her wish that they would leave for their homes because the boy and the girl "were in the seventh heaven of sleep" without enough covers or sheets. As long as the guests were in the room, Um Jalal could not spread out the mattress on which they put the bed clothes. She would listen to them between naps, and when she would lose hope, her head would tilt down onto her shoulder, and her snoring would rise intermittently, becoming deep and regular, leading her into an agitated sleep. Aisha would go into a stupor, moaning in a choked voice because the hardness of the wall worsened the pain in her back. Between wakefulness and sleep, she would see armies of ants swarming over her legs, digging into her flesh with their pointed heads. As she wrestled with sleep, she would jump amongst rocks and stones, until her consciousness focused again, and she would wake up. She would change her position and gather her dress around her.

As morning would break, Assayed and his friends would grow tired of relating their memories of the port at Haifa and the refinery workers, the battles of Jerusalem and Bab el-Wad, the massacre of Deir Yassin and the fall of Alama and She'ab and Saffourieh to the Zionist gangs. The oldest in the group would sum up their evening: "All our uprisings were haphazard and lacked organization. It's true that there were battles and unrest and commercial strikes and shooting, but it was all spontaneous and without proper organization. If we had been in control of our country, this would not have happened to us. God curse the English. They caused the immigration to Palestine and prevented us from possessing even one bullet. Anyone caught with a bullet would go to prison for a whole year under martial law which broke our backs. They did us so much harm without any fear of God. It's enough that the English brought the Jews, the source of our troubles. They slaughtered them in their own country, then brought them over and installed them on our land."

A discussion of the Nazi, Hitler, would follow. They would argue over whether he was the reason for Jewish colonization of Palestine. The secondary school teacher would conclude the argument by repeating for the thousandth time that the first Jewish migration to Palestine had been in 1904, when Hitler was still a child on his mother's knee. By then, the room would be enveloped in a curtain of cigarette smoke forming cocoons, and the two children, Husam and Ibtissam, would be sprawling on the floor like dismembered bodies, parts haphazardly thrown about. Finally, Assayed would recall that his wife and daughter were still squatting in the corridor outside the room, and he would yawn loudly so that the group would break up. The friends would leave, singing old songs in low drunken tones, careful not to make too much noise on the street so that they would not get told off by the Popular Committee as they had been on a previous occasion. When quiet reigned again, Assayed would go and shut the door, then go to the leftovers sticking to the plates and lick them off his index finger with a greedy enjoyment. Then he would go and wake up his wife and Aisha. Without bothering to ensure that the other members of the family had adequate sleeping arrangements, he would hoist his inactive body onto the bed, lie on his back, and quickly begin to snore. He would make a boisterous noise even in his sleep. In that jarring oblivion of his, as his chest rose and fell, Aisha would try to fall asleep again, engulfed by a feeling that her body was no more than a bunch of dry grass forgotten by the harvesters in a field one night.

Um Jalal noticed that Aisha's face was as pale as turmeric, and that she was badly in need of original olive oil from the home country to improve her health and also her colour would once again become rosy and fresh: "Over there, the land and its bounty. One would drink a glass of olive oil before going to the fields and one's face would appear as fresh as a round loaf of bread. Oh, for those days of bounty and harvest. Where is the land? Don't worry, Yamma, soon when things get better, I'll arrange a visitor's permit so that we can go to Palestine and visit my relatives there. Don't worry. George's oil will arrive from the West Bank within the next few days, and we'll get some of it."

Um Jalal would say this knowing full well that she would be unable to arrange a permit to visit, but it was wishful thinking which she voiced in front of her children whenever she felt hemmed in by a despair she was unable to conquer. She used to comfort her daughter with the impossible visit like one singing to a baby that could not fall asleep. Nothing would restore Aisha's health, and she grew thinner and weaker. Even during her worst moments of serving at school, in those dawn hours when she would tear herself away from the warmth of her bedclothes to wring the coarse mop in the icy water and the cold would scar her hands with cracks that would ooze with pus, even during those moments, she had not felt a greater unhappiness than she felt then.

The wedding! The wedding. The end of August was approaching, and soon September would be upon them and George would be drawn to another place and other people, and everything would be over for her. She accompanied her mother here and there, and learned by heart all the preparations that were made for a wedding: the trousseau, the wedding chants and the henna. But she soon came to feel that her continued accompaniment of her mother was unnecessary because no one paid her any attention or gave her a thought. Hana did not try to ask her again if she could work with them on the literacy course. She worried that her mother might find out about the feelings she was hiding. That would be a scandal too momentous to bear. Woe was she! If only she had remained a servant over there. If only she had been blind and not met him. If only she had continued living among the solitary convent women. They did not interfere with her like her mother, who was always going on in a complaining tone about her daughter's thinness and peaked face.

A poisonous smell like the melting of a metal in acid would suddenly rise wherever she turned, stopping her from breathing properly and blocking her appetite. It would infiltrate her nostrils against her will, evaporating and slowly melting into her tissues and her airways. She would smell the odour of an impending catastrophe, not knowing what would follow it. During those times, she used to secretly rummage through the things her mother was keeping for him on the floor of the cupboard inside a cotton sheet. She would stealthily feel his white jacket, fingering the white linen at the collar and sleeves. She would spread it across her chest, caress it, touch it, pass her fingers over its pores, enjoying the friction of the rough fabric against her skin, removing a loose thread from one of its stitches, or rubbing its folds to smooth it out. She would plaster it with kisses, rub her forehead on it, feeling that she would be humiliated if her secret were discovered. It would involve her in a scandal which was incomprehensible and totally unacceptable. She remained afraid of clearly admitting her feelings to herself, so how could she possibly contemplate the knowledge of others? But George knew. The secret was revealed suddenly the day he had visited them after the last bout of clashes was over. He saw her as he had never seen her before, overflowing with longing, wrapped in a mantle of dumb yearning. Her body was sublimating, almost as transparent as a mirage. She resembled saffron flowers as their reddish orange colour turns to an autumnal yellow. She had grown smaller, her body shrinking as though its parts were drawing closer together. He realized that she was in love. Her brittle wilting, like falling autumn leaves, told him. But he could not guess whom it was she was in love with. He felt all of a sudden that he had grown older, because those whom he had considered to be children had started to change. Every intimate change around him used to affect him like a splash of cold water that would awaken him, and he would remember that he had left his own home town many years ago, and that time was increasing his hidden longing. The unexpected change in the young girl took him by surprise, and he became more aware of the age difference between them. He was used to the fact that life had pushed him into growing up very quickly. Old men considered him as an heir to their wisdom, women treated him as the most intelligent son, men looked up to him as their ideal because he was a fighter, and children treated him as the most patient of fathers. He had grown used to treating boys and young girls with a spontaneous paternalism. Aisha was not quite a child; she was something in between. He became aware of her and saw her. The wide pink dress with its thick pleats. Her pigtails falling onto her shoulders. Her thick unplucked eyebrows. Her infinitely sweet smile, at variance with her hidden tension. And her voice, which would disappear as though she had swallowed it whenever a guest or visitor would speak to her.

This time, he saw her as he had never seen her before. Thin, exhausted, her weakness causing her to almost spill over onto the doorstep as she crossed it. She had become endowed with a strange, discomfiting beauty. The beauty of pain and suffering which becomes particularly concentrated in the pupils of the eye, causing them to stand out like a shining black stone at the bottom of a translucent marble pool. He was surprised by the change that had overcome her. He was even more surprised when she blushed in his presence, and he began to feel that there was a riddle somewhere around. Did he know her beloved without realizing it? Could it be one of his friends? However, he suddenly forgot all about it when Um Jalal broke the good news to him that Hana's parents had consented to the marriage. Hana with whom he was so taken. Ever since he had returned from that trip abroad, his thoughts and attitudes towards women had been confused. Hana was the only one who made him comfortable, and allowed him to feel there was a way of being free of that confusion. He knew perfectly well that the criteria set by his mother and the conditions made by his sister regarding the right girl for him did not apply to Hana because she was not blonde and did not have blue eyes. She was not retiring or quiet, timid enough for "the cat to eat her dinner" as the saying went. She was quite different from all that. His trip abroad had shaken his previous sense of security. He had met many women who had appeared perfect at first, when it came to their appearances, their education and their independence. They had simple jobs or important careers. But what had initially given him enjoyment, and later imparted to him a lasting shock was how easy they were. The ease of reaching the farthest, most secret parts of their bodies without having relationships with them that called for the kind of intimacy which one only offers to one's partner for life. Women for free! That's what he felt. One could easily exchange jokes, gifts and hints of complete sensual love until one got to their beds, only to discover the next morning that one was no more than a passing stranger to them, and that they were willing to make passionate love with many other such strangers. He encountered them in restaurants, at the Party school, cafés, the metro, and on streets where no one would expect to find them. Good women, always ready to give all that they could to help their friends. But their free availability did not inspire reassurance. He could not just accept that the problem lay in his being the son of an ignorant peasant. He longed deep down to return, get married and have children. He wanted to find a special person who would understand him and know how to talk to him. He could never accept the silent rural world in which his mother had spent all her life. For these reasons, he had been taken by that girl and had become interested in her. Love? Admiration? It made no difference. What mattered was that he felt comfortable with her, and had a burning eagerness to listen to her charming chatter. She was the daughter of a refugee peasant who traded in electrical parts in the camp. This enabled him to give his family financial stability, ensuring that the girl received more care and pampering than other girls in the camp. Because of her privileged position within the family, she had been allowed to have a say in choosing her husband, something that would be very difficult for other girls of her age to do. He had sent her many messages, but she had refused to meet him alone. He had found this reassuring. However, she indicated her acceptance of him, making things easy for him, and not letting him down.

Hana. She was the exact opposite of what his mother had wanted for him. Her beauty was lively and boisterous, spreading warmth wherever she went. She was always moving, talking and laughing, telling jokes and listening to them as though she had been created only for fun and socializing. She would tease people around her, joke with them, jump around, her voice rising above others, as though everyone were her family, and the whole world were her own small home. She would touch the coarsest of things, and they would immediately become familiar as though they had only been created to await her arrival. She was someone who could tame inanimate objects and solve the most intractable of problems. She would lose her temper and argue when something displeased her, and would change the texts of messages she was assigned to send on the wireless by throwing in a comment or curse for the benefit of the enemy picking up the coded words. She wouldn't mind the scolding of her superiors for adding such remarks, which got her anger off her chest. She would giggle and transform any reprimand into a small joke without causing resentment or a negative reaction. She would say what she pleased, and her superior could tell her off to his heart's content later on. What mattered was saying what she thought, however chaotically.

George thought that their life together would reign in her reactions. He recalled how she had sent him a coded message responding to his secret craze for her. Her glances made him feel that he was more special than others. She would keep laughing at the unsuccessful jokes he made whenever he came into her office. The fact of the matter was that the seriousness which characterized his life prevented him from being able to tell the jokes that others told so well. He tried to draw near to her by adopting her own nature, so he began to tell her funny anecdotes about people around them. She responded by laughing very hard, and he realized the essence of her temperament: she would lavish her admiration on what he was saying no matter what it was. He picked up her signal, and sent intermediaries to her parents. On her part, she began to treat him as though he were her official fiancé, even before their engagement had been announced. She arranged her work shifts in the office to coincide with his. She would bring him *falafel* sandwiches and fenugreek cakes, which her mother made very well. She would spend the evenings discussing the situation and the latest news with him whenever her wireless was not keeping her busy. Their relationship became more natural and spontaneous, and he no longer needed to engineer conversations that would attract her attention.

His friend Hassan, who also worked in the Signals Department, told him that Hana had been given a secret name, which their comrades used jokingly amongst themselves. They called her "the fierce one" because she clashed with whoever she did not like. Hassan said: "She's a good girl, but she's fierce. It's true that she brings other girls into the organization, and she is an official in the Signals Department, but I have to tell you that she has a reputation for being very bad tempered if she takes a dislike to anyone. No one dares to go near her. Many have tried before you and failed . . . Be careful Ahmad, sorry, I mean George!"

Hassan had used his real name because he was the only one allowed to keep the lists of real names, which were kept secret. But he sometimes used those names when talking to his close friends.

But George was George. Perhaps his other name was one of the reasons for his uniqueness. In fact, Hassan was almost sure that George was his actual name, and that the other name was the result of a mistake made when the names were being registered. In the world of the Resistance, it was possible for one to live for twenty years without giving one's real name, because it could be kept in secret registers until the announcement that one had been martyred.

George wanted the marriage to take place so that he could discover her, enter the warmth of her life and the intimacy of her emotions, which she would not reveal to him. One evening, he had found her alone in the office. He had held her hand in his, not letting it go. She panicked for fear that someone would see them, and her voice shook.

She trembled, and it seemed that her fear of their being alone overcame the happiness blossoming on her face, and her features became anxious. He said: "I love you more than I had thought. When will you marry me?"

"I do too, but I can't do anything until my parents have arranged things."

She stared at him childishly, her face wearing an expression of desire tinged with nervousness, optimism with premonition, confidence with fear.

❧

Aisha did not know whether she was hearing the cooing of a pigeon or the sound of a faraway bird in the quiet of dawn. She began to awake at dawn to the sound of the cooing, which was coming to her from nearby as though it were the echo of the unknown that she would never discover. She tried to find out the source of the sound, but could not. No one raised pigeons in the alley or the neighbourhood. In the morning glow, she looked closely at the nearby walls, the openings in them and the fences on the nearby rooves, but she couldn't see it. The pigeon was hiding somewhere, gurgling and cooing, crying in the early hours of the new dawn, then falling completely silent as the light burst forth. Aisha would lie in bed as the light made its way to the cracks in the window. Every day, she would listen for ages to what she thought was a dawn conversation in which her wounded heart participated. The cooing would become a coded dialogue, opening the pages of her heart, making her feel that here at last was a fellow sufferer, who was confiding in her and listening to her. One day, Aisha got up and went about her housework. Suddenly, she raised her head and looked at the window ledge. There stood a white pigeon with a shining brown collar. Aisha stretched out her hand, motioning to it to come in. Then she thought of sprinkling some food before it. Aisha ran to the kitchen. But when she returned with a handful of wheat, she could not find the pigeon. It had flown off. Nevertheless, it returned . . . It always returned at dawn, but Aisha was never to see it again until the day she left Tal Ezza'tar.

No one had expected Hana's father to be kidnapped as he made his way back to the camp from West Beirut on a very calm, ordinary afternoon. Everyone had expected the crisis to end one way or another by the end of summer. Some of those who had been overly optimistic became the victims of the mobile road-blocks set up by the Christian militias, although the Christian leaders categorically denied that such road-blocks existed. The elderly electrician was on his way back to his shop, bringing with him some spare parts for cars. Then, the catastrophe happened.

When the news arrived at their house, Um Jalal beat upon her chest with anxious foreboding: "How doomed to ill fortune we are! We waited so anxiously for things to calm down, and now the man has been kidnapped. We've been singled out by bad luck. What a catastrophe! How will poor George be able to get married until the problem is solved? If only they had waited two or three days before kidnapping him, at least his poor daughter's wedding would not have been postponed. Now, the wedding can't take place until the man shows up."

Her mother took her to Hana's house. On the way, she stammered with agitation: "May God ruin them. Damn them and all their road-blocks. A road-block! My word! As though we hadn't got enough problems and hardships, they go and grab George's father-in-law. Woe is me, the poor Shalabi! The unlucky one was invited to the feast, but she could find no place at the table!"

Relatives and friends thronged Hana's house. The parlour was full of visitors, who sat on the sofas and the small straw stools borrowed from the homes of neighbours. The very old ladies sat on throws spread in the hall outside. Militiamen with guns slung across their shoulders stood at the entrance of the house. The crowd grew and shrank within the room like waves rising and breaking whenever a group of visitors departed and another arrived. Everyone expressed anger and distress by mixing curses with expressions of sympathy and grief for Hana's father. The family would retell the details of the incident, and how the poor man had gone off without understanding that the improved conditions were as transient as the plums in April.

Irate, sorrowful talk prevailed, getting lost amongst the many cups of coffee being served to the guests. Clouds of smoke masked the faces of the neighbourhood's young men, who thronged the house, opened to the public with sudden hospitality. Um Jalal found a way of expressing her solidarity with Um Hana. She drew close to Um Hana, whose eyes were swollen and whose hair was torn, and whispered the secret: "Pull yourself together, sister. The problem will undoubtedly be solved. George has gone to the liaison committee to work out a way of searching for him. The least you can do in a situation like this is not to allow your home to be so open. Okay, I understand your serving coffee! But the cigarettes! What a waste. Think of the expense. It would be better if you were to put them away in the bedroom."

Um Hana looked at the stainless steel tray overflowing with every imaginable brand of smuggled cigarettes, and her eyes, red with weeping, flashed: "The pity of it! Is it a matter of cigarettes only? I wish our friends and our enemies could smoke all the cigarettes in town if that would make them bring him back, Um Jalal."

"Trust George, my dear. He will . . . see to it . . . Pull yourself together and take heart. He will definitely be back with you in two days at most."

And Aisha waited for the absent George. George, who did not come. She grew depressed, was torn between the flood of sadness around her and her crazy joy at the indefinite postponement of the wedding. Because she, because, because she wanted. Wanted to. No other solution. Another house. A different place, or another girl or family, or, or . . . Aisha waited. She did not fidget, nor did she urge her mother to go home. Maybe George would come. The large number of people going and coming disturbed her, as did the pessimism of the atmosphere, and the morbid expectation that the kidnapped man would be killed and would not return. She hated herself for her secret approval of the idea that the man would not return so that there would be no wedding, so that it would be indefinitely postponed. It would end before it had begun. The jacket would remain at the bottom of the cupboard, and she would be able to smell it for a long, long time without fearing that its owner would leave and not remain hers. She would touch its fabric with adoration, her heart contracting because the jacket's owner would remain elsewhere, far away. She would wear the jacket, cover herself in it, although it was too large for her. She would fleetingly look to see how it fitted her, carry it in her arms and talk soothingly to it. She would spread it against her skin, and sleep inside it. She would sleep. Its owner would remain theirs, hers. The man. The *Feda'ee*. The shining halo and the smile glittering within the rich pupils.

He would continue to belong to her, she who wished that she were not herself. If only she had been like that girl, Hana, skipping, bouncing and jumping like little girls did. Talking to the young men, chattering with them, acting coquettishly, slanting her mouth as she chewed her gum without being scolded for it, not being confined or prevented from going out. Everyone looks at her with admiration and affection. Then George – he comes. He looks at her. He loves her, then . . . if only !

If only she could stop being Aisha, whose family force her to wear a scarf when she goes out, who walks with her bosom bent forward, almost folded over her torso out of modesty. If only she were not who she is because . . . no one sees her or pays her any attention. She is present on this earth, yet does not exist. She's like a bus stop, where one stops to buy a box of matches, then turns away and walks off.

How she wishes she had remained far, far away, over there.

7

~⊂⊙⊙⊃~

It had been a long time since Assayed had walked into the house singing a verse from one of his favourite old songs the way he was doing on that late autumn day. Aisha was troubled, and her heart fell. It occurred to her that Hana's father had returned and that a new date for the wedding had been set. Assayed called her, and she came out of the kitchen without having a chance to wash her hands of the brown stains left on her fingers from peeling potatoes. Tear droplets brought on by the diced onions hung from her lashes as she looked at Assayed, waiting for what he had to say to her. Assayed joked with her, called her Ayyoush, put his index finger on her chin, and said to her with a tenderness that aroused her suspicion: "My daughter Aisha. You're so lovely now that you've grown up. A young woman better looking than any other."

She pulled back, drying her palms behind her back with her dress. She froze her posture and did not move again so that he would not notice her fright. He called to his wife in his usual noisy manner: "Prepare her, Um Jalal. Prepare your daughter because her fiancé is coming tonight."

Um Jalal's jaw dropped open, but she quickly said: "Fiancé? You mean they're coming to ask for her hand in marriage this evening?"

He slapped his pockets with pride: "That's right. Why not? Isn't my daughter a young lady? We've aged, Khadijeh, and it seems we're going to become grandparents without realizing how time has passed."

Aisha was dazed and filled with apprehension. She stared so hard, she felt her eyes would pop out.

She dragged her feet back to the kitchen, followed by her mother: "What's up? What's going on? Has that husband of yours gone mad? Who told him I want to get married?"

Um Jalal answered good naturedly, her hands busy mincing the tomatoes: "Keep your voice down so he doesn't hear us. Child, this is very good news. Why are you upset? All young girls wish for marriage."

"Who . . . told you that I wanted to get married? Does one get married just like that?"

"What else would you do then, my dear? . . . Become a university professor? Or a teacher of French? What are you talking about? The boy is a decent young man and there's nothing wrong with him!"

"But I've said no, and that means no."

"Yamma, the bridegroom is respectable and nice. He's a university student at . . . let me remember its name . . . the Arab University. They say he's studying economics. He also works for the Democratic Front. He saw you the day we were at Hana's house when her father was kidnapped. He went to George and told him. And tonight, with God's blessing, they're coming . . . may they bring good health and happiness."

"Yamma, d'you think marriage is something that one just stumbles into? By God, I won't accept."

"For the sake of Prophet Mohammad, what's the matter with you? D'you want me to oppose your marriage? Marriage is a girl's destiny."

"No, by God. No."

"Don't bother rejecting it. Your father has said yes, and that means yes. What is it that you have in mind? I hope you're not intending to become an old maid and remain at home so that people will say my daughter couldn't get a husband?"

"Okay, I'll get married. But not now, and not a man I don't know."

"It gets better and better! It seems you want us to arrange you a rendezvous before you accept! Now . . . you can see how bad the situation in the camp is. Where are we to find someone better?"

"Okay, take it easy. When things settle down. Why d'you want to get rid of me?"

"Enough you hussy. Okay, you're our daughter. But your father is satisfied with the man, and that means he's good. Now, if you don't like that, you go and tell him. I have no influence over anyone, not even over myself. After all, George says he's good . . !"

"Yamma, explain to me, what has George got to do with this? What business of his is it?"

"Oh, stop chattering. They're best friends, very very close."

"Why should it be his concern? All I need is George getting into this."

"Don't make a mountain out of a molehill. His friend Hassan wants to ask for your hand in marriage and has asked George to come with him. Your poor father is so happy. Let him experience one happy day in his life. He hasn't had the pleasure of marrying off his son . . . so let him have the pleasure of marrying you off."

Aisha cried. She showed her agitation. She let loose a flood of tears, stifled gasps and moans so that her mother would feel sorry for her and intercede with her father. But no one listened, and Aisha imagined that the whole thing was a punishment for her, while the others saw it as an honour and cause for joy. Um Jalal ignored her the way one ignores a naughty child kicking up a scene to be allowed to play in the mud. Talking was no use as the mother moved between the sink and the kerosene cooker, loaded with potatoes frying in oil. It was useless. Aisha gathered up her courage, swallowed her tears, and came out of the kitchen to speak to her father. He was leaning on the throw with his elbow, smoke rising from the thin tobacco wrap between his rough fingers, as he watched the cloudy circles rising inside the room. The only sound around them was that of the kerosene cooker, its rhythmic groans drowning out everything else. Assayed became aware of her. He turned to her, and their eyes met silently. He threw her a threatening look which reined in her tongue and made her speechless. With his honey-brown eyes, he looked like a wolf ready to pounce on its prey. He put out his cigarette as he watched her. He crushed the burning stub on the floor as he looked into her face. He began to undo his belt.

He pulled it off and laid it on the floor next to him, determined to show her the hiding that she might get with the leather belt, ready for that purpose. She would never forget the day she had refused to give him the golden chain the nuns had given her for a present. He had whipped her with his belt, and she had almost died, until her mother had pushed him away from her. He had roughly pulled away the thick belt curled around her neck and left without saying a word. The bruises had marked her skin for a long time. Thick long lines that had changed from crimson to blue, then to a greenish black, then to purple which had become tinged with pale orange. Now, as he was pulling off his belt, Aisha remembered the pain, and in that instant, she forgot what she had wanted to say. Actually, she didn't forget. It was her tongue that was unable to speak. Did one speak to a monster? And if she spoke, what would she tell him? Would she tell him that she did not wish it? But he did wish it. Her knees felt loose and her leg joints became shaky and unable to support her. The pain, again. Her vision clouds over, and she runs up to the roof.

From then on, everything proceeded in a circular movement like a cord around her neck. Everything went round, coiling like a rope, surrounding her and tying her down. That evening, the fiancé came and spoke to her father. She insisted on remaining in the kitchen, and saw nothing but the crate of grapes the man had brought with him. Her mother said: "See what good taste he's got, dear! You're lucky that he's so well-mannered. God willing, he'll bring lots of good things to your home."

Aisha stares at the wine-coloured grapes, which seem to be her own blood, spilt in the prime of her youth. No one cares about her or her anxieties. Everyone is happy except for her. They are all enjoying themselves at the feast of her slaughter. The banquet tonight is celebrating her body and soul, which are being sold in exchange for bunches of appetizing grapes. The cheap Ibtissam runs around her in circles, saying: "Now we can have another wedding. We and George. Aren't we lucky! Hee hee. . . . "

The mother mutters as she is about to take out a tray of tea-filled glasses: "Oh God, please end our troubles and hasten the return of Abu Hana. If only he hadn't been kidnapped before the wedding! God keep us. What had the poor man got to do with anything? Perhaps he's been killed, we haven't heard a thing about him. Nothing has been of any use, neither the Liaison Committee or any such thing!"

George was talking about something she could not make out because of the racket being made by her brother and sister as they fought over the sweets her father had brought home that afternoon.

George . . . even he. As though it were not enough that everyone else stood against her! Confusion was almost destroying her sanity. Him? George? How had he been drawn into her predicament? If only she knew, she could escape, go anywhere, become a maid on the western side. People would always need servants, even during wars. She would go to Ras Beirut where the rich lived. She would work in any home and not go out onto the streets at all so that Jalal could not find her. If he did, he would drag her by the shoulder and force her back to get married against her will. If those bastards would not feel ashamed of themselves and stop all this, she would certainly flee. Even if George were for it! George, who was so fond of his friend to the point of ruining her life to please him. She wished so hard that the clashes would end so that she could leave the Tal and take charge of her life. And the Beloved. What a fool she had been! He was just like everybody else, wanting to marry her off. The phrase her mother used to always repeat when complaining fitted her own situation perfectly: "Those who have no luck need not even bother with trying and worrying."

By then, they were drinking sweet coffee and eating the rice pudding which Um Jalal had taken great pains to make. And the bridegroom! His name was Hassan. She whispered the name to herself. Perhaps that would help her find out what that Hassan wanted with her.

Hassan was the brother of Fayez, who had been martyred in the clashes between the army and the resistance in May 1973. Who in the camp did not know of the hero who had held back the attack on the camp with his own body? Hassan had only joined the militia after his brother's martyrdom. He had been a politically-active student at Beirut's Arab University. His fees were being paid by UNRWA, which in return for covering his tuition fees had taken his name off its list of those entitled to financial support. The day his brother had been martyred, Hassan had picked up his gun and sworn to take his place. Hassan had paid no heed to his family's pleadings that he continue his studies and spare them the worry of constantly fearing for his safety.

Hassan was his mother's only surviving son, the rest of her children were girls. Ever since then, she had wanted him to get married, but Hassan had refused, always making excuses. What had made him suddenly insist that his parents should ask for her hand in marriage on his behalf? Why had he only now decided to take a fancy to her when she was going through the darkest time of her life? Aisha wondered. She would run away. There was no doubt about it. She would leave the area for ever. But! The roads were closed. When would all this end? Who was this man whom she did not know, who was intruding on her, impetuously, just because he had set eyes on her on one sad occasion? Who was he to become, that simply, her husband?

She secretly stared at him through the crack of the kitchen door. All she could see was that he looked no different to the other young men littering the streets of the camp. There was nothing distinct about his looks or his speech. He was neither dark nor fair; neither young nor old; his beard was neither cleanly shaven nor was it long, as though he did not care about grooming himself. His brown eyes were neither light nor dark. His ordinary moustache was neither thick nor thin. As for his figure, there was nothing special about it at all: he was neither tall, nor short. Anyone setting eyes on him would forget him after a second or two at best. So why pull her into marriage now?

She would escape.

The beginning of September.

Clashes. Once more. They did not. They did not give her a break. What was the use? The battles, the war. Disaster striking anew.

The clashes flared up again, not giving her an opportunity. To run away, to breathe or to do anything.

The battles rolled on like the glass marbles with which Husam used to play. Shining spheres in the boy's hands, spinning with coloured spikes running down their transparent middles, rolling on the earth, picking up its dark specks, getting covered in them. Then going into the ditch. They would all die that way. Her beating heart told her so. It said so to her. The chalk pale frightened faces in the room. Her mother beating her bosom with distress, as she kept the two children in the corner: "Oh God, how have we offended you? . . . Isn't the hardship of our lives enough? Now the whole world is coming down around us? Where will I find work now? How are we to come and go? How?"

The spheres. The shells. The marbles. The fire. They roared above them in the sky. They flashed. A war of thunder and lightning. Chariots of chaotic noise clamouring over the rooftops. Exploding. Flying like thunderbolts. Burning human flesh. Destroying people, humans, pigeons, water, clay, water, blood. Assayed remained completely and unexpectedly silent, gathering his body like a porcupine near the edge of the bed. He could see no one. But he listened to all the radio stations very attentively.

He drank one glass of *arak* after another, remaining speechless like one who had taken a decision in his own mind. He was calm, not cursing or accusing or complaining. He would only discuss the situation with his neighbours who appeared on their rooves during the few hours of calm. At times like those, he would unleash sharp criticisms against Egypt for concluding agreements with Israel that brought down wars and troubles onto them. When his neighbour the carpenter would ask him to prove it, he would be unable to mention any argument other than the one he had picked up while listening incessantly to various radio stations: "That bastard Sadat doesn't give a damn about us and our problems. It's all because of the Sinai agreement. Since it was made, we haven't known a moment's peace. All we've had has been shooting, problems and worry. Perhaps they started this war to distract us and keep us from opposing the agreement. I'm sure of it."

The clashes lasted a few days, then stopped.

The first thing that Assayed did after the battles ended was to verbally inform Hassan, his daughter's fiancé, to bring the sheikh over the next morning and make ready to sign the marriage contract immediately on the understanding that the wedding would take place a week later. The message he sent was that if Hassan would not agree to this, then Abu Jalal would irrevocably call off the engagement. Um Jalal protested that one week was not enough time in which to prepare her daughter. She said she had not even been able to send word to Hassan's family, so how could things be carried out without allowing customs and mores to take their normal course. Assayed answered with determination: "Don't interfere, woman. Leave us be, and mind your own business. Tomorrow the marriage contract will be signed, and the wedding will be in a week. If you're happy, fine. If not, it's too bad. D'you want a repeat performance of George and Hana's engagement? There she is, that poor girl, neither married nor divorced. She doesn't know whether her father's alive or dead! She doesn't know whether she'll get married or go to hell! I say that's how things will be, and that's the end of it."

So what could Aisha do? They would blame her in future and say that she had got herself into trouble through her own choice. She is neither able to go on with her secret love story, nor can she find salvation in a career or a job. As she confronts her clear feminine destiny, the same eternal treatment meted out to millions of women like her awaits her. Even qualified women with careers and means of their own are no different to Aisha in our part of the world. They do not know how to enjoy the independence of taking their own decisions, however much society may appear to appreciate them. The point is that Aisha, of course, cannot risk an adventurous escape. The camp's exits and entrances are blocked by barriers and fortifications, and she won't be able to find transport unless she can collude with a driver she knows, and she knows nobody. So what is she to do, then?

Not a thing. She will not.

Will not. Because she cannot.

Because. There is blood, war and clashes.

As usual, she cried for a long time and was unable to sleep.

She buried her head beneath the covers, careful not to allow her choked sobs to reach her father's ears. Since night began, she has been thinking of a way to kill herself without hitting upon an appropriate method. She hasn't got enough money to buy asprin tablets. Anyway, the pharmacy is too far away, on the eastern road, near the entrance of the camp. She hates everything to death. She hates them and this place and Hassan, who has turned up in her face like a black lottery ticket. She knows full well that there is no way of hiding from them, but she is not fully convinced of the need to die. She doesn't like the idea, doesn't want to, however hard she tries to convince herself. She stretched herself out like a stiff corpse, spending the night lying on her back, the fibres of the cover pricking her and her hot breath rebounding onto her face. The cooing of the dove came to her, its singing quenching her pain like fresh water, but for the very first time, she detested listening to it. The pigeon seemed like another voice for her own weeping. And she was weary of all the waves of sadness that had lashed her since her return to the camp.

On the first calm night after the fighting had stopped, Aisha stole up to the roof, leaving everyone else in a deep, exhausted slumber. It was dawn. Aisha climbed the rough concrete steps like a ghost fleeing an approaching nightmare. The sky was a purple black. the air felt fresh and clean, The plant stems were bent in a sleep that would last till the first moments of light. The acacia tree crouched like the skeleton of the mythical roc, surveying the other houses and nests. High buildings surrounded the camp from far off like the watch towers in the concentration camps in one of those television series about the Nazi war. Suddenly, Aisha heard a rustle behind her. She started, and her hair stood on end.

"Dastour!" She turned her neck round to see a dark mass stretching out its hand to touch her shoulder.

Um Jalal said: "My dear, in God's name and His will. Don't be frightened. It's me next to you."

She stepped backwards, not reassured by the voice. But her mother drew close and put her arm around her. The first light of dawn was rising as the birds twittered around them. Her mother pulled her towards her, cradling her daughter's face in her hands. She said with an unaccustomed tenderness that reminded Aisha of the day she had met her as she left school: "Bless your face, which is as lovely as the moon. Have we upset you, my child?"

Words clogged up in Aisha's bosom, and all she could do was bend her face downwards, allowing her tears to flow down cheeks already soaked with much weeping. She did not know what to say or why.

The mother drew closer to her daughter, pulling her towards her and embracing her. The girl did not draw back as she had done all her life. Instead, she collapsed on the mother's shoulder in a flood of tears. For the first time in her life, Aisha received the smell of her mother without disgust or revulsion. She accepted the putrid odour of perspiration mixed with the aroma of coffee, cigarettes and salt lurking in the heavy body, bursting with complete motherhood: "My poor Aisha. Let yourself go, dear. Don't be upset. You're my darling daughter. Don't cry. Calm yourself down, my dear."

Aisha swallowed her words, drank them in with her tears, stuttering as she tried to speak: "If you're too upset, don't talk. I feel with you, and I know. Why upset yourself? Perhaps your luck in another home will be better than your luck in our home."

"But Yamma. I don't want to get married."

"I know. You're scared of marriage. We were all like you before getting married. All girls feel that way. That's what destiny brings. All girls end up getting married."

"But I don't know him, Yamma. How can I marry a strange man? Keep me with you. Let me stay here."

"Dear Aisha. My darling Aisha. The boy is nice, and there's nothing wrong with him. We know him well, and so does George."

Aisha answered heatedly, forgetting her grief: "George. George. What has George got to do with this?"

"Well, you're like his sister. If only you knew how much he cares about you. If you could hear how he always asks after you. He was worried about you when you were ill, and he encouraged both me and your father to accept *Ustath* Hassan. Yes my dear, when he graduates from university, he will become a highly respected teacher. The boy who wants to marry you is respectable. Perhaps he will make it up to you for staying here with us without anything to do. Perhaps you will have children who will give you something to do. Perhaps when you see them smiling, you will forget the whole world. Maybe because he is a member of the organization, he will let you work like some of the other girls! Now isn't that better than your father's tantrums and scenes which we have to put up with?"

"Really? Is that how George thinks?"

"Yes, my dear. He has your interests at heart. After the bus incident in April, it was he who encouraged us to bring you back from school. He was concerned for you and afraid of what might happen to you if you stayed amongst strangers."

"It would have been better for me to have remained there."

"If you'd stayed there, you would have been cut off and without family. Perhaps they would not have accepted you and said: 'Go back home, may God and the Prophet go with you.' The Khawajahs never liked us, Aisha."

"But must I get married?"

"Aisha, accept your destiny. It is pre-ordained and must take place. That's it. Today, the Sheikh will come to conclude the marriage contract. Why kill yourself with crying and sorrow? Why, when in the end, you're destined to get married anyway?"

Aisha was not convinced by what Um Jalal said. But she thought: would it be possible for something to change in my life if I get married as my mother is saying? She thought about what her mother had said about George. Was he like them, governing her life without asking her? Was he the source of the catastrophe, engineering her departure from school? Could he think of nothing but politics and not realize the horrors that those politics of his had brought down on her? She had heard him referring to the Khawajahs by a strange name, which had come up on some news bulletins. He had called them the isolationists. But how strange! Had he not understood that her isolation over there had been for her own good? Would it not have been better for her had she remained isolated over there until she had received a certificate and found a job?

George. George. He was like Judas, turning her over to them like an easy prey, then pretending that he was doing it all in her best interests. She did not want to believe it. At the same time, she could not understand: why were things happening the way they were? Why should she be the daughter of such people? Why did those people live in the camp? Why did the Khawajahs open fire so fiercely on the inhabitants as though they wanted to destroy them? Why was she inside that place now? Why should she be in love with George and get proposed to by Hassan? Why was George helping Hassan to marry her? Why should Hassan ask for her hand in marriage at a time when the roads were closed, the exits blocked and stepping outside the camp meant risking a hundred sniper bullets? And she? What should she do, Oh God? What should she do about her tragic disappointment in George? And in them? And in herself?

As for what was taking place at Hana's home that day, it was truly bizarre. Um Hana suffered an almost constant migraine, the pain keeping her from opening her eyes until her daughter had used up all the lemons remaining to their friends and neighbours. A whole day of horrific pain, so that anyone who saw Um Hana thought she would die of it. Then the fit passed, and she begged her daughter to try on the wedding dress so that she could see her in it. This would have been a very normal request had the household not been in a sate of grief that was almost mourning. Hana gave in and decided to grant her mother's wish, despite her inner misgivings at trying on the dress in such a depressing atmosphere. Her mother brought out all the parts of the costume – the white tulle dress, the silvery shoes and the white gloves. She rummaged through her cupboard, bringing out a bunch of wax orange blossoms and the fake crystal earrings she had worn for her own wedding. She asked her daughter to put them on, so she could see them and test their elegance as a prelude to reusing them. Hana uncomfortably complied with her mother's wish. She stood in front of the mirrors, the decorated veil and tiara on her head. Then came a knock at the door and repeated requests by Um Jalal to borrow the dress the next day. She also told them that they had a special invitation to attend the wedding. Um Hana was not pleased, and pessimism weighed down her spirit. But she did not express her frustration with Um Jalal, who had rudely violated the custom of not borrowing a bridal dress before it had been worn by the bride for whom it was intended. Due to the family's close relationship with Um Jalal, she pretended to welcome the idea, allowing Hana to free herself of the suffocating task forced on her by her mother. She immediately changed back into her jeans, finding that she could no longer do without the comfort of wearing them. The terrible premonition that had entered her mother's mind as a result of that omen never occurred to her.

Noon. The clergyman.

Many people. A banquet at the bride's home. Aisha. Assayed. Hassan in a navy blue pin-striped suit. A feast of *kubbeh* discs. Trays of cracked wheat made into a dough with minced meat. *Ma'moul* cakes on a large square tray borrowed from the neighbourhood bakery. Women from the bridegroom's family. Neighbours. Acquaintances. Women who have come together from every corner, as though the camp had been emptied of them and they had been thrown into the single-room house. Waves of people arriving. The place swallows them up, then spits them out, and new waves arrive. The lamb, slaughtered that morning, is in the huge copper cauldron over the burning wood at the entrance of the neighbourhood. The smell of meat has drawn everyone able to smell it. However, everyone politely ignores the cauldron boiling over with sauce and white patches of fat. Some women carry their ladles and bend over as they stir the pieces of boiling lamb. The sight of the meat makes the children salivate. No one notices or cares about the patches of crimson blood caked onto the walls.

No one sees or cares. And she listens to them, but does not hear. The crying of babies in their mothers' arms reaches her. The sound of the drum beating between the hands of the dressmaker Najah with a strong monotonous rhythm. The gold earring resembling a small bell swings across her ear as she beats the drum musically. Hands clap with incredible enthusiasm. They don't know her, yet they are all so happy.

"Ala Dal'ouna . . . Ala Dal'ouna
I beg you, my dark-skinned beloved
I beg you, Oh *Feda'ee*, joy of our eyes."

And then! Suddenly. Aisha hears a line that arouses her sorrow:

"I begged you so to change your mind,
Time tilts but does not adjust itself.
Oh you who always plait your hair,
Your poisoned dagger has wounded my heart."

But they were all not there. She was alone. She stands there in the sand. Things fall silent. Nothing but her and the sky and the sands. The rhythmic beating of the drum and the pieces of yellow sulphur pouring down on her, almost burying her. Aisha lies on the ground, and more and more yellow flakes fall on her. They cover her body, piling up high, resembling a grave. Far away drums begin to beat in preparation for her funeral. She tries to get up before she is buried and dies, but cannot. The beating of the drum increases.

"Boom. Dum. Dum. Boom . . ."

Aisha awakens from the spiritual coma into which she had entered. She looks around her. Most people have left to prepare for the wedding in the evening. She is alone on the throw spread on the floor. Her sister is beating the leather skin of a small earthenware drum. Her brother is dancing and somersaulting like a monkey. Her mother is in the kitchen with a few other women washing the dishes after the banquet.

Only then did the noises in the alley assail her ears. She discovered the remains of the expired banquet. The traces of the departed guests. And the legal contract which had been concluded.

It was all over now. The bridegroom had gone, and she had not seen him, although he had shaken hands with her. She had not heard him although he had spoken to her.

Hassan! Oh Hassan! How strangely the name echoes in her ears. Who was that man who had become her husband? When her mother had pressed her into stretching out her hand and shaking hands with him after the contract had been concluded, she had seemed dead. She did not want to notice or see anyone. Now, she wanted to reassemble the pieces of his fragmented image. She must remember him and firmly plant his image in her mind.

Hassan: his dark complexion almost honey-coloured. Curly hair parted at the side. A nose that matched the mouth, like most men in the camp. Was it that most Palestinian men looked like that? Dark lips surrounded by a coffee-coloured line that emphasized his swarthiness. A moustache. A slight scar over the left eyebrow, cutting across the hair roots and preventing the eyebrow from reaching the temple. He puts his hand to his cheek and day dreams. Where do his thoughts go? A faint smile on his face, as though he were keeping to himself a secret sorrow over something unknown. A shine in the eyes and a smile of deep admiration whenever he set eyes on her.

"The crazy man. God would punish him. Why would he not set her free?"

They had come and gone. Soon they would be back to take her. All that Aisha knew was that they had brought the sheikh and written something on paper, and then called her. Her mother had dragged her forward against her will to say "yes" to the turbaned sheikh. And she had said it because she was frightened of the multitudes crowding into the house and at its doors, and in the street. All of them had frightened her, and she could do nothing more than bow her head and say yes to her funeral. She will kill herself. She must do it. Pour kerosene on herself and burn. But she is afraid of fire. Even when the kerosene cooker gets out of order and she has to make it work again. With a knife? The blood? No, no. All that scares her. The mere thought of it is nauseating.

The best solution is that she should be hit by a bullet during the next bout of clashes. She will go to the roof, stand facing the wind, then receive a bullet to the chest and die.

But was she really capable of doing it?

Throughout all the rituals, Aisha was unable to feel anything except for being moved by a few verses from the songs the women sang at her wedding:

"Yamma, call him,
He for whom I longed,
As I spoke to him."

Their touching voices would ring out, pulling at the strings of her heart, and she wished that she were a real bride, not a stiff image of one, as she sat on her chair, bedecked with artificial flowers. Their voices poured out like the pieces of bright crystal on the church lanterns in her old school. Their singing brought her back to her surroundings. The words pierced her breast, penetrating her sorrowful memory. They were singing for her, and she was banishing the songs:

"Oh nation of Mohammad,
Bless the Prophet's name.
Aisha, wife of the Prophet,
Her leaves are those of the olive tree,
Her leaves are those of henna,
Which decorates the gates of heaven."

Later, she would take long looks at herself. She would face the mirror hanging over the sink on the wall. She would study her puffed eyelids, and touch her short tresses of hair. Anyone who had seen her a month ago would have taken her for a boy. She had the face of a sad, frightened pale child. But her dangling gold earrings left whoever looked at her in no doubt. There was a sarcasm reflected in the crooked smile on her lips and in her inquiring eyes. Bitterness welled up inside her onto the scratched metal surface in which she was surveying herself. The wedding. The night of the consummation. Aisha had not wanted henna painted on her. The women had brought in the big copper cauldron, brimming with the paste, its colour like a mix of coal and mud. They had thrown the cauldron down in the middle of the room, which was full of shoes and plastic slippers belonging to the neighbourhood women and their children. They sang for her:

"You who paint the brides with henna walk at night,
Step on the plough and on the saddles of the horses.
You who paint the brides with henna, walk in the day,
Step on the horse and on saddles of money."

The henna paste. The strong smell, like metallic paint. The yellow sulphur-like colour. She didn't want to. Attempts at persuasion poured down on her. They sang:

"Let me through girls,
So I can paint her with henna.
The moon lives in her face,
And the star is there too.
Put out your hand, stretch it out,
So I can paint it with henna.
Your fringe is a like an ostrich feather,
As the breeze blows gently through it."

Because she is the bride. She must be painted with henna. She? Not a girl or woman crowding into the room did not have some of it on. But she would not. Then, some of the sharp-tongued ones scolded her: "Shame on you. Put some henna on. Who refuses henna on the consummation night?"

At last, she stretched out one of her small fingers on its own. They dipped it in the brown dough, laughing in her face and singing:

"She lowered her eyes and put out her hand to be painted
They have gone off to hunt the gazelle."

They laughed and danced, and she cried. They whispered about her: "The girl is a wreck ever since she went to that foreign school. The poor bridegroom. God help him."

And her tears fell once more, as though they were about to slaughter her. One of them stung her with a remark from behind: "The tears of the immodest ones are ever ready to flow."

And she cried because she knew no other way of protesting at her condition.

Since the morning, the crowd of women had done nothing but pursue her, touching the intimate parts of her body. Fingers stretched out at her, making a sugary lemon paste, examining her body, intruding between her organs as though she were a doll made of dough available to every hand to sculpt and remodel into something different. Many arms dragged her into the room, took her clothes off, and removed the hair from her entire body with pieces of the sugary paste. The women plucked her like a chicken, leaving deep blue bruises on her body. The spotted marks left on her body by their dextrous hands resembled those left by her father's leather belt when he had beaten her. They used a thread to pluck her eyebrows. They pulled out the down over her upper lip on the pretext that they were ridding her of her moustache. She wailed, raged and objected. She almost succeeded in escaping and slipping out of their many hands, without bothering to put any clothes onto her naked body. This prompted Um Jalal to intervene and pull her out of their grasp before they had completed the job. Sarcastic sayings tripped off their tongues as tears streamed down her face. Her tears were a bad omen to them, causing pessimism to creep into their hearts, which was contrary to what was expected of a bride. Out of earshot of her mother, they wondered: why is this girl as grief-stricken as though she were going to her own funeral? The women were frightened of what this presaged, and they dropped nasty hints within earshot of her as they went out into the yard. But Aisha was preoccupied with the shame spreading across her body like a hellish flower that would grow that night, exploding into blood that would trickle down her legs.

That night. Him. Hassan.

Their eyes were prying, staring greedily and curiously at her body, as they laughed and told dirty jokes and anecdotes about men and women coming together. And about the blood that would flow in that secret place as proof of her honour. Aisha averted her gaze, turning her face away so that the continuity of their talk would be interrupted and she could pretend that it was not directed at her. Her thoughts were taken up by a mysterious dream of escaping; opening her eyes suddenly and finding that she was outside the camp, far away from them all.

Every now and then, Ibtissam would jump in front of her to tell her what was going on at the bridegroom's house at the edge of Dekwaneh. She told her of the crowded banquet, the slaughtering of lambs, and their cooked meat being offered with rice and cooked yoghurt. Ibtissam begged her to hurry up so that they could get to the bridegroom's house in time for the Sha'rawiya and Shamaliyah dances at the entrance to the alley, near the carob tree. Tunes floated up from both the double-pipe instruments, the *mijwez* and the *arghoul*. There were bottles of Pepsi Cola and Fanta and a large copper jug full of coffee with cardamom. And at the wedding, the lights at the entrance of the building were on in the middle of the day. And there was a whole company of young men with drums, flutes and accordions, and women dancing inside the bridegroom's house, shaking their hips and their tummies.

"Come on, hurry up, let's go," Ibtissam said, winking at her older sister, "the bride", whom the women had prepared by giving her a hot bath with *eau de cologne* and scented soap. Then they had slipped her into the white dress borrowed from Hana, and put on the tulle veil and the wide satin belt. Aisha did not take in what her sister was saying and did not respond.

Gradually, the clamour of the wedding procession that would take her to the bridegroom's house drew nearer. One of Um Jalal's distant relatives got up and began ululating and chanting:

"Oh pigeons screeching above the trees,
I never thought the beloved would really depart.
Oh pigeons crying above the trees,
I never thought the beloved would reject purity.
My heart leapt like a feathered bird,
Poor love-sick one, how shall you live?
If my cousin strikes me with his dagger,
I shall wipe away the blood and do his bidding."

Aisha was taken by surprise. She became agitated and burst into the bathroom to escape those present. No one criticized her for going.

The women were busy ululating and chanting about the bride who would be leaving her father's house for another man's. They sang nostalgically:

"Oh Yamma stuff my pillow,
I left home without bidding my sisters farewell.
Yamma, Oh Yamma wet my handkerchiefs,
I left home before I had bid my youth farewell."

In the bathroom, she was choking like a slaughtered rooster. Her eyes fell on a pair of scissors that had been left on the window sill. She picked them up and began cutting off her hair in front of the broken mirror, which stood on the overturned tin washing tank with the burnt edge. She cut off her hair in terror as her sobbing rose, drowning out the ululating and chanting outside. She cut the tresses as though they were superfluous waste paper. Her weeping turned into loud wails, its rhythm rising in her ears. She heard her mother's pounding on the door. She paid no attention and did not open the door. Um Jalal went crazy, thinking that her daughter was about to set herself on fire, using the kerosene burner. Um Jalal pounded on the door with her fists, with all the strength of her fat body, shouting loudly: "Come on, open the door, what are you doing to yourself?"

Aisha opened the door, which had been about to fall inwards. She stood before her panting mother. She trembled, and the tears rolled down her face, spattered with the make-up applied by the hairdresser. She stood there shaking like a wet bird, her tears mixed with kohl trickling down her cheeks, leaving a trail of soot. Um Jalal thundered: "You have really and truly scandalized us. Whatever did you do this to yourself for?"

She was unable to continue the scolding because her ears picked up the sound of the bridegroom's family delegation as it turned onto their street. The crowd, with their shouts and beating drums, drew near to the house, and there was no time to berate Aisha and beat her, venting her frustration with a blow that the little madam, for whom nothing was good enough, had never dreamed of. She froze in panic, facing her daughter with her dishevelled, unevenly cut hair, which revealed her scalp in some places. Um Jalal was completely taken aback, she didn't know what to do with the remaining cropped tresses, which looked like a sponge on Aisha's forehead. She raised her hand, then dropped it helplessly as she surveyed the horrific disaster. A secret grief entered her heart at her daughter's uncontrollable madness and at what her insanity had prompted her to do. She ran towards the veil, which was lying on the bathroom floor next to the drain, picked it up and put it back onto Aisha's head. She shook the clusters of hair off the white wedding dress. She took a piece of clothing lying nearby, wet it, and used it to wipe the bride's face. The dirty circles of kohl disappeared from her face, and it regained its clarity, embellished with a slight rosiness. She cleared away the remaining bits of hair from Aisha's neck and shoulders, fastening the veil onto her head with hair pins. The tulle flowed down her neck and back, hiding the way in which her hair had been haphazardly cut. Before, it had been piled onto her head like a crown. Now it looked like the torn hides of calves at the butcher's shop. Um Jalal did it all with speed and dexterity, her lips moving silently all the while.

"What a scandal for us, what a scandal. Why have you done this to yourself."

Now, Aisha looks at her hair in the mirror and sees that it has grown a little. It is a quarter of a finger long, and completely covers her scalp. She studies her features, and her stomach turns, churning up pity and shame. Pity for herself and shame for what happened on the night of the wedding. The door closed on them in the same room. The place, his place. The house! Hassan's house. Hassan's family. Not hers. Not at all. She does not know this man, who is a stranger to her, and is called her husband. She is not used to his appearance, his speech, his behaviour towards her. She sat down on the edge of the bed, averting her gaze from him. He was moving here and there. He changed his clothes, and she stared into her lap. She was as silent as a gravestone. After a prolonged silence, he asked her: "Aisha, aren't you going to bed?"

She interpreted his question as an immediate invitation to fall asleep. To go to sleep. To fly through the world of dreams. She lay down on the bed, trembling whenever she heard the veil rustling around her head as though it might scratch her scalp, and make it bleed. But she refused to remove the veil, telling him weakly what her mother had told her to say: "I can't take it off because the hairdresser made a mistake when she was cutting my hair and ruined it."

He tried to calm her down, laughing and saying: "Never you mind."

He turned his attention to arranging his things, and she turned her back, standing between the curtain and the corner of the wardrobe. She hid there and changed into her nightgown. Then she came back, yawning, and announced her intention of going to sleep at once. He asked her: "Just like that? We're still only newly-weds, and you can't wait to fall asleep."

And that was exactly what she did. She laid her head down onto the pillow and immediately fell asleep because of her drowsiness, nervousness and tension.

As Aisha recalls what happened to her, all she remembers is something heavy descending on her. She felt crushed and unable to breathe properly. She gasped and pushed him off her. He was on top of her with all the strength of his body. Oh what a nightmare. She was unable to break free because his strength and eager kisses pinned her down. God help me! He's killing me. Killing. Removing, pulling, pressing, holding down. It all happened in a flash, or perhaps it took the whole night long. Something evil, lethal, disgusting. She cannot understand or explain it. The man burst into her, assaulted her body. She was lost and lost herself. Then, she regained her senses in her new room, feeling the dishonour and shame that would cloud over her for the rest of her life.

In the morning, both their families came to visit them with a tray of *knafeh*. She would not leave the room or see anyone. She turned her eyes away from her mother, when the latter came eagerly into the room to inspect the bedclothes, wanting to reassure herself as to her daughter's honour so that she could convey the news to the bridegroom's family. Aisha did not see her mother, or, rather, she was unable to see her. Hassan noticed how pale her face was. He attributed her shame of her body to embarrassment directed at her mother and his family. He took Um Jalal out of the room, saying in a firm, but teasing tone: "From now on, no one is allowed to interfere with me or with my wife, Aisha. Everyone minds their own business."

Um Jalal answered: "But you know that I must see proof of my daughter's honour so that I can tell your parents."

He said: "Your daughter's honour is with her, and she is accountable to no one from now on. Leave her alone, both you and my family."

8

❧ ⊙ ❧

"Curse my mother and my father," she said to herself as she looked in the mirror that day. Aisha was facing her wardrobe looking for something to wear, behaving like other newly-married women, who try to vary their appearance every day. One half of her image trembled on the cupboard's left door mirror, while her other appeared on the right one. Half of her appeared here, the other half there. Each mirror reflected a separate part of her. Each image opened onto an inverse side of the other. Aisha opened both sides of the door, and the heavy wood creaked, the two girls disappearing together. Aisha decided against a patterned dress she liked, and put on a house-dress. Then she stood behind the door listening to Um Hassan's morning movements as she made coffee before the rest of the household awoke. She struck a match, removed the saucepan from the gas cooker and put the coffee pot on in its place. She swept the mats, and threw the broom behind the door. Aisha emerged from her room and saw her squatting in her long black dress, the plastic men's shoes that she was wearing revealing the backs of her heels, which were covered by short socks.

"Good morning Yamma. How are you this morning?" said Um Hassan.

"Fine, but I couldn't sleep. There was shooting all night long. Hassan didn't come last night. There must be a state of high alert!"

"When one sees one's beloved, he forgets his friends. My sons were always that way when it came to the Democratic Front."

She fell silent as she stopped stirring the coffee, staring silently at Aisha, before a smile shone across her face, framed by glistening silver hair that added a youthful elegance to her deeply wrinkled face: "No one means the same to him as you do. My goodness, Aisha, he fell so deeply in love with you when he saw you. He just went out of his mind. He said: I want to get married this instant. Go and ask for her hand in marriage. I had tried so hard before, but he wouldn't accept anyone. He wanted you only. But these are such bad times, keeping newly-weds on alert and on duty."

She sighed as though to apologize for her son's absence. She stepped up to a cupboard whose missing door had been replaced by a white sheet, pulling out a copper tray, and small coffee cups decorated with a pattern of small gold palm trees. She poured out the shining brown liquid, and the fresh smell of cardamom floated about. She turned her face sideways, shaking her head as she made a mock spitting gesture and said: "I spit on them! May God kill those treacherous Arabs."

Aisha was embarrassed. She wanted to comfort her over her son's absence, but did not know how to address her. Should she call her "Amti" or "Khalti?"

"Khalti, don't be upset. I don't want anything. If he wants to go on alert, then let him go on alert."

"No, my child. That's not the problem. The trouble is that this Arab nation just won't leave us alone. They've been after us since the Palestine days! What do they want of us! I wish they'd leave us be, get off our backs. Haven't we lost enough martyrs already?"

Her gaze flew off and rested on the black frame around Fayez's photograph. Two tears trickled out of the corners of her eyes, which reddened whenever she became emotional. Fayez's picture began to form within the watery glow burning her dark wrinkled cheek. Aisha surveyed the martyr once more. His appearance in the picture. A good looking, fair-haired man. Green eyes surrounded by dark, heavy lashes.

Teeth stained by smoking, and an exaggeratedly sweet smile. The writing below the picture read: "The Martyred Lieutenant Fayez Assamhadan." The date he had been killed was also there: "May 1973."

The woman said in a voice that had become as oblique as a shadow: "Look how good looking he was! All that youth, and he was martyred. He was always being taken for a foreigner. You see, half my children look like Arabs, and the other half resemble westerners, like their father. Your husband, God keep him, is dark. Curse Palestine. We love it so much and have lost so many of our children for its sake."

Aisha's gaze shifted to the second photograph hanging on the wall. The mother in her white head cover and long dress standing in the martyr's cemetery. She is carrying a water jug and sprinkling the speedwell and basil plants around the grave. Marbled headstones spread out behind her in infinite columns inside the finite square.

"What can I do? What descends from heaven, the earth receives. May God keep my remaining children."

The last syllable of the last word floated above them, and something gave within Aisha's heart as the melodious voice rang out. It felt as though a heavy hand had struck at her heart and smashed it. She realized that she had come to love this sturdy, petite woman who was considered her mother-in-law. Tradition called for disliking one's mother-in-law. But she felt that she loved her more than her mother, more than her husband, more than all her family. She felt that something mysterious that she could not understand drew them together. Was it the flowing of tears? Or was it the remembrance of a time that had passed, and a place that could not be regained?

Um Hassan sat down on one of the side seats covered with a thick rough fabric, and crossed her legs. She handed Aisha, who was sitting opposite her, a cup of coffee, and made ready to speak. Aisha knew that her proud companion had decided to abandon her silence after the night of high anxiety that she had spent without any word of Hassan.

"Yamma, Aisha. What days you young people are living through! Do you think these lives of yours are good ones? Oh, my dear! What have you seen? Was that a wedding? Weddings, my poor one, were lost and gone a long long time ago, from way back then. If I told you about my wedding, you wouldn't believe it. We were in Palestine in those days."

Um Hassan shifted her weight, and cleared her throat: "When my husband married me, I was still a young child. I was too young to have a bosom or breasts. They clad me in clogs and closed my eyes. The bath-house attendant stuck lit candles on my fingers until they shone like a crystal chandelier. She took me in and out as I changed my seven wedding outfits. The wedding bath went on for seven days at our expense, and all the guests and loved ones bathed. And the henna. It was beautiful. They painted patterns on my hands and feet. If only you could have seen the lute, the drum and the tambourine. Or the dancers that were brought to dance. One of them pinned gold coins on my head dress. The trousseau your father-in-law brought was magnificent: two lamps and two decorated glass water jugs. A slender-necked bottle shaped like a duck for sprinkling rose water. A carafe with matching glasses. A copper bed frame, and a set of white cotton sheets. My wedding was really something else.

"On my first night with him, I put the quilt over my head and was frightened. I was frightened he'd gobble me up. He pounced on me like a cat. But later, I got used to him. A fair-skinned, well-built bridegroom, he was. When we would sit down to supper, I'd say to him: take my hand and give me yours. He was so blond and had bluish-black eyes.

Aisha could not believe that the handsome man her mother-in-law was describing was the same old man still fast asleep and snoring; the grandfather who wore thick concave lenses and suffered from glaucoma. It was him, the very same man whose yellow moustache trembled, and whose heavy, shaking limbs were unable to carry him downstairs to sit in his small shop.

Um Hassan tilted her head as the memories began to fill the room with a light that enhanced the morning sun rays: "We were living in Alama, in the country, amongst the plantations and the olive trees. There was bounty all around. Amongst the blossoms, the orange blossoms. Oh, how beautiful it was in the countryside where the peasants live. Weddings in those days were for everybody, not only for certain people like today. The women would cut wood with their scythes, and bring it back in bundles over their heads, singing happily as they came. Some of the older women in the family would play the lute, some would chant and others dance to their music. The men used to bring young men from Hitteen to sing ballads and they would yell out their approval saying, "Ah, yes!" There would be entertainment for a whole week, the men chanting refrains, the women singing, and the whole village would turn into a wedding. There's so much to tell, I don't know where to begin."

Um Hassan moved her hands as though she were protecting her face from a breeze in the fields. Throwing her head back, she said: "We had fig trees, grape vines and olive trees. A woman used to go to the fields and work with her man. She was just like him. They used to harvest lentils and wheat. There were no schools back then, and families used to marry off their sons and daughters to each other. It wasn't like it is today, strangers getting married and only getting to know one another when they wed. I had my first son, Fayez, when I was fourteen. I had Hassan when I was sixteen. The month I had him, we fled and left home."

With an automatic strength, she held back her words, which had turned into something resembling the stone that one rubs before prayer, hoping to pierce it and squeeze out whatever water might be inside it when none is available for ablutions. But her overwhelming sadness broke through her silence, and she spoke once more: "Eh . . . We came out of Palestine. We were in the orchards picking olives when Assafsaaf, which was the nearest village to us, fell. The Haganah gangs slaughtered a lot of people, and also raped many women. My neighbour's niece was slaughtered in front of her father. We had no arms. We thought it would be a good idea to leave for a short time so that what had happened to the people of Assafsaaf and Ain Ezzeitoun, which King Abdallah had surrendered, and Deir Yassin would not happen to us. We went north. We didn't see anything, and never looked back, because we were so sure that we would return a few days later. In Bint Jbeil, we found that the UN were putting people into cars and taking them to Burj Esh-Shemali. People were surviving on almost nothing. When it snowed on us in Burj Esh-Shemali, they moved us to Nahr El-Barid in Tripoli."

As Um Hassan spoke a cloud would move across her face, and another would quickly replace it. As she reminisced about the land, the figs and the spring greens, bright rainbow colours would shine in her eyes and on her skin. She would return to the prime of her youth, her face would blossom and she would be engulfed by a sheen which

109

would then darken and shrivel up when she mentioned the exodus and the snow. Her face went white as though all of its blood had drained away.

"What can I say? One minute we were well off and living comfortably, the next we were poor and had absolutely nothing. We would sit in the tents with the rest of the women and cry, saying:

"We have left the country of grapes and figs,
And come to the camp to beg for flour.
We have left the country of grapes and almonds,
And come into exile to beg for olives."

"What sin have I committed after doing good?"

"But let met tell you . . . when my son Fayez grew up, he went to university. We were forced to leave the Nahr El-Barid camp and come to Ezza'tar so that he could go to university. While he was at the Arab University, he joined the Pan-Arab Nationalist Movement, and when the Resistance started, he became a member of the Democratic Front. He became a political official. Two years ago in May, the army came and began shelling the people in all the camps. Fayez was martyred."

Um Fayez continued: "Hassan was a member of Fatah at university. He used to work at the factories during the summer holidays to meet his expenses. When his brother became a martyr, Hassan took up his gun and said: with blood we shall redeem you, Oh martyr. And he became a member of the Democratic Front."

Her body was shaken by a slight tremor, like someone who had a fever.

"Fayez was the life of the house. He and his Lebanese wife lived on the floor below us. God Almighty gave me patience to cope. When I heard that he had been martyred, I ran to the office, I ran at the door and kicked it, and it flew open. There he was lying on his back. I drew close to him, bent down and kissed him here and here," she said, pointing to her cheek and forehead. "Then I raised my head and said, 'Yamma, I congratulate you.'"

They removed me from him. Fire ran through my body. I screamed, I rent my clothes as I ran after them to the mosque. I ran behind the car, and my sister ran behind me, pinning up my clothes with safety pins. I threw myself over him at the hospital and said: I shan't let him go, I want to die with him. Tal Ezza'tar was being so badly pounded that we couldn't bury him. They took me home with him. He lay in the corridor for three days with us standing around him. The corridor between us and the neighbours is as wide as a mattress. He lay there, all covered up, and I lay over him without shedding a tear. If I had cried in front of them . . . his father and brother would have collapsed and died soon after. His poor wife was going out of her mind. For three days, gunfire was crackling outside, and we were all around him. One would faint, and I would resuscitate him. Another would cry and I would comfort him. The martyrs lay dead on the streets, and no one could move them. Ever since that day, I have had heart problems because I stopped myself from crying. I felt that life was not long enough to put out the fire inside me."

At that point, Um Hassan realized that she had gone too far in immersing Aisha in her lake of grief, and she asked her apologetically: "Yamma, if one is ruined, broken-hearted and homeless, away from one's brothers and sisters, can one be happy? I have put one young man under the ground. We were dragged around and made homeless. We've become nothing more than some flour and a bit of water that never runs out. Yes . . . those who are dead are dead. Things will inevitably calm down and you will have children. One's grandchild gives more pleasure than one's child."

Um Hassan looked at Aisha's abdomen as though she were expecting an answer to her oblique query. Aisha lowered her eyes, ignoring the silent question which hurt and embarrassed her. Grandchild? Was that why Um Hassan liked her? She pampered her and would not let her do any of the housework, burdening her own daughters, Khazneh and Amneh, with it. They complained about this, both in front of Aisha and behind her back. No, Amneh was the only one to express her frustration, while Khazneh said not a word. But was the calculating Um Hassan just trying to extend her own existence through her offspring. Was that why she had married off her son, so that he could remain near her, despite the fact that marriage had not kept Fayez? Would the situation calm down, as Um Fayez was saying? Would Aisha's suffering diminish and would she get used to the cat-like attacks, which she felt she would never come to like?

Never, she would whisper to herself every morning and every evening. She reminded herself again as the silence ebbed away, and the noise of the waking sleepers began to pervade the house.

Hassan bent his head and hid behind the sandbags after a stray bullet whizzed past his temple. George bent over double and cautiously emerged from behind the fortification, made up of sandbags and empty diesel barrels. Hassan was studying the positions opposite through a pair of binoculars, and George was looking them up on a map. "Well, I've known this for a long time. I swear that getting out of Tal Ezza'tar will be as difficult as death itself."

George answered: "As you can see, fortifications are all-important."

"And this blasted forest. I'm damn sure it's full of booby traps and snipers."

"As though we didn't have enough problems already. Where did this problem of blasted Phalangists come from? By God, I don't know how Palestine is going to be liberated. First Black September, then Kahhaleh, then Beirut. We just don't know where to turn." George touched his beard, which had grown quite long. He recalled the ten-year old Ibtissam repeatedly asking him:

"George, when will you shave your beard?"

"Not until Palestine is liberated!"

She would answer: "But uncle, is it ever going to be liberated?"

He would give her a tender smack on the neck and say: "Ibtissam, all that affection and pampering and talking to you, and you've already turned into someone without hope?"

Again, George remembered Aisha's face. Whenever he thought of the little girl, the image of her older sister would immediately come to mind, like the relationship between a captured bird and the thread which ties it, as the saying went. He could only remember her as a pair of black eyes fluttering like flags on a murky night. Strange, how she generated a pity deep within him for a reason he could not grasp. Even after she had married, she remained that way on the rare occasions on which he saw her. She would look at him with her sad eyes as though she were blaming him, and he would have to avert his gaze, pretending not to notice. He could not put his finger on the nature of the problem. Was she blaming him because she was unhappy with his friend Hassan!

In the end, he was forced to discuss the mysterious atmosphere surrounding Assayed's daughter, who seemed perpetually unhappy, with Hana. Even her husband had become worried about her fluttering, distracted stares, which seemed to go nowhere in particular. He began to investigate the state of affairs at home during his absence. Was anyone harassing her during his absence, he wondered? But Um Hassan reassured him that the young girl's ill-health could be due to an early pregnancy. She was treating her like a princess, not asking her to do anything, not even to carry anything. What was wrong? Hassan kept turning the question over in his mind because he never found the opportunity of having a frank talk with his shy bride. No sooner would he arrive home than it would be time for him to go back. He even did not have time to have breakfast, shave or have a bath. He was being kept busy by a series of assignments which did not give him the chance of scratching his own head, as his mother would say. The clashes did not stop. The shelling would begin after midnight or at dawn, and go on till the morning, or noon of the next day. People would take advantage of the few truce hours during which the shelling would stop to buy household necessities or bake their risen loaves of dough. But by the beginning of February 1976, when achieving some sort of breakthrough seemed impossible, people were being mobilized to build fortifications. The militia would oversee work in every neighbourhood. Earth would be loaded onto trucks, then shovelled into sacks. Filling sandbags and erecting protective barriers on all the roads and public footpaths to deflect sniping, which was causing an increasing number of casualties, became the main preoccupation in the camp and around its edges. But an agonizing worry had taken hold of Hassan because of an incident the previous day. The fighters of Al-Barq Al-Arabi had pointed their guns at a civilian truck, intending to confiscate it, thinking that it was carrying sacks of rice. After an argument with the driver, who had to call on the militiamen in the adjacent neighbourhood, the men at the Al-Barq road-block were surprised to learn that the truck was loaded with sandbags being used to build fortifications. They resorted to unconvincing excuses to justify their actions. Hassan asked George in a loud voice: "Hey, George. There's evidence that they're acting like pirates. What's this about confiscations? Can they be confiscating civilian rations for trade purposes under the pretext of patriotism?

But George left hurriedly to continue his daily round of the fortifications, leaving Hassan without an answer to his anxious question. "We have enough problems in this mess. We don't need incidents of that sort added to them," thought Hassan.

Aisha looked through the window at the steep slope separating the camp from the Christian areas. She wanted to breathe in fresh air instead of the suffocating air of confinement imposed by the clashes. The shelling would stop, only to start again with added ferocity. The roar of machine guns and missiles would stop, but more shells and bullets of different sizes would soon pour down on the camp like heavy rain. That meant that even the nicest dividend of her marriage was denied her – that of visiting her mother and father. She had regained their sympathy and won the right of belonging after a long rejection. During her first days of marriage, she had visited them on an almost daily basis. She would go in her high-heeled shoes, her handbag hanging on her elbow, dark brown lipstick badly applied to her lips, making her look like a cat which had just eaten its kittens, as Hassan's sister, Amneh, observed in a whisper. She used to look forward with joy to the time when she would leave the house, heading for her family's home. She would return refreshed, her pale cheeks slightly flushed. Those daily excursions had broken a barrier that had excluded her soul from the world and other human beings. Dilly-dallying on the way had become her favourite hobby. Aisha had wanted to find something she enjoyed in her new situation. Stepping out had become a pleasure, but then, all hell had broken loose. She had begun to learn to adapt to the privileges that marriage had offered her. She could not be a daughter to her family except that way. Assayed respected her and was tender towards her as though her marriage certificate had proven the fatherhood he had tried to avoid. Her mother began to consult her about everything she intended to do, especially about how best to convince the Red Crescent employees to give her a regular monthly salary for working as a cleaner instead of simply employing her on a daily basis. Ibtissam would use different excuses all day to stay with her at Hassan's house, helping her to tidy her room, taking advantage of her inattention to examine her lipsticks and paint her nails with bright, shiny varnish. Oh God, all this had stopped when the unending hell broke out. There she was, looking through the window to get some fresh air. All she could think of was the flimsiness of the tile-covered metal roof of her parents' house. She had only become aware of this as the clashes had escalated. After living in her in-laws' house, she realized that the walls and roof of her parents' house would not withstand a heavy blast of wind, so how would they hold back such a storm?

During the second half of the first month of the new year, when it became clear that the clashes would not end, Um Hassan insisted that Aisha's family should move in with them. Um Jalal, worn down by the state of her home's dilapidated roof, had no objections. She tried hard to convince Assayed of the need to sleep in a safe place, but he answered with sarcasm: "Look woman, if I'm to die, I'll die here. Why go and trouble poor Um Fayez?"

Assayed insisted on staying at home.

Hassan used to make affectionate fun of the solidly good relationship between Aisha and his mother. When he used to jokingly claim that he had discovered the reason for the rapport between the two women, saying that tears were their common secret, Um Hassan would retort: "Is there a reason for crying? Everything about our situation is sorrowful."

The young Husam, who continued to play on the streets even during the worst sniping, would visit his married sister's home daily without any fear of the shelling. He would come just to get a few pence, which he would plant alongside the vine in the barrel on the roof of their home, hoping that his dream of seeing them sprouting into gold coins would come true. No one in either family was able to understand the secret of that strange conviction of his, but planting coins became an established tradition which no one questioned, and Husam's journeying between the two houses in his torn yellow jumper became a daily ritual.

That morning, Aisha seemed profoundly different when she got up looking pale and walking heavily. The whistling of the kerosene cooker disturbed the quiet, emphasizing her late rising. White beans were boiling in a red sauce inside the big pot. The rising bubbles brought back to her the scene of cooked tomato sauce which the women had put out on the roofs to dry out for preservation. Aisha was overcome by nausea, her stomach turning at the acid smell. In the middle of the room, Amneh bent over a mass of dough in a copper basin, mixing it and slapping it with her palms. The cotton balls edging her scarf swung in time. She had a frown on her face, daydreaming as she punched the dough, which was becoming more malleable. All of a sudden, she turned to Aisha and said: "All the glory goes to rice, and the cracked wheat can go hang."

She sighed, pursed her lips and turned her face away in disgust.

Um Hassan scolded her daughter: "Good Lord, what a way to start the day."

She continued talking to Aisha:

"Good morning, dear. You look pale today. I hope everything is alright?"

"I'm okay, aunt. Where's Hassan?"

Amneh's voice rang out, mimicking Aisha: "Ah, my dear. He's gone. Ah . . . "

Um Hassan snapped angrily:

"Shut up, now. Behave yourself if you know what's good for you."

Aisha ignored the attack directed at her, and said: "Okay, aunt. Did Hassan wake up and leave early?"

Um Hassan nodded at her and continued to stir the cooking meal, the invisible question trembling within her breast. Could she be pregnant? Thinking of that possibility tickled her with feelings of joy. She would accept all of Aisha's eccentricities, which deviated from the behaviour expected of good daughters-in-law, and would slaughter a lamb at her feet if only . . . nothing would upset her then, if only she could give them a child. The pallor on the bride's face was a good omen. The constitution of the family's men was capable of planting the seed of conception even if women did nothing more than shake hands with them!

Amneh pulled her palms from the soft mass of dough and wiped them with a wet cloth. Then she brought a piece of white muslin and spread it over the dough so that it would rise. Her tall well-built figure came into view as she stood up and stepped barefoot across the mat. Aisha trembled secretly because of the tremendous discomfort she felt in the presence of that evil girl, who, as Um Hassan put it, would simply not behave. With her long, white face, her straight hair flowing beneath her scarf, and her thick crimson lips, she seemed like a monster who gobbled up little children. She did not resemble her older sister, Khazneh. She had nothing at all in common with her. Slightly-built and lame, Khazneh had contracted polio at a young age, and the UNRWA clinic had not known how to treat her. After the situation had deteriorated, Khazneh had not been able to to return to her job at the Christian fabric factory, so she had started helping the other girls in the camp to fill sandbags and prepare meals for the militiamen manning the positions at the edges of the camp. As for Amneh, her only way of amusing herself was by picking arguments with those around her, or by plucking her eyebrows and removing the hairs on her legs one by one.

Amneh gathered the edges of her long striped dress and searched for one of her plastic slippers amongst the pile of shoes and sandals at the doorstep. She walked out deliberately, showing her anger. Um Hassan pleaded: "Hey, yamma, go and check on your father. Go downstairs and take his place in the shop so that he can say his prayers."

Amneh threw a glance at her mother and didn't even bother answering her. Um Hassan continued: "If she doesn't go down there, I'll go and take the old man's place myself."

"Poor old man," Aisha thought to herself. She imagined him sitting in his chair for long hours unable to perform his ablutions, purifying himself instead by stroking the stone he kept next to him, praying as he sat in his chair, unable to work because of the weakness of his sick eyes. Unless someone were on hand to lead him upstairs to his home, he would stay in his shop on the corner, his presence unfelt except for his soft mutterings and his black cloak with golden embroidery around the edges. He would motion customers towards the merchandise they required, and they would serve themselves, finding what they were after with the help of his hoarse instructions and nods of the head.

Hana stood in Aisha's room, her face reflected in the mirror of one of the wardrobe doors, while Aisha's face appeared in the other half. Hana was talking and gesturing with her hands: "And the cinema! If only you knew how I loved it before the war. I used to go with my uncle to the cinemas in El-Burj and Martyrs' Square. The film I liked most of all was 'Take Care of Zouzou'. I was wearing a new blue woollen costume which my mother had bought at the Sursuq market. I wish you had seen how good looking the main star was. He was blond, but very likeable. The important thing was this: Suad Husni was a poor girl, yet she managed to solve her problems. Since then, I've been going to all her films. Oh! If it wasn't for the war."

Aisha remained silent, leaning against the pillow, her left hand to her cheek. Hana said: "My uncle used to bring his party's pamphlets and hide them amongst my books, so I began to understand politics. I used to burn papers he was afraid would be discovered. I asked him to get me into the organization, but he told me I should wait until I grew up. At school, one of the sisters contacted me when I was in secondary two, and I began working for secret cells. I worked in the Signals Department. Wireless work is so nice. But I wish the peaceful times would return and I could visit my uncle again on the western side and go to the cinema with him.

She continued, "If things would calm down, you could work with us, because perhaps you're in a difficult position. You're a recently married lady and can't go to the combat lines. We used to give literacy classes, but we've stopped because everyone is on alert. Ah, if only you knew what it felt like the first time I fired heavy arms. I had received a lot of training with kalashnikovs and guns. I said in front of our male comrades that it was also possible for girls to fire heavy arms, and they laughed and said the only thing women were good at was talking. I made up my mind, picked up an RPG launcher as I stood next to the anti-aircraft guns on the Al-Meer hill, and I fired five times at an enemy position. I wish you could have seen their disbelief! They offered to train a brigade of women fighters. Their commander agreed, but things never quietened down enough. What a pity! They allow us to receive militia training, but only with kalashnikovs and hand grenades."

She fell silent, then continued bitterly: "Everything pales beside my father's kidnap. The Liaison Committee is simply useless, although George has made lots of inquiries. He was upset with my mother for not allowing our marriage contract to be signed. We needn't have a wedding, but at least we must sign the wedding contract. My poor mother . . . I really don't know whether I should listen to her or to George. No, No . . . the war is still on. When things calm down and they've located my father or found out something about him, then, God willing . . . "

Hana left after giving Aisha all her news. At last, Aisha had realized what the difference between the two of them was.

The woods! The green woods. Hassan looks out at them through the window, but can only see the tops of the faraway fir trees. He touches Aisha's thick hair, tied back with a patterned scarf that has small red squares on it. He smiles in her face, like a father amused by his little girl's waywardness. He says: "Ayyoush! It's impossible that you should go out before a few months have passed. You're still a recent bride, and no one will understand it. Okay, you're bored staying at home, so just bring out the sewing machine and sew. Do some embroidery. Do whatever you like. But going out when there's a state of alert! No, that would be impossible. What will my comrades say? It doesn't make sense for you to be running around all over the place when we're newly-weds and you've never had anything to do with the organization! It's best for you to be reasonable, otherwise my family will think you've gone mad."

He pointed at a spot in the woods from which faraway crackling could be heard.

"It's possible that the attack on the woods will begin today. Perhaps we should have launched it a long time ago."

Hassan recalled the exhaustive argument at the meeting of the Joint Forces about whether to occupy the woods or ignore them.

The Thabet Woods formed a loose strip that separated the Jisr El-Basha and Tal Ezza'tar camps, cutting both of them off from Nab'ah and Sinn El-Feel. Ever since the clashes had begun, Hassan had supported the prevalent view, which favoured the occupation of the woods, because whichever party controlled them would have the camp within firing range. As more people complained about the increasing sniping at them from the woods and the rising number of casualties, serious thought was given to occupying them. However, it was the occupation of Karantina that had prompted the joint leadership of the organizations to take the decision. The previous July, enemy forces had launched their first attack on Karantina, but had been unable to enter it. Now, in the early days of the new year, and despite several cease-fire agreements, Karantina had fallen, and many of its inhabitants had been killed in horrific atrocities which a few of the escaping survivors had described. The news provoked a stunned silence amongst the inhabitants of Ezza'tar. They feverishly resorted to their radios to seek the details. They crowded around telephones, but none of them could satisfy their need to know. Only the press could describe the event in all its detail without being censored, but newspapers could not find their way into the camp after the siege. However, what the people of Ezza'tar did manage to find out was enough to bring home to them that their camp was the next stage in the plan to wipe out Palestinian communities in the eastern area. The Phalangist leaders had often declared this to be their goal.

As Hassan walked towards his position, he went over all the duties awaiting him as part of his assignment of deploying the militia groups. He was completely absorbed in checking out the various fortified positions, for everything would depend on them within the next few days. The only trenches that were ready were the ones along the Dekwaneh and Meer Hill. A week ago, the high earth barricades had been removed from the Slik-Karkaba axis. The digging of trenches had begun on the hill facing the Sallaf area. Now, he had to tour the different positions to ensure that everything which had been prepared the previous night would go smoothly, without error.

The sky was clear and shone like a crystal plate. He felt like whistling his favourite song, "Inta Umry". He sang it inwardly, unable to sing the tune out loud as had been his habit until recently. "Your eyes brought me back . . ." a shell whistled past him, and he took cover behind a wall, then ran, thinking that the decision to take the woods should have been taken from the very first hours of the siege of Ezza'tar. His amazement had increased at the argument of the representatives of the Al-Barq organization, who declared that the orders they had received from their headquarters did not authorize them to participate in the attack because it would further provoke the enemy. Anger raged within him at such logic. Was the issue at stake not to provoke the enemy, or to defend ourselves first and foremost? And which was the party besieging the other and rejecting its existence, us or them? What crooked logic, Hassan said to himself. But he forgot about the whole issue the second he arrived at the entrance of the first building from which the attack to occupy the Thabet Woods would begin. Amidst the noisy chaos of the men's shoving feet and the squeaking sound of weapons being mounted, Hassan turned around and saw it behind his shoulder. The shining glisten, the bright sparkling . . . the first morning sunlight on the lovely pine trees in the woods. In days gone by before the war, he had always admired the trees. That was the place where he had first discovered birds' nests and the pine cones out of which dry dark seeds would fall. He and his friends used to gather the cones, make a small fire and burn them. The tasty seeds would pour out inside transparent wings, which, once rubbed, would become edible. Many a time, he had leaned his head against an old tree over there and fallen asleep as he listened to the crickets. He had captured many a spider, letting them go because of the fragility of their slender legs and their dainty movements. The birds had sung then like a choir. Now, one didn't even dare to listen to the songs inside one's own head without being stunned by the shells that whizzed about day and night. As he climbed the stairs, Hassan shouted as though scolding someone, "Inta Umry, you are my liiiiiife." Suddenly, George's face appeared, saying: "I promise you, we all know you're a bridegroom, but kindly run upstairs so that we can organize some new supply kits to replace the missing ones."

The bridegroom broke out in a cold sweat of embarrassment, as though he had committed a reprehensible action and been caught out by his friend.

Khazneh had never before felt that she was light enough to fly. She felt she was cruising over a spring field. The woods were green, but never before had they given her such a sensation. Her body had felt heavy as far back as she could remember. Her cumbersome steps had given her a sensation of pulling herself forward like a wagon stuck in the mud. She had contracted polio as a child, and the only treatment the UNRWA clinic had given her had been asprin tablets. She had survived, dragging her leg behind her. She had crossed these woods many a Sunday, picking greenery with the other girls. Spring greens, sorrel and mallow. They would all turn into appetizing meals prepared by her mother, who was good at keeping down household expenses. These were met by Khazneh's monthly wages. She would bring home her salary and hand it over to Um Fayez so that she could take care of the extended family, including Fayez's children. Oh, the field was so green, although it was winter, and the yellow camomile flowers sparkled like gold in its midst. A grasshopper jumped in front of her. It was dark green, pushing its folded legs upwards, propelling itself forward like a flying ship. Not walking, but flying, circling, soaring, jumping, although it was no more than a floating insect. Praise be to the Prophet! God bless Him, even insects are sometimes more agile than human beings. And she stretched her steps towards the Red Crescent first aid centre in the mosque at the edge of the woods, without fearing the bullets of the snipers around her. She ignored the flying pellets that traversed between the arms of the snipers and the sky above the woods. She walked as usual, even better than usual, harbouring a profound belief in fate. Nothing shall befall us except that which God hath decreed, as it is written in the Quran. She had always wanted to enrol in armed resistance training courses for women, but she had not dared to. There would have inevitably been those who would have criticized the paralysis of her bad leg. She had done a first aid course two years before, using an aubergine to learn how to administer injections. She had also become proficient at taking temperatures and blood pressures. Now, here she was doing first aid work at the forward positions, filled with confidence and enthusiasm as she walked. Perhaps her confidence matched that of able-bodied people, and perhaps it even outstripped it. It was better that things should be this way than letting everybody believe that her only role was to serve her family, since she was not ever expected to get married. Doing first aid work was better than spending her time attending to the demands of the young and the old, of falling asleep while listening to her father's boringly repetitive accounts about the days of Safarbarlek and Turkey. How he had escaped conscription and hid near the Houleh lake with his cousin; how the cousin had hid the gold coins inside the back of his trousers, fearing the wrath of the Turks. He would smoke his rolled cigarettes and mutter: "Curse the Turks." Cousin Abdallah had become so weighed down by the hidden coins, he could no longer walk. When they finally got to Alama, Abdallah started shedding the gold coins unawares like someone who had acute diarrhoea. Later, Majid's wife found the money amongst the goat droppings as she was sweeping.

Her father would tell the story over and over again, always with the same enthusiasm. "We remained in hiding until Turkey was defeated. That's the way of the world: it's pot luck." Khazneh's job was to listen, always. Her luck decreed that she remain silent and listen to everyone.

Four days after fighting and taking up positions in the Thabet Woods, the joint command decided to abandon them. Holding on to them was difficult, and occupying them exhausted the militia that was protecting the camp. The liaison committee sternly warned of the grave political implications of Palestinian expansionism. The expansionism argument was unconvincing to the people of the camp, for they had existed long enough without bothering to worry about anything outside their own windows. But they had hoped to end the threat posed by the Phalangist shelling of their camp. This had proved hard and costly. They did not have enough forces to ensure their continued control of the Thabet Woods, which commanded the camp's main roads, and the movement of every creature within it. On the fifth day, the decision to withdraw was taken and carried out. And on the fifth day, Khazneh returned home, dusty, her hair dishevelled, but unconcerned by Amneh's mockery of her for joining the military. A new thing occurred in the house: Khazneh would relate an incident she had experienced to anyone she came across.

"One of the fighters came to me and said: 'Sister Khazneh, there are five wounded people in a building at the corner of the woods, let's go.' He carried my first aid kit and ran ahead of me. We were unable to go into the building through the main entrance because it was being shelled. Four women dangled down a bath towel from the ground floor. I held firmly on to it, and the young man hoisted me up, and the four women pulled the chord. When I got in and saw the wounded, I was at a loss. I saw two children, a woman and two young girls. I didn't know where to start. But I remembered that in first aid classes, we had been taught to begin with the most serious condition. After I began to bandage their wounds, the medical bandages ran out. So the women tore up their household sheets and gave them to me with boiling water and salt."

The famine grew and the shops closed because they had run out of food. The inhabitants, who had depended on daily wages for a living, were unable to earn enough to meet their needs. The rations that people had amassed in their homes ran out. The middle of January went by, and things did not calm down as the liaison committee had promised. There was no more kerosene in Um Jalal's home for the cooker. Nor was it possible to refill the gas cylinders, because the distributor had disappeared and could not be found.

When the shelling would stop, and this was a rarity, Aisha would visit her family. She would enter the house and marvel. How the concrete would break and the metal roof would twist if it were hit by a shell! She marvelled at the plaster that fell off the wall; at her mother's eagerness to serve the people whom she knew; at the boy Husam, who wandered the streets, and at Assayed, who would make much of her despite being in a continuous daze. Once, she had wanted her mother to teach her how to make bread, because Amneh had repeatedly criticized her for not being good at anything. Um Jalal taught her how to mix the flour and water, how to wait for the dough to rise, and then to cut it into round pieces. The mother put a white muslin cloth over the tray to keep the flies off it, and Ibtissam carried the tray to the bakery on her small head, her hand hanging down with a natural balance. Five minutes after she had left, Ibtissam came running back with Husam. They were dragging something heavy, struggling to push a large conical shape. Um Jalal and Aisha stared in disbelief at the object the two children had proudly brought. Husam and Ibtissam had energetically dragged home a rocket they had found in the opposite field. Assayed came out of his habitual daze, shouted, ran up to the rocket, and dragged it back to the garbage pile where it had been lying. The rocket had fallen, but its detonator had been faulty. No one had gone near it, except those two devils of children, as Abu Jalal referred to them. At the doorstep as she was leaving, Aisha once again experienced a bitter taste in her mouth as she recalled her past. George no longer visited because he was preoccupied with his new duties. She could do no more than surrender to the fate of her acidic days. But she was not alone. That applied to everyone else living in the Tal which was named after the green thyme herb: Ezza'tar!

In the last few days of the first month of the new year, the hardship imposed on the camp by the siege eased. Suddenly a woman was killed under the cover of darkness by a sniper's bullet. She died carrying a large frozen leg of lamb. Her corpse was the signal which prompted armies of people to head for the frozen meat plant between Mukallis and Jisr El-Basha. The famous frozen Sobka meat, plus boxes of ghee, chocolates wrapped in shining paper and original Limelight Flour all moved along the winding dirt tracks as people's hands snatched them, running home with them under shelling and sniper fire. Some made it, and others were killed. The hands of the hungry people even reached the chicken abattoir, without realizing that the next attack would lead to the fall of the whole factory area, or what was left of it. Less than a month later, despite a ten-day cease-fire, the second attack from the direction of Mansourieh began. The people were unable to use the apples lying on the streets. The fruits had been removed from the fridges and lay slowly rotting beneath the gentle winter sun.

That was a sight I shall never forget. The day I managed to enter the camp of Tal Ezza'tar, being one of a few people who had managed to reach it between two sieges, I saw the apples scattered around on the streets, their skins shrunken and wrinkled. But they had kept their pretty red colour. I had said to myself: "Ezza'tar? Why don't they call it Attuffah?" At that moment my grandfather's home in Wadi Attuffah, the valley of apples, in Hebron flashed into my mind's eye. And I remembered my mother, Hayat, in the mid-fifties. She had lived at my grandfather's house temporarily before moving into the attic above the school, which was afflicted with measles and frost-bite. How innocent I had been. I went to my grandfather simply to tell him how I had heard my mother complaining to Hajjeh Salimah about the hassle and pain of living with my grandfather's fourth wife. I had told him. I was three years old. My mother and Hajjeh Salimah had later accused me of blowing the whistle on her and reporting her grievances to the tribe elder, who wore a red tarboush with a silk tassle. But, what I want to say is this. Every place I saw later would always remind me of my birth place in Palestine. And in Tal Ezza'tar, I recalled Wadi Attuffah in the West Bank of Palestine. My amazement increased at the dry fruit littering the place like freckles on a face that has seen too much sun. Everybody was sitting in the sun, both old and young. They had all come out of the shelters, corridors and passages to get a touch of the amber rays. Old women with patterned tattoos on their faces, which had been acquired long before their arrival in this place. They sat with their grandchildren in their laps, while the women were busy airing the sheets and blankets in which the young ones had slept during the confinement. No one looked at the scattered fruits which covered the ground like stones forgotten since the beginning of creation. The car turned and went up into the Tal. At the clinic, I was able to meet Um Jalal and the doctor who worked there. When I told them that I had come to do a newspaper report on the steadfastness of the camp on the anniversary of the emergence of the resistance, people called one

another from here and there and they spoke to me. Hassan. Khazneh.
George. And Hana, the wireless operator. During a free moment, when
I got the opportunity to look through the clinic window at the
buildings opposite on the eastern side, I was overcome by fear, and I
understood what the siege meant. Spontaneously, Um Jalal went into
the next room, which was sectioned off by a flimsy cloth curtain, lit the
kerosene stove, and made us some tea. The doctor explained how bad
the situation was and the shortage of medicines despite the precious
boxes that the liaison committee had succeeded in delivering in military
trucks. He asked me to write about the implications of not having a
central hospital with an emergency operating theatre.

The doctor's name was Ashraf Mahmoud Badran. He told me that
he had studied at the American University of Beirut and worked in one
of the Gulf countries for two years and become a volunteer with the
Resistance. I noticed his elegance despite the total misery outside.
When I met his wife, Dalal, during the second half of that year, she said
that he was always that way, paying attention to his appearance in spite
of everything. I do not want to exaggerate the description of his clothes,
especially since he spent the entire period of the second siege in the
same shirt and trousers. But he who is elegant is elegant, to quote my
mother, even when wearing sack cloth. The doctor complained bitterly
about the absence of medicines and antiseptics; of the lack of back-up
generators to keep the operating theatre going if there was no electricity
supply; of the scarcity of medical tools. He pleaded insistently: "Go and
write that steadfastness will be very difficult if this situation persists."

From afar, I saw George approaching. I recognized him as soon as he
crossed the doorstep. Um Jalal had seized a brief opportunity, when the
doctor had left me to check on a patient, to tell me about George. She
drew near me, saying: "I wish you'd talk to George. No one knows
what's going on as well as he does! Such a good-looking young man,
and intelligent as well." As soon as he entered, I recognized him because
Um Jalal beamed all over. She said in her hoarse voice: "My dear son.
Have you got a cigarette?"

I secretly attributed this fat elderly lady's admiration of the young
man to opportunism borne out by the greedy way in which she smoked
and raided his cigarettes one after the other as he was busy talking.

In his khaki uniform, which embodied the coming together of two opposites – power and gentleness – George told me about the attempts to break the siege around the camp: "Our goal in trying to break through to Nab'ah and Burj Hammoud was to open a channel that would penetrate the siege. The Thabet Woods were the only way to ensure a supply line for food and military support. We tried, but we could not hold out there. When all is said and done, we haven't got professional military forces. A militia can defend, but it cannot attack. We still hope that our brothers can open up a passage or breach the road from the mountains, because the situation is hopeless if no one does something to support us. We have a tremendous shortage of arms, and also a lack of variety. All we have are kalashnikovs. We haven't got enough ammunition for our rocket propelled grenades. Our brothers out there must feel for us and help us. The spontaneity on which we depended in the past is no good. Hassan, the militia leader, will tell you about the siege experience. But write, please write."

The slightly-built Khazneh walked in and said, panting: "Hassan will be here in a few minutes."

Everyone began to ask me about the situation in West Beirut.

I was unable to remember many things at that moment. Despite the horrors of destruction and the shells falling on the other side of the city, it all paled in comparison to the terror I had experienced on my way to the Tal and the feelings of collective panic and sense of being abandoned and rejected that anyone visiting this spot felt.

I had come in the car of a Lebanese friend. All along the dividing line between the west and the east sides of the city, I had not set eyes on a single human being. We had come as soon as an end to kidnappings between the two sides had been announced by the liaison committee. I had not given much consideration to the possibility of mobile kidnap road-blocks. I depended on the safety guarantee enshrined in the medical profession of my friend. Would they think of harming a doctor? That was the safety guarantee I had given myself. I had not thought about it for long. Either I went or I did not go, and I had wanted to go. But my inner self was filled with calm because I was expecting. I had a certain feeling throughout that period that the war would not get me because of the feeling of ripe fertility inside me. Why? I don't know, and I am unable to understand or analyze that feeling. On the empty road that had once swarmed with people and vehicles, only one car was moving: ours. All we noticed was Beirut's famous forest stretching along the dividing line, as if to insist on its old name, the Green Belt. But the high pine peaks were the only witnesses to the absence of any living creature in the sky above and the land below. Hundreds of vacant villas and houses along the flashpoints, which cars crossed with the silence of intruders. The facades of buildings bore black marks and holes made by mortar shells, but their appearance still bore evidence of the luxurious flats they housed, with their shining wooden doors and modern architecture. We did not see a single human being, or even a single 'chick', as they say in this city when they want to exaggerate. Near the empty buildings of Jisr El-Basha, patriotic songs blared out of hanging loudspeakers, though I couldn't make out to which side they belonged. But their loud racket amid the fierce silence emphasized our complete isolation from the world we had left behind, and our journey into the unknown. In Beirut, one feels that one is both the centre of the world and the world's next victim. A shell from an unknown source is fired, and you think that all the newspapers in the world will be interested in its origin and trajectory. What a feeling of warmth the cement jungle imparts along the Al-Jadida Road or in Barbour. On the other side from which we came, all the roads are covered and shadowed. At least that was how I felt; I don't know how I managed to forget the shelling that killed two boys working at a garage on our street. Nationalist Beirut had spread an umbrella of security over everyone who had contributed to realizing its dream of democracy and change during the first part of the civil war.

Hassan arrived at last, to tell me about the militia and the popular committees responsible for dealing with day-to-day problems in the camp. A young man with an air of vitality wearing a blue track suit. I was unable to guess his age because the sedate, deliberate way in which he spoke did not go with his dark curly hair, and the daintiness of his thin nose. The droopiness of his thick, talkative mouth indicated that he had passed from youth into a new kind of middle-age. It seemed that his presence inspired a respect amongst the crowd similar to that enjoyed by the doctor or George, who was in charge of the organization. Hassan told me how the women had helped sew the bags that had been used for the fortifications, using household sheets and duvet covers. Everyone worked, young men and young women alike. Only children had nothing better to do than to play in the piles of sand and earth. Hassan stood up like someone performing a military salute and said emphatically: "I beg you, tell them that we haven't got any water from artesian springs. They wouldn't listen to our pleadings to build an underground central hospital that would be fortified against shelling. I don't know what they're doing over there, and why they are not reacting to our situation with the seriousness it deserves!"

I told him: "The organizations definitely haven't got enough money, otherwise they would have acceded to your request long ago. If they'd had the financial means, they would have done so."

His answer took me by surprise: "Yes they do. The oil countries give them a lot."

That was the first lesson of conscience that I learned during that war. That one should voice one's convictions irrespective of slogans. We had not yet arrived at that stage, because we were wallowing in the romance of the revolution, especially on the other side of the city. But Hassan had exactly expressed the well-known saying, "he who puts his hand in hot water feels different to he who puts it in cold water."

Hassan continued.

"We are suffering a tremendous food shortage. If we had had generators, we could have stockpiled food reserves underground, then . . . "

And he stopped talking and looked at George as though consulting him so that he would confirm what he was about to say: "There's the problem of the black market. We have begun finding stolen television sets hidden in some homes. If we were able to meet people's basic daily needs, we would start working immediately on controlling such robberies."

He added by way of explanation: "They go to the shops, taking advantage of the chaos. . . . "

And he did not finish what he was saying.

His personality made me stop and think. I had never before met such a daring and spontaneous militia leader. In most other positions that I had visited during my reporting, the militia leaders and heads of popular committees were old Palestinian resistance fighters who had started their work before 1948. While they had not lost the enthusiasm of youth, they used to exhibit extreme obedience and retiring embarrassment in their relations with the heads of their organizations, especially their military superiors. Hassan was the only one who seemed to have a distinctive presence in front of George, the organizational and military leader. I still remember the burning tone of his voice as he told me: "Go and tell them. We want a hospital and generators. We want food and supplies and aid. We want medicines and antiseptics. And more important than anything else, we want fuel. That is the most essential of all. Steadfastness does not come out of a vacuum. They should understand us before making demands on us."

The problem Um Hassan faced that day revolved around her secret suspicions that her daughter-in-law's ill-health would not allow her to remain pregnant. But the fact was that Um Hassan was unable to bring up the subject with Aisha. During the morning when the shelling would become less intense or when it would stop during a perfunctory truce, she would steal away to the house of one of her female relatives to get her worries off her chest. Um Hassan would have feminine talks with women of her own age, who understood her and were not like today's younger women. Her cousin said: "You must get a piece of frankincense. You boil it in water, and she must drink one spoonful of it first thing in the morning for forty days."

Um Hassan replied: "The road to Sursuq market is closed, and there is no apothecary in the camp. Bless the sheikhs of the olden days, they used to make charms out of threads in seven colours. The sheikh used to coil the threads into a sphere as small as a coin, and he would recite verses from the Quran over them. The he used to dip it in oil and put it in a piece of gazelle skin."

The hostess said: "Take care of her. Don't let her visit a home where there is much joy or sadness. See to it that she stays calm and tranquil. Beware of letting her carry anything heavy, otherwise she will strain her back and miscarry."

"No, my dear, of course not. Children are the candles of the house. I can still hardly believe that the lad has got married and will soon be preoccupied with the sweet little baby. I swear by God, I prayed by kneeling one hundred times for him to get married and settle down instead of running around with the Fedayeen. May the Lord God protect them through the glory of the Prophet Mohammad. May God let Aisha conceive and bear boys, through the power of the Eye that does not become distracted or sleep."

Um Hassan chanted in a low voice:

"May strings of pearls hang from his walls,

May only son Hassan have a very full house."

Then she added, by way of explanation: "He's the only bunch of grapes in the midst of a vine." "Oh, the grief of his becoming an only son after there were two."

She turned to her cousin and said: "We used to sing this one during the 1936 Uprising when we were little."

The woman was no longer there. She was making tea in the nearby kitchen. Tea had become as precious as hard currency. Um Hassan continued talking to herself and singing:

"Oh mother of two sons, weep for one.

And mother of one son, weep for him too."

She sniffled and her tears welled up. She shouted to her:

"That's enough Um Suleiman. I haven't come here to test your hospitality. Hold on to your kerosene for a rainy day. Come back, my dear, and sit with me a bit before I leave."

Like a passing arrow, Hana entered the clinic. They introduced her to me: "Hana, the bravest wireless operator in the entire camp. No one is quite like her. She does the night shift in the wireless room, and goes with the girls to the military positions."

I looked at her. Her eyes were green, her hair was tied back in a pony tail. She had a feminine air despite the seriousness which her difficult assignments imparted to her. I asked her: "It's unusual for a girl to be on duty at night all by herself!"

"I'm not afraid of the night. Sometimes I used to be on duty at night, and I was not scared. The young men would be tied up along the combat lines and I would keep operating the wireless. At first, my parents wouldn't agree to my work because they were worried about me. But I've done a three-month militia training course. I did it when the revolution entered the camp, and training began. They offered a course for girls. I was fourteen years old. It was a very strenuous course, and I was in the third preparatory class at school."

"Do you face any problems?"

"One is affected by the situation in general. All that time under siege, and the kidnapping! Of course one has personal problems, but those can't be solved until the general situation improves. I'm the fastest at solving problems. In the camp, they say that I am a handful. My mother brought me up that way when I was young. She used to let me do whatever I liked. I could buy anything I wanted. I was not close to people. But my work made me feel the need to interact with them so that I could find out how they thought. I recruit girls and young women and develop their thinking and explain things to them. Look at Khazneh. She used to work in a factory. Now she has become a first aid worker at the front lines. Let her tell you how she offered first aid at the Red Crescent clinic during the battle for the Thabet Woods."

Khazneh nodded excitedly to indicate her agreement with what Hana was saying. "I was a worker at the Ghandour factory. I took first aid courses in the camp after the incidents of 1973. Before the battle for the Thabet Woods, the fighters asked us to go on alert and be ready for anything. On the day of the attack, our job was to set up posts to treat the wounded. During our free time, we prepared storage facilities for the fighters' weapons. The day of the attack, I climbed the wall with the Fedayeen. I leapt towards the Hayek hospital and entered it, and I started passing things out to my brothers, the fighters. We returned victorious to the Red Crescent clinic." She continued, "During the battle of Thabet Woods, some of our brothers were surrounded and unable to return to the camp. The other girls and I took them some food. On the way, we encountered many difficulties because shells were falling like rain in winter. But we were not frightened, because our only concern was to get food to the brothers."

Khazneh had not fully had her say yet. She said: "After the battle of Thabet Woods and the martyrdom of some fighters, we formed groups to raise the morale of the brothers. I help out with sorting and distributing supplies and I work at the medical health centre when needed."

I looked at the slim, lame girl with the pale face, the deep cracks around her mouth standing out when one looked at her for the first time. Was it really possible for her to be doing all this? Everyone in the room regarded her with a compassion that confirmed my suspicions that she had only become endowed with such vitality during the war.

Um Jalal bade me farewell at the door of the car. She asked me: "Why didn't you take pictures of us? Excuse the question, but my son, Jalal, is on the West side, and that would have assured him that we're alright."

She drew closer, before she could hear my explanation for not being able to bring a camera, craned her thick neck forward to prevent anyone from hearing her, although the others had remained inside, and said: "If you come across him, tell him that Abu Jalal is suffering badly. He needs some money for cigarettes and alcohol."

The words stuck in her throat, but she continued: "Yes! What can I do? He got used to drinking when things were not so bad, and now he can't even get his hands on a couple of coins. Where am I to get him the money from?"

She left me before I was able to understand what it was that she had wanted to say about George. She had uttered the first syllable of his name, but turned round and went towards the voice calling her from inside. It seemed to me that this was one of her most basic traits: not to ignore the call of anyone she loved.

During the period of anxious peace experienced by the camp, the residents did not dare leave their homes and hiding places, harbouring hopes that the situation would improve. It was during that time that Abu Muhammad Ad-Doukhi infiltrated the tight siege outside the camp to check on his nine, or ten, or thirteen children. He told me this as he repaired a broken window in my house. I asked him about his sons, and he answered with the same verse that Um Hassan had chanted to her relative, about the mother of one and two sons. I was frightened and surprised. What was this sense of high tragedy with which we Palestinians lived our lives? I asked him, "Abu Muhammad, are you sure?" He laughed until his gipsy-style gold-covered teeth appeared. He said: "Of course, daughter. I must return to the Tal at whatever cost."

When I heard that my son, Muhammad, who was sixteen years old, had joined the militia and was doing well, I didn't know what to say to him. The only thing I could do was go to the cupboard and get him a woollen jumper, a towel and a few other things which I can't remember. I thought they might help someone stranded away from his home.

During that period, there was family talk of Amneh marrying Jalal, dependent, inevitably, on an improvement in the situation.

Also during that period, a cat and mouse game began between Aisha and her mother-in-law. Um Hassan very strongly believed that Aisha was pregnant. Aisha did not think that she was, but she went along with the game, playing it adeptly because it gave her unexpected privileges of pampering and attention. Aisha understood Um Hassan on every score, except when it came to that blind obsession of hers with the baby. She would respond with a mysterious nod to coded questions which took the form of innocent references to familiar sayings such as: "Stones are only supported by their gravel, and men are only supported by their young." The mother-in-law would sit cross-legged on the ground, or she would squat while baking bread as though she were building a throne. Holding a mass of dough, she would move it from one hand to the other, then spread it out until it became thin, large and round. In a soft voice, she would sing songs and ballads harking back to her old peasant days. Recently, she had begun singing songs about yearning for children as though to fire up those around her with that same wish. Aisha began to think that a certain insanity had taken possession of her mother-in-law. She would sing:

"Oh people, their house has no one,
They left it as dew flies away.
Oh people, their house has no children,
They left it as pigeons fly away."

Sometimes, Um Hassan used to raise her head, and direct a hawk-like look at Aisha, her mouth pursed, and two long furrows between her eyebrows. Her thoughts would immediately become apparent, but Aisha would ignore her and turn away. Aisha thought that the recent disruptions to her body were a reaction to the complete change in her conditions since marriage, rather than a sign of the much-desired pregnancy. She felt a nausea every now and then, but thought it had nothing to do with pregnancy because she had suffered bouts of it while still living at her father's house.

9

‿❧❦☙‿

Ten days before what people consider the beginning of spring, the big siege, the second and last, began. The roads and entrances to the camp were completely blocked, and the possibilities of crossing, which had been undertaken with very great risks before, were completely non-existent. Al-Ahdab, a Lebanese army general, carried out a bogus *coup d'etat*, pushing things even further into crisis. This plunged Assayed into a new fit of depression, and he was sure that the Tal Ezza'tar camp, which was being held hostage, would not be released this time. Assayed based his predictions on radio news bulletins, which repeated the newspaper headlines. It was not difficult for him to come to the conclusion that things were being secretly plotted. He repeated the words of Raymond Iddeh, a Lebanese Christian politician who supported the Palestinians, that the Phalangists in Jbeil were arming themselves. He predicted that the great conspiracy to uproot the camp would be carried out following mid-month reports that a Phalangist delegation in Syria had met with President Assad and his foreign minister Khaddam. Assayed roamed the neighbourhood proclaiming that his suspicions had been proven recently, referring to a radio report about a meeting at the palace between President Franjiyeh, the Maronite Christian leader Chamoun and Jemayel of the Phalangists to announce that Syria considered the Phalangist working paper as the basis for resolving the crisis. Towards the end of the month, when Assayed learned of Jordanian support for Syrian mediation, and of Washington's announcement that its navy was on standby to evacuate American citizens, he went around the neighbourhood yelling that he was the first to discover the conspiracy. No one was surprised at the way in which his daily chatter included criticisms of the Arab countries, or when he referred to foreign politicians by their first names as though they were personal acquaintances. He never tired of mentioning the American, Dean Brown, who had come to Beirut to prepare a report for his president, Ford, supporting the Syrian initiative. April came, and Assayed went from house to house in the neighbourhood declaring the accuracy of his predictions. There was King Hussein supporting Syrian intervention in Lebanon; the Phalangist Party was occupying the port of Jounieh and had established a local police force, courts and a complete system of services; and Kissinger never stopped announcing American opposition to any foreign intervention in Lebanon, while praising Syria for containing the extremists.

"The conspiracy! A conspiracy," Assayed would say as he twisted his moustache, which stood out like cactus thorns. He would say it, his facial muscles contorting as though he were swallowing an instantly fatal poison.

Aisha understood not a word of what was being said or broadcast about Kissinger or anyone else besides him. The constant misery imposed on everyone by the famine was enough for her. Um Hassan's attention was diverted from her by the scores of bread loaves she was making in her home for the fighters along the defence lines. They would bring her fuel, and she would spend most of her time baking bread on the thin baking tin at the entrance of the building. As she squatted, her underwear and the men's socks she was wearing inside her plastic shoes would show. The old man stopped going downstairs to the shop, which had run out of everything. He had sent the simple first aid items he had, like oxygen, bandages, antiseptics and asprin tablets, to the health centre. Amneh loafed around in her flannel pyjamas and the coloured skirt which she never took off. She would often go to the house of

Zeinab, her brother's widow, to help her take care of Fayez's children, who spent most of their time at the nearby shelter. Before the war, Um Hassan frowned on the close relationship between Amneh and Zeinab, fearful that it would strengthen the widow's position and encourage her to remarry and take the children with her. Now, she welcomed Amneh's constant surveillance of her.

Nature blossomed in April, and Aisha learnt from her brother and sister that the roses had burst into bloom at the church near Dekwaneh. The two children knew the area very well because they used to scour it for cigarette stubs, which Assayed used to smoke. When enemy shelling would stop every now and then, the two children would go out to look for old newspapers which Assayed would use to wrap up ground seeds or dried ground *mouloukhiyah* leaves to make cigarettes.

The pleasant breeze . . . The spring of Beirut despite the repeated shelling, the irresistibly inviting fresh air awakened feelings of love for the outside in Aisha's soul. Not only outside of the area, but outside of the house. She looked at Khazneh closely and with an affectionate envy. Even the repressed Khazneh, as they used to refer to her, had changed and gained rights she had not previously had. Aisha wished she could be like her, that she could move outside the house, even during the height of the shelling. While Um Hassan was occupied with starting a fire in the wood beneath her large round, thin baking tin, Aisha left the house with Husam and Ibtissam on the pretext of visiting her parents. And so, on that sunny morning, she began her journey with her brother and sister to see what lay behind the road connecting the two houses. A bullet here and a bullet there. Husam took her first to the bonbon factory. They slipped past behind the mounds of earth fortifications along the road separating the two sides. The factory was in no-man's land, so the boy had preferred to go to it at ten in the morning, during the fighters' morning break, during the brief lull which allowed the people of the camp to enjoy the warmth and light outside their shelters. Joining the people's stealthy movements from place to place, the two children slipped away, followed by Aisha, who was almost jogging. At times they ran, at others they crawled on their stomachs until they got past the metal fence around the abandoned factory. Through a side door, which no one would have discovered except for those devilish children, as their father called them, they entered into the smoky space of a very large and long hall. The forgotten machines were dwarfed amidst the dust, resembling people who had frozen in their sleep. The air inside was stale and static as though it had solidified a thousand years ago, and no one had been around to move it or shake it. Aisha was repelled by the emptiness pervading the abandoned space, but her brother and sister paid no attention to the expression of discomfort on her face. They called her, and pulled her to a wide room off the main hall, walking ahead of her into a fairyland of sweets, toffees and chocolates in golden, coloured wrappings. As Aisha stretched out her hands to scoop something up out of that mythical spring of sweets, something inside her sang out drawing her into a oneness away from the rest of humanity. With her brother and sister, she sat down eating and gorging herself without finding enough time to devour everything she craved, knowing that she could not take away one sweet, even if it were hidden in her mouth, so that no one would discover her trip and the secret of the regular adventure carried out by the two children. Aisha became submissive towards them as never before, because they appeared to her as two experts who knew the place, its entrances and its exits. Her haughtiness towards them melted away with the chocolates, which brought her together with them.

Their next stop was the lentil factory silo, which was not in no-man's land like the bonbon factory. The people of the camp had discovered it as their supplies were running out. They had finished all the meat and apples refrigerated in the nearby plants. The thrifty women, who had cooked the frozen meat and preserved it in glass jars for bad times, had roamed around in groups looking for new sources of food. Getting in was not as difficult as the bonbon factory. When mothers ran out of ways of providing food, they would send out their children to bring back whatever they could from this factory without fear. Another surprise awaited Aisha inside, she could not believe what she saw. The floor was full of small mountains of brown grains as smooth as sea sand. The granules intermingled, and the gradations of their colour only appeared when Aisha drew near and spread some out onto her palm. The soft grains slowly slid between her fingers, falling back onto the small mountain. Aisha became aware of the presence of other children roughly the same ages as her brother and sister. They shouted and jostled as they played a strange game. Instead of busying themselves with filling up the empty jars and boxes they were carrying, they were scattered over the small hills in the large hall, sliding down them and jumping on them, washing their faces in the grains as though they were a magic powder, diving in as though in a swimming pool, running up them as though they were a slide at a fun fair. Aisha was amazed by the scene. She wanted to shout at them to stop and leave with their supplies. But her voice froze in her throat, shrinking and not coming forth. She felt confused for a while, then listened to the instinctive call inside her brain. She climbed the mounds, doing as they did, losing herself in their playful shouts. No one would come here to hear the sweet shouts and see the games taking place here. If one of the grown-ups were to actually come here, he or she would not be able to believe what they were seeing. A salvo of 500-millimetre machine-gun fire reminded the children that they should be leaving. Some withdrew, while others ignored their fear, trying to gain a few extra seconds inside the playground. As they left, gnawed by disappointment at their forced departure, Husam suggested that they search the piles of rubbish around the wall for cigarette stubs so that they would not get a beating from Assayed that day. Aisha bent over the garbage mounds outside the factory, and, to her great surprise, she found a small mirror. She wiped it with her fingers, and stared into it to see her face. The mirror reflected the happy face of a young girl tinged with warmth and alertness. Aisha denied what she saw, unable to believe it. She turned the mirror once more to have another look, and a quick flash shone in the air. The naughty Husam jumped up to snatch the mirror from her, then choked a whisper in her ear: "Put that away if you know what's good for you, or else you'll give us away, and they'll start shooting at us."

Aisha stuffed the mirror inside her bosom.

The shooting stopped for a while. Husam listened like a veteran soldier, whose war-sharpened perceptiveness and instinct allowed him to predict the moment when the next clash would begin. He stretched his long ear, almost like a little donkey's, and said: "They're not starting. They still haven't rested enough. That's just a bored fighter shooting uselessly. No one's going to join in with him for another hour. Let's go to the church."

To her very great and constant surprise that day, Aisha immediately agreed without hesitation or argument. It seemed as though Husam had changed in her eyes, turning into a human being full of wisdom and skill. Aisha forgot about Um Jalal's warning to the two children not to go to the lentil factory without telling her first. Husam avoided the memory of the bitter beating he had received with Assayed's belt for indavertantly mentioning something a few days ago that indicated he had been to the place.

Aisha accompanied her brother and sister to the Church of Saint John! Saint Joseph! No. The Church of Saint George. It was in the Kharroubi district, not far from the Dalal Ash-Shamali building. It was at the end of the uphill road towards the Za'tar factory. There was a school behind the church which the enemy forces had occupied and were using as a permanent headquarters. The enemy barricade was on the first floor of the school, obscured by piles of sand and cement filled barrels. But they were asleep, Husam reassured his sisters. Aisha could not believe herself, and she walked hesitantly. Damask roses hung in layers across the fence. The roses! Red, white and pink, each the size of a porcelain plate. Roses bursting forth, climbing the fence, colouring the world with a long-awaited freshness. They stretched upwards, carrying all their secrets in their petals. The roses. It was too good to be true. All that shelling, black smoke and dynamite exploding here and there. All that blood splashing about and smearing the walls. And this, itself! Lying meekly, calmly, innocently, not knowing war yet. Roses growing on their bushes, transmitting their magic smell through the dust of death, untainted by the dark colour that had overcome everything in the camp. The roses. She put out her hand to pick some, but her gaze fell onto the church building. Its windows were open and the gold on its murals glinted. The imagined taste of the bread and wine of holy communion trickled onto her tongue. They prayed over it, soaking it in the oil of the Virgin, and she sucked it. No. How many times had she imagined its taste on her tongue, but never had the opportunity to taste it, not even once. "If you suck it, you become a Christian, and we cannot take the responsibility of baptizing you," Sister Mary had said. She remembered how she had attended a wedding at a church once. A woman there had asked her: "Where do you come from?" She had answered, "I'm Palestinian." Disgust had immediately appeared on the woman's face, and Aisha had felt it would have been better for her not to have accompanied the nuns to the wedding. But. Palm Sunday! They would carry candles and palms. Husam nudged her with his elbow.

"Look! There are some cigarettes here. Help us pick them up."

But Ibtissam countered, "No, it would be better to pick some sorrel."

As they argued, Aisha stretched out her hand to pick some roses and touch the velvety texture with her fingers. A hoarse voice suddenly rang out from somewhere she could not see: "Evil girl . . . you, how dare you pick roses!"

Aisha froze as she saw a bearded man looking at her from behind the fence, the muzzle of his gun sticking up next to him.

She said in a frightened tone: "Why are you talking that way?"

He turned away mockingly and said as he walked off: "It's okay this time. Next time, I'll choke you."

And he fired his gun into the air.

Aisha was dying to tell her secret to someone, but she found no one to speak to except herself: "He kept sniping at us, shooting at us, but in the air."

The next time, Aisha, her brother and sister, had an empty water container with them. The same man came outside as his comrades took their morning nap. There were no more cigarette stubs in the grassy church yard. Ibtissam pleaded with him: "Let us fill the container with water."

They had brought the container with them to get some water from the bottom end of Dekwaneh, where a few pedestrians had broken some water pipes beneath the asphalt of the road going downwards towards some buildings. Aisha had not mentioned in front of her mother that she was going with them. And the children had said nothing about the whereabouts of their intended destination, because their parents would have gone berserk if they had known. Everything had gone extremely well, if only it had not been for that man standing there in the early morning in the school yard, playing with the water hose, spraying water upwards.

Ibtissam implored: "For God's sake, we need a bit of water because our supply has been cut for a long time."

The man answered, "Why doesn't your older sister speak? If she asks, I'll give you some water."

Aisha did not utter a single word. Sweat ran down her back, and she felt like running away. But she froze instead. The man, who was wearing a western-style straw hat, shouted: "Look here, if you asked night and day, we wouldn't give you a drop of water."

He directed the water jet at them, and their bodies were soaked with big drops of water. They were frightened and ran back.

The roses! The roses. But the roses had become so difficult to get at.

The frequency of the shelling increased after the sewers linking the camp to Nab'ah and Burj Hammoud across Sallaf-Assaloumi were blown up. The people of the camp tried to find another way of breaching the siege. The sewers had been the last passage linking them to other friendly areas.

The Joint Forces decided to attempt to breach the siege in another way. They took Hassan's suggestion to send able men to crawl for long distances inside the sewers. One of the attempts succeeded, and two men arrived at Nab'ah. But they were unable to return, because the sewer had filled up with water for some unknown reason, and moving through it became impossible.

Aisha was once again confined, surrounded by the stale air of houses. The shelling increased day by day, and she slept and slept as though the echoing of cannons were a soporific injection to which she had become addicted. She would slide beneath the light quilt and dream. Songs rise over the shining marble alter. She is still a child, running barefoot on the cold stairs. The damask roses. They are red, pink and white. Each is as big as the palm of a hand. The church is all golden. Hymns inside. The roses on the fence. The roses!

They would dress the girl in white. The boy would wear a long brown gown with a black belt. Like saints. The girl. The clothes of the Virgin Mary. They marry them with prayer. And Aisha! Forbidden. The nun says: "You want to watch, look from outside."

They had taught her politeness and good manners, always.

Every day, her cup of coffee would be brought in to her in the corner of the room, where she had moved her bed, sleeping on the floor for fear of the shells. Hassan would pass by, bend over quickly, talk to her and leave. He would go, he would leave, he would arrive, he would come. And she would remain silent or would yawn. The anger of being confined blinded her, and she no longer saw or paid attention to anyone. The rare occasions on which she went out, in the middle of battles or when they stopped, gave her a feeling that there was still a world out there, although it was debris. Everyone chose to hide, except for her. The bride. The fifteen-year-old young woman. The owner of the high-heeled shoes lying in the bottom corner of the wardrobe. She had nothing. Not even the blessing of slipping out in the shelling whenever she wanted to. The world shakes. She hides beneath the covers. She closes her eyes and sees darkness. She stares at the darkness.

Um Hassan held her peace. She was sure that Aisha was going through the moods of a pregnant woman. She did not dare to broach the subject with her daughter-in-law, who would only wake up to go to sleep once again. But that almighty shuddering that resembled an earthquake forced Aisha to jump up in panic. She saw the cupboard leaning over as though it would fall on her, and she leapt up in fear, shouting and asking what was going on. Only later did she discover that the enemy were blowing up the sewers to prevent them from being used to break the siege. As for Um Jalal, who found out immediately because of her presence at the medical centre with the fighters, she was terrified, and ran outside to find out the direction in which the two children had gone to look for cigarette butts for Assayed. The latter had gone so crazy, that he had consumed every drop of surgical spirit and eau de cologne in the house. She hurried down the street looking for them, muttering what she believed were incantations that would protect them: "Dastour. Hadour. In the name of God, who created demons and mankind." The earth trembled and shook once more. Um Jalal ran towards the two children, who had not gone very far. Shrapnel was flying all around them in the swirling dust. She pulled them aside, and pushed them and herself into some empty barrels beside the road until the smoke and dynamite settled.

At first, the women in the camp were pleased that the sewer opening had been blown up. Water flowed out, smooth and clean, as white and clean as calico. It was not merely water to them, but seemed as beautiful as white birds landing on the debris, broken stones and earth. Aisha ran with the other women who had come to see the miracle which the explosion had caused. They were overjoyed and ran home to bring jars and big plastic water containers. They ululated and threw chants into the air, which had been torn by the explosion. When they returned and crowded around the water, their joyous features contorted once again. The water had revealed its dirty origin, and was mixed with garbage and excrement. The women put their white kerchiefs over their faces and held their noses in disgust. They walked away muttering curses against the Phalangists, who were the cause of all the trouble.

During that period, Um Jalal began making candles at home to augment her livelihood. As the siege had tightened and power lines had gone down, the people of the camp had discovered an abandoned factory which contained quantities of unmanufactured wax. It was not a candle factory, and the wax inside it was there to supply some other industry. People's senses had become so finely tuned to finding anything that would make life easier, that they got to that factory as well. Those who were too poor to get fuel, gas, or kerosene, were able to light up their nights with these candles. They would put the wax on a tin plate, put a piece of cloth in the middle to make a wick, and get the light which their besiegers had sought to put out. Um Jalal's real problem was that the medical centre had to terminate the services of its daily cleaners and rely on volunteers. Um Jalal did not go home, or leave the centre. She stayed on as a volunteer, cooking and making bread and rendering every possible service in exchange for a few supplies of flour, dried beans and tinned foods. However, the problem of finding food grew when the siege was resumed, and there was no indication that things were improving. A slight hope emerged that the food problem would be solved when all the militia groups formed a joint committee for supplies. It was agreed that each organization would set aside part of its supplies to be distributed amongst people. But the experiment did not last more than a month for several reasons. The reserve supplies of some organizations ran out, while the supplies of the biggest one were never released because it was alleged that they had gone bad. But Um Jalal, with her usual acumen, discovered the matter when she noticed the signs of flour being unloaded outside the house of an organization official. The tell-tale sign was a long line along the ground, originating from a truck that had been carrying weapons. So she regularly gave Husam and Ibtissam a small measuring spoon to scoop up the flour which fell to the ground while being unloaded and remained there.

She would not give away her secret to anyone she knew so that, if worst came to worst, she could rely on this source, made possible through coincidence and negligence. When she tried to approach the popular committee to get some stored dates, she was surprised to learn that the Al-Barq organization had stolen the dates, and transported them to some Arab capital. Some swore that the organization was trying to market the dates, which had been given as aid from a Gulf country and had entered the camp before the siege had begun. Um Jalal unbuttoned her clothes and prayed aloud that members of Al-Barq would be blinded by the plague and paralysed by strokes. But she knew that divine providence would not hear her, because Bilal Hassoun remained at his barricade along the combat lines between the factories. He had already done very well out of the factories, whose owners had given him protection money before the war. Now all the doors of those factories were open to him.

Bilal Hassoun was a bully and strongman, and the people of the camp did not know where he had come from. He began his career as an ordinary member of the Al-Barq organization. There were many rumours that he had worked for an official who was known to be rich. He had risen from an ordinary cadre, to a local official, to being in a position that enabled him to collect protection money from the Christian factories and shops within the borders of the camp. That was the man who had caused Um Jalal to bare her chest on the roof of her house, revealing her breasts, to ask God to hear the prayer of an opp-ressed woman and punish him. That night, she had gone up to the roof and decided that she would solve her problems herself until God Almighty allowed things to ease. Inspired by her suffering that night as she squatted beneath the vine, from which small bunches of unripe grapes were growing, the idea of making candles and selling them at the medical centre to other workers and visitors occurred to her. Since then, Um Jalal had become well known for turning out candles of an unmatched quality. She would collect empty meat and sardine tins, melt the wax and pour it into them and put a string right down through it. When the wax became solid, she would cut the box and remove the candle. As the siege progressed, Um Jalal's industry became more advanced. She would bring X-ray films, coil them into tubes which she would tie tightly, and then pour melted wax into them. After untying them, she would get dainty, pretty candles. George was amazed at the delicate creativity of this fat woman with the thick voice. It would never have occurred to anyone that there was anything delicate about her, except for her small gold earrings, which shone in the candle light as they swung next to her thick neck. But the improvement in Um Jalal's situation did not stop her from complaining as soon as she met George. She would continue to grumble that the wife of the official, outside whose house she used to secretly send her children to gather dropped flour, had lots of matches, sugar and good candles. George could not understand her. What did Um Jalal want? And why was she taking out her frustration on a strange woman whom she did not know? There was a sense of solidarity amongst the people of the camp, which made Um Jalal sound out of tune. He did not know what it was that was bothering her about candles in particular. And Um Jalal was unable to explain to him the difference between her candles, which melted the skin of her hands because they were so hot, and the proper, respectable candles which that woman always seemed to have, along with other supplies.

On the one thousandth and fifth night of his shell-shocked memory, Assayed said that he would stop drinking as soon as the battle ended, and the road out of the Tal opened so that he would be able to go to the western side and see his son, Jalal.

At the height of the battle, George told Assayed's young children that they reminded him of his own younger brother and sister.

Ibtissam asked her mother: "Why does Aisha look down on us?"

Um Jalal answered: "Shut up, you, and leave your sister alone."

Ibtissam replied: "My sister is so good-looking! My sister is a real stunner, but none of us knew it, until that time we tried to get water at the road-block near the church."

The road-block was beyond the church, near a high building, beyond the school in which the armed isolationists were stationed. As for Aisha, she buries her head beneath the pillow and sleeps. She sees a huge slope of broken rocks beneath her, and pieces of yellow sulphur falling on her as she enters the churchyard, and goes in to the alter. She walks in, crosses herself and bows before the beautiful lady carrying her son from Nazareth, born under the star of Bethlehem.

He is a Palestinian, Aisha discovered. And she was frightened of her dreams in which George appeared walking through the churchyard towards her, opening his arms and coming towards her with an expression on his face that she had never seen in her life.

Aisha was frightened and buried her face further and further beneath the quilt.

10

Tallet Al-Meer. Al-Meer! During Ottoman days, that word had referred to a man of high standing. The hill would have had no importance had it not been for the anti-aircraft guns that were deployed on it. The hill was at the end of the camp near the industrial area. When the anti-aircraft guns were in action on Tallet Al-Meer, Zeinab, the widow of the martyr Fayez, and her children used to come out of the shelter where they spent most of their time. Zeinab was not alone in this respect. Most of the people, who felt at such times that they were protected by the bravery of the tough young men on Tallet Al-Meer, did likewise. Abu Ibrahim was the commander of Tallet Al-Meer. When he was wounded, people barricaded themselves inside the shelters with an unprecedented hopelessness. Students and workers used to look in on Abu Ibrahim and his men every day. The main pilgrimage of the day in the camp was to that hill, whose name the inhabitants had not even known for a long time, had it not been for the siege. Abu Ibrahim strode through the trenches in his light beard, his khaki beret and his tightly-laced military boots. The ninth day of the last round was the day of his martyrdom. A shell landed on the anti-aircraft gun and destroyed it completely, wiping out Abu Ibrahim and his men.

Hassan licked his lips after eating his *mujaddarah*, which he liked. Then he threw the plate from his hand, trying to forget the sense of catastrophe that had borne down on him when the news was confirmed. The enemy were on Tallet Al-Meer, and they could completely command every single movement inside the camp from that vantage point. He did not talk very much to anyone in the house. Instead, he went looking for George and all those in charge of the organizations so that they could hold a meeting to redistribute responsibility for all the combat lines. The camp seemed to turn into a focus of terror after the hill fell and Abu Ibrahim was martyred. Hassan left without speaking to anyone in the house. The taste of grief filled his chest, as he thought of the hill, which had almost fallen a month before. He thought of the people who had run to the offices of the various organizations in angry protest. The dignitaries of the camp had gone to the offices of the various factions to express their outrage and disappointment in those to whom they had entrusted their lives. The elderly ladies had come out of the basements in buildings and shelters, and gone to the offices, their words hinting at implicit curses if . . . if the fighters were to take the safety of the inhabitants of the camp lightly and allow the hill to fall. That forgotten hill had never enjoyed such fame before.

And now. After Abu Ibrahim, and the blow received by his group and the destruction of the three anti-aircraft guns. The hill. Weeping, or something akin to it flooded up through Hassan's throat. He said to his mother and Aisha before walking out: "Abu Ibrahim has been wounded."

The man had not been wounded, he had been martyred. But no one was able to deliver a blow so crushing to the hearts of the camp people all at once. Who dared to stab the people by telling them what they could not stand to hear about their hero?

Assayed was not able to spread the information he had always attributed to special sources through the neighbourhood. Shells were falling on the camp with a mythical intensity. On 22 June, the first day on which the siege of the camp had become completely impenetrable, about eight thousand shells hit the camp in one day. Many fires broke out in people's houses, and at the Kneider wood factory and the plastics factory. The bombardment continued uninterrupted from five in the morning till ten o'clock at night. And so the morning truce periods which people had taken advantage of to move around while the attackers slept came to an end. No matter what, war is war.

Khazneh ended her last night at home by burning her curly hair. She went to bed exhausted, and kept tossing about near the plate of burning wax until her hair caught one of the sparks, starting a fire in her curls. She was startled out of her sleep by Amneh shaking her into consciousness. Amneh threw a thick blanket over her, almost suffocating her, and rubbed her head with its thick fibres. The little blaze went out, leaving a blackened spot and the remains of burnt hair. "Why does natural hair leave gluey remains when it burns?" wondered Aisha, as she watched with great pity Khazneh's hair being ruined. In any event, Khazneh never spent a single night at home with them after that. She remained on alert at the medical centre at all times.

Water! "We have created all that lives out of water." Abu Hassan was listening to the Quranic reader Abdel-Baset Abdel-Samad with a kind of Sufi rapture. As his head moved, his white beard trembled. No one in the house had bothered to shave it, and it had grown like thick grass, spreading upwards along his cheeks, which protruded beneath his glasses. As the shelling raged on, the old man sang and gave praise along with the reader's voice on the transistor radio. For the first time in her life, Um Hassan felt the heaviness of old age weighing down this good old man, who spent most of his time on the ottoman without complaining or speaking. "The poor man," she thought to herself. Her work for the young men, baking tens of bread loaves for them, helped her to forget half her problems and to ignore the sound of half the shells raining down on the camp as she worked. As for him, what could he do? She was trying hard to understand why Hassan had insisted it was necessary to bring Zeinab and her children over. And she was looking for an excuse that would deflect her son's anger when he returned and found that Zeinab had refused to leave the shelter in which she had settled with her children. Um Hassan imagined that her son would scold the widow, who spent most of her time trying to make them aware of her independence, while putting them to a great deal of trouble by demanding extra favours every time her children needed something.

Yesterday, they had given her some bread because she had said she was no longer able to bake outside the door of the shelter after a group of boys standing there had been hit by a shell. Now, God only knew what she would ask of them in the middle of this mess if she did not bring the children and come to stay with her in-laws.

Water! It was as though he knew her thoughts. Hassan came on one of his flying visits and asked for Amneh. It was up to Amneh to take water to the children in the shelter because their mother had, as expected, refused to come and stay with them. Um Hassan said she did not think that the cowardly Amneh would agree to take the water. He told her she was to tell Amneh that no amount of objecting would do any good, and that he would return in the evening to take her to the water.

Could Amneh refuse? Hassan returned and took her with him to show her the way to the water pipe so that she could take water to Fayez's two sons and two daughters.

The world was dark, murky. The world was not itself. The only light came from flares falling here and there. One walks and wishes one could hear the sounds of cockroaches or mice, because they mean normal life, instead of hearing the whistling of shells that are falling like curses. Amneh walks, and Hassan moves ahead of her with quick steps, forgetting that his sister is not used to jumping. She is behind him, going through alleys, collapsed walls and passages, empty of everything except for demons and earth. Tilting arches that used to be parts of walls, windows still shaking from a nearby explosion emitting a moaning noise. Her heart jumps inside her a thousand times. Hassan disappeared behind a collapsing house. She called, "Brother . . . Brother." He was out of sight. She went berserk. She began crying and wailing because she no longer knew where she was. During normal times, she had known every inch of the camp. Now, because its landmarks had been so drastically changed by the shells, which were still landing as though on some place in hell, she no longer knew where she was. She shouted, cried, and struck her face, imagining she was very far from home, and that she could never return. Never, she could not . . . because she was lost, did not know her way. A while later, Hassan appeared like a ghost. She recognized him by his military uniform. He soothed her, "Don't be frightened, but hurry. This place is exposed."

She thinks to herself, "In this devastation, everything is exposed." It's as though she is in another world. And she cries once more, although she is following him, and he turns back to check on her before every corner and bend. The only water pipe still oozing out life was near Dekwaneh. All other water networks inside the camp had broken down. There, Amneh began seeing ghosts arriving, carrying pots and containers. Some returned carrying large plastic bags swollen with the precious liquid over their shoulders. They were walking, unsure that they would be able to get back with the bags before drops would start leaking down their sides. That scene would break her heart at sunset or in the evenings in days to come when she would see the sad procession waiting for hours for the shelling to let up around the open water pipe. Then, people would come out stealthily through the holes in the ruins and the broken doors, coming forward step by step, one after the other, to take that which they had awaited for long hours. In order to reach the water, people had to spend time in an area only one road away from the enemy ambushes. They were on one side, and the enemy was on the opposite pavement. There was sniping, shelling and mortars along the road leading up to the water. She would ask herself at length, every time she had to go and get water, whether or not she would complete the mission. One died a thousand deaths in seconds. What for? So that one would be no more, and others could live on? She thought that in the hour of death, one's life became dearer than those of one's children, and they were not her children. But she had no choice. In any case, they were Fayez's children. On the way to the pipe, a shrapnel-wrecked car stood near a corner. There was a sniper renowned for his many victims and his accurate aim. Every time Amneh would pass that spot, she would stop there for more than twenty minutes and think: would she be able to finish her journey without dying? If anything happened to her, would she be willing to die for children to whom she had not given birth? She had often thought of going and throwing the jerry can in Zeinab's face, but she was too ashamed of what other people would think. What would they say about her if she provoked a quarrel with the children's mother? She used to have a long imaginary dialogue with Zeinab, but she would always chicken out at the last minute and avoid starting it, especially since Zeinab remained in the shelter all the time surrounded by other women.

She would swallow hard, and wish that she could tell her how simple and easy it was to walk there and back when things were normal. But when one was carrying a jerry can on one's head, the process became killing, deathly. Many a time, Amneh would stand at the corner near the wrecked car, debating, should she continue or go back? She had turned back often, the ghost of death preventing her from believing in the necessity of going forward. She would return, knowing that the children would be upset, and that they would remain thirsty until she returned once again. However, one incident changed much in her life. If only it had not occurred!

Near the water, where the water pipe was, and a very hot day it was, a tall man with broad shoulders suddenly appeared. Amneh thought he must be one of the militiamen controlling the area around the water pipe. The area owed its name to that of the commander of that military axis, who had become well-known for his fierce defence of it. The Ali Samer Axis was its name. The man emerged unexpectedly from amongst the ruins and ordered her, and another woman who was with her, to go back because the shelling of the water source was expected to intensify. Amneh was flabbergasted and was unable to determine whether the man was authorised to give such an order, or whether he was an opportunist trying to get to the water himself before the shelling got worse. Many people were jostling to get ahead in the queue; some used their arms, and a few even used their weapons, to push the girls aside. The other woman did not believe him, and began speaking to him in a scolding, mocking tone: "Lay off us, man. I've got children, and if they don't drink, they'll die of thirst."

The man was rude, and possessed not a whiff of courtesy. He shouted at them once more: "Hey! You and her! I said get away from here."

Although the shelling was getting stronger and the shells were getting nearer, the other woman refused. But! Anyone who saw the water flowing, bubbly, sweet, gushing, shining with its white foam, forgot the rest of the world. How, then, was someone who had gone through the horrors of hell to get to it to respond? The other woman did not move away, and began to fill up the tin she was carrying. But Amneh moved away. Something inside her bowed in obedience to the authoritative tone of this man – a tone which hinted he knew what he was talking about only too well. Something inside her was overwhelmingly enraptured by the rudeness of his commanding tone. She did not know him, but if she had, it might have occurred to her to answer, in the words of the song: "Yes, master!"

Strange! She remembers Abdel Halim Hafez's song, and forgets the searing midday heat, the shelling, the dust that resembles flies and the flies that resemble dust. She forgets death as it swarms over their heads, and the sound of the cannon muzzle as it turns towards every corner, including the water source. She forgets everything, and thinks of nothing except asking about the name of the rude stranger. As though in a pure dream, she moved off while looking at him. She stared. Behind her was the wall supporting the water pipe. People used it to take cover from the sniper. Then, it felt as though a terrific earthquake had struck the ground on which they stood. Dust and earth swirled before her eyes. She peered. She looked closely. The wall was a pile of rubble over the woman. That other mother, whom no one knew. People's heads and necks appeared from behind walls and through holes to make out the victim of the shelling whom they had not seen before. They all hid again, and the man disappeared, uttering a stream of curses against everything in existence. Amneh's knees buckled beneath her, and she felt unable to move them, so terrified was she by the spectacle of the woman's death. Then she abandoned her jerry can in the middle of the road and ran, thinking of nothing except getting home. She left everything behind without so much as a thought for the jerry can, which would later prove difficult to replace. She decided to save her skin, her eyes, her ears and her hearing. The only thing she picked up was: "Ali Samer warned her, but she didn't listen."

"Ali Samer." So, that was Ali Samer, whose fame was spread across the horizon. That was him! She always asked her brother about him.

Amneh returned to the stand-pipe several times in spite of herself. But the old fear which had plagued her disappeared and was replaced by fear of a new kind. She no longer feared that she would die in that place. It was as though the protection he had spread over her, coincidentally saving her on that day, was still surrounding her. If it had not been for him, she would have been dead without a doubt. The thought gave her a secret pleasure. Her fear became focused on the question of whether he was married or not. And would the war end so that she could meet him?

During war, the rule becomes the exception. No one knows how the fighters found a calf, nor does anyone know how it came to the camp in the midst of the shelling. It was hunted by the fighters, who had forgotten the taste of meat for quite some time. They grilled its meat in the shelters close to the entrance of Dekwaneh. When they tried to throw away the head, trotters and intestines, Um Jalal appeared. None of them knew how the news had reached her before all the other women. Um Jalal came and negotiated with them, offering to supply whatever they needed in exchange for the offal. They asked for salt because they did not like eating the meat without salt, which had not been available for over a month. On Um Jalal's instructions, the two children went off and returned with some salt. That day, Um Jalal became the richest woman in the camp. She went home and cooked without worrying about the strong shelling. It was her first feast in a long time. To offer enough to eat to Assayed and the children. As for Assayed, he appeared to be a new person. He grew flexible and submissive, almost losing his supper to the cat, to quote Um Jalal as she described his state to Aisha. She said she hoped the war would end and things would return to normal so that she could lead a reasonable life with Assayed, who had turned into a well-behaved man in the end. She was sure that her son would take care of them on the western side of Beirut, and that it was high time for her to start taking things easy, now that she had married off her older daughter and was awaiting the marriage of Jalal himself. Um Jalal said many other things about the people working with her at the medical centre. Then she remembered to mention the warm regards that George and Hana had sent Aisha. She expressed a heartfelt wish to dance at George's wedding. Um Jalal talked and talked, then went off again to her work at the Red Crescent clinic, where she was spending most of her nights. She would place one sandbag in front of her, another behind her and sleep with the two children next to her if the way home became impassable due to heavy shelling. Assayed was the only one to remain in his home, which he did not leave until the last day on which the camp fell.

Aisha had never contemplated how frightening a process childbirth was until she became certain of her own unwanted pregnancy. Despite the difficult circumstances, she accepted her condition with an indifferent resignation akin to the resignation with which the people of the camp faced the successive disasters befalling them. Hassan noticed the developments affecting Aisha. He could not help smiling inwardly because his wife was experiencing something she disliked, but was not crying as she always did. Hassan was surprised, but he was soon overtaken by joy – he was to become a father. But he did not have the time to show his happiness or to distribute sweets as would have been expected under normal circumstances. The camp was being turned upside down. People were being forced to leave their homes, cramming themselves into already overcrowded shelters. The hospital was unable to cope with the phenomenal pressure of casualties. There was almost no water to be had. The medical centre was unable to offer first aid unless patients brought water from their own houses. No anti-tetanus vaccines were available. Nothing was available. Therefore, he could not pay any attention to himself or do anything of a personal nature. He had to participate with the others in solving those problems first.

But Aisha! The pregnant Aisha had to evacuate her room to the basement of the building after the window panes on the second floor had been shattered by a shell falling nearby. One shell. It had not hit a specific house, but it had damaged five nearby. It took out the kitchen of the neighbours with whom Um Hassan had quarrelled over an electricity line fifteen years ago. But the real catastrophe was that their neighbours' supplies were set on fire and burnt up, prompting Um Hassan to share what she had with them. She began to cook a double portion of pulses, or crushed wheat or lentils, sending half of it to Um Mazen's house. As the frenzied shells fell more heavily, spreading like crazy serpents, it became necessary for her and her family to leave the house and go to the basement. Once there, Aisha, who had never before visited a shelter, experienced everything imaginable and unimaginable. She was no longer able to distinguish the owners of the basement flat because so many of those present were living at such intimate close quarters. Children and mothers, fighters coming to see them, living or dying suddenly and without warning.

The basement house! Voices echoing in a deep lair. The wailing of confined children and their running noses. The kerosene cookers emitting soot as they burned, and the smell of kerosene with the orange-blue flame. The arms of women moving the stone mill to crush lentils for use as a flour substitute. Discovering this new camp! It did not occur to anyone outside this besieged patch how thousands of people were living without basic necessities. No rice. No sugar. No wheat or flour. But there were lentils that were crushed and ground, mixed with water, then fried on kerosene cookers or tin baking plates under which scraps of wood and paper were set alight. When there was no milk, they used lentil water as a substitute to feed their babies, and they used lentil yeast to make new bread. Lentils became a mercy from God, quieting cries of hunger. Those who were unable to replace torn sandbags near their fortifications took cover behind lentil sacks. They hid behind them waiting for God to ease their plight. Had it not been for the blessed presence of the lentil packaging factory inside Tal Ezza'tar, hundreds would have starved long ago.

In the basement house, Aisha watched a blonde girl who was going through her last months of pregnancy. According to Um Hassan, she was the same age as Aisha. Aisha was surprised at how blonde the girl was, especially her eyelashes and eyebrows. She was even more surprised at the colour of the girls' tender complexion, which looked as though it had been washed with bleach. The girl didn't know a thing about the camp or its inhabitants. She resembled a blind, disabled child. She was a stranger to the camp, brought there by her family from the West Bank in Palestine to marry her cousin, who was studying at one of Beirut's universities. The girl had lived for a while in a room on the roof of one of the buildings on the New Road, then she had come to the camp with her husband, a student volunteer. The girl was unable to concentrate. Georgette would tell the story of her marriage and her arrival from over there as though she did not understand why she was here. Her only preoccupation was to constantly await the return of her husband, who was now fighting along one of the front lines. He had not appeared for days. No sooner had Aisha met her than Georgette went into labour. It loosened the bones in her back and her knee joints, and she groaned and panted until the pain almost stifled her breath. There was no one to take care of her, so the women decided to call in a midwife from the camp. All messages sent out to the other shelters in the camp were fruitless because there were only a few midwives in the camp, and they lived in areas which were not easy to reach. As they waited for some sort of midwife, the older women spent their time giving Georgette boiled cinnamon, tea and dry mint to try and speed up her delivery. They tried to convince her not to be frightened, an infant remains in its mother's womb for nine months, nine days and nine hours. Eventually, Um Hassan was forced to send for Um Jalal, who told her that it was impossible to receive the girl at the medical centre, where the floor was covered in coagulated blood due to the water shortage. The girl was afflicted by increasing terror and instinctively shrank inwards. Her contractions went on for three whole days and nights without the slightest sign of a delivery. They brought Khazneh, who had never in her life attended a delivery. She remained with Georgette, pulling and pushing as best as she could in the square corridor leading to the bathroom.

It seemed that she had subconsciously decided not to give birth because of her fear over her husband's disappearance, despite all the reassurances given by the women around her. The girl did not speak, moaning became her language. She became the dilemma of all the inmates of the over-crowded place. Abu Hassan did a four-genuflection prayer, begging God to help ease her pain and relieve her misery. He prayed although unable to perform proper ablutions. He substituted that by rubbing a stone the size of his palm, which he kept in the pocket of his cloak. And as though heaven's compassion had been roused by the rivers of sweat that streamed down her body, the girl gave birth. Thanks to the collective prayer of everyone, the child was able to meet its father a day-and-a-half later. But the window of hope was narrowing every time a new piece of news arrived. Every day, Aisha would hear of several new casualties and martyrs.

Georgette's visiting husband reported that: "Each of us knows that if he is hit, he will not make it. There are no medicines or medical treatment. So we all fight to kill or be killed." He scoffed at the rumours being spread by the Phalangist radio station that the fighters were sheltering in underground tunnels. It seemed that their enemies were unable to explain their stubborn determination to defend the camp despite the tonnes of shells falling on it. He said: "Just look at Tallet Al-Meer! None of us ever thought that it would become such a danger! It commands the whole camp, and anyone on top of it can see us as though we were standing in the palm of his hand."

And the child. How beautiful he was, despite his choked crying after the women had severed his umbilical cord with a pair of sewing scissors. They washed him with a small quantity of water from a box, and put

Arabic kohl on his eyes. Aisha looked at his delicate feet with their lines and folds. He moved them as though kicking the world around him. Deep down, she laughed at the edge of his tongue, which resembled the tongue of a cat licking milk. The seed of tenderness entered her heart, like a cotton plant which grows to cover large fields. Cotton. No. She would buy cotton bibs for her baby when the siege ended. Actually, the baby girl. She wanted to have a baby girl whom she would raise as she liked and spare her the suffering inflicted by backward parents. She would pamper her, coo at her, and love Hassan for her sake. The war would end and then she would be able to look at his face and see him, get to know him, and he would be her friend. He had promised to find her a job after the war. Despite her continuous frown, she had asked enthusiastically: "A job working in the Signals Department? I'd like to have that for a job."

He answered in the hurried tone he usually used when he had important work ahead of him: "Yes, with the Signals Department. Why not, my dear? You're more than capable of doing it."

The only man. The only human being who had believed that she could. Everyone. All of them had treated her as a girl brought up by the nuns, who would remain that way for ever after. They still secretly made fun of her, despite the war, which had directed their attention away from her and made them as helpless as her. Giving birth to a boy? So be it. She would agree to having a cat if that would change her life. In that respect, she was in agreement with Um Hassan, who was kind and attentive towards her, giving her any nourishment that she could provide in this new hardship. Boy! Girl! It made no difference. One day, she would have a little doll to coo at like Georgette's baby. The girl would grow up and reach her own age now, and she would become a friend to her, she who had been deprived of friends and companions. Soon, God willing, when the fighting stopped, as Um Jalal always said.

Khazneh could not help vomiting when twenty-three corpses in their coffins were blown apart in the front yard of the health centre, which had always been a depressing place. She had never imagined that she would live to see coffins being ripped apart and flying about in the air. They had been lined up for burial. When the shelling had started up, their bearers had left them to take cover in the entrances of nearby houses. Khazneh could not believe what she was seeing, the corpses, turned into little scraps of flesh and blood, landing here and there. She hated the little piles of sand lined up opposite the clinic because she had once seen the bodies of the children who had been hit outside the shelter near the nursery lying on them. She had covered her eyes with her hand, and not opened them until she was inside the building, away from the white glare of the light. The image stayed in reverse even when she had closed her eyes. She had seen the world as if on the negative of a photograph. The children! She would never be able to recall the scene without feeling that she was about to fall down, her maimed leg pulling her down below the edge of grief, where she would die and never be reborn.

This was not Khazneh's problem alone, nor Georgette's, whose young breast was not producing enough milk. Her new-born cried most of the time, because he greedily sucked her nipple without satisfying his hunger and quenching his thirst. He was too young to be able to digest the water of boiled lentils. It was also not Aisha's crisis alone. She began to worry about her own fate whenever she realized that the shelling was intensifying to the point of madness, never stopping. She used to pass the time counting the shells as a way of warding off fear. She would look at her small wrist-watch, which she had been given during the first days of her marriage. She would follow the small hand as it ticked past the seconds, noticing the race between it and the muzzles of the heavy cannons directed at the camp. The shells were falling quicker and quicker. From sixteen a minute to eighty-six a minute. She was forced to use her fingers to count so that she could stay accurate and not miss out one. She saw less of her mother, who was busy preparing meals for the fighters in addition to her other work. All the women worked all the time, helping out with one thing or another, even the old ones. Aisha took it upon herself to help Georgette and her baby. Georgette was unable to give him a name, because his father had not found an opportunity to return from his front-line position since the time he had first seen his new-born child. But at least it seemed that Georgette had regained her health quickly, and her pale face became rosy again.

The attackers began entering the edges of the camp. Panic spread when people discovered that two shelters had been stormed near what had been the taxi station for Fakhani and Sabra. There. At the bottom. The other end of the camp. Near the soap factory. The inhabitants of the shelter near the George Matta factory arrived, their throats dry with fear at the sight of the murderers who carried axes and had knives hanging around their waists. Some were able to carry away bundles of flour and lentils. Others could barely believe that they had saved themselves, and had left behind their precious tins of powdered milk. The siege was completely air-tight from three directions. A serious threat appeared from the fourth direction in the shape of the Phalangist position behind the church. The solid building allowed the attackers the opportunity of sniping at people, and hiding behind it like a shield. Finding a solution was essential. The only possible solution was to mine the church. It would crumble, providing a chance for protecting the fourth direction, where most of the inhabitants had gathered.

The Joint Forces assigned the mission to Farid. A group of the best fighters in the camp would go and blow up the church, depriving the enemy of free movement in all their positions behind it. Farid was a veteran fighter specialized in mines and well-known for his skills in previous battles. He had fought in the battles of Irbid between the Resistance and the authorities in 1970. Then he had fled into the woods, and come to Lebanon, where he had joined a Fedayeen base in Arqoub. Now, here he was with a group of fighters, having managed to enter the camp between two sieges. Anyone who saw Farid, with his slightly built body and his thin moustache, found it hard to believe the long string of achievements he had chalked up to his name, truly making him one of the few experts around on mines. According to Um Jalal, who had often seen him visiting some of the wounded at the health centre, his only fault was his excessive smoking. Although smokers understand each other and the urgency of the need that flows in the blood, this Farid, despite his almost constant silence and appearance of dignity, resembled a steam-train puffing out smoke day and night. As soon as he put out one cigarette, he would light another. No one would have noticed during normal times, but given the situation in the camp, this habit of his attracted attention. How could he be getting Marlboro cigarettes when everyone else was living on cigarettes made from seeds used to feed the birds, dried *muloukhiyah* or grape vine leaves wrapped in newspaper.

Her son-in-law, Hassan, had praised the man's integrity in response to her criticisms and hints that he might have found a warehouse overflowing with cigarette boxes and not told anyone. Hassan ridiculed her suspicions, and said: "The man is free! What d'you want with him, aunt? All that's left to him in this world is a cigarette. His family are all in Gaza. He's not married and hasn't got children, and you feel that a couple of cigarettes are wasted on him. Let him smoke as much as he likes. Why not?"

Um Jalal walked away, large masses of fat protruding from her back beneath her shapeless dress. Hassan recalled Farid with special sympathy. The homeless one! Unable to enter any country because he had no passport. Living in airports and travelling in planes. He had once tried to travel to an Arab capital to see his mother, who had come across the bridge, but he was unable to. The old lady had waited as airports took delivery of the young man, then threw him off to airports farther away. His Palestinian travel document got him to Scandanavian countries after passing through African and Asian ones. Farid would enter a country and immediately become an inmate in an airport lounge until the authorities rejected him, putting him on the first departing flight. Farid had told them a lot about other Palestinian families living in transit lounges. He would guffaw as he told of how they would hang their underwear in the public bathroom. Sometimes, he would become tearful as he recalled the humiliation he had faced with security men and policemen. In the end, his case had turned into something akin to a play from the theatre of the absurd which no one would take seriously because it was merely entertainment. Finally, one of the PLO offices was able to solve his problem through intensive lobbying of important people in the host country, and it was decided that he would be deported to Lebanon. Thereafter, Farid completely turned his back on plans to see his mother, and on his good intentions, which had only brought him harm. He never, ever thought of trying again, and his brothers had informed him of his mother's death a year ago.

Although Farid had been accused of belonging to a terrorist organization, the name of which struck fear in the hearts of officials in European airports, Hassan believed that he had never even harmed an ant in his life. Duty was duty. And it was duty in any situation. It was enough that Farid had almost become the victim of his own organization when clashes had broken out in the early seventies over the concept of a Palestinian state on part of the homeland. The organization had not accepted the idea, and considered it a transgression of the sacred charter which called for the liberation of all Palestine. We cannot give up our land to the enemy, they had said. The whole of the levant will revolt one day, and we will liberate Palestine to the last inch. The result was all too clear now. The Arab governments wanted to liberate their countries first, had been the comment of Farid. His incessant smoking provoked the anger and coughing of the middle-aged women dying for a Marlboro cigarette or any real tobacco wrapped in white paper.

The hateful church was nothing more than a wall to the fighters of the camp. They would remove it and excuse the enemy position which was crushing the people with their sniper bullets and shells. Hassan failed to understand why religion had turned into a sword against human beings. Until that moment, he could not understand how they would be able to blow up the church despite the teachings of the Quran chanted by his father, which instructed him to respect other religions. Hassan had never in his life tried to pick up a Quran and read its verses. He had become used to respecting it from afar. He had treated religion as though it were meant for old people and sheikhs who went on pilgrimage to Mecca. It was not for him, or those who were his age. The continued problems of day-to-day living had prompted families to give top priority to the education of their sons. His family had always said that the Palestinians could not win the struggle to survive without education. No home, no country and no friends. How could the Palestinians struggle to survive without that weapon? It would gain them the protection they needed, and they would rebuild their shattered lives until they could return to their countries. Religion. He could not remember that anyone in his family had ever prayed, except for his elderly father. His mother had considered that working to solve the problems of being homeless refugees was a form of worship. Preserving the life that God has created is the most noble form of worship, she had always told them. So Hassan asked himself why the enemies were waging their war in the name of religion. Was it because they had a lot of money, houses and factories that spared them from being overwhelmed by the problems of daily survival? But they were not all that way. Their poor were at the front, and those waging the war appeared on the social pages of the newspapers at their boisterous parties.

Why do they want to evict us from here? We work in their factories, our women sweep their homes and kitchens. Thanks to our work, they have the time and means to enjoy Europe's beaches. Yes, that was it. Hassan remembered the long summer holidays which he had spent working to save up towards his school fees. He had worked at the chewing gum factory, at the ghee factory and at the Foremost Dairy factory, where wages had been low and working hours long. He no longer remembered the number of times he had worked at this place or that. He felt that he had been through all the places around the camp, and knew them well, except for this church. He had never known it, nor had it occurred to him before that it was here.

From afar, the church looked like a circle of darkness. Abandoned, remote, isolated, as though its only occupants were ghosts. All lonely places had given him goosebumps since he was a child. He had always longed for crowded places, and liked their smells, however putrid or acid. His brother had been the complete opposite. He had liked quiet, and being alone, away from the noise of neighbours and the commotion of friends and acquaintances. But Hassan greatly enjoyed watching people's expressions, studying their features, and listening to stories and myths of the past. His mother said that he was sociable like her, that he could not stand the shade if familiar voices could not be found in it. She had been greatly surprised by his unexpected whim when he had married Aisha. His mind had flown and followed a woman who did not resemble him. A little girl with a strange mood who never smiled. None of those around him had known why he had chosen her, her in particular, although several young women admired his happy disposition and joyous presence. Those had been Um Hassan's secret hints at the beginning of his engagement. But she soon dropped them after she had been won over by her daughter-in-law's silence and ability to listen well to her problems.

The church. Hassan looked at it as he advanced with the group, taking cover behind the sand fortifications. An insensitive building constructed in the modern style that had invaded Beirut in the sixties. It was covered in dark marble, which gave it a gloomy look despite the red tiles hanging over its sides. It had many windows, but what lay behind them was imperceptible in the sunset. From a distance, as one's gaze traversed the long path leading to it, thickets and gardens appeared, adding to the mystery surrounding it. This church of Dekwaneh was at the junction of the city and the countryside going up to the mountains. It occupied part of the open space that led into the western mountains of Lebanon. Overgrown whiskers of cypress trees appeared over the wall, suggesting a sense of belonging to the city of pine trees, of cypresses and of war.

Although Hassan was very familiar with the planning of the mission, his gaze kept moving across to Farid. Everyone was watching Farid. Steel hearts and a very high degree of self-control did not dispel the feelings of all the group that danger hung over the head of that one specific man. He was the one assigned to go around the huge building, which loomed like a huge phoenix. Intermingling shadows bent around the corners and windows, heightening the alertness of nerves and eyes. Intermittent fire from far away machine guns. The tank cannons around the camp whistling and shaking after firing shells. The ground shook as Hassan put his ear to it, listening to its insides. He wanted to reassure himself that Farid was not in danger. Would they see him and get him with their machine guns? Only one person could infiltrate to carry out the mission, and the rest had to cover him. The explosives' wires stretched across the black ground like snakes. Farid pulled them towards him then darted or crawled, making his way into the church on his stomach. Their hearts stopped as though suspended in mid-air by a hair. It would probably take an hour for Farid to fix the mines to the foundations of the church. He had always told them, as a cigarette had hung from his lips, "The first mistake is the last." Anyone doing his job could not make a mistake, "or else . . . ". He used to say it sarcastically. They tried to catch their breaths, and inhale a dose of the evening breeze and hold it inside to avoid making the slightest sound.

They all watched through a hole in the wall. They had chosen the sunset because visibility was at its worst. It was the safest hour. The eyes became accustomed to the darkness at night, and scores of flares would be used. The only thing they could not take care of was the sunlight, which faced them from behind the enemy lines. Farid arrived and managed to enter the church through an open window. Some of the windows had remained open since the beginning of the war. The fighters breathed a sigh of relief although they knew that the next phase would be the most difficult one. An hour passed and their eyes were still glued to the building. Things had to be going really well. Farid had even managed to hide the noise of drilling into the foundations. No one saw or heard a thing. If things went well, the camp would soon be spared the activities of the snipers and the merciless shelling. An hour or two of quiet only meant that those manning the enemy position were taking a rest.

Farid appeared on the window ledge, like a ghost in the last haze of dusk, as he made ready to return. They all held their breaths, watching as he began to lower himself to withdraw. Then, at the last moment, the very last, a sniper's bullet rang out. One shot, two shots, three. And Farid fell, not outwards, but downwards into the church. Farid yelled and fell. Perhaps that shout of his was the last mistake of which he had spoken. Perhaps if he had not yelled, the men could have pulled him out during the night. But! The way he was hit so suddenly meant that he confirmed the sniper's suspicions. Then, all hell broke loose.

Fire, shells, tracer, snipers' bullets. All the instruments of hell broke loose along that front, which had been relatively quiet up till then. It seemed that the earth had opened up to shake off everything on its surface. As though the Day of Judgment arrived. Amidst the whizzing of firing weapons, the young men imagined Farid lying on the floor of the church without anyone to save or protect him. They concentrated on keeping the enemies occupied so that they would not be able to enter the church where Farid lay.

11

❧❧❧

Things continued that way for five whole days. The state of high alert continued along the church front as they awaited the right moment to enter the church and bring out Farid, whose moaning could still be heard between bouts of firing. Every now and then, his comrades would hear his loud groans and go out of their minds. They stuck to the new front – the church front. There seemed to be no way of pulling him or bringing him out. Somebody had to go in there and bring him out, while another had to go in at any price to light the fuse. The building was so solid that it was not affected by what was falling on it. All the windows were broken. But Farid was still there. The landscape changed in front of the church. Fortifications rose in pyramid-like piles. Shells ate at the facades of the surrounding buildings, turning them into ruins. Many inhabitants migrated to the few remaining shelters, which became even more overcrowded. They had to find a solution. So they assigned their two most competent men to save them from the inferno. The two fighters were Hassan Assamhadan and George Haddad.

"Ta . . . ta . . . ta," Um Jalal stammered in a daze when Husam told her what he had heard from one of the fighters heading off for the church front. Impossible. It occurred to her that this must be impossible. But she was tongue-tied with terror. She started to run to her daughter's house, but she soon became wary of spreading panic in Um Hassan's home. Moreover, she had no right to interfere in the work of the fighters, based on some tittle tattle picked up by her son hanging around with them.

She did not know what to do or where to go. She was confused. She wailed. Then, amidst the thunderous shelling, she headed for Hana's office, which was not too far from the health centre. Without being stopped by anyone, she entered the room where Hana was sitting behind a small table with the wireless apparatus, amidst glasses with dried tea leaves in them. She was bent over the wireless, engaged in a strange activity. She was responding to the curses of her Phalangist interlocutor, whose voice could be heard loud and clear through the receiver. She was talking back to him in the same way.

"You whore."

"You son of a whore."

"We will fuck the hell out of you."

"Curse your father and his father, you dog, son of a dog."

Um Jalal stared, open-mouthed, not knowing what to say. She could not understand why it was necessary for Hana to respond to those bastards using the same language that they were using, especially such curses which only men used. Hana raised her head to greet the elderly woman. "What is it, aunt?"

Um Jalal lifted her arms, gesturing with her hands. "The church! The . . . the . . . "

The girl realized the fear which the other woman was feeling, and asked: "So, have there been any new developments?"

Um Jalal stammered back: "I mean . . . Hassan and George."

The girl, who was careful not to show her fear of any disaster, calmly answered: "They've been there for a long time, aunt."

Um Jalal's reason returned. She felt embarrassed to be telling her troubles to a girl the age of her daughter.

She panted, speaking hurriedly to avoid spelling out her fears: "I'm very worried about them, and I don't know what to do."

"Don't worry, aunt. In the end, we will sort things out and resolve the situation. Look at my mother, God help her for what she's going through."

"God will help us," said Um Jalal as she left for the church front.

Hana turned her attention once again to the wireless to resume her war of curses with the enemy at the other end. Perhaps to help her forget the present for a time, the situation and its conclusion, which she did not dare even think about. By pretending to forget it, she distinguished herself from her female comrades and only expressed her overriding terror far away in the depths of her heart. That repressed panic was deep inside, forbidden to show itself. The only thing left to her was to relieve her tension through curses. She secretly worried about Um Jalal. What if the elderly lady betrayed her secret to George? He had only seen her at her best, an ideal girl in every way. What if Um Jalal went and told him that she spent her free time between incoming and outgoing messages listening and retorting to curses? If that happened, Um Jalal would cause her a great deal of embarrassment which she had to find a way of dealing with as of now.

In the hail of fire which they passed through, each on a different side, they survived moments of incredible danger. But the greatest danger lay in allowing the situation to remain as it was: a war of attrition, more vicious than anything along the other fronts around the camp. The church must be uprooted. It must fall so that the position hiding behind it would be exposed. Or else.

The first mistake is the last. He said it with determination and humour as he lay half-conscious on the cold tiles of the church. On its beautiful white marble, thought Aisha, as she trembled with Georgette's baby, which still would not feed. His mother's meagre milk left him to chew her breast and stretch it without getting enough. He pulled it with his lips, bit it with his toothless gums, then rejected it in desperation. He would spit it out and start shouting and wailing. The baby would not accept lentil water. He would stubbornly close his fleshy lips whenever he tasted the cloudy yellow liquid, although several other babies had grown accustomed to its unpleasant taste. In the beginning, Aisha tried to help Georgette so that the baby would accept his new diet. But she could not keep up her joke that the baby was an aristocrat and belonged to the Bourbon family, or that he was a relative of Marie

Antoinette who had offered to give the people cake instead of bread. Things were developing into a tragedy with this newly-born child, who was rejecting the taste of life because he did not like it, driving his mother to near insanity. She would cry and moan whenever he screamed. The father did not come because of the hardships of the siege. The child grew thinner until he was almost skin and bone, frail of body and pale-faced, his lips chapped. At one point, Georgette went out of her mind and would have almost struck him, had it not been for Aisha's interference. The child would purse his lips together, and no one could open them again.

Aisha did not know that her husband and George had been chosen to enter the church. She heard the story of Farid wounded and trapped inside the church because it had spread as soon as it had happened. She was not sure of the details because of the long time separating Hassan's visits. The day before, he had visited them for five minutes at his mother's wish. She had missed him and sent him a message after he had been absent for ten whole days. He had eaten his lentil soup without waiting for it to cool, and left. His mother had run to the door calling out: "Stay. I still miss you. We didn't see you properly."

He kept going, saying: "We have work to do. When we've done, we'll rest. Yamma, take care of Aisha."

"Shame on you. She's dearer to me than my eyes."

"Farewell, Yamma."

He was speaking to his mother, but he looked at Aisha, and she got the feeling that it was she he was addressing even when he was speaking to his mother. He looked at her and said: "Aisha, take care."

And he left.

The only person who felt refreshed that day was Assayed. For the first time, he was getting cigarettes without going to a lot of trouble. Due to coincidence, which is the reason behind every great invention, he had found that flowers make the best cigarettes. He had grown depressed when the two children and their mother had disappeared off to the health centre. He picked a rose from a nearby pot of plants. Then he went round gathering all the roses, carnations, gardenias and the Arabian jasmines. He crushed them and rolled them up in paper pulled out of the children's copybooks. When his new cigarettes were ready, he began thinking of going out and showing them to the young men. The nearest front was the water front commanded by Ali Samer. But according to information imparted to him by Um Jalal a few days before, he thought that most of the young men would be at the church front. So he prepared to go out, but took his time as the shelling grew stronger. He squatted near the door waiting for a period of slower shelling, because he was unable to move in all that insanity. As he smoked, he imagined how they would welcome him, and the congratulations he would get for his wonderful invention, especially from the tobacco-loving Farid, who would be the first to appreciate the importance of his new invention.

As Hassan began crawling towards the high wall of the church, Feirouz's song rang out in his head. He needed to focus his attention on the long path full of bullets skimming over the blades of grass, which nothing had stopped from growing. Yes. The green grass. He even cast his thoughts back to the battle of Thabet Woods. Still, he could hear Feirouz's song. He sang it inwardly, unable to remember all of its words because he did not have the time or place to do so. He made a resolution to himself: when he got out of here, he would go through all the songs, and search for the one inside his head. He must look for this wonderful song, and perhaps replay it on a tape recorder several times. Suddenly his friend Tawfiq flashed through his thoughts. Oh, if only he had not teased him then, when the enemy had re-attacked Tallet Al-Meer. I was with both Fares and Tawfiq. We went up to . . . no, we were thirsty. Thirst. Ah – there was half a jug of water. Tawfiq was lying on the ground. "Give me some water," he said. I teased him and replied, "I don't want to." I started scooping up water and splashing it on him. He said, "For God's sake, let me have a drink before I die." I gave him a drink of water. But I've always felt sad when I think of him. The Phalangists were infiltrating the hill. Our weapons weren't any use. Kalashnikovs and B-7 rockets were not enough. I went fifty metres down the hill to get the missile thrower we had found by chance. I ran down. I picked up the gun and climbed up again. It was just beginning to get dark. When I got up there again, I called to him: "Tawfiq." He did not answer. I drew closer. I found him bent over his gun as though in prayer. The handle of his gun was broken. His stomach was covered in blood. I was frightened. For the first time, I felt fear. But the song! "I loved you . . . I loved you . . . In summer . . . " No! "In winter," The words rush into his head while he is on the ledge of the high wall, beautiful, ugly, black, white. But it is a wall, in all cases. If only he hadn't teased Tawfiq over a drink of water. He had even spoilt the last drink of water in his life. The sun had still not disappeared. A turbulent haze hung around, from the scores of burning shrapnel falling down on them like an evil metallic shower. And his friend, his beloved George. So soon after his engagement his marriage had been postponed, until only God knew when. He had not become so attached to any of his other friends at university. "You poor things," Um Hassan would say. "Miserable things. What have you seen of your land, or your country? You're all paupers, the lot of you. All you teachers! All you students. Not one of you has known the pleasure of the shade beneath an olive tree or a grape vine. Here you are forced to fight, when you've hardly been weaned. My poor darlings." He did not like being pitied or having sympathy lavished on him. And he could not understand why his mother was unable to appreciate the privileges of the modern age, which allowed for things lost to be regained instead of crying over them. He was proud of his generation, which fought despite everything to regain the pride that had been lost since the exodus of 1948. His family swore that they had fought as best they could. They had taken up arms and fortified themselves in the hills. They had confronted the Zionist settlers in several battles, but the enemies had won because they had superior weapons. Guns dating back to Turkish times had been no match for the modern guns, mortar cannons and Bren guns. He secretly believed them most of the time.

He attributed their misery and defeat first and foremost to backwardness and the huge civilization gap. When he had grown up and gone to university, he had discovered that there were two civilizations living alongside one another in modern times. One was the civilization of repression, which used the most developed tools of technology to repress people and evict them from their homes, as in South Africa and Palestine. The other was the civilization of the oppressed, who could possibly win, but only possibly . . . but if one was in one's home and country. But here? Amongst strangers. How could one go on amongst those who only cared about importing cars and arcade games, and the latest brands of washing powder appearing on television screens? And here? From that cursed building dedicated to the service of God, scores of people had been killed by snipers' bullets and shells from behind it. God?

He did not know whether or not he existed. He had discussed this at length with George. George was a Marxist and the whole issue had been settled as far as he was concerned without the need for a long argument. Religion was the opium of the people, he would say, and that was it. As for him, he believed in a higher spirit at times, but not at others. Sometimes he felt that there was an invisible compassion in the universe which no tangible power could produce. At other times, he would be overcome by panic at the sheer cruelty that unmasked itself in life. Could God be so vicious and cruel? He had to concentrate on what was ahead of him, on the square black and white tiles of the church, which he had reached despite the flood of machine gun fire outside. He would go north to mine the building, and George would go south. Suddenly, he saw Farid lying at the end of the large hall. He was surprised, as though he had not expected to see him there in such a state. It was as though he had forgotten what had happened, expecting Farid to welcome him and offer him a cigarette. Despite the horrors he had encountered to get there, it had not occurred to him that Farid would be in such a condition. He crawled to get to him. The field of vision was completely open. The church windows had views to both sides. On one side, they overlooked Dekwaneh, from where they had infiltrated, and on the other, the school where the enemies were barricaded on the ground floor. Every movement inside the church was visible to them now that the glass had been broken, and only shards of it were left stuck to the wooden frames like sharp knives. As he drew close to Farid, he crawled with difficulty over debris, wood and broken glass. His knees bumped against a candlestick with pointed tips, and torn bits of artificial flowers. He was covered in earth and plaster peelings from the floor. He recoiled at the putrid smell which seeped through his nostrils and struck his palate. He drew close to Farid. He saw his wounded leg before seeing his face. And he realized where the smell was coming from. Beneath the torn trousers was a wound like an open mouth. It was directly on the joint. The leg was swollen, and the skin was as black as coal. Little worms wiggled over the wound. Farid breathed with difficulty, sounding as though he were snoring. He did not open his drooping eyes, as though he had not been aware of the noise made by their break-in. Hassan was amazed at Farid's shrunken size. His body looked as though it had been pressed beneath a steam-roller.

As he had crawled, pulling his kalashnikov rifle behind him, he had only thought of the original Farid, who laughed and puffed smoke in everyone's face. If he had not been amongst those who heard shouting and moaning after being hit, he would have expected him to greet him with an embrace and a kiss. He noticed something else which aroused his suspicion, prompting him to look closer before even trying to ask. He saw slender wires attached to the injured body and wound around it. At that moment, every part of his body was seized by a violent shudder. His teeth chattered until he thought that he could hear them banging against one another under his scalp. Farid had been completely booby-trapped. The timer wires around him would blow him up if they were not removed by the person who had wired him up. No one could save him except the criminal who had booby-trapped him. Hassan shook. He looked around him and wanted to call George, who was at the other end of the hall examining the wires around the marble columns by the alter where communion was given. Outside, the battle raged on as violently as ever. The Phalangists manning the forward position had noticed the break-in, and were responding with all the viciousness and spite they could muster. George had his back to him and to Farid. He was squatting as he studied the possibilities of blowing up the place effectively. The organ stood behind him. Hassan had never known how beautiful it could sound until one of his professors who lived in Ras Beirut had played him a recording of a piece by Bach. He had been enchanted and told the professor that if circumstances had been better, he would have studied music instead of commerce and business administration. Bach's organ music had sounded as though it were descending from heaven. He wondered whether the broken organ could ever be played again. That might not be possible. Those people. The church people are too busy fighting us. The old Beirut, which used to put up with the people who drank UNRWA milk has changed, even the street cleaners and factory workers are no longer the same. Interests have changed. Oil has arrived. God himself has cursed us ever since they began fearing us. They think we will take over their golden stock exchange. "Curse them," to quote Um Hassan. Hassan sighed as he remembered his mother. The song came to mind once again. Was he recalling it deliberately so that he would not smell the stinking odour around him? He looked at Farid. He couldn't see much, but he was still breathing, imprisoned in a coma whose end no one could predict. If only he had brought the first aid kit with him. Perhaps he could have cleaned the wound before going back to George so that they could decide whether undoing the wires bringing him out was possible. He stretched out his hand and stroked the wounded man's forehead. His features were swollen, distorting his appearance, so that he no longer looked like himself. Who would have believed that the injured creature crumpled on the floor was Farid? Then a shell fell a metre away from me. I shouted three times, but the fourth time, I had no voice. A piece of shrapnel had entered my lung. I cannot breathe. No one can hear me. I took my gun and I don't know how I ran. Blood was coming out of my eyes and I called George, George. I couldn't see any more. Blood was pouring out of my eye. A piece of shrapnel must have entered my right eye. I heard a voice shouting: Hassan. I wanted to kill myself if it were them calling me, wanting me. And Farid stares at the sky above the organ with his closed eyes. And George. George Haddad, whose real name I am the only one to know. Ahmad Al-Ashi. I cannot see. Blood has covered my eyes, and I cannot see.

George did not turn. He could not have turned. The wave of pressure picked him up then threw him down into the broken ribs of the organ, away from the windows. The smoke of the shell rose like steam in a Turkish bath. The explosion pulled George from the altar and threw him into the organ, which crouched nearby like a huge beast. Tunes flew out of the pipes, playing out like a mad orchestra. Long notes tangled with one another and floated out like a nest of wild hornets. The shell screamed and whistled in his ear for some time after it had exploded. The sound came in wave after wave. And Hassan? He hardly had time to regain his balance and pull himself out of the trap of the organ when . . . He hardly had time to shake his clothes. He looked over there in the opposite direction and saw. Hassan. His beloved Hassan, who had been tending Farid in preparation for taking him out. His dear Hassan. Blood pouring down his face and covering his eyes. Blood spurting from his chest. Flowing like a fountain.

Pouring out and streaming down. He must get him out at once. He ran over to him in great leaps, reaching him in a split second. Hassan has no voice. No speech comes from his throat. His injury is severe. Farid is still in the same condition on the floor. At a glance, George realized the situation. He saw the booby trap hanging from Farid's body, which by then was also covered by piles of turbulent dust and small pebbles from the explosion. So. The important thing was to get Hassan out in any way possible. The important thing was Hassan. He would not blow up the church because he did not want to blow up Farid with it. Curse the damned church. The barking of dogs and the cacophony of the organ had masked the catastrophe which had befallen his friend. George Haddad ran, carrying Hassan across his shoulders. He supported him with his arm and pulled him as he pulled himself. Behind them was Farid asleep-alive-comatose. Beneath the arches of the church covered with the gold-tinted faces of saints. The wide, ugly sturdy arches which remained unaffected no matter how many thousands of people died beneath them. The rays of light in which dust particles swirled, mixed with blood. And more importantly Farid, who was dying and craving to see his mother. He had been around the world without being able to see her again. There was no time to even feel anything. The most important thing was to get Hassan out of this den of endless ill-fortune.

Um Jalal did not see Hassan because she arrived as they carried him up and ran towards the medical centre. She could not understand what they were saying, or make out what was going on. She simply followed them until they took him in to the doctor. His face was covered in blood, but she recognized his clothes. The crowd was calling Khazneh and searching for her in the clinic. The doctor ran out of the operating theatre to save him. And Um Jalal did not comprehend what had happened. All she knew was that the omens of evil which she had sensed had finally come true. It was not the careless Assayed, who wandered so aimlessly around, who was dead as she had expected. It was her pride and joy, the husband of her eldest daughter. She staggered to her daughter's house, unable to run. All the way there she beat her cheek, paying no attention to the shells pouring down like rain. Crying was all that mattered. She wailed and cried and struck her cheek. She looked into the basement room where the inhabitants of Um Hassan's building had congregated. She did not think to ask anyone's help in breaking the news to her pregnant daughter. She let out a long wail as she stared at her daughter, who was shocked by her mother's condition. She lunged at her and embraced her, almost throwing her to the floor as her excited body lost its balance. She howled: "God help you, your husband's gone."

Aisha did not understand. She looked inquiringly at her mother. She looked at her again filled with the innocence of disbelief. Then the news seeped through her being. It reached her consciousness. Breathing became difficult, and she leant back onto the floor where she had been sitting. Then she collapsed in a faint. The women in the shelter surged towards her crying and shouting in a collective wail. Some tried to loosen her collar so she could breathe. One of them ran up to her kitchen despite the increased shelling and brought back a bottle of rose water and eau de cologne with which to sprinkle her. No one noticed Um Hassan, who had entered at that moment to find out what all the chaos was about. She had left her iron oven with the remains of doors burning in it since gas was unavailable. She was not told. Merely from their looks. She parted the crowd, which had stopped sobbing and fallen silent as she entered. She saw her daughter-in-law lying unconscious, and Um Jalal beside her collapsed on the floor like a kneeling camel. Without asking a single question, the mother comprehended the situation with pinpoint accuracy: "Woe is me, how black is my fortune."

She shouted. But she did not fall to the floor as the other two women had done. She went back towards the door. She parted the crowd with her hand and ran forward although the other women tried to hold her back, fearing the effects of the terrible shock on her. She ran. She flew with her thin legs clad in men's socks and plastic shoes and her white headcloth to the medical centre. The intensity of the catastrophe froze her tears into a ball of ice that descended onto her heart, pricking it with pins, and worsening her heart condition. Her blood dried up and poison surged through her spine. The fire inside her flared up from that moment and forever after.

The horror of the tragedy. The horror. Grief drove her crazy, lighting up her old fire with unprecedented fierceness. During that dark night, Um Hassan rent her dress, crying to God and pleading in front of everyone. Hassan had not lived to see her. The murderous piece of shrapnel had torn a hole in his chest wide enough for a finger to go through, as Um Jalal had said. His injury had turned into an infinite death. Grief and futility without hope. Um Hassan wailed. She tore open the fabric of her gown, bearing her chest, so the Lord could see how he had allowed this injustice to crush her. No one looked at her although she mourned for a whole hour outside the medical centre, walking around with sad, defeated steps. People left her alone because they saw that she had a right to address God in such a way. She then beseached him, "My God, you have orphaned me, your obedient slave, who has always borne patiently the suffering you inflicted on me. You squandered the seeds of the last pomegranate which I had thought was mine. You have broken my back. We have suffered so much, Oh God. We have been eating lentils and more lentils, and we haven't complained. Bread! Nothing but the mouthful we have offered the fighters before ourselves. Water? We don't even have enough to wet our mouths. No gas. No kerosene. We baked over the wood of collapsed houses, and broken doors, yet we accepted all this. For every glass of water we've drunk, there has been a glass of blood from the person who brought it. Lentils in the morning, lentils at noon and lentils in the evening. And that we accepted and endured. Why do you want to break our backs? What have we done to you? The old man is smoking dried grapevine and castor leaves, and we did not complain. We said, its the price of this problem of ours. Why don't you do to our enemies what you are doing to us? Or do you consider them to be the lady's children and us to be the slave's children? We accepted everything. Why are you hounding us like this?"

Um Hassan struck her face and wailed: "My backbone has been broken."

Then she walked away with the crowd of wailing women who had gathered around her, crying and saying: "The poor thing, she's lost her son. He who has no luck should not even bother trying. He who has lost his son has lost his happiness."

At first light, a group of men headed for the road leading to Beit Miri. Reaching it was not easy. They were threatened with death at any moment. But they were the friends. Students or ordinary men whom no one knew. They had not played any prominent or distinctive roles along the front lines. Nevertheless, a fire burned within them. They could not sleep without doing something. All they could do was defend the camp. After the battle for Thabet Woods, the camp had discovered that defence was the only course of action open to it. But these men had decided to attack, if only once, so that Hassan's martyrdom would not be in vain. The elderly Abu Mazen joined them. It was the kitchen of his home which had been shelled, prompting Um Hassan to forget the old family quarrel and treat his family as though they were members of her own household. He did not have any weapons. He carried his winnowing fork and walked. A worker from the chocolate factory, whose brother had been killed by the Phalangists went with them. Another volunteer took a spade and hoe with him because he was short of ammunition. With them went Abu Al-Walid, an expert at mines and a friend of Farid's. He had given up his profession because of his amputated arm, but he was one of the most active men working with supplies and ammunition. They learned from the scout that enemy military cars went to the mountain positions at dawn. They set up an ambush. The chocolate factory worker carried the RPG launcher, which he had never before used even during training. He crouched in readiness, and as a landrover passed, the rocket-propelled grenade flew towards it, exploding and setting it on fire. With the winnowing fork, the spade and the hoe, the other three prepared to finish off whoever was in the car, but no one came out of it. Seconds later, Abu Al-Walid showed them how to plant mines on the street. They planted one on a dirt track and another beneath a high pile of rubbish. They did not have enough time to dig, so they planted the third along the road which the tanks used to climb towards Tal Ezza'tar. As they turned back, each of them felt that if he were to die after that day, he would go with peace of mind. Behind them, as they infiltrated back into the camp, the first mine exploded beneath a truck. The second went off beneath a passing Chevrolet. They waited an hour for the third, but heard nothing, so they returned.

In the far away shelter by the Boutajy building, which barely stood its ground because of the shells pounding the area around it, Amneh stayed with Zeinab and her children. People coughed and gasped as the plastics burned in the factory, which was being shelled with phosphoric incendiary bombs. Smoke and dust got into their eyes and noses. The worst part of it all was that the shelling was concentrated on the pillars of the building, in which some five-hundred people were sheltering. Zeinab and Amneh feared that a huge catastrophe was imminent; that the shelling, which had become almost continuous, would make it impossible to get to the water source. No one inside the shelter was able to go out for water, so they all resorted to the only possible solution. They scooped up the dirty rain water from the floor of the shelter. Carrying out yet another insane excursion, one of the inhabitants had managed to reach a nearby well and extract some water full of worms and blood. Everyone closed their eyes and noses as they drank the only available water. Zeinab had four children: Samir and Samira, the three-year-old Abir and Nisreen, who was two years old. Samira was about ten, and Samir was nine. Zeinab, about whose problems Um Hassan had not tired of complaining in more normal times, was close to thirty. Her mother-in-law did not trust her hazel eyes and her quiet appearance, which gave the impression of submissive malice. It was obvious to everyone that the friendship between Zeinab and Amneh was based on a kind of complicity against the rest of the family. As the artillery concentrated its fire at the shelter following the burning down of the plastics factory, the biggest danger facing Zeinab was the news that reached them about Hassan's martyrdom. It was impossible for Amneh not to go home for the funeral of the family's second martyr, and for Zeinab not to remain with her children, because leaving them alone was unthinkable. Nor was it possible to risk taking them outside as shells fell at the rate of one every second.

Amneh went as she was expected to. She went all the way home, risking death, fires burning behind her and debris piling up ahead of her, almost blocking her way. The wrecking of buildings continued, and the piles of rubble increased until she began to think that she was lost in some strange place, such was the horror facing anyone going from one street or one place to another, although such journeys had only taken a few minutes before the siege. Amneh returned to her family, "expecting to kill or be killed," as she said to her dazed mother. But all she had seen along the way had not shocked her as much as the sight of Assayed did. The overpowering, capable man had turned into a rag because he had cried so much, his sobbing at times outdoing the weeping of the women. He resembled a blind man, and the grand awe-someness based on his physical strength and cruelty had disappeared from his features. It was hard to believe that this man was Assayed. His cheeks were wrinkled. His jaw hung open, and some of his front teeth had fallen out due to some sort of accident. He had lost weight, and become like a shadow. He remained dazed as they discussed the funeral. He did not move from his place and Um Jalal later swore that she had seen a pool of tears beneath his bent head.

Assayed risked it and went with Aisha, Um Jalal and Um Hassan to the Kharroubi area, where there was a plot of land being used as a military cemetery. The others were all unable to go for one reason or another. Amneh remained with her father, who was seized with an almost fatal bout of high blood pressure. George remained at his front with the other young men. Khazneh remained on alert at the medical centre, where they discussed moving the patients to other safer locations as the centre came under deliberate and intense fire. Assayed carried a spade and hoe and walked with the sad procession. Each of them stretched an arm upwards to help carry the wardrobe door on which Hassan lay. The load was very heavy. Um Jalal attributed the heaviness of Hassan's body to his desire not to leave the world. Silence and the inability to cry cut through Um Hassan's breast. The possibility raised by Um Jalal took her by surprise, increasing her daze. Her tongue grew heavy, and she was only able to release a long "Ah" of complaint to the God who had ignored her and had not answered the prayers she had offered day and night.

The moon was out that night, as it had been on that last night when Hassan had hoped to live so that he could know the rest of the song by Feirouz, which had played inside him for such a long time before he was hit. The moonlight was the voice of Feirouz. Her mysterious song hovered here and there above the little crowd as it climbed the hill towards Kharroubi. Aisha thought that for the first time she had come to resemble that young girl, dressed in black with the two pigtails, standing at the crossroads asking passers by about a lover she did not know. If Hassan had lived, perhaps he would have one day become her beloved. Had he lived! Perhaps that constant missing of things would have stopped haunting her. She had come to know nothing else in the world except him. He had taken her from her family. He had even deprived her of hating them, of her old dreams of the other man who had proposed to Hana and not given her a thought. He had taken her from herself, which wanted to hate him but had not succeeded. So what was left to her? All that was left was the black dress she would wear for the rest of her life, and those weak pulses against the wall of her abdomen of a foetus which meant nothing to her now that its father was dead. There was the moonlight and the fig tree at the top of the hill, which Assayed had chosen as his tears flowed in grief over the fate into which he had forced his daughter. His old cruelty had turned into a tenderness which he had not known throughout his life. He had made inquiries about the best burial spot, and had found out that the first floor of the house in which many bodies had been buried after the tiles had been removed, could no longer take any bodies.

Hassan was still in his military uniform. George had wanted to remove it, but the other young men had refused. They had said, "He is a martyr. Leave him in the clothes he is wearing and he will go to heaven in them, if it is not forbidden to us like all the other lands we have been prevented from entering." They lowered the rectangular wooden board beneath the tree, which looked like a ghost in the dim moonlight. Shafts of light and searchlights shone as they stood beside the ditch which Assayed had prepared. He brought a piece of carton from the adjacent plot of land and fixed it next to the trunk of the fig tree so that they could recognize Hassan's grave later on perhaps when the war ended and some party on earth or in heaven would intervene to convince the Phalangists and other isolationists to end the siege around the camp. As they all said the Al-Fatiha, the first verse of the Quran, over the martyr's grave Assayed burst into tears again, and he put his arm around his daughter on the way back. After dropping Um Hassan and Aisha outside the basement of their building, Um Jalal accompanied him home, and he made a vow to which she was the only witness. He promised he would completely give up drinking and that he would devote the rest of his life to taking care of his orphaned grandchild. And he cried at the thought that had just occurred to him: that his grandchild would be born an orphan, and would never know its father.

12

ഛൟ൙

Water relieves the plight of the thirsty and is the one desire of their hearts. Khazneh was forced to leave work and go to the water pipe. She skipped along as she dragged her heavy left leg behind her. There was no longer enough water for the wounded at the medical centre. Nor was it possible to boil and prepare lentils without water. She went at night, or at first light, waiting in the ruins with the other volunteer girls. Her head spun and her vision wobbled, though she didn't know the reason why. Perhaps it was exhaustion, as the doctor had told her, or her fascination with the activities of the new nurse, whose hands seemed to have revealed miraculous powers. Elias Addoughani, who had worked as an ambulance driver, lived in a Lebanese community close to the camp. He had chosen to stay with them, abandoning his ambulance, which had broken down. Its batteries were removed and used to operate the wireless. The Lebanese Elias continued to perform tasks which a whole team of nurses would have not been capable of. During the past few days, he had plucked up the courage to carry out difficult surgical operations, which the doctor had pronounced a success. The man was not daunted by anything, however difficult things became and however much others cried or complained. Khazneh began to enjoy working with him. She would hold down the wounded patients, so that they would not move as he stitched their wounds without anaesthetics. He told jokes and shared bursts of humour with everyone, as though the unexpected success of his medical performance had given him an overpowering sense of rapture. He would look at Khazneh slyly and say: "Auntie, my auntie," winking at her with a frank sense of complicity. And Khazneh would feel happy. She would shine with pride for all to see. There was Elias treating her as a partner in performing miracles. Elias brought his untidiness into her world, causing her to suddenly go into daydreams. But she continued to steadily pick up and perform the basics of her first aid work. She once asked him naively: "So! Are you married?"

He pointed at the engagement ring shining on his finger and said: "Anything for you, girl. I swear by God I'll throw her in the street for your sake. Just wait and see. As soon as the war ends."

He would use his charm to skirmish with her. She would laugh without believing him, feeling deeply grateful towards him. Here was someone coming along amidst the insanity of the bombardment to joke with her. He would look into her small eyes with great affection, as though he had known her since the beginning of time, giving her the self-confidence she had always lacked. She would feel that circumstances . . . ! If it were not for the present circumstances, she would have been able to study nursing and get a certificate that would allow her to work at a real hospital. At the height of the tragedy, he had wanted to devise a gimmick to amuse the weary people around him. He went to the earthen barricades protecting the centre and planted them with beans, broad beans and chick peas. They sprouted and became a joy to behold because they were Elias's mobile farm and his nutrition centre, catering to people's needs twenty-four hours a day. He would pull out the green sprouts and give one to a desperate wounded man breathing his last, asking him to chew it, listing its inherent benefits and vitamins, and mentioning all the maxims in Jumblatt's book on nutrition. until the patient felt that he was about to partake of the plant of life, or picked up on the joke and started to banter laughingly with the nurse-doctor. Khazaneh carefully and gradually asked Elias about the details of his past life as she made plans to continue working with him at some other place in the future. He promised her that he would create as much trouble and fuss as possible unless she were appointed as his assistant wherever he was. He said: "By God, we'll throw the fiancée in hell for you. Nothing is too good for you. All that counts is that you should be pleased with us."

Most of the patients around them had guffawed with laughter at the huge difference, of which they were all aware. Elias was engaged to an extremely beautiful girl, who had turned down many men before accepting him. And Khazneh? No one could have even thought of Khazneh if he had not been someone with a very good sense of humour in the first place. Khazneh alone was deadly serious, but was not offended by their laughter, although she fully realized the reasons for it. Yes. She began to call him "teacher." He was enchanted by the title and began to repeat it, until it caught on. No one would refer to him by his first name without preceding it with "teacher." Elias remained her teacher even when she began to spend most of her time bringing water due to the drop in first aid services and the shortage or near-total lack of medicines.

Khazneh's experience was nothing earthshaking, according to Um Jalal, who had overheard her telling Elias that she had been returning with some first aid volunteers carrying tins of water on their heads. "A shell landed two metres away. We were saved by a miracle because the roof of the house we were walking past protected us. The sisters began walking faster. I said: slow down, let's all stay together. I was unable to walk as fast as them. I dragged my leg and tried to catch up with them. They had got about ten metres ahead of me. I began to run and called: girls, wait for me, for God's sake, slow down. None of them listened. Then suddenly, this shell fell right in their midst. I heard their screaming as I hid in the entrance of a destroyed house. Oh, what a sight, how ugly it was. You know the rest. Not one of them lived. When I set off, I had a tin that could take thirty litres. The shell was so close, the tin flew off my head. I searched for it near me, a second later, after I realized what had happened to the sisters, I turned and the tin was smashed to smithereens."

Um Jalal then related her own experiences in a tremulous voice, the white hair streaming down from her temples like the ashes of large fires. That was how the nurse-doctor saw her as she interrupted the conversation to silence Khazneh as she spoke so that she could tell her own tale. He was treating the hand of a girl, which had been hit by a fragmentation missile, which had removed the skin and torn the muscles.

"By God, Khazneh, everything you are saying is just a fraction of what I went through. Would you believe that I went to get water for three days, day after day, and returned empty handed? How could I possibly? How could this miserable one or my daughter have any luck? Look at what happened to wretched Aisha! Talking isn't like seeing. Anyway. The first two days, I waited in the alleys and narrow streets until dawn as the shells whistled by. If you could have seen your aunt! I said: 'By God, I'll put up with everything to get a bit of water for the poor wounded patients.' It turned out that my bitch of a daughter, Ibtissam, was following me, and I only found out when I entered the garden. Yes. We left the pipe as morning dawned and ran towards the garden. Of course that daughter of a so-and-so was following me as though I were still breastfeeding her. I told her: 'Have some shame and go back inside with your older sister.' But she paid no attention. She said she wanted to help me carry the water. I told her: isn't it enough that you won't grow any taller because you've carried so many water containers? You look just like a dwarf. Who will want to marry you in the future if you remain stunted? By God, the animal, if you'll excuse my language, wouldn't listen to me. The company of her brother, Husam, has turned her into a tomboy. So anyway, we went into the garden. There weren't many people there. Two men and five women. And then the shelling began! Shelling as though the sky had gone crazy and was raining fire down on us. We all spread beneath the trees, but the snipers could see us and were aiming at us. To cut a long story short, we were trapped in the garden, unable to leave. Suddenly, there was a lull. We thought that the least we could do was get some water before leaving. One of the men went up to the well to draw water. The sniper's bullet hit him in the heart. He fell into the well, face downwards. So his friend crawled over and tried to pull him out.

The poor fellow who had fallen into the well was as dead as a door-nail. His friend reached out, and then he got hit in the shoulder and his leg. By God, we stayed there for six hours not daring to move because the moon was out. We hardly dared to breathe. And that daughter of mine kept crying every so often. I hushed her and said: 'Stop it girl, or else they'll hear us.' In the morning, if it had not been for the *Fedayeen* who helped us to crawl away without being seen by the enemies and showed us the way, the five women and I would still be there."

Um Jalal suddenly fell silent as though something had occurred to her. It was as though the whole story she had just related was not really what she had wanted to say. She wished she could vent her grief and depression after what had happened to Aisha and her husband of three months, but she was too embarrassed. She did not know what to say.

People were dying night and day. Life was the exception and death the rule. In the basement, Aisha once more struggled with Georgette's new-born child in the hope that he would accept a mouthful of sweetened tea. But the child pressed his chalk-white lips together with a stubbornness drawn from the illness that had overcome him, leaving him with no strength to resist the wilting away of life. Despite her tear-swollen eyelids, Aisha focused her attention on the weak little mass. Perhaps if that child survived, life, which was so horrific, would change a little bit for the better. It seemed that Georgette had completely given up hope of any improvement in his condition. She left him in Aisha's lap, and leaned her head back against the wall. No one had been able to gain a few more centimetres of space in the overcrowded place before. Sleeping, even sitting comfortably, was difficult. Now, because of the condition of the baby, who seemed to be on the verge of dying, and due to Aisha's widowhood, everyone cramped themselves further to make more room for the two girls. Aisha tried as hard as she could with the child, who had quietened down, and was no longer screaming as he had been during his first days. He simply issued a few soft moans that were closer to intermittent sighs or gasps. The child would not accept. His mouth remained closed, his eyelashes hanging over his eyes as though he had gone into a coma.

It's the suffocating heat and humidity of Beirut, Aisha thought, fearing that those around her would discover what the dearest wish of her life was at that moment. If she could have, she would not have asked for what people would have expected her to. She would not have asked that God give her a long life and bring back her husband, Hassan. She would just have asked for one moment to go out onto the beach with this baby, expose him to some fresh air, put him in the breeze,

187

offer him a dose of the air which was so absent in this place, leaving him slowly to die. Oh God! The sea! Its blueness. She was beginning to forget colours. They were fading from her memory. She was losing touch with everything related to nature outside. At night, she dreamed of the glow. She would see the piles of yellow sulphurous earth sweeping towards her. The sunset, the fiery horizon wanted to burn her. The glow. The horizon. Gunpowder on fire, near her, about to devour her. She cannot see anything except the glowing mass breaking out in front of her. The glow! It's rays are blinding. The poisonous light of the incendiary missiles. She had wanted to dream of the sea a month ago. She kept on wishing she could bring its blueness into her dreams. She watched the flame of the kerosene cooker as the women fried the lentil dough and made cakes out of it. But she would forget to recall the cool sea blue that she wanted. Nothing but death and black clothes and the glow. She wanted to go to the beach with the baby, she kept telling herself whenever she could close her eyes, whenever she wanted to retreat into her weeping. But all she could see was that glow, that dying.

Um Hassan did not continue to wail. Grief churned in her throat like stones as she baked bread for the young men, dragging herself about as though carrying on her back the heavy piles of flour she was baking. A while ago, before Hassan's martyrdom, she used to jump, run and leap so that anyone who saw the back of her without catching sight of her face would have mistaken her for a young woman, in the prime of life. Only now did her real age show, in the shadow of her latest catastrophe, which she would never be able to overcome as she had done the previous time. She shuffled about, kneading the dough and tending the fire, which was burning the remains of window sills, doors, clothes and furniture. Every now and then, she would pull the elastic belt around her waist and tighten it. She would touch her nose to wipe away secret tears, pretending to blow her nose. No more than a few drops trickled down the chin of a woman who was good at hiding behind her pride. She spoke to Hassan between her and herself: "Where are you Hassan, still asleep? God have mercy on the earth covering you, my darling. You see? By God, I see nothing but your image. I'm burnt by your loss, and your wasted youth."

On that hot July day, it occurred to Amneh that the tragedy had been going on for more than a year. She was hurrying back to the shelter where Zeinab and her children were, intending to have a row with her brother's wife. She would carry off the children and take them to the basement shelter so that she could stay with her parents after the calamity of Hassan's martyrdom. No one had the right to keep her away from her parents in such difficult circumstances. She would confront Zeinab and force her to bring her four children with her to her old mother so as not to add to the family's sadness and misfortune. Madam Zeinab! The respected lady Zeinab. The dear mistress. She must understand, must realize and must feel with the family. Amneh could not see why she had played along with her for so long over the issue of being independent. That was unimportant now. The Hajjeh, mother of the two martyrs, Fayez and Hassan, was more in need of care, whether Zeinab liked it or not. She would drag her and the children home against the will of heaven itself. Did she, Madam Zeinab, think she was the mother of Queen Nazli, the pampered wife of King Farouk? She ridiculed her. She had no right to keep the family's children apart and keep Amneh by her side under such terrible circumstances just to escape her mother-in-law. A new kind of guilt flared in Amneh's heart. How many times had she helped this woman to mock her mother? And now? She would not put up with her for a minute longer. Would not. Would not. She would make her understand that there were others whose situation inspired sorrow and pity. An unexpected sword struck her heart. Ali Samer could die tomorrow, and she would be like her. Like Zeinab, whose heart was filled with bitterness. Or the stupid Aisha, who kept pampering herself from the first day of her marriage until the day Hassan had been martyred. Would she become like them, she who had always considered herself to be above them? Not for any clear reason, except because she was Um Hassan's daughter. As she stumbled over the stones of some debris, she became aware of this matter of resembling her mother. She had never realised before that she harboured great respect for her mother. She did not listen to her, or obey her orders, and always ignored her advice. Now, amidst this hell of gunpowder and flying shrapnel thundering down on her, she discovered that the only reason for her extra pride in her destiny, which she thought was different, was due to the fact that she was the daughter of a strong woman, who had been raised amongst the threshing floors and olive groves, a woman whose hands had grown used to hard work at a very young age. But who could guarantee that tomorrow Ali Samer, tall and broad, with moustaches fit for an eagle to perch on, would not die? She had continued to admire him since the first time she had seen him. She had summoned up her courage and searched for him near the spring of death beside which a frightened crowd had stood. She had seen him several times since then, and could scarcely believe that she had managed to look into his eyes to make him aware that she was in love with him and cared about him in the middle of the shelling. In the middle of death and oblivion. Yes. He might forget her. Who could guarantee that a man busy fighting death and the enemies would not forget her the next moment? Who? But she had done that which had been prompted by what her mother had described as her hard heart. Um Hassan said that her heart was harder than her mind, and that would cause her unspeakable problems one day. She had looked straight into his face, and had turned around to look back at him after she had had to leave, despite her fear of being treacherously hit as so many of those going to the water pipe had been. She loved him, and she wanted to let him know this. It was up to him to under-stand and not to forget her when the damned war ended, if indeed it ever was going to end.

As she walked through a corridor of brown cloudy smoke Amneh saw herself as a sleeper sees his soul. She saw her body passing through fields of stones, crushed rocks, and pieces of debris flying about in the air. Amneh saw herself as if in a dream, as though she were crossing a desert too hot for any human to bear. Sweat flows profusely from her, dripping down her forehead, her shoulders, and beneath her arms. Powdered gypsum, or something like the white plaster used to decorate the walls of houses, stick to her hair. The clouds grew thicker, then lifted to reveal what Amneh finally realized – the shelter. Collapsed. Crumbled. Shelled. It was definitely no longer in its place. It no longer remained standing. Something the mind could not grasp. But the crowds of traumatized people. They came in shocked waves. The sound of their wailing mingling with the hoarse moans coming out of the shelter convinced her, forced her to see what was happening. She went over to a man carrying a spade. He tossed it away, and threw himself on the debris to dig with his hands. All she could get out of him was that the shells which had set the plastics on fire at the Boutajy factory had cracked the walls of the adjacent building, whose basement had housed the shelter. The enemy had shelled the five-story building continually for several days, concentrating their fire on the exposed columns which supported it, until they had cracked and collapsed. The roof had fallen in on everyone beneath it, blocking the exit. No. Everything had collapsed over them, and there was no longer any door or exit. The man was crying, shouting, screaming. His howling was lost amidst the successive waves of wailing voices coming from beneath the battered ground and from above it. People ran around here and there carrying hoes, but they were not of much use in removing the rubble of five floors, which had collapsed over the shelter, whose door had completely disappeared. At that moment, many different emotions surged through Amneh's bosom. There was a horrific shame at not being with Fayez's children when the disaster had occurred. There was an inexplicable devilish feeling of malicious joy at the fate suffered by her brother's widow, who had adamantly refused to move in with her in-laws, although Amneh knew that it was none other than herself who had helped her to carry out that decision. At the height of the confusion that took hold of her from head to toe, she was overcome by an excitement, which she knew to be despicable, at the thought of Fayez's widow disappearing off the face of the earth and sparing her all those burdens which she was not used to. It was as though she, Amneh, had given birth to four children. Their mother sat in the shelter, while she defied death and destruction every second for their sakes. Zeinab, who expected them to be grateful to her for bearing their children, and who treated Amneh as though she were responsible for taking care of them, deserved this fate. Amneh stood in her place for a minute. Then the cries of the people crushed below the ground and the fallen building shocked her. She realized that her brother's children had almost certainly been killed or injured. She could not help herself, and her tears flowed. She sobbed and wailed, throwing herself down to help with the digging so that she could find Samir and Samira and Nisreen and Abir. It was beyond her control! She had raised them and cared for them with their mother and they meant more to her than ordinary relatives. Amneh snatched up a digging implement, brought by members of the popular committee, and resolved to dig with everyone else, even if it meant getting killed. The shelling still directed at the shelter was delaying the digging. But those who worked busily amongst the chorus of wails and shrill cries for help all around, listened carefully, trying to pick up the gradually weakening screams in the hollow below, so that they would know where to dig. Amneh worked like an imprisoned genie trying to escape from a bottle. She and the man with the spade headed for the sound. They heard the muffled moan of a man beneath the rubble telling them that he and his children were still alive. Amneh and the man were able to open a small hole between bent iron bars into which they dangled a bottle of water. She continued digging with the families of those who had been buried, from two o'clock in the afternoon until three o'clock the next morning. During that interval, and until it became possible to enter the shelter, Amneh did not try to look at the bodies which other rescuers pulled out. She did not want dead people. Simply, she only wanted those able to live, because she had come to hate the kind of life that was saturated with death day and night. She would not care about bodies or remains, because she only wanted them alive. She did not want bodies or dead people. If they were still alive, then would they kindly present themselves. She would be willing to receive them. She wanted them to live so that she would know they deserved the terrific exhaustion which descended on her as she dug for all those hours, alone, without anyone else from the family. If she were to die, no one would know what had happened. No one at all, ever. Except for her. On the morning of that day, late in July, Amneh descended into the shelter with the first wave of rescuers. A terror that she would never again experience in her life paralysed her. A terror that would crush her and would reshape and polish the hardness of her heart, making it even tougher than before. Inside the shelter, Amneh saw about four hundred bodies so disfigured that it was impossible to recognize them. They were all unimaginably mangled. A very small number of people had survived, but they too had sustained severe injuries to their limbs. Most of the mutilation had affected the heads. One woman's intestines had spilt out, and she had died only a short time before. Next to her was a child, about three years old. Amneh, taking her for Abir, pounced on her. The child was unconscious. When she looked closely at her, she realized that she was not Abir. So where was Abir? Amneh tried to carry her, but her head was trapped by a metal wire. Other people brought a saw and freed the child. It was five in the morning. There was no one looking for the child. The dead woman was almost certainly her mother.

Amneh thought no more of the child. Her relatives would appear sooner or later. She knew she had to leave and return to her unhappy family to break the news to them. Amneh dragged her body, though an overpowering urge to fall down pulled her towards the ground. But she resisted it with all her strength. To throw herself down and sleep or die on this despicable earth which insatiably swallows the bodies of human beings . . . She remembered Ali Samer. No. She doesn't want to die despite her intense grief. She will live and go to him, look into his eyes with insolent desire and make him understand that she wants him, and he will propose through her parents if they live. She wants him, there is no question about it. She will not die. She will wait even though going to the water source has become almost impossible these days.

At the entrance to the basement, Amneh expected to see the neighbours tending her collapsed mother. But she heard nothing implying that a new catastrophe had taken place. If not her mother, then the neighbours, or at least Aisha. She stepped fearfully into the crowded room, hesitating to announce the sad news. Then she saw something her eyes could not believe. The "virtuous" Zeinab and her children were sitting amongst the women, children and old people. When she caught sight of Amneh, she called out in a heartfelt tone: "Where on earth have you been? We've been very worried about you. Where were you?"

It was as though the devil himself had appeared to Amneh. She stuttered and stared so fiercely at Zeinab that Um Hassan thought the whites of her daughter's eyes had displaced her irises and pushed up her eyelids. Amneh shouted as though she did not know what she was saying: "What? Are you still alive? Everyone around the shelter thought you had died long ago."

Amneh broke into long hysterical sobs. Her jaw went loose and hung down, her tongue falling to the bottom of her palate, so she had to force out her words with difficulty as though she were handicapped: "By God. I don't know what to do with you lot. It's all my fault, my own doing, anyway. I'm the stupid idiot who thought that you and your children were there. Why did you keep crying and begging me to go back to you? Why? So that you could put me through that horrible black terror? By God, I'll show you what you are, you bitch."

She attacked Zeinab ferociously, trying to pull her hair and slap her face at the same time. Um Hassan prevented her, holding her wrists. Amneh tried to break loose and attack Zeinab again. She spat in the face of the dazed Zeinab, who had not yet understood what had happened. She screamed: "You will tell me this instant why you played your filthy trick on me. Why did you leave the shelter without telling me?"

As Zeinab realized what had happened, she knew that the battle between them would not end unless she announced the reason that had prompted her to move without telling Amneh. She did not think for long. The important thing was to end the standoff, which had turned into a scandal right in front of all the neighbours. She knew very well that holding anything back would do no good. She stood up in her worn out scarf, its tip pointing towards her back. She placed her hands defiantly on her waist and said: "Alright! There's nothing wrong with it! I'll tell you. I needed to relieve myself very badly. I told Samira to hold back her brother and sisters so that I could go outside. You know that there isn't a bathroom in the shelter. The children wouldn't listen to their sister, and they followed me. She followed them because she wanted to report them to me. They came to where I was in the entrance of the next door building. Suddenly, God preserve us, God is Great, what was to happen? As you said, the earth opened up and swallowed the shelter. What was I to do then? I picked them up and came running to my mother-in-law. How was I to know that you would go there and not find me?"

"Ah's" and chuckles arose as Zeinab announced the real reason that had saved her and her children from the collapse of the shelter. No one paid any attention to Georgette, who turned to her baby, not daring to hold him. She was frightened to touch him, and couldn't summon up the courage to voice her suspicion to anyone for fear that it would come true. She remained silent in the hope that her fears would not be confirmed. The child, who had not been named because his father had not returned. The child, her son, was frozen in his place. The drops of sweat had stopped dripping behind his ears. He had gone quiet, and cried no more. He was silent, but she dared not speak. An hour or so later when Um Jalal dropped in casually to check on her daughter, she became suspicious about the baby's silence. Every time she had passed, his crying could be heard until his voice had become part of the everyday atmosphere. Um Jalal became uneasy about the situation, and wanted to find out what was going on. She called to Georgette: "Yamma, Georgette. Pass me the child, may God bless and keep him."

Georgette picked him up from where he was lying next to her and gave him to Um Jalal. In that instant, everyone present realized the fate of the child. His head dangled from his cloth wrapping, swinging like the neck of a slaughtered bird. The baby was frozen, his limbs rigid, keeping a silence that none but the dead knew. Um Jalal's thick lips trembled, and she turned to the dazed Aisha, who seemed perpetually lost in an unknown land. She asked her in panic: "Aisha, how long has the child been like this?"

Her question seemed to explode Georgette's repressed terror. She began to wail and cry, pulling the baby to her bosom: "Where are you my child? Where are you my darling? When will you suck some milk and end my grief? Where are you my child so I can suckle you? I wish to God you would suck and live. I can't bear this filthy life in which I never breastfed you. I wish I could die with you. I want to die."

Georgette let out a great scream, throwing herself over the baby's body, rubbing her head in his white clothes and swaddlings, stained with brown spots from the dirt and mud in the shelter. Georgette began tearing her hair, and slapping her face madly. The women rushed towards her, trying to pull the baby's body from her lap. Ibtissam broke away from the crowd so that she could see the dead child. Um Jalal shouted at her: "Stop it girl. Get out of our faces. The last thing we need is for you to get possessed because we won't be able to treat you. We've got enough calamities. We don't need anything happening to you."

Um Jalal was expressing her firm belief that whoever stared at the dead for too long would be possessed by jinns who would send you mad for ever. She pulled her daughter fiercely and pushed her back so that she would not see the dead child.

The mad Georgette. That was the name she became known by later after her speech became confused. She would talk of the blood of her family splashed onto the walls. She said that her mother, father, brothers and sisters-in-law and all of her family had been hit by a shell. Death! It had taken them all. She had no one left to her. She kept trying to dash out of the room to go to her family in the middle of the shelling, calling to her new-born child in heart-rending tones.

Um Jalal left Ibtissam with her older sister, hoping that would help make her more alert and conscious of her surroundings. Since Hassan's death, Aisha had worn a black skirt and dark blue blouse. She had remained lost in a daze as though she were not there, not sleeping or waking up, not aware or interested in anyone or anything. It seemed that the baby's death and Georgette's disappearance had finished her off, leaving her unable to care about anything in life. Georgette had kept up her crying, saying that she would go to the top of the hill to see the flesh of her family which was sticking to the walls. One morning, Georgette left, and no one knew which direction she had taken beneath the shells raining down and the black gunpowder descending down as though in a storm. There was talk later of the girl who was walking beside the walls calling out to her baby. My son. I'm looking for my baby son, the apple of my eye, she would say to people who asked her to come in to shelter from the heavy shelling.

13

Along the front lines and military positions, news spread of the orders which were being irritably repeated over wireless receivers in recent days. We want you to remain steadfast. George, who no longer had time even to distinguish between night and day, was upset. He threw down the paper Hana brought to him, shouting bad temperedly. He who has his hand in water is not like he who has it in the fire. He roared and made threats. He was angry that all outside attempts to break through the siege had failed. A new attempt by the Nationalist fighters to cross over to them from the West Side through Furn Ash-Shubbak and Ein-Arummaneh had failed. There was another route. If they were to go around and come down through the mountains, they would no doubt reach the camp. Deep down, George was convinced of this. But the leadership had not taken the decision to come down through the mountains. They did nothing more than sending small groups of fighters – something that would not affect the outcome of the battle in the slightest – and helping them out by shelling the enemy forces, even though their own positions were right next to those of the enemies, almost overlapping with them. Sometimes, they shelled an enemy position which was less than ten metres away from their own forces.

George believed, between him and himself, that the shelling aimed at the enemy in defence of his own forces was inaccurate and was hitting them as well, because their positions and the enemies were so intermingled. He kept shouting in Hana's face: "Steadfastness! Steadfastness! They want steadfastness. That's all they tell us all the time. What the hell are we doing then? Perhaps they think we're dancing! Or that we're singing 'Ya Ein Ya Leil.'"

Hana wanted to calm his reactions. She attributed them to the bad temper which was getting hold of everyone. She did not know what to say to him to soothe him. In the end, she knew that the reason for his anger was that they had been hit by shells fired by the artillery of the Joint Forces. He revealed to her his suspicions about the lack of sufficient seriousness with which the leadership considered the fall of the camp and of the delays hindering the evacuation attempts of the Red Cross. All she could do was recall a verse of poetry about how man does not do justice to himself even as catastrophe strikes. She only knew half of the verse, which she had learnt at school "If I shoot, I am hit by my own arrow."

My God! What could George do?

Um Hassan's conscience continued to prick her whenever she mixed water with flour to make bread loaves which grew fewer and lighter by the day. Her heart ached as her thoughts wandered and her mind was preoccupied with the sense of tragedy and loss which remained with her since Hassan's eternal sleep had begun. A few days before, the son of their neighbours, with whom they had become reconciled at the beginning of the siege, had come up to her and asked her for a bit of hot bread. She had refused him and scolded him. She had turned him away because she could not be tolerant towards anyone since her son's death. Now, she was having pangs of conscience as she moved around and the smell of hot bread, which was more valuable than gold, filled her nostrils. She remembered how Um Mazen's youngest son had approached with embarrassment, and interrupted her as she worked: "Yamma, for God's sake, I want two loaves from your good hand."

She eyed him from top to toe as though she disapproved of the request by this child, born virtually yesterday, who had taken to wearing a brown beret and jeans. She pursed her hard lips, a frown appearing on her forehead as she told him off: "Yamma, you can see for yourself. I have so much work, I can barely cope. This bread is for the fighters at the front lines. You're a member of the student militia and a civilian. Get off my back and go find someone else to feed you. I'm committed to those who can't leave the front lines for a single minute, and I don't distribute a loaf here and a loaf there."

The boy did not protest at her words. His forgiving spirit was stronger than her rudeness. It was almost as though his request had been intended to gather the loose flour of her spirit as it fell to the earth. He had happened to pass by and the pleasant aroma of the bread had appealed to him, especially since he had been eating nothing but lentils night and day. Um Hassan was absolutely sure that God would not forgive her pompous hardness towards a poor boy in need of a piece of bread to melt in his mouth like appetizing butter. Before leaving, he had looked at her and moved his tongue inside his mouth as though to tell her of the dryness that afflicts the inside of the mouth when soft foods, vegetables and fruits are unavailable. Seconds later, the boy had gone to lounge around with his friends from the militia in the opposite building, which had still been under construction when the war began. He had stretched out on the concrete floor and stared at the uneven plaster, which had still not been finished. He had told his friends that he would make them a cup of tea. He had daydreamed for a short time, hesitating before getting up. Then he had looked for some wood with which to light a fire. He had caught sight of a cupboard door lying in the middle of the road. He had turned to his friends jokingly before going outside and said: "When I die, search for a cupboard door like this one because it's the right size for me."

Then he had laughed as though he were fighting the sullen silence imprisoning the faces of people everywhere. He had gone out and brought back a few pieces of wood he had found. He had squatted and started a fire. But a shell had landed on him. It had been a direct hit. The people in the basement had come running out to see what had happened on the street outside. Ibtissam had been the lightest and quickest amongst them. She had seen the boy's brains splattered about, mixed with earth. She had seen pieces of his hair sprinkled on the ground. She had seen enough to give her the shivers all night long. Her mother had brought the Al-Rajta cup and made her drink out of it after reciting verses from the Quran over her. Um Jalal had accused the boy of jinxing himself: "He brought the bad omen down on himself. Why did the poor fellow have to say that he wanted that cupboard door? Five minutes later, they brought it and took him on it to the cemetery. God protect us and have mercy on us."

Guilt continued to plague Um Hassan's conscience. Perhaps he would have lived if she had kept him there and given him what he had asked for. Perhaps, maybe. She could not shake off the boy's image, which filled her mind's eye. She suffered a great bitterness as she thought of the many people who had begun toasting lentils and eating them uncooked because of the water shortage. The old man, Abu Hassan, listened to Quranic verses on a small radio, but its batteries were gradually running out. The sound grew smaller and smaller until the people crowding into the basement had to scold their children so that they could pick up the bits of sound coming from the outside world. They began to listen to reports about the attempts being made to bring them out through the intervention of the International Red Cross, which seemed powerless. Amneh said with malice: "But we know that neither side will let us out. Our loved ones and relatives have to consider the morale of the people on their side of the city. If we leave and withdraw, what will become of morale? As for our enemies, may God one day show them and avenge us through the intercession of all the Prophets. They are sitting there making as much trouble as possible. And there we are stuck in the middle like a hapless tourist in Jericho burning in summer and drowning in winter. No help from one side to another."

Um Hassan, who was overseeing the distribution of the small amount of remaining water amongst all those present, answered: "Spare us your wisdom and close the subject. Get up and do some useful work. Go down and get some water."

Amneh was embarrassed and confused. She loved disobeying her mother, but she was not used to being humiliated by her in front of other people. She thought it best to provoke a row that would kill off the idea of her going to the water source. She said: "Yeah, yeah, Yamma. I'm the only one who has to work for everybody. Look at that monkey, Ibtissam, jumping here and there. Why doesn't she come with me?"

She had asked the question knowing that mentioning Ibtissam would sabotage the whole idea. But Um Hassan, with her newly-acquired temper, had not fallen for Amneh's ruse. She agreed and asked Ibtissam to go to the water source with Amneh. Their destination was a garden which had a well. People did not go there as often as before because of the intense shelling and sniping around it. Amneh took along the midget Ibtissam, who would probably never grow any taller because she had carried so many heavy water containers. The two of them headed for the garden. At the hedge surrounding the garden, Amneh asked Ibtissam to stand there and wait for her, saying: "I'll fill up a few buckets, and you can empty them into the containers."

She recalled Ali Samer's front line with yearning and sadness. Going there was no longer possible. The shelling had targeted the pipes until all of them had been destroyed. It was no longer possible to take a single step into that area, so violent were the battles. At night, the enemy would come out with a megaphone and call Ali Samer: come on, you son of a tramp. There would be an exchange of curses between opposing positions throughout the night, and they even might abuse their opponents by name.

A group of militiamen were fortified inside the garden to help the women pull buckets from the well after the incidence of civilian casualties had increased, causing some of them to fall into the well as they were pulling out water buckets. Heroic Amneh, who had earned that new title, was able to pull several buckets of water and take them to Ibtissam who was waiting outside. Suddenly, or perhaps as was to be expected, sniping started, and shells began to fall. Ibtissam took cover behind the fence, but when Amneh did not return, she began to cry. Her tears flowed as the flares spread out like lightning, alternating with the incandescent phosphoric bombs. Ibtissam did not know how long she cried and cried. It seemed that all the tears she had held back throughout the war had been destined to fall then. When Amneh appeared to her after a long time, she was startled and stared as though she were a ghost coming out of a grave. She was as frightened as if she had seen Beelzebub himself. She had not imagined that Amneh could still be in the land of the living. Amneh shouted at her: "Get up you wretched thing, let's run for it before the shelling gets worse. God bless you, get up! Come on now, come on."

They grabbed the two water containers and ran as though they had been stung. Near the basement, Ibtissam felt that her leg was on fire. She kept running as she carried the water containers. Her leg was burning like a raging fire. She did not stop running. She felt like her feet had sandbags in them. She could no longer take a single step further towards their basement doorway. She fell to the ground, not feeling anything. She couldn't even walk or crawl. At that moment, Um Jalal came out of the shelter. She pulled the girl in, stretched her out on the floor and saw the shrapnel that had hit her. Her little toe was broken and the flesh was hanging out. Um Jalal gave her a drink of water, said a brief prayer over her, bandaged the wound with a piece of gauze she had been carrying between her breasts for emergencies, and carried her off on her back to the clinic.

George's appearance changed. His beard grew longer, its edges were uneven and the strands of hair starting at his temples were twisted and tinged with white. He became thin, and the skin around his jaw was loose as though he were suffering a permanent tooth ache. He was seeing more of Hana than before. The combat area had narrowed, and the front lines had rolled back like the ebbing away of the tide. He secretly admired the way the girl controlled her fear. He explored her depths and understood the terror which caused her extreme sarcasm, as opposed to the crying of most girls of her age. He pitied her and became more tender towards her. It was no longer just a matter of admiring her. Things had changed, and people's conditions left no room for anything other than the will to survive. Whoever lived was the lucky son of Abu Zeid Al-Hilali, that legendary survivor of great cunning and whoever died was no more than an ordinary person – simply one of scores every day. Everybody knew this only too well. Um Hana took refuge in the far corner of one of the shelters, as though she knew nothing of life except that which was transmitted by her terrified memory, while the girl continued her work without even wanting a short rest. George would tease her by saying he could not make out her roots due to the obvious cowardice running in her family. She would glare at him and raise her voice, saying that she resembled her maternal uncle. "Two thirds of a child comes from his maternal uncle." And she would remind him about her uncle, who had spent years in prison in an Arab city because he had joined an opposition party. "My uncle, brother," she would say. He would respond: "Okay, I understand about your uncle, but why are you calling me brother?" She would engage in a garrulous, joking argument over whether he would make a good brother for her, or whether he were her fiancé. She would tell him about her mother's dreams of marrying her off at a brilliantly grand party to which every friend and relative would be invited. The mother! Her mother. She had dreamed of organizing her daughter's wedding in one of West Beirut's most luxurious hotels. Her plans had been linked with the kinds of fabrics she would wear, the furniture she would buy, and the food she would offer. As Hana said, "My mother considers that every penny my father has saved throughout his life must be spent on the wedding. She used to fight with him even before I went to secondary school so that she could take a look at his accounts."

Throughout that period, they had never been able to complete a conversation which they had begun. Something would always interrupt them. Either the signals machine would start transmitting, or Hana would have to receive new wireless messages, or someone would come in and call George out urgently. Sometimes it seemed that the decisive battle for which everyone was waiting was about to begin. He would leave without enough time to give her a passing look, leaving a secret regret in her heart; but her strong pride made her defer all her longing to the future, although she could scarcely imagine it. During the successive violent explosions of the continued shelling, they discovered a new and intermittent enjoyment like the dew that watered the trees. Stolen kisses between one explosion and the next, one earthquake and the next. The world was in one valley, and the thin lover, whose eyes ached with lack of sleep, and the dedicated girl who had not let her morale fall, were in another. As the siege grew tighter and the rhythm of death grew stronger, the girl abandoned her trembling hesitation. Whenever the young man drew close to her, she told him she would call herself "an idiot" from that day on. Oh God, how had she not known the paradise that was an embrace before? She should have. Should have. She would say it even as she broke loose from his arms during his brief visits. She would leave him amazed at the speed with which she would snatch herself and jump to the apparatus whenever a new incoming signal was about to begin. She would tell him breathlessly after receiving the message, "I should have met you when I was a little girl." His silent gaze, straight at her would make fun of her, and he would ask, "What good would such a childhood acquaintance have been? What would we have done, Hana, if we had been children? Would we have played on the street together?" Then he would add, "Thank God that we met and got to know one another despite these strange times." Often, he would not finish what he was saying. The office was open to everyone, and they rarely managed to win a few moments of privacy. But the more he loved her, the more he wanted to tease her. So he would start calling her: "You stupid thing, you stupid thing." But he understood exactly what she meant, although he made fun of her. He completely understood that one always hoped to have enough time for love, and that if one's time did not allow it, then one would wish to borrow the time from one's childhood.

Hana did not know how to explain it to him. Since her childhood she had not thought highly of young men because talk within the family had been so focused on their eligibility as bridegrooms. If she had not met this particular young man, if their admiration had not been mutual to the extent that she had encouraged him to draw closer, she would have decided to spend her life as a working woman. Even as a child, she had never found baking, cooking or cleaning the house enjoyable. She had only considered water useful for taking baths and for wetting her throat with home-made lemonade with fresh lemon peel in it. Only jobs which were meant for men attracted her. She enjoyed discussing and arguing and gesticulating to emphasize her views. She loved finding solutions to problems so that she would not become like her mother, who wanted nothing more out of life than to sit and smoke a water pipe with the other women. She would feel dizzy and bored whenever her mother imposed that kind of a visit on her, or forced her to sit with her neighbours and friends, who let loose an endless stream of complaints and shrieks. In her exasperation, Hana would swear that she would never become like them, or resemble them in any way.

The only thing which Hana concealed from George, despite the honesty of their new relationship, was the way she cursed over the wireless. She continued to skirmish with her enemies during the rare moments when the apparatus was not being used. She cursed and swore at them, responding to their obscenities in kind. Hana was too embarrassed to share the more shameful side of her vitality with George. If she was unable to confront her enemies on the street, she would use the weapons that a lower-middle class woman like her mother would use if she were in her place. These women would have mustered up all the curses at their disposal. But Hana was using the same oral weapons in the most masculine of ways. She was not shy of responding in the same language that they were using, outdoing them at times. She was not embarrassed to be common like her mother's friends, who smoked water pipes and let rip curses when their impotence allowed them nothing more. But in every other respect, she would not have agreed to resemble them in any way.

Bad smells lingered everywhere. People took to wearing masks to protect themselves against the pollution in the camp, which was engulfed by swarms of black flies with shining bodies resembling copying paper. Pieces of metal sheets pierced by shrapnel and jumbled up with rotting organic remains filled the newly-formed ditches caused by the continued shelling. The ground turned into little hills and ditches, losing its old evenness. The staring Aisha scratched her skin, digging her nails deeper and deeper into her complexion, which became lined with scars and brown patches of blood. It was no use talking to her. She would listen, but would not respond. During one of these times, Um Jalal dropped into the office while looking for George and confided her troubles to Hana. Assayed sat in his house and would not agree to move to the shelter. Um Jalal quarrelled with him, so he had furiously kicked her out of the house. "The house?" Um Jalal said. "May you be spared all evil. It's like a ruin. But he's staying there and refusing to budge as though it were the Yeldiz Palace!"

That evening, as George walked into the office, Hana was unable to say a single word about the problem of Assayed refusing to leave his home, despite the promises she had made to Um Jalal. Things were very delicate, and the situation was extremely critical. The second patrol had arrived via the mountainous route. Its members brought news of several other patrols whose members had returned to the western side without making a second attempt to reach the camp. The office was in a state of turmoil. The groups which returned had not been disciplined, and this meant that no firm decision to save the camp had been taken.

George welcomed his friend Mazen, who had arrived with the fighters crossing the mountains with open arms. He embraced and kissed him, "I thought you would be martyred on the way."

Mazen pulled away, looking at him with shining eyes.

"No, I was the one who thought that you would be martyred."

They both laughed, as though the simple discovery of having the same thought in common was extremely funny. George punched Mazen affectionately in the chest and said: "I heard that you were getting married."

His comrade laughed, almost falling onto the ground, as he said: "No. I'm the one who heard that it was you who's getting married. I said to myself: George has always been the son of a lion, but now he's about to become the son of . . ."

Hana sarcastically interrupted the conversation: "It seems our brother has forgotten himself. Have you come to fight the Phalangists, or to fight me?"

Mazen laughed and said: "I oppose all forms of injustice, slavery and siege."

Hana said in a half-joking, half-serious tone: "Leave us be in our misery. May God keep you happy and far away. The saying goes, may you who are waiting be spared the evil of those who are coming."

Mazen retorted, "There's another saying that going to a funeral is better than going to a wedding."

George sprang up and said: "What's this new war? Okay then, I have a saying too: The bride is for the bridegroom, and running is for the less fortunate."

Mazen said: "So that's how you've ended up, like the monster who gobbled everyone up, except for his wife."

The conversation then moved on, following its inevitable course to the issue which was burning in everyone's thoughts and expressions. George said he did not know what the brothers outside were waiting for. They must decide on one of two things: either to continue negotiating so that the camp could be evacuated and the civilians taken out, or else to make their way to them and help them out, instead of merely giving them advice. George pointed out sharply that whoever had been able to get Mazen's group into the camp, and a previous group of ten men as well, could also get in one or two hundred men. So what were they waiting for out there? George was absolutely sure that they were still waiting for some form of mercy to descend from heaven, for some leaders of the Arab World to sympathize with them and exert pressure to lift the siege. In his opinion waiting for their pity was useless as their inability to act was clear and obvious to all. He set his teeth and asked his comrade: "I swear I am unable to understand. Fifty thousand attempts to storm through, and they still can't get to us. If they had been able to, they would have done it long ago. Since the battle of Thabet Woods, they haven't been able to reach us. At the beginning, it was easy. It was only a matter of two steps and they would reach us via Furn Ash-Shubbak, Ein-Arummaneh, and the Chevrolet route. But since the Thabet Woods battle, that has become impossible. Now there are several barricades in the Thabet Woods, Sinn El-Feel and then Qal'ah and Jisr El-Basha."

George picked up a news pamphlet that was lying nearby and read out loud: "The *Al-Hamishmar* newspaper gave extra detail of what had been discussed at the meeting. It said that Kissinger had told the Israeli ambassador that Israel should almost certainly not be anxious about *Fedayeen* attacks on the Occupied Territories or about Syrian control in southern Lebanon, because the confrontation between the PLO and Syria would continue."

He fell silent, then brought his fist smashing down onto the table, covered with black dust and stones. No one knew quite how they had got there. Hana, who was sitting behind it, jumped back with a start. God alone knew that she was discovering the man's temper for the first time in her life. All she had seen of him before was his smiling, well-behaved side. Now she was seeing the hidden aspect of his personality, which she had secretly wondered about for a long time. His features were full of contradictory feelings, and she couldn't make out whether he could bear them or not. She was witnessing the raging of his repressed anger, which he only allowed himself to show in rare moments. It was truly strange that a handful of men from the outside could have infiltrated the impossible siege while those who had been urgently called on to do so had failed. It was also strange that allies should be involved in a conflict that served the enemies.

"I'm your close friend, hear me out," said Mazen. "You and I trained together in the south. The basic preoccupation within the resistance movement is Ezza'tar, but the problem is that they don't know how to go about it. The joint command tried to penetrate the siege and get through by the Shiyyah–Ein-Arummaneh route. Every day there are martyrs, and every day people are dying as they try to break the siege. But they can't. That is the truth. Why that is, no one knows. But if you were to ask me, I'd say it's an organisational defect. Large groups, each belonging to a different organization or faction. Some are made up of students, others are trainees. Some are volunteering for the first time in their lives. Others, perhaps, are using guns for the first time in their lives, and they must face the army of a state, not only militias! But when it comes to the actual will to do something, people are getting killed every day because they're really and truly working at it."

The calm look of former days began to spread across George's strained features. He continued to pose questions: "I'm not asking about those in Shiyyah and Ein-Arummaneh because I know there isn't the slightest possibility of breaking the siege after the fall of the Jisr El-Basha camp, which linked us to them. No, I'm asking about something else. Where are those who are fighting in the mountains? We keep hearing about Sanneen and Aintourah. What can they want with Al-Matin and Ras Al-Matin? Why don't they come down here to our rescue? They've got all the heavy weapons and other means that we're deprived of. Why don't they come down here, since they're near us? If they'd come down in a straight line, they'd have been with us a long time ago."

Mazen sighed and exhaled with all his strength, like someone fighting a bitter battle within himself. Hana interrupted: "Enough of this, my friends, stop this argument! For starters George, you know that the command will not allow the camp to fall easily. Getting to it would need them to occupy the whole city, or half this large capital from one end to the other. In other words, they'd have to occupy the entire eastern side to open up a path and unblock the road. On the other hand, Mazen, it's impossible for them to infiltrate down the mountains with heavy weapons because the enemy's artillery is waiting for them! And it's not only one state that's fighting them either. Whoever said that the way down here is open to them? Calm down, both of you. You're losing your tempers and taking it out by criticizing people over there who're at their wits' end."

Hana did not finish what she had been saying. An explosion. They were forced to interrupt their conversation and fling themselves into the corridor for cover. Recently the shelling had targeted the hospital and the offices which the fighters used and where they received their wireless messages.

The hospital. God alone knew the pain stored in Khazneh's weakened feet as she carried the wounded and moved them to small centres scattered around the camp. Fuel had run out at the clinic, and it was no longer possible to use the operating theatre, despite massive efforts to light it and run some of its equipment using whatever car batteries were available. The shortage or complete lack of medicines, serum and antiseptics prompted the medical team to break up the clinic and relocate it to smaller medical centres to protect the patients, whose lives were threatened by the shells that kept pouring down on the building. Khazneh left the clinic with the feeling that she was leaving a part of her body behind. It was the dearest place she had ever known, she who had always borne the charitable kindness of others without having the opportunity of giving freely as she was doing now. Elias Addoughani had begun to comfort her after he had realized the nature of her feelings towards him. He had kept promising her that she would become his senior assistant even if that meant breaking up with his "breathtakingly beautiful fiancée", as he had always described her. She felt as though a dagger were ripping her heart apart. Why? Khazneh didn't know why she was upset. The only thing she knew was that she was perturbed, and felt as though her blood were haemorrhaging from her quaking feet.

"I wish it were me, not you," cried Um Jalal, as she carried her daughter Ibtissam to the clinic, whose patients had been moved elsewhere. The deep brown cuts caused by the shrapnel had begun to fester with little worms. Um Jalal shouted at the doctor: "I beg of you, worms are eating up my daughter's foot."

The doctor purified the wound with salt and water, although he inwardly knew that this would not be enough. It certainly would not be enough. The infection of the wound, brought on by the heat and being shut up with the crowds in a shelter, could cause gangrene in the foot of this little girl, whom he had often seen bravely carrying water with her mother. The doctor advised the mother to try and get the girl out in one of the Red Cross cars.

"But doctor, you're the best informed man around. The cars come every day and stop at the entrance to the camp, and the Phalangists won't let them in."

"And you're the best informed lady around, Um Jalal," said the doctor, with his canny look that always made her feel good when he was addressing her. He added: "When things are resolved and the road opens up, we'll get Ibtissam out immediately."

The doctor hid his pessimism about the probable need to amputate the foot if the siege did not end.

Ibtissam did not dare to tell anyone about the memory she kept recalling. Whenever pain buzzed through her wound like wasps, and whenever she saw the tiny worms sucking her blood, she would fearfully recall what had happened to her one day as she returned along the road from the lentil factory with Husam. They had just finished their daily visit to the bonbon factory – something they had continued to do until a short while ago. She was sure that her foot had been wounded because she had lied to a boy, Othman. As Ibtissam had returned uphill towards Um Hassan's house, she and Husam had run into this boy, who was about the same age as themselves. Husam was twelve and she was eleven. The boy was a bit younger, although he was in their class at school. They had met the boy, Othman, at the water pipe. He was carrying a large square can of water. He caught the smell of sweets wafting out of their mouths, and he asked for one sweet, but Husam refused to give it to him. Othman swore that he would pay Husam for the sweet out of his next pocket money, which was a quarter of a lira a day. But Husam teased Othman with a hidden malice, reminding him of the falafel sandwich of which he had refused to give him a bite. Othman was one of those clean, tidy children whom one rarely found at an UNRWA school. Every day, he would get beaten up or insulted and cursed by one of the thuggish boys such as Husam known for their bad behaviour. Othman had begged both Ibtissam and Husam to let him taste a morsel of one of the sweets or toffees they had with them. He had said he didn't want all of it, just a piece. He had gestured with the tips of his rounded fingers. Only, just. He had promised to pay for it later on with the price of a chocolate bar. Ibtissam did not know what sort of a devil had taken hold of Husam that instant. What harm would it have done him to give the boy one lick of a very small lemon or caramel flavoured piece? But Husam had refused. Othman had turned to Ibtissam, begging her for some. But a hidden nastiness had filled her heart, making her lie to him and steadfastly swear that she had no sweets at all. As they had walked up the hill, Ibtissam had not known that the shell was around the corner. Um Hassan had been standing on the balcony, and Husam, jumping like a monkey, had entered the building before her, while she had carried their plastic jerrycan with both hands. The boy had not gone to the nearby shelter, where his mother and eight children were living. Instead he had kept on following her and Husam as though the sweets were a magnet pulling him. He did not call it a day, but carried on trying to get a sweet. Ibtissam had not known the insane stubbornness of childhood until that moment. At the same time, she could not admit that she had been lying by giving him one of the sweets hidden in her pocket, although it almost seemed that he could smell their presence. At the corner, a woman and her sister had sat before a kerosene cooker, frying lentil dough cakes to feed the children inside the shelter. Um Hassan had heard the hissing of a shell, followed by another, and she yelled from the balcony: "Yammaaaa take cover."

Ibtissam had picked up her plastic slippers and run towards the entrance of the building.

Um Hassan had shrieked with a clarity undimmed by the sound of collapsing walls in the nearby street: "Yamma, God bless you, run."

The boy had not run. The poor boy. The heavy tin had been on top of his head, so how could he have run? The boy had not run. The next shell and . . . only human remains. Ibtissam had imagined that a hand stuck out from them to beg for some sweets. And the women sitting by the kerosene cooker . . . also. Only. Human remains of skins, flesh and bone. As she sat watching the small brown worms swarming inside her foot, she knew that God was punishing her for lying. Not because she had refused to give the boy some sweets, because that was up to her, but because her lying had ended the boy's life. Had he not sensed that she had been lying, he would have left her alone and joined his family in their shelter instead of following her and Husam.

Ah! Husam. The other crazy boy. No one knew where he was staying. He claimed that he was spending his time at the front line positions to help the fighters. Um Jalal would say: "God knows better. Who can tell about another human being, even one's own son?"

It was the day of judgment without any doubt. The Red Cross cars would arrive and leave every day. They would draw up at the entrance of the camp, then depart after being prevented from entering. And Ibtissam! What would become of her wounded foot? Would she live or die? Um Jalal sadly hinted at the possibilities to her daughter's mother-in-law, who was lost in a frightening daze. Um Hassan became like a hard rock, unshaken by anything, undisturbed by lightning or thunder. A human skeleton with tight features and hard lines on her face. A speechless statue. Even when the fighters achieved the miracle of finding new flour after it had become completely unavailable, not a syllable had passed Um Hassan's lips in praise of the great discovery made by the head of the camp committee. A brilliant idea had occurred to Muhsen. He had thought that the empty flour bags in the UNRWA warehouse must have the remnants of some flour stuck amongst their fibres. Many civilians volunteered and had gone to the warehouse to shake the empty bags. And what had been the result? "Exactly two hundred kilos of flour," shouted Husam, who acted like he had sprouted a moustache because of the huge manly tasks in which he had participated. Many people had stood there shaking the sacks until they had gathered two hundred kilos, as measured on the UNRWA scales. And so it became possible to feed the fighters, whom it was difficult to nourish with the flour of crushed lentils. Since Hassan's martyrdom and the incident of the shell that had killed the neighbours' son before her very eyes, Um Hassan no longer felt the same old pleasure at making bread for the fighters. The old lady, who had aged suddenly, did not complain. She did not protest or change the ritual of sitting by the fire, which continued to burn, sometimes on curtain fabric and sometimes on twigs of wood of which only God and the mischievous Husam knew the source. All that happened was that she became quieter, calmer and less concerned with new developments, as though living were an obligatory task that one had to go through like conscription. Even if the fire were to have burnt her, she would have looked on in eloquent silence, closing her eyes and muttering phrases that she alone understood. Even on that day when Khazneh brought several jerrycans of water and emptied them into the large barrel propped up in the basement corner, Um Hassan wasn't pleased or moved.

Khazneh told her how the doctors at the medical centre had gathered the fuel from all the lanterns and had poured it into the motor of the pump for the centre's well. They had extracted the last of the water in the well and distributed it amongst the civilians once it had become impossible to perform operations without medicines, serum or medical supplies. They had pumped out the last drop of water with the remaining fuel after being absolutely sure that there would be no more operations, however small or simple. Water! Only Zeinab fully appreciated it, because it spared her the agony of having to give the children only a few drops, which were insufficient to quench their thirst. For a day, she was able to give them water as though there had been a promise of rain. That happiness only lasted for a little while. The tens of bodies that had gone to sleep on the floor of the basement awoke the next day to water flowing around shoulders and backs, waists and feet. The playful hand of a child had tampered with the barrel's tap, loosening it and allowing the water to drip onto the floor in the thick darkness.

Amazement or stupor? It made no difference. What counted was feeling and alertness, Khazneh concluded with great sadness as she looked at Aisha. It seemed that everyone else was in one world and she was in another. "Aisha, Aisha," she called tenderly, but the rapt girl did not hear her. Khazneh left without anticipating what would happen the next morning. She left behind the smell of wet straw which evaporated from the drenched mats, the rancid odour accumulated on the hot bodies and the stench of sweat, gunpowder and dust.

The last pipe. The only water pipe that had not been hit by shells broke. People had followed the pipe and its intermittent leaks, with its meagre flow each day at dawn until it had shattered. It then only flowed towards the opposite side, which was sparing nothing to wipe them out.

The wireless machines worked at their full capacity that evening, on which it became known to the whole camp that the end of the battle had drawn very near, closer than the jugular vein. Bilal Hassoun, most of whose men had fled, had spread strong rumours widely about the amnesty that the Phalangists would grant to whoever threw down his weapons and left. Who would leave? Who? The signalling machines worked continuously describing the latest developments to the leadership outside. Since the last drop of water had trickled out of the pipe, a decision had finally been reached to evacuate the civilians under the supervision of the Arab Deterrent Forces and the Red Cross. There was no other solution.

I return to that last night on which Um Jalal had been forced to go to the dangerous well. She had almost been killed by a sniper's bullet at its fence one night. I see her lowering the bucket into the well, trying to bring out water for her children – the widow, the injured girl and the mischievous boy who will not be still. She searches for a few drops for Zeinab's weakened children, their voices still loud despite the fever running through their bodies. Um Jalal threw down the rope and waited with a few other women to pull it up again, but it stuck in its place like a stone. She could not understand why, and she continued to pull until it occurred to her to look down the shaft of the well. She jerked her head backwards when she realized that the black bundles floating in the water were human hair, of women or girls, it made no difference now. Um Jalal thought of Ibtissam. She remembered how she had bled into the bucket when she had been hit. But a more urgent thought occurred to her. The news of the imminent withdrawal from the camp had spread. It was said that the wireless machines had received an order saying, "Soldier save yourself." She knew that these were the last few hours before leaving the camp now that the only source of water had dried up. Despite the nausea, the thought went through her head. The attackers would do terrible things to the girls as they left. What would she do with the virgin who was still her responsibility? What would she do with Ibtissam? How would she explain to her? No, it was impossible. No. Better to think of a way of getting rid of her now. She would kill her before she would be engulfed by such an indelible shame. How would the little one ever be able to face up to the world if? No. She would leave her lying at home, and go, and she would die of thirst. That was easier than the other terror. She remembered how she had left the girl with Assayed in the entrance of a collapsed building near their house. Ibtissam. Oh, Ibtissam, what shall I do?

The mother thought all this as she emptied the fragments and tangled body parts from the bucket, leaving some shallow, blood tinged water. She lifted the container with the blood-tinged liquid and walked.

She left the well and the hair of girls floating over the murky water. On her way, she did not miss the sight of exhausted women, tripping as they carried containers filled with bloodied water, some of it splashing down their faces.

Um Jalal's dreams were always on the brink of dawn at the moment when a black thread can be distinguished from a white one. She had settled down and it seemed to her that she had just closed her eyes as she sat at the entrance of the collapsed building. She had lost the courage to look into the eyes of Ibtissam, who was lying on a wooden board beneath a ladder. She came to as the hand of Assayed, who now had a long beard full of white hair, shook her: "Get up, we must go."

Um Jalal immediately understood the importance of that phrase. So, it was the departure. She pulled her heavy, sleepy body together, and recalled the images of her intense dream: "I saw myself asleep. I opened my eyes and found myself carrying my things and leaving. I went to a white, white desert. I walked through sand that was white as snow. I arrived at my family's home in Acre. I entered the neighbourhood and walked amongst the houses one by one. I found that I'd remembered all the roads, the trees and shops. I knocked at the door of our house, and the people living in it answered. They said, 'What brings you here?' I said, 'This is our house.' They said: 'The house belongs to your parents, but you're married in Lebanon, so what do you have to do with it?' I answered, 'No! So what if I'm married? This is my home. The home of my parents and relatives.' As they spoke, I roamed amongst its walls. We have a lemon tree at home. A big citrus tree. They'd cut off part of it. That made me cry. I sat in the yard, and the neighbours came over to welcome me back. Then I saw policemen coming after me, knocking at the door to take me away. Suddenly, I saw our neighbour Ghazaleh, who lives right next door to us. She said, 'You're a grown-up young lady now and you have children.' She and I went out together and the wedding was in full swing. The lights were blazing. There was light upon light. A real wedding. When I woke up, I said to myself that it was a bad omen. The snow. My goodness, the snow. A white, white desert. And a huge land, and all of us singing and dancing on it."

Um Jalal repeated her dream to Assayed, whose face wore an unexpected expression of relief.

215

"Your dream is meaningless. The important thing is that we should get out of here. Thank God that we're still alive."

Um Jalal looked around anxiously and wondered: "What about Ibtissam? How are we going to get her out? I heard that they're killing girls on the way."

Assayed, with his red eyes and melancholy face, did not understand what his wife was implying. "If you're referring to her injury, I'll carry her on my back."

He added: "I vow that I shall never drink another drop of alcohol if we make it out of here. I'll even stop smoking."

There was nothing more left for Um Jalal to do. Just a second so that she could bring something, and she ran up to the cracked roof of her house. Its metal sheets revealed fissures and torn fragments like the savage teeth of saws. Suddenly, the vine flashed before her eyes, and she forgot what she had come for. The vine was still climbing the wall, but its clusters of fruit, which she had eagerly awaited, had only now ripened. They arose, lovely and full of juice. Um Jalal stretched out her hand, then held back. This was the first time in her life. She had never before felt that something was too beautiful to be touched by human beings despite their desperate need for it. What a pity! The bunches! They must not be picked. She would leave them rounded carrying their jewels. It was better that way. The ripe fruit shining like clusters of precious stones. Leave them. She would not take them. Her hand returned to her side empty. The sound of a heavy vibration from an unknown source arose around her knees. Were the shells following her up here to declare an end to her life?

Something hit her lower abdomen. Suddenly she was able to make out that it was Husam. He sprang towards the vine like an arrow on fire. She grabbed hold of his arm and pulled him back towards her, asking: "Why have you come up here, you animal? I was going to bring you some grapes. Have some shame and go back down there before you get hit by a shell or some other catastrophe. Down, you."

The boy wriggled loose, roaring: "Hey you, let me go. I want my money."

Um Jalal understood what he had in mind. He was referring to his small coins, which he had buried in the earth of the barrel in which the vine was planted. He had hidden his few pennies there in the belief that one day they would grow and blossom into a golden tree.

Assayed carried his daughter on his back and swayed as he walked like someone approaching the edge of a steep cliff. For the first time in months, he tried to train his weak eyesight, which had become accustomed to the darkness of entrances and crumbling corners, to look at the light once again. He did not recognize roads or directions, and he marvelled at the camp. Had the shelling changed it to such an extent, or had his perception wilted and faded in the absence of alcohol? Um Jalal was pressing on ahead of him with a great agility he had not known she possessed. In the weak light of dawn, she was making her way to Dekwaneh Square. He found out from her that the fighters had given the go ahead to leave the camp at the beginning of the previous evening. Most of the camp inhabitants had tried to follow the fighters and leave by the mountain passes, but the clashes had intensified there. So everyone had headed back to the camp. She said that people were making ready to leave along the road passing Dekwaneh Square, as Bilal Hassoun had advised. He had reappeared, justifying his absence by claiming to have been negotiating exhaustively with the enemy. He advised people to head for Beirut along a single route, saying that the safety of those who did so would be guaranteed, and that no harm would come to them. Assayed gave in to his disturbed, raving thoughts. He began to recall a mysterious dream he had had during a fleeting nap. He had not expected to have such a dream at all, and could not put it out of his mind, it trickled through him drop by drop.

"I suddenly found myself at the borders of Palestine. How would I walk and cross them! By God, I had no idea. Barbed wire and lots of television aerials on the roofs. I saw myself entering, wanting to get in. I flew upwards. But I found that I had gone backwards and was in Beirut. I was upset and said to myself, why am I still here? I closed my eyes and saw myself riding the Blessed Al-Buraq horse on which the Pophet Mohammed himself ascended to heaven. Its head was that of a pretty girl's. I found myself in the middle of Palestine. I saw my family, but didn't recognize them. Someone on the street decided to pick a quarrel with me. I put my hand to my side and pulled out my revolver. I wanted to shoot. I held the pistol. But then I woke up."

The final seconds, and the camp is no longer itself. As she left the office Hana discovered how much it had changed while she had stayed in the office, behind doors fortified with sacks of lentils. She was now used to darkness and dimmed colours. Her hearing had become much more sensitive, allowing her to pick up the slightest movement, even during the height of the shelling. Her compulsive listening to the rustling friction of the wings of the cockroaches as they rubbed against each other had disturbed her a great deal. They had crawled about in the corners of the quiet room, fighting and increasing in number although the world was collapsing over people's heads. As a child, Hana had believed that insects only multiplied over garbage and human waste. As she sat confined to the wireless machines, she thought that the insects would disappear through the cracks in the ground in an attempt to get at those who had been buried beneath it. Only now did she realize the enormity of the ruin that had befallen the place which had been so familiar to her. A strong depression took hold of her, and a steel hand surrounded her neck, almost choking her. How many times had her eyes burned with the embers of suppressed tears, which she had not dared to let flow for fear of lowering the morale of others. But throughout that great preoccupation of hers, she had never imagined that things outside were this way. Everything was broken and wrecked. All the houses and buildings had collapsed, one over the other, brick over stone. She saw nothing but smashed columns, twisted iron bars and huge ditches. Had someone told her that this would confront her, she would have preferred to stay where she was, and not to move, whatever happened. Truly.

She thought back over the violent quarrel she had had with George as he tried to convince her to join those leaving via the mountain passes. Her reply had been blindly and stubbornly biased in favour of her mother. Her mother had sent word to her to wait for her so they could leave together. When she had informed George of her decision, he looked at her with wonder and amazement, saying: "How strange you are, Hana. Your mother is a civilian, and no one will take any notice of her. You're the one that counts. What if they recognize you? How will you save yourself? What God in heaven will prevail upon them to leave you alone?"

"No one will recognize me. I'll change my appearance and clothes, and no one will know who I am."

George had become insistent, but she had not agreed. He had grown angry, but she had not given in. "Whoever sees how strong and independent you are, would not guess how attached you are to your parents. Let your mother leave on her own. Nothing will happen to her. Let her get out with the other women, and put my mind at ease."

"Isn't it enough that my father was kidnapped? No, by God. I am responsible for ensuring my mother's safety before my own."

Hana walked on, driven by a strong sense of bitterness. She had not thought that the world outside was that ugly and antagonistic. She missed the protection and tenderness that George had given her, but she pressed on to the shelter where her mother was hiding with a strange conviction that there was no longer an opportunity or time to change her mind.

Confusion broke out in the shelters. The news spread like wildfire running through dry stalks. Everyone gasped upon hearing that same phrase, "Soldier save yourself." They immediately gathered the children, or began to plan how to save their older sons. It seemed that the outdated phrase, which none of them had heard except in the stories of the Safarbarlek during Turkish times, had awoken within them things that they had expected and others that they had not. Each of them became aware of a mythical echo in his or her inner ear. An immense pulse to which they had not grown accustomed even at the height of the shelling. A great flood of savage, bloody torrents. Suddenly, a thin trail of blood had appeared on the face of the stormy sea in which they were floating, affirming that resistance of the storm could not continue for ever, that a savage killer shark would appear. That it would inevitably come even to those who tried their utmost to stave off such a time. Each of them had become accustomed to postponing any thought of this pulse of time, which had never stopped rolling towards them with the full force of its insanity. The bodies ravaged by wounds had been a dam preventing it from pouring down over them. The streams of blood had been a sacrifice preventing the sharp, pointed teeth from drawing close to them. The flying limbs blown off by the shelling outside on the roads had been a ransom protecting their lives. Even the young Ibtissam raised her fingers to cover her eyes. She smelt something strange mingled with the hot air, weighed down by the smell of rotting corpses piled along the sides of the road leading out of the camp.

The terror. And the bodies. And Amneh, whom Um Hassan had

sent ahead to find out what was happening at the top of the road. Some of the neighbours had already left. But Um Hassan and Um Mazen were delaying their departure, hoping for a miracle that would avert the horror of falling into the hands of the besiegers. As the decision to surrender had spread through the shelters, crowds had surged either towards the mountains surrounding the camp, or towards Dekwaneh, that terrible compulsory route. The amputated hands and feet scattered along the Dekwaneh road, their veins being sucked by blue flies, were the true testament of the fate awaiting those who chose to head in that direction. The fighters prepared to leave by the rough mountain paths up to a small village called Mansourieh, hoping to break through enemy lines there, and then to continue on to the Nationalist-controlled area. Most of the young men and women joined those going up into the mountains, prompted by an instinctive certainty that risking the unknown was better than following the voices offering people safe conduct which had suddenly blared out through several megaphones from the direction of Dekwaneh.

Amneh, with the newly-acquired military experience she had gained from her water-gathering trips, noticed that the faces of the bodies lying along the road were turned towards the camp, and she concluded that they had been shot in the back. The sounds of the clashes on the road to the mountains made her aware of the new battle around the camp.

She heard from some of those running past that a clash had broken out with Abdallah Hamdan's group, which had been one of the first to leave via that route. Soon the returning groups appeared, heading back towards the streets of the camp. The surging crowds of people were forced down again towards the Dekwaneh road. As for the fighters, the ferocity of the shelling forced them to withdraw into the camp. They took refuge in some of the deserted houses, but the camp inhabitants did not realize they had returned. In the chaos and confusion of forced departure, amid the crying and rising sobs of children, the inhabitants could not tell who had returned or who had left. The collapsed walls and piled up rubble seemed frozen, and haphazard earthen barriers thrown up by the saturation shelling rose high as though caused by an earthquake that spews out the fever pent up deep beneath the ground. In place of the familiar houses, there were huge piles of concrete, stones and twisted sheets of metal. Amneh could easily have got lost if she had tried to get further away from their house. She wanted to stop passers-by and ask them what was going on in their streets and neighbour-hoods, but no one would answer her questions. Everyone was running around and panting as though it were doomsday. Only those carrying the wounded or children walked slowly. People were ghosts walking hurriedly in the noon light. Blue circles, formed from the vapours rising from the putrefying bodies, floated around them in the noon glare. Amneh saw a man carrying his wife on his back, her feet dragging behind him on the ground. The man was ill, or so he seemed to her. The woman was wounded and unconscious, or perhaps she was . . . a few dogs were following them with a silent greed, awaiting the moment when the man would drop the woman from his bent back and leave her behind.

Amneh returned and related what she had learned to Um Hassan, who was discussing how to make a move with her neighbour, Um Mazen. They were complaining about the difficulty of moving. Um Hassan was complaining about her rotten luck, which was causing her to leave in a procession of women and children without a man, except for her old husband. Um Mazen was awaiting her husband, who had gone to search for his fighter sons, and had not returned. They decided not to head for Dekwaneh via the road passing the mosque because Amneh had found out that it had turned into a cemetery for the wounded who had taken refuge there, unable to walk any further. Many of them had gathered there in the early dawn hours, but the enemy forces had come and finished off those inside it with hand grenades and machine guns. The women decided to take an unfamiliar road that would lead to the western side of the city without passing the main Phalangist centres they knew of. They would walk west along the road passing the thyme factory, then the lentil factory, in the hope that maybe, just maybe. Um Mazen said she was still awaiting news that would reassure her about her sons, the fighters. She mentioned Ali Samer as being one of them. Amneh's heart melted, and she suppressed a broad smile that was about to appear on her face. At last, here she was discovering who his family were! Could Ali Samer be the son of their neighbours, with whom they had had such a long quarrel, without her knowing it? But how? His family name was not the same as theirs.

They were from the Jaber family, but his surname was Samer. How could this be? But mention of the water front line confirmed to her that it was indeed him. But she postponed her questions and would find out the answer once they had made it out of this mess.

As for Aisha, she seemed so remote from everything going on around her, Amneh thought as she followed her with her gaze. It seemed that she had lost her ability to speak since the day Georgette's son had died. Was she so frightened for the safety of that small thing she was carrying within her? Amneh had never been convinced that Aisha was pregnant in the first place. The whole thing was no doubt an illusion which she had created to win some extra attention. Or else why had she stopped mentioning the pregnancy and ignored it as though it were not a fact? Aisha's continued crying and the tears flowing down her cheeks gave Amneh a feeling of uncontrollable contempt. Her present bout of crying would no doubt bring on them the same ill-fortune which she had brought to her marriage.

The people of the neighbourhood had gathered at the top of the street and begun walking in an ever-growing procession. From beneath the ruins appeared new faces they had not known before, or which they needed time to recognize because they had changed so much. Um Hassan walked, supporting Abu Hassan with her arm. He had wrapped himself in his Katiyyeh head-dress with a pattern of black and white squares on it. He wore his striped gown and his Arab cloak, with frayed golden embroidery round the edges. His wife propelled him forward despite his stick, with which he tapped the ground twice before each step he took. Um Hassan, with her long white scarf hanging down her back, and men's pyjama trousers showing beneath her dress, continuously recited the Quranic verse of Al-Kurjy followed by other verses that would protect whoever said them from evil, keeping away the hatred of enemies and opening the road to salvation. Zeinab walked beside Um Mazen's daughters-in-law. One of them had awaited her husband, who had ascended into the mountains. No one could tell her what had become of him, or whether he had made it. Um Mazen had been unable to wait for her husband, who had gone to scout out news of his sons. Walking with them was the wife of the other martyred son, who had been fatally hit on Sallaf Hill. Each of the daughters-in-law led her children, who hung on to ends of her dress. They were joined by a crowd from their street, followed by a crowd from the next street until a long procession had formed. They made their way haphazardly forward, weighed down by a feeling heavier than dread after hearing news brought by those returning from the mountain passes, which were covered with boxthorn and prickly gourd plants, and especially after one of the young men who joined them told them of the massacres taking place inside the camp, outside the church and near the Fawzi photography studio.

The terror. The strewn corpses. The wild dogs biting the bodies hoping for a limb or some human flesh. Squinting eyes and shaking heads, and Um Hassan talking to herself, "I wish I were a bird so that I could fly, rise into the sky away from this injustice, this hunger and thirst which Fayez's young children are suffering. There we go, Yamma Hassan, there we go. Some die, and some flee." She walks with Abu Hassan and sees the edge of his white trousers. How proud she used to be of their cleanliness. Now they have turned into something more like a dirty sheet showing beneath his gown. The old lady is secretly glad that his weak eyesight and thick glasses prevent him from seeing properly the hell they are crossing, and not realizing the impending end. He tried to ask her in which direction were they walking? She warned him in whispered tones to lower his voice and be quiet for fear that the enemy would notice them. He had a distinctive way of raising his voice when asking about something which his weak eyesight prevented him from understanding. The sounds of clashes could still be heard in the mountains. Salvos rang out from several directions. The rhythm of artillery shelling began to die down, as though it were coming from a far off land. Abu Hassan dragged his heavy steps as he mulled over the dream he had awoken from as he had opened his eyes to say his dawn prayers.

"I am walking across the land of Palestine, guided by the morning star. I walk carrying the gun across my shoulder. Suddenly, a horseman appears on a blue mare, coming slowly towards me. A horseman as green as the spring is approaching. He asked me, do you want anything? I said to him: I want your well-being. He said, where are you going? I answered: I don't know."

❧❧

In the meantime, Khazneh separated from the rest of the medical team, which had waited in vain for the cars of the Red Cross. Instead, members of the Al-Barq organization had come in and asked them to surrender and leave via the Dekwaneh road, where safe conduct would be provided to everyone.

Khazneh bade farewell to the team, including Elias, hoping to meet up with him at the first aid centre on the western side of the city. Khazneh headed for her family's home with the intention of catching up with them and helping them to leave. In her pocket, she carried a bottle of valium pills to help calm down the children. She ran as fast as her heavy leg would permit, to link up with them before they left via this route or that. Khazneh thought that if they left with her, wearing her medical uniform, their safety would be assured, or so the doctor Ashraf Badran had told her. If she were able to find them, she would accompany them wearing her white nursing uniform, and no one would think of harming them. Khazneh tied her white nursing dress around her waist like a belt, careful not to put it on for fear of drawing attention to herself inside the camp. She would only put it on in Dekwaneh, so that it would not get dirty and look undignified to the enemies. She would keep it wrapped around her waist, then smooth it out and slip back into it over there. If she were lucky, she would find them ready to move immediately. The neighbourhood was empty, like many others. Ashes and black smoke wafted out through the holes in the collapsed or wrecked walls. Debris covered by more debris. She turned her face away from the bodies of the young men thrown in the middle of the street. Warm blood still flowed from some of the bodies. Sheep, not human beings. That is what was done to them by those who slaughtered them. Sheep, by God, sheep. She realized that she was talking to herself out loud like someone mourning, she who wanted nothing other than safety for her family. Her voice frightened her, and she swallowed it like one who had committed an unforgivable sin.

When she came to the basement of the building with the three wrecked floors, she found the dark curtain hanging across the open door. The curtain fabric flapped alone amongst the vapours and the fires, which had reached this neighbourhood after the nearby streets had fallen and the others deliberately torched. Her heart fell as low as her heels. It descended to the depths of the ground in astonishment and confusion as she saw the signs of their absence. She looked at the water covering the ottomans and furniture and failed to understand why. And how? Did they all die at once? Where are the neighbours, then? She did not think for long. She retraced her steps with the utmost speed to catch up with the medical team as it crossed, so that she would not be alone even in the absence of her family.

She carried herself and walked. Aisha had not known what carrying oneself had meant until that moment. A strange dream passes through her thoughts of resting her head against that stone on which the body of an unknown young man is lying. To put her head on his shoulder and fall into a deep sleep that she has never known before. To fall asleep and fly to the music of the flute, which has never left her memory since she heard it as a child. She wants not to smell this dark, polluted, dirty stench of thousands of putrid, rotten disintegrating corpses, their blood clotted, their purplish, blackish, brownish, bluish colours covered with dust. Oh God. You have done all this to us. Why, my Lord? I ask you, if you are still up there on high, why? The pain in her right wrist. She cradles her right wrist in her left hand, feeling as though someone were coming to slaughter her on the spot. "Aisha, Oh Aisha. We hardly had time to get to know you and love you," Hassan had told her. And I never had enough time to get to know you, either, and to know the colours of your hair and face before you went to the church. Um Hassan mutters "Woe is me. Ah. Huh, you Arab boys, huh." She has stopped drinking coffee in the morning. She has stopped looking at others and making sure that they are alright with her former morning tenderness. She no longer has anything to do with Aisha, as though she were not carrying her son's seed within her. But why? Why dear God? Just because of the child? Is it possible? Can one love someone else and take care of them just to increase one's progeny? "My God, you are my protection," says Um Hassan. She says, speaks. Is it possible? She walks now, the old man leaning on her, her figure upright and emaciated, her face deeply lined, her small eyes shining. She, Aisha, will give birth to a boy or a girl, but Um Hassan will have no say in anything to do with her from now on. She has ignored and neglected her, treating her like a silly cow. Yes. That was it. As though she were a stranger to the family, an intruder, as though she were. By God it's as though I were a beggar or a cripple. The thirst. I've never in my life been so thirsty. But I won't ask them for anything. I don't want any water. If I could put my head against some stone on the road and throw myself down and stay with those who've stayed. By God, I don't care about a thing. I don't miss anyone except Georgette. That small thing is growing inside my tummy and tingling and running like cold water through my intestines. It reminds me of the poor, miserable girl. What then? Meat they say. By God, I shall never eat any meat for the rest of my life.

She swore and continued swearing to herself that she would never taste that hateful bitter flavour, which reminded her of the smell that was making her intestines convulse with nausea, her insides churning up into her throat, as she fought not to throw up. On top of all the catastrophes, they would have to stop for me to vomit. "Ah, that's all we need," the crazy Amneh with the long tongue would say. She who gossiped and fabricated news and lying stories. She'll direct her resentment at me. Tomorrow we'll see, madam Amneh, whom you are wronging. The yellow desert of her nightmares returns. The yellow sulphur. No. But it is. No. It's the smoke from the burning of the wood and the concrete and the flesh of people. The burning of hair and nails and bones. Oh, the horror of the nausea jerking about within her insides. And the ugly vomit which she is resolutely pushing away so that the confused, lost procession which cannot find anyone to guide it along the correct road out of the camp will not have to stop. It turns and walks as though inside a maze. We crossed the Za'tar factory. A large ugly building full of halls. Tal Ezza'tar no longer smells of thyme. That green herb which heartens and opens the appetite. Oh! How she adores the smell of thyme now. If she arrives safely, she will eat thyme and smell it every day. Every day. Without olive oil. Just green thyme with sesame seeds mixed in. The dryness. Losing the feeling inside her mouth as though it were made of metallic fibres. The parched feeling. By God, thyme. Just a drop of water and a mouthful of thyme. Corpses with odours rising from them. Their faces towards the camp. Young men in their prime. We saw a pile of them. We saw them. We were frightened. People stopped. The old men with us said: "We either move forward, or we turn back."

At that moment, a Lebanese fighter wearing the badge of the Guardians of the Cedars came forward. He was carrying things he had gathered after breaking into a Palestinian shop. It seemed that our passing had interrupted him as he gathered them. He motioned the long procession to follow him. He took us. He led us through the lentil factory. We sank into the piles of lentils up to our knees. Lentils slipped over my feet soft and cool. The grains spread a gentle powder over the perspiring feet that had stepped through burning fires. The lentils. Pile upon pile. As we pass through the thick mounds, I stop crying and am cheered as I remember Ibtissam and Husam. Where are they, my God? Will my mother be able to take care of them and save them? Ibtissam and Husam and the piles of lentils that we drowned in, bathed in, sprinkled on our faces and hands, and wanted to use for ablutions on the suggestion of one of the boys, who swore that his father used it for ablutions before prayers when there was no water. My father! Assayed! Where is he now? Is he still bad-naturedly sticking to his street refusing to leave? He cried bitter tears when Hassan was martyred. He hugged me, put his arm around me and said, "Forgive me, my child. I hadn't intended it to be this way." If anyone said that war changes people, it has changed Assayed more than anyone else. He seems to have turned into a completely different man. Whoever is wearing slippers or shoes sinks into the lentils and comes out without them. They're all coming out barefoot. Even I. No. My sandals are buckled and won't move. I wish I could put some lentils in my pockets. Why? I don't know. Perhaps because I like this place. The cobwebs in the corners have grown, and are like arches above our heads. Goodness, they stick to the head of whoever passes them, making it seem as though one's hair has gone white. I've also gone white because they've stuck to my head. Oh green Saint George, where is the day that you have foreseen? Over there. A woman crying and asking, "Brother, have you seen my children?" One of them says to her, "We haven't seen them. God will punish you for your sin. You've lost five children, and now you're crying over them? No, I haven't seen anyone along the way." She left the procession and cried and wailed like a maniac. Georgette used to cry. Not a spoon of milk, not a drop. If only my tears would become milk so that I could give it to my son, she said. I never knew how she went out, left without telling anyone. Um Mazen had with her a pistol that had belonged to her martyred son. Amneh drew close to her and said, "Take care now aunt, they'll see it and give you a bad time." Um Mazen said: "That's something to remind me of my son's sweet memory and I don't want to

227

give it up. I've attached it to the waistband of my drawers, and no one will see it." But the domineering Amneh convinced her, saying, "But aunt, you still have children who are alive. What will happen to them if they find that pistol with you? It would be better for you to throw it away." Um Mazen said, "Where am I to throw it with that Guardians of the Cedars man walking in front of us and his friends ahead of him?" Amneh said: "A sewer is ahead of you. Throw it in while no one is looking." Um Mazen pulled the pistol out from between her legs and threw it into the large sewer we were walking next to after leaving the lentil factory. Near the hill of the General Command as we went towards Sallaf. I saw them. Shoulder to shoulder, carrying their arms. A long line of Phalangists or Ahrar or Guardians of the Cedars, by God, I can't say which. But the shivers. My hair stood on end. A line going up, and another coming down. All of them in military lines. My goodness. My word. Enough to frighten stones. We got to where they were. They took charge of us. I bear witness that there is no god but God and I bear witness that Muhammad is his slave and Prophet. They stopped us in the yard and said, "All the men should step out to one side. They separated the men and put them into cars and left. Someone by the name of Suleiman tried to hide amongst the old people and the women. He tried to escape. He was young, wearing a size nine to ten jumper. He ran and they ran after him. We heard bullets behind us. No one was able to turn round and look. Those walking next to him saw the blood streaming down his face and head. His mother was there, but she did not even dare to say, "That is my son." No one was allowed to turn round and look behind him or her without being killed. But the biggest catastrophe was that they started taking away little boys aged ten and above. They said it was because they had clean-shaven heads, which meant they were helping the *Fedayeen*. A woman stood defending her son. She begged them, saying: "He's a child, leave him." They said, "No, whoever has shaved off his hair is a *Feda'ee*." She replied, "Fear God! We used to shave off childrens' hair for fear of lice. For the sake of the Prophet, let him be." They said to her, "What prophet? Go to your prophet Arafat and let him bring back your son." And they pulled him, pulled him from her arms as he cried and screamed. She threw herself on him. They simply shot her. The man shooting her behaved as though he were shooting at a rock, not at a woman. Everyone secretly and silently said, "God have mercy on her and on her son." Nobody dared say a word. We're in front of the Al-Murr buildings, and the military cars swarm around us like ants. They put the young men they had captured into the cars and drove off. They left us alone, a long line of women and old people with a few children.

Abu Mazen was lost. He heard from people running past that his family had left via the cemetery road near Mukalles. He passed the tile factory at which he had once worked, though he could not remember it very well. He had worked at almost every factory in the area in his day. He had been around but when his children had grown up, he had stayed at home, taking care of things there. At the cemetery, he noticed many old ladies. A line of weak old ladies on their own, he remarked to himself. He did not realize that their children and young men had been taken prisoner. But what amazed him most as he passed the concrete headstones over the graves was a skeletal woman. The skeleton was that of a young woman with long dirty blonde hair hanging down her neck. The skeleton was bent over one of the graves in a posture of permanent mourning. "Could it be Georgette?" wondered Abu Mazen. As he left the cemetery, he was taken aback by the spectacle of some old ladies being held by a group of Phalangists. They looked so very strange, one of them eating soap as though it were a falafel sandwich, another swallowing black tea leaves spread out on her palms. And the men laughing and joking amongst themselves as they surveyed the scene before the muzzles of their guns with enjoyment. The tall old man could not help but intervene. He felt that this could cost him dearly, but he was not the kind of person who would withdraw once he had decided to do something. In his white head-dress and his brownish khaki trousers, he went up to the men wearing sleeveless white t-shirts and black ribbons around their foreheads, and he asked them to set the old women free. Between give and take, shouting by them and scolding by him, they discovered the identity of their elderly interlocutor as one of the women called out to him. One of the men said: "So! You're the father of Ali Samer?"

The old man had never in his life refused to take up a challenge, nor had he ever abandoned a fight. He spoke up. "I have that honour. Why only Ali? I have many like him. But my son Ali is the best known of them." He added hurriedly: "Stop mistreating those poor old ladies. Where are the rest of their families?"

But he was faced by silent stares, the shadows of their faces mingling with the headstones on the graves. He continued his conversation, ignoring the evil that was turning them into scarecrows of fire. His face turning into a handful of white flour, he asked them: "Are you members of the Phalangist group or the Ahrar group?"

And he remembered what he had heard about the atrocities committed by each of them.

The road-blocks that had been erected just past the Fawzi studio struck fear in Khazneh's heart. The first road-block, she passed through without being hindered. Hundreds, thousands of people, human beings who were no longer that, carrying bundles that contained nothing but scraps and remains, torn things that no one would need, the clothes of the dead and the things they had left behind, everything for which they had no need save that of convincing themselves that they were still human beings and that their exit was normal. She was perfectly sure that none of them had had the chance of choosing what he or she really needed. They had almost certainly carried those things, wrapped up in worn out cloth, to prove that they were not lost animals waiting to be slaughtered. By some miracle, a white cotton mass resembling a hairy balloon with an empty core crossed her field of vision. It was a dandelion, the devilish *Iblees* plant flying and passing amongst the shoving shoulders and surging bodies. Khazneh silently blessed the Prophet and marvelled at the wonders of creation. Even *Iblees*, the plant that bore the Devil's name, passed with dignity and majesty through the slimy blood-coloured light. Even *Iblees*. But humans, no! Khazneh wiped away the sweat pouring madly down her face. Even during the worst crises she had suffered even during her first battle at the Thabet Woods, not so much salty water had dripped from her body. She feels the intense thirst rubbing the lining of her mouth with bitterness. Where did she get all that liquid seeping out through her skin? It seemed that her skin had split up above holes that were filled with wounded wells, leaking sour water. Her body was absorbing the poisons in the air and secreting them back through the cracks in her face. Every drop dripping from her was the size of a grape from Um Jalal's vine, which had grown this year on the dew of bombs and the steam rising from the sea, and the poisonous vapour clouds floating over both sides of Beirut. Now she was crying, not tears, but sweat. A new idea invaded the cells of her confused head, giving an even stranger air to everything around her. She recalled her mother's words about how they had cried tears of blood as they had left their village in 1948. She said to herself that the people of Ezza'tar would cry tears of blood or bloody sweat for the rest of their lives if they managed to survive this massacre. She shivered despite her outward resolve as she noticed the fists of the children holding on to their mothers' clothes. Dream or reality? The haze of sweat-tears lifted from her eyes as she watched. She saw. She heard. She felt. She suffered pain because of the weight her feet carried. One of the guards called out to a twelve-year-old boy trying to hide behind his mother's dress at the checkpoint. Khazneh saw but could not believe what she was seeing with her own two eyes. "You, bald one, come here," and he pulled him away from his mother's arms. The mother said, "I beg you, he's my son. Leave him be, may God keep you for your parents." The armed man said, "Get away from here if you know what's good for you, otherwise I'll do to you what's been done to others. Leave the boy with us so that he doesn't grow up and become a trainee." And he pushed the boy towards a second armed man as the mother walked on without saying a single word for fear that they would pull away the other little ones holding on to her skirts. If only she had shouted or cried, Khazneh would not have experienced so much terror. A terror that resembled a bullet burning the brains, sucking out all that it had been accustomed to, all that had been stored in its cells before that moment. It bloodies the eyes, ruins them, weakens one with wounds, ensuring that no healing shall be granted even if one is visited by death a thousand times.

From then on, Khazneh saw nothing but blood. She passed the towering church which all the battles had not succeeded in destroying. She marvelled at the changed appearance of the building. It was neither destroyed, nor completely intact. Fallen, piled up stones, and high thick walls and people standing outside them in lines. Was her eyesight playing tricks on her when she saw the building moving towards her, crawling like a giant ship that had suddenly set sail from a mythical port. Medieval flags fly over it, and knights parade on its roof upon pure-blooded saddled horses, wearing cloths flowing down their flanks. They carry quivers filled with poison-tipped arrows, and helmets and shields and pommels and whips and shining iron swords. As for the church, it continues to crawl and stretch forward with a slow deliberate movement, while they take no notice. Khazneh rubbed her eyes so that she could verify the movement towards her of the building-ship that she was seeing. She looked more carefully and saw rows of young men lined up in front of the wall of the church. Now they were hitting them on their backs with hammers, the stone pestles used in stone mortars to grind wheat and mix it with raw meat for *kubbeh* dough. But the hammers! They were hitting them with those hammers which had been specially made to pound red meat for that traditional dish. They ordered the prisoners to kneel and poured petrol over them. It caught fire in a split second, and some of the prisoners fainted. They sprayed bullets on those who were kneeling, after placing iron bars in the fire and using them to burn crosses onto the bellies of those who remained standing. The smell of charred flesh filled the air. Burning flesh. They began tying up the prisoners with ropes to parade them on the eastern side of the city in trucks specially brought over for that purpose.

Khazneh drew closer, almost out of her mind. She did not care if any harm came to her. Her gaze roamed as she tried to identify the young men who had become helpless victims against the wall of the church. The church that floated on waves of blood which rippled over the earth. A white gown caught her sight. Over there. It was him. They were all there. The eight male nurses and the six female ones. They were all there. The man whom her heart recognized before she had seen any of the others was on fire. Elias Addoughani had been arrested for helping the Palestinians, despite the fact that he was Lebanese. Or else, why was he wearing a white gown and accompanying the nurses from their medical centre? Khazneh drew closer to help him, and she saw the blood pouring out of his body like thick foam as he convulsed on the ground. Only much later on did she realize that she and the doctor had been the only ones to survive the massacre. Before he reached the compulsory check point, a Phalangist fighter had sprung over to the Palestinian doctor, who had operated successfully on him in the early days of the conflict. He had told Doctor Badran that he would take him away from where they were. True to his word, he had pulled him into a corner and sent him off with some of his people to turn him over to the Arab Deterrent Forces, who took charge of his safety. Fifty metres away from the rest of the medical team, he had heard the bullets and their screams. He was so shocked, he felt that his mouth had twisted and his heart had stopped beating. He could not believe what had happened. And from where the Phalangist fighter had kept him before sending him off, he was able to see through a crack in the window shutter ten people he knew, as their bodies crumpled and fell over scores of other burning bodies.

Khazneh's feet sank into the mud, or something that was like mud, sticking like glue and pulling her down. She would have fallen had it not been for the tremendous effort that she made to prop up her body. She stood amidst the rolling human crush, her eyes instinctively searching the faces of those descending towards the gathering in the square. Her instinct drew her in one direction, and her panic in another. She could not make up her mind where to go, without anyone she knew or who knew her. Someone she could speak to, who could speak to her. An uncontrollable panic took hold of her amidst the confusion and clamour, which overcame any attempt at thinking or reason. Might she have gone mad, Khazneh asked herself, as she heard the name of her brother Hassan being called loudly above the crowds. She listened, and heard the voice calling out the same name, "Hassan Abdusattar Assamhadan," through megaphones. "Hassan Abd . . . Give yourself up." Possible? Was this possible? They were calling him, unaware that he had been martyred. Her grief at Hassan's death was doubled and she felt that he had been martyred all over again that day. They even showed no mercy towards the dead. She could no longer comprehend. No, no, impossible. Did they want to get him out of his grave? After? After they had killed Hassan, and the nurse Elias and the child they had taken from his mother because he was bald. She shed more bloody tears because she knew full well that the heads of children had been shaven to make sure they did not get lice, and that she had shaved some of them with her own two hands.

She was thin, which had changed her appearance from the days she had enjoyed strength and good health. No doubt the stale air, the tension, and living on the edge as news arrived in telegrams and coded messages, had destroyed all the joy that the young woman had stored up in her previous life. Or perhaps it was that in the last hour before they left the camp, she discovered that she would have preferred to have gone with the fighters by the mountain route. When she met her pale-faced mother, with the tears locked up in her middle-aged eyes, she felt no sense of belonging to her. This woman was not her mother, but some other woman whom she might have known and become familiar with during another time, but not now. A terrible feeling of pity for the anxious mother overcame her, and a pained sadness lashed her conscience for not leaving with her beloved fiancé. Now, she would have to suffer a long period of uncertainty and waiting until she was sure that he had survived. Her thoughts would remain an ember of glowing restlessness and grief until she would see him again. If only she had joined them. It was not right for someone like her to abandon her team at the very last minute. The memory of the siege returned to her, of being confined with them even when the electricity had been cut and they had lived by candle-light behind the lentil barricades which had not escaped the shrapnel. She was sad and regretful, but did not express her feelings to her mother. There was no point in mentioning that which could not be changed. She and her mother were valleys and valleys apart. How could her mother understand that her Hana's life had become completely severed from hers, and that she could no longer tie her daughter to the wheel of her previous life. Hana felt that the battles completely separated her from her earlier civilian life. She was only concerned about him, her lover, and her work with the signals machine. For the first time, she had taken off her jeans and checked yellow and olive shirt. She put on a pair of wide green trousers beneath a black skirt, like any other ordinary woman in the camp. She smeared soot from the kerosene cooker onto her forehead and cheeks, making herself look like one of the women who had come out from beneath the ruins. With twenty or more other women, she headed for Dekwaneh Square.

She passed through the first road-block with her mother with no problems. And the second. At the third, leading into the yard of the Hotel Training College, he stopped her. A masked man stretched out his hand and picked her out from amongst twenty women or more. She ignored him, rearranged the white scarf with which she had tied back her hair into a pony tail, and walked on. The bayonet of a gun barred her way, as the armed man addressed her: "Hana of the signals.

We've been after you for a long time. We've heard you and you've heard us, and we've taken a fancy to you. Come on with us."

He pulled her by the wrist behind the road-block where a Landrover car was parked. At first, the girl was so taken by surprise that she was unable to do anything. But when she found herself being pushed by the strength of a strange man into the military vehicle, as he demanded that she climb into it, she got hold of herself, dug her feet into the ground, raised her hand and slapped his face as hard as she could. She cursed him as she had never cursed before. She said all the rude words that modesty would have barred her from saying under ordinary circumstances. Words she had learned to say well during long months of exchanging them with these men. "So, you . . . you so-and-so and you son of a . . . Isn't all that you've done to us enough. Now you're here to . . . our honour."

Um Hana's mouth dropped open. She listened in disbelief, as though the girl speaking were a completely different girl to her daughter. She did not have time to see how a second armed man had come up behind her daughter and hit the back of her neck with the butt of his gun. She immediately fell motionless to the ground. The armed man picked her up and threw her to the floor of the Landrover. He and some of his friends, who had stood nearby, drove off with her to some unknown destination. The white scarf that had fallen from her head as she had resisted was all that was left of her. For several years to come, her mother would take it to fortune tellers as she searched for her daughter.

As Um Jalal entered the Hotel Training College in which people were being held, she wondered about one of the women who had worked with her at the medical centre. The woman only had one seventeen-year-old son. She had made him dress in girls' clothes, put a scarf over his hair and given him a bundle of clothes to carry. But the armed men at the last road-block had become suspicious when they had tried to molest him, mistaking him for a girl. Close scrutiny allows nothing to be concealed for long. They shot him and left his body in the open. Um Jalal with Assayed and Ibtissam and Husam managed to arrive at the large school without any significant hindrances. Assayed carried the injured girl on his back. His miserable appearance deflected the ill-omened obstacles which faced others. The Hotel Training College was a large building with small rooms. Dirty paper which the fighters had thrown about was strewn all over them. The place was drowning in piles of torn-up rubbish. The pages bore evidence of better times when the college had been a real school. What a surprise it was when Assayed ran into his friend, Khawajah Abu Nimr. Khawajah Yacoub stared at his old friend, who pounced on him and embraced him. As they stood together for a short while, they exchanged their traditional phrases of censure, and it seemed that they had only parted the day before. Each of them blamed the dastardly times that would not allow one to meet one's friends. But Khawajah Yacoub began to look left and right, saying, "Excuse me. I came to see my son, Nimr. He has left university and become a senior official."

He added, "Of course, I'll tell him to let you through. If you, who are my dear friend, don't get through, then who will?"

Then he added slyly, "But what news of Jalal, may God protect him? Does he still work with the Fedayeen?"

He did not wait for the answer. Instead he prepared to leave by rearranging his *culpac*, which he never took off even in summer. He said: "I'll come and have coffee with you tomorrow morning because I've heard that people must stay here overnight for some formalities. But never you mind, my dear friend. Abu Nimr will solve all your problems. Don't you worry about a thing. Don't be afraid, Sayyed. Have no fear. I'm the only one who knows you."

He left quickly, as though he were afraid of being discovered as he stood with the shabby, strange-looking Assayed. Assayed stopped to catch his breath, as though he had finally found his life's dream, and said to his wife: "What did I tell you? The friendship of a lifetime is worth the whole world. The Khawajah will now let us through. I always knew it in my heart."

He began talking to her with an excitement that surprised her after his period of prolonged silence following his son-in-law's death. Um Jalal wondered whether he was himself, or whether he had been overcome by mental confusion. The woman marvelled at the change in her husband. It seemed as though new blood was flowing through his veins. Um Jalal, who was looking for any ray of hope, like someone making a great effort to sew together a worn-out gown, became optimistic. She attributed it to one of the Prophet's sayings, "Be optimistic about good fortune and you shall find it." Maybe, just maybe. God might ease things, and she would complete her journey with her husband and children to the other side of the city. At dawn, she said the verse, "Have we not made your heart glad," several times as she watched the sun of the new morning rising and waited for the day to begin so that Khawajah Yacoub would save them from the abattoir of extermination into which they had fallen. The Phalangist forces were using the college as a centre for eliminating the young Palestinian men leaving with the rest of the people. Um Jalal and her husband and children had hidden behind a door until the morning for fear of attracting attention. She had struggled to stop hearing the moans and screams of the dying that filled the place. The two children fell asleep, and Assayed laid down his head in her lap for the first time in thirty years.

George returned to the camp with Mazen and his group. They went to the school building, which the shelling had not succeeded in destroying and was mostly intact, and they hid in the classrooms. It was the longest day in the lives of all those young men, who had to hide until darkness fell. The daylight hours were taken up by hand-to-hand fighting between the Phalangist forces, which were combing the camp from house to house, and fighters hiding behind the few doors and walls which had not yet collapsed.

As Mazen returned to the camp, pain swooped onto his conscience like a swarm of locusts. He remembered that he had not told his mother what had happened to him. No. That was not the problem. Not his mother, but his wife. He remembered that he had not told them about the decision taken by the command. Perhaps they would decide to stay and wait for him with the rest of the family until he arrived to assess the situation and the possibilities of leaving. It was not possible for him to leave the school to see them and check on them. It would have been better to visit them before he had gone up to the mountains the day before. Now he would not know whether they had been able to arrange things with the other women. He envied his single brother, Samer, but felt a keen yearning for his wife and two children. The youngest was only a few months old. The day passed in an ugly silence that floated amongst the men, squatting, sitting or standing behind the closed doors. Not a moan or a single sound. Through the cracks of the closed windows, the combing operations out on the street could be seen. Many armed men roaming amongst the houses, coming out of them carrying television sets, electric irons and small portable radios. Perhaps that was why they had not come near the school on the first day of the fall of the camp. There was no loot to speak of in an empty school. The sounds of intermittent individual clashes in other parts of the camp gave the attackers the impression that the neighbourhood was calm. They thought the silence indicated a total absence of people. It was the longest day of their lives – George, Mazen and the rest of the young men. Time was scarce, and wound tightly around their necks like a noose that had not yet been fully tightened. None of them could think of a single action they could successfully carry out. Simply staying alive was the greatest of achievements. They had to remain silent so they could listen to the footsteps of the enemy, and face them with their guns as they had agreed beforehand. They would not allow themselves the humiliating fate of war prisoners. Either climbing up into the mountains or death. Sunset was the answer to a cosmic mystery, which they awaited with all the yearning of their lives. Once it set, they would be able to move and slip away under the cover of darkness to find their way. But what Mazen did, in the evening of that hot summer day at the beginning of August, unsettled George and the rest of the group. He insisted on infiltrating back to his home before withdrawing. None of them could stop him. So they agreed with him that he would go to his street and return before nine so that they could complete their withdrawal. They wanted to make good use of time before midnight, and before their enemies began shooting flares to reveal the routes being taken by what were left of the Palestinian groups. Mazen jumped from roof to roof, and through one destroyed wall after another, and through broken window after broken window until he managed to get home. He found it empty. At the stone doorstep, he found the body of a woman whose throat had been cut, holding a baby to her bosom. She was the same age as his wife, and her figure and short hairstyle were the same. He covered his face with his hands and hid his eyes behind his fingers. She must be his wife. Who else could she be? He could not bear to go closer to her or to turn over her corpse. Death struck him with a fear of himself and his ugly selfishness. He had not thought of her throughout the previous day. He had not wondered about her as everyone had swung between life and death. He could have at least sent one of the young men to his house to tell his family what to do. But no, he had not cared except about himself and his group, which was now under siege. He turned around, disappointed and raging against himself, intending with all his might to find the necessary way out to escape the noose and save his group, whatever else had happened. The loss did not push him to despair so much as it prompted him to try and save what was left. The tragic death of his wife and child was nothing more than a drop in the ocean of his fear of himself. He had never known before that his selfishness would push his nearest and dearest to their deaths. He had turned his attention to the fate of the withdrawing groups of fighters before thinking even of his family. He and George and the other group leaders had been so preoccupied with making plans to split up the withdrawing groups and map out their routes. They had been busy searching for guides to lead those who were leaving into the nationalist areas. The only objective in Mazen's mind had been to improve the chances of success because he was convinced that the withdrawal could be organized. Since the first days of the battle, they had lost all their supporting positions, and they were only left with light arms, pistols, kalashnikovs, RPGs and hand grenades. They had fought with a very limited supply of ammunition and confronted the all-out attack, which they would have been able to hold back had their water supply not totally run out. Mazen recalled how he and members of the militia had gathered kerosene from the lanterns in people's homes to operate one of the water pumps at the medical centre. His heart ached over the martyrdom of his two brothers. The older one, Abu Afif, and the younger one who was less than twenty and had been killed in the building opposite their wrecked house after looking at a cupboard door and jokingly asking his friends to carry him on it to his grave. Now his own wife and child had been slaughtered too, before he had had enough time to tell her what to do. At that moment Mazen loathed himself, and his over zealous preoccupation with the battle. He hated his dedication to his professional duties at the expense of his humanity, and he hated his son who was still alive, because he knew this. The important thing was that he hated him, and that was all.

Khazneh loosened the nursing uniform tied around her waist and let it drop to the ground with a deliberately hidden and hasty movement, fearing that someone might notice.

The noon sun shone high in the sky, but Khawajah Yacoub had not shown up. Every second of waiting was consuming whatever remained of Assayed's life. Within hours the lines on his face deepened and his eyes sunk as though he were about to die. Um Jalal comforted herself by saying that the delay in the Khawajah's arrival did not mean that he had forgotten them or was pretending to forget them. Furthermore, Assayed was not wanted by them, because he was too old. What did they want with an old man? But at midday, two men less than thirty years old came. They spoke with the same accent that Khawajah Yacoub had. They asked for Assayed and found him. They led him to the gate and warned Um Jalal not to follow them. The woman froze in her place with panic. Husam followed them unnoticed. He saw what everyone else at the Hotel Training College heard. One bullet from behind. Then they picked the old man up threw him to the floor of a military jeep and drove off.

❀

They gathered many men and loaded them into trucks, leaving the women, old people and children. One of them noticed Samir, who was holding onto the hand of his grandmother, Um Hassan. They pointed at him. "That one is blond and has green eyes. How do the Palestinians have someone like that? Take him. It's a pity for the Palestinians to have someone like him."

Zeinab threw herself at her son to protect him. Um Hassan froze. "He's my son. Leave both of us alone. Fear God. It's enough that his father's dead. I'm Lebanese from Karkaba. Brother, have mercy and pity our state. By God, I'd kill myself if anything happened to my son."

The armed man said: "By God, if you had not been Lebanese, I would have killed all of your children. Go on, take your children and make yourself scarce."

In Dekwaneh, Khazneh saw a forty-year old woman, her head uncovered, carrying a bottle and hitting a fifty-year old man with it. She hit him on the head with the empty bottle, then borrowed a pistol from one of the fighters and shot the man dead. She swore that she would kill ten Palestinians in return for her son's death.

But Um Mazen, who kept silent as the armed men called out the name of Ali Samer, felt relieved that she had managed to throw away her children's identity cards in the sewer over which the procession had passed. It never occurred to her that they had managed to find her husband Abu Mazen, at the other end of the camp, and that at that very moment they were tying one of his legs to a jeep, and the other leg to a stationwagon and that they were pulling him along the ground as each car drove in an opposite direction. All this was taking place in front of hundreds of people standing in Dekwaneh Square.

Um Jalal carried her daughter on her back and bent as though she were a branch about to snap. She reached a truck belonging to the Arab Deterrent Forces. It was parked a few hundred metres away from the massacre. The Arab soldier spoke first. "So, you've come at last?"

Um Jalal replied bitterly. "Yes! We've come. We've come to you."

The old Abu Hassan cannot clearly see what is going on. He senses the disasters occurring around him from the screams of terror near him. There was nothing he could do. He continued to think about his dream: I found my family heading towards the Khadra's house. I went to the Khadra's house. I threw a stone into the chimney. My father came out. What have you done to me, Ahmad? All the cattle have been slaughtered. You've ruined me, Ahmad. From my father's house, I said to him: I stayed in the wilderness for three months. I came across a shepherd. I told him: I'm hungry. He milked a goat for me. I drank a cup of milk. My father comes on horseback and says: I'm going to give you up to the soldiers. I reply: By God, I won't give myself up. I'll shoot myself before I surrender. And so it continued. Then Turkey was defeated.

Before Mansourieh, the infiltrating group ran into Muhammad Sheha-deh's group. An hour earlier they had clashed with a Phalangist group. The two groups met, then each went a different way so that casualties would be minimal in case they faced an unpredicted hindrance as they withdrew. Mazen reconnoitred the road every fifty metres. He was lost in dark thoughts about the reason for the tragedy that had befallen his wife and child. He was carrying out his duties with more than usual efficiency, driven by a hitherto unknown terror: the fear of being captured. Death inside the camp was so much more simple, beautiful and wise. One either lived or died. But here in this frightening wilderness, it would be better to kill oneself than be taken prisoner. He looked back and saw George preoccupied and dazed, as though he were walking in a vacuum. Poor man. They were all like that. Myself and you and him and all of us. Which of us can tell whether he will meet his loved ones after today? Who can guarantee his own life for one minute to come? The sky seemed to him like a grey cave, clouded over with dampness and decaying air. He tried hard to push away images of his wife as she was dying, or the young child holding on to her arms. He tried long and hard, but did not succeed. So he surrendered to those images in an utterly mechanical way, and it seemed that his body moved in space while his spirit was imprisoned at the bottom of a very deep hole. The images continued to flash before his eyes as he sprinted ahead of the crowd, then reappeared to them to report his observations. They had moved as evening fell. George had dropped out of sight as he slowed down to oversee the withdrawal of the fighters at the rear. Such a measure had become necessary after one of the fighters whose feet had not enabled him to keep up, had been lost when they first started out.

The group headed for the valley. The path was rocky and strewn with brambles. They had to cross the valley below the small bridge. After half the procession had crossed the stream, shooting started coupled with yells of, "Surrender, surrender!" They heard many curses of the kind their ears had grown accustomed to along the front lines in the camp. The water was cold, and those whom the shooting had taken by surprise could not spend the night in it. They climbed out of the stream, each of them seeking his own retreat under the cover of darkness before the moon rose, and in spite of the very hazy starlight. When George came out of the coldness of the water, which seeped through to the bone, he found the group broken up and had to make his way on his own. He heard moaning nearby. He looked around and found a member of the group writhing on the ground. He had been severely injured, and his intestines had come out of his abdomen and poured out away from the torn khaki fabric of his pants. The injured man begged him, "Leave me. Go and get some first aid. Don't carry me with you. You won't be able to drag me along this rough path. It's best that one problem should not turn into two. I beg you, leave me."

Alone and inundated with feelings of defeat, George departed, leaving the wounded man by the bank of the small river in the hope of finding the group so that they could return and save him. He passed rocks and thick trees, his feet moving faster than usual. Maybe, just maybe. Maybe he would find them before it was too late, and they would be able to help the wounded man and treat him. He could not carry him on his own without a stretcher for fear that the exposed insides would be crushed. George saw death before him as a savage instinct in whose darkness a human being gets lost and is unable amidst its maze to help one's comrades. He kept on seeing corpses in the camp's alleys, blue flies swarming over them, gnawing at their sinews. Death! He had not known a thing about it before. Even during the darkest hours of the siege, things had seemed easy and clear. It was either "Life that pleases one's comrades or a death that angers one's enemies," according to Abdul Rahim Mahmoud, the Palestinian poet who had been martyred during the Battle of Ash-Shajara. God, oh God! His memory filled his soul with the scent of yearning for the West Bank. And for Toulkarem. The large green vineyard full of crystal-clear water that flowed like light through the orchard canals. He would have had to become a farmer had he stayed on. But education! The father and his insistent desire to see him educated, a "university graduate." And, go, Ahmad, to Cairo, no matter what sacrifices the family may need to make. The family was made up of girls, and getting their secondary school certificates was enough for them. Marriage was the fate of all girls. He got goosebumps. Why? He did not know. Perhaps it was because he had remembered his name for the first time in several centuries. Perhaps because he was recalling his origins in these moments of life and death. What had brought him here? What had made him choose a familiar name that one heard a thousand times without thinking of the identity of the person to whom it belonged? And now, the very sound of it pleased the ear, causing it to consider each letter one by one, so that it would not fall into the same trap sprung by sectarian names. Why had he chosen that name? So that he could enjoy having a name that convicted the person to whom it belonged before the charge had been proven? And what was the proof sufficient to protect the others who carried the same name against trial and indictment? Was it true that they were different to the Christians of the West Bank? "Strange. We come from there, where we don't know what the meaning of the word sectarianism is," he used to tell the pretty, tender, over-enthusiastic Hana. She had loved him in the way that silly girls do. All she had understood of love were the songs of Shadya and Abdul Halim. He had loved her too in her foolishness and naïveity, although his family had expected him to send word proposing to his cousin. A pang struck his conscience, rising from his very deepest of feelings. Why had he allowed her to leave alone? Why had he hurried away and left her on her own? He had run off to his group to try and ensure its safety. Hana, God alone knew what would happen to her. She had tried to give him the impression that she was as strong as a steel sword. But whoever said that strength would be right to tackle the problems he might face? Who could guarantee that her sharp tongue would not loosen up and provoke a row at the road-blocks, preventing people from departing? How could he tell? How could he know?

What would assure him of her safety? No. Nothing at all. He was totally unsure in this lonely wilderness, amongst the rocky outcrops which obstructed the path. The night crickets are excited. Bats surge curiously over his head. The faraway sounds indicate that there are clashes in other areas. The battle! Oh hell, when he had left her and gone to gather those who were departing, what had made him so sure that she would make it? And who but he should have taken care of her? But he had treated her as usual. The strong, domineering comrade who never got tired or gave up. He had been taken in by the illusion every-one had of her, although he knew better than others that her character was the result of being an only child. Her parents had allowed her the privilege of accepting or rejecting things to a much greater extent than others would have. Oh God, a bitterness caused by the hunger that was consuming him entered his mouth. In the past, he had only cared about the collective fate. In this enemy wilderness, he was surprised by strong impulses which he had not experienced before. For the first time, he saw himself as responsible for his own personal happiness, even before that, for his own individual survival. Before, there had been the country, the family, the extended family; then the organization, the establishment, the party. Everything, except for himself. It seemed that veils had all of a sudden been pushed away from his eyes, throwing him into a blinding light which he was not used to. He finds himself confronting the night, the breeze and the dry weeds rustling under his feet whenever he moves. He sees himself alone in the universe, as he was when his mother gave birth to him, in an even worse state. When he was born he had not been able to realize his cruel loneliness as he does now. He watches the moon apprehensively, wishing it would stop rising so that he can press on. From far off, new rustling draws closer. He takes cover within the groove of a large rock to watch from there, but sees no one. Hanging between the sky and the earth, sitting in the lap of the huge stone, George saw the flash of bullets coming towards him. He heard a voice calling others whom he did not know. He stuffed himself into the hole in the rock and held his breath, hiding his body from the wandering, fatal, speedy, fast killing bullets. The sound reaches him, and he can do nothing but listen to the shots ringing out, whizzing and whining in his ears. One of the bullets ricocheted off the rock and fell hotly onto his thigh. He was not wounded. Again. Here was fate playing with him, like a feather floating in turbulent air. He was not injured. But if he had been, would he have rotted in his place as had happened to Farid inside the church? Would he die instantly, or would he be a witness to the disintegration of his body before his very eyes? The confusion, the pitch darkness and the bullets flying about in the dark blue sky, hitting the body of the huge rock. Then the shots stopped, and the sounds coming towards him suddenly stopped.

Many families had gathered in the Annaf'ah Square. Frightened and silent, they cowered on the ground. It was a mechanical centre for testing cars, and it was being used to vet people before they boarded the trucks that would take them to the west side. Everyone cringed fearfully, drenched in the sweat of fear of a new call for one of them that would be his or her death warrant. The armed men roared curses as they carried paper napkins, which they spread amongst the squatting people, gathering their watches, rings and gold chains, and the money hidden between the breasts of women. One of them stopped in front of Zeinab, who was sitting on the ground with her children, who clung onto her. He pointed at her wedding ring. Zeinab's weak fingers pulled off the ring and gave it to him, tears flowing from her eyes. The armed man's superior, who was walking past, came up and asked him to return the ring. The armed man shouted with surprise: "But why, my dear comrade? By God they're not worth it."

His superior answered: "Enough scandal. Tomorrow they'll all go and tell everything they've seen to the media."

His warning was accompanied by a threatening look to which the armed man immediately gave in, and returned Zeinab's ring to her. He moved on to another part of the large playground to continue gathering his loot out of the sight of his superior. Um Mazen whispered to Zeinab, "What have we done in our lives so that they should be killing us just because we want to return to our country, child? What do they want with us? Why don't they free us? What are they holding us for?"

After hours of squatting in the sun while men and boys were picked out to be driven in trucks heading for the Phalangist centres, one of the armed men came and shouted at the people, bringing news of an end to their ordeal.

"First the children. They must gather and board alone. Then the women must gather and board the trucks. The old people will be last. Those who disobey will fall dead where they stand."

Outside in the glaring light and searing heat, the armed men were shouting: "Whoever refuses to curse Abu Ammar will not be allowed to board."

Mazen dicovered George's disappearance after the group had scattered. They walked slowly and heavily. The rising moon revealed their shadows, and the group had to slow down so that it would not be discovered once again. Mazen passed his hand over his shirt pocket. The piece of paper was still there. Hassan had left it with him at the beginning of the war. Hassan used to say that it was the paper of prophecies. Their two families did not speak to one another, but the organization had brought them together. It was a large national movement that encompassed all tendencies and ideologies. Their comrade George belonged to a leftist group, but he was a personal friend. The paper of prophecies! Hassan had made fun of his strange paper. He said: "Mazen, one day soon, you'll see. If they manage to get us out of Ezz'atar, the whole area will break up into small states and sectarian principalities like dwarf kingdoms. By God, here the future of the whole area will be decided. All the sacrifices and losses we are offering are not in vain."

It truly was a strange paper, showing a map of the Middle East that Hassan had primitively drawn and coloured, outlining the borders of the sectarian principalities he had imagined. Mazen put his hand in his breast pocket and touched it again, wondering to himself whether time would see Hassan's prediction coming true now that they had left. Mazen heard Nazmi as he tried to suppress his chronic cough, his chest rattling. The sound was closer to a sob, and Mazen whispered, "Take heart."

Nazmi replied, "Did you think I was crying! I wish my tears would flow, it would be better for me."

Khazneh entered the Hotel Training College. Her weakened feet drove her along with the crowds being propelled towards it. The armed men were pushing them, saying: "Walk to your deaths. Where do you keep springing up from? Where are all the shelters that had space for you?"

George pushed himself out of the hole in the rock after they had left, and he walked in the all-encompassing darkness after the moon had disappeared. The arches of his feet hurt him, and he felt the pain of muscle lacerations spreading through them. Since his childhood, his feet had been painful because they were flat. The heavy military boots caused more pain in his hardening muscles. By some miracle he dragged himself and walked in the opposite direction from which he had come, because this was his only guide as to how to proceed.

They were asking the woman whose husband they had got hold of during the final round of elimination before boarding the trucks, "How would you like your husband to die? Shall we shoot him, or slaughter him and let his blood flow?"

Aisha saw them and swallowed back the gasp into her chest. My husband! Where? No one had asked her about her husband. She looked shrunken and small like a secondary school student. But her chest was tight with depression, and she wished that he were leaving with the others through the mountains.

At the detention centre into which Khazneh had been forced, armed men asked the hundreds of camp residents who were there to go up to the third floor. Many people froze in their places, guessing at the motive behind the demand. But the machine gun rounds fired amongst them and over their heads made them run in every direction. The old men and women with no teeth ran as eagerly as the injured children with frightened looks who were with them. Khazneh saw herself running with them, jostling and hiding amongst them, others pushing her and trying to take cover behind her body just as she was trying to do with them. This was an extraordinary pastime for the armed men, who did not even bother to find out about the casualties they were causing as they amused themselves. Khazneh became dizzy and lost her bearing for the first time in her life because she had run and turned around with such unprecedented speed, then sheltered amongst the thronging bodies which secreted the metallic, sour sweat of fear. They made them go up and down three times. Then they ordered them to the trucks.

An armed man standing near the truck pointed at her. He tried to bend over and search her, and she said, "I haven't got any money."

He retorted, "Whoever hasn't got any doesn't board."

Khazneh pulled four-hundred liras out of her bra and gave them to him. As the armed man made way for her, he said, "You taught us courage and steadfastness, you dogs, so put up with it."

The light of dawn spread in rippling circles over the valleys and hills surrounding the mountainous precipice towards which George walked. His eyelids had known no sleep although he had lain down over a smooth rock to rest at dawn. He was crossing pine forests. Shooting still echoed in his ears after he had passed near areas that raged with clashes. The Phalangist groups wanted to kill any young men from the camp they could get their hands on. During the night, he had bumped into corpses that had gone rigid, stones hidden by the thick foliage and insects which whined in his ears and stung him. During the day, he had to find a hiding place big enough for him and his gun until evening fell and he could continue his journey. Inside the rock, the tender stone that concealed his presence from the enemy, he remembered her. He could not feel happy, secure or joyful without thinking of her, she who was never out of his mind. She who was crazy with anecdotes, jokes, laughter and curses. The daughter of the camp who thought herself to be the daughter of a city, just because she had worn jeans and run in the militia training grounds and mixed with fighters in the offices. The poor thing, the very thought of her made his heart sink whenever he wondered what might happen. His savage yearning for her seemed to reflect an unknown fate which his heart would not reveal. He wanted her, and did not want any harm to come to her. A dark cloud passed before his eyes. If only he had stayed with her, and she had stayed with him.

The sound, which resembled the whining of black flies as they swarmed over dead bodies, was still ringing in his ears. Evening. The suffering of the entire day accumulated in his body, exhausted by thirst and hunger. He found some weeds which he tasted, then spat out because of their bitterness. He tried to chew some pine needles, but was unable to because thirst had dried up the cells in his mouth and his tongue was swollen with little ulcers.

Cigarettes! A blessing in this life and in the life to come. So he had discovered as he walked alone without help or a companion. He walks through tangled thickets, beneath pines that shine with a black-green colour, amongst hard rocks, firmly wedged in their places since the beginning of the world. In the wilderness, amongst the crickets and their monotonous chirruping, and the shadows of the fierce eagles high above. He walks without a compass or map, trying to follow the signals mapped out by his instinct. He notices some burning grass on the side of the opposite mountain, and realizes that he is still in enemy-controlled territory because the shelling is coming from the West side. He walks, although his legs are too weak. Hunger gnaws his stomach and insides with a thousand teeth. Foam covers his tongue like someone panting hoarsely. There is no chance of a bite to eat in this wilderness, nor a drink of water, nor a smoke of tobacco. No. Nothing but death which mocks him. Would it not have been better for him to have died there contented and happy, closing his eyes amongst people he knew, who cared for him, instead of being prey like this to earth and heaven and everything in between them?

On the ground at the Annaf'ah Square, Um Mazen was supervising her daughters-in-law and their children as they boarded the trucks. One of her sons was a fighter in the south, and he had brought his wife to live near her and had been unable to get to them during the siege. The oldest and youngest were martyrs. As for Mazen and Ali Samer, her heart told her that they had managed to survive. The two others were fighters in the northern camps of Al-Baddawi and Nahr El-Barid. She would no doubt manage to find shelter for the large family she had brought with her. She looked at Mazen's wife and two children, and her heart sank. What if she were wrong, if her daughter-in-law had become a widow and the burden of providing for another widow in the family were to fall to her? No, her heart told her that nothing had happened to her son. Her daughter-in-law was behaving with unusual calmness. She thought: "Mazen's wife is careless and pampered, but now she has turned into someone whose dignity, balance and sense of responsibility are exemplary." She would tell him this, no doubt, so that he would be pleased when he came through the blockade and met up with her on the western side.

Another group of armed men for the Ahrar group arrived, cocked their guns at them, and said: "Say: Long live Chamoun."

A Phalangist fighter jumped up and yelled at those boarding the truck: "You won't be allowed to board if you don't say: Long live Pierre Jemayyel."

"Come and kiss my boots."

Then he fired new salvos amongst the legs of the women and children standing near the back of the truck.

Inside a deep ditch, Mazen and his group hid, waiting for the end of the day. They were at the entrance of an enemy village in the mountains. Nazmi, the Maronite from Haifa, crouched near him. He had lived in the Jisr El-Basha camp since his childhood. "If my mother were to see me hiding in this ditch, she would curse the hour that allowed her to give birth to me," Nazmi whispered. Mazen nodded and continued to draw geometric forms on the earth with a piece of straw. "Long live the Arab nation," he replied.

George found himself at the beginning of the unpaved road. He chose a winding footpath, and stretched his heavy steps across the ground once more. It was a lonely night, only interrupted by the faraway bleating of sheep and their bells, which echoed across the hills as they returned to their pens in the evening. He could not go near any of those inhabited places to ask for help or a drink of water. His face was covered with a chalky dust, and anyone who might have seen him would have taken him for a ghost. He thought of using a trick. He would suddenly jump over a farm's fence and make strange noises so that he could snatch some food while the inhabitants were startled into paralysis. But he decided that hunger must be making him rave unreasonably. The farm dogs and the guns of their masters lay in waiting for the wanderers who had left the camp. He picked up a few broad, smooth stones and placed them over his stomach between his body and his shirt. Their pressure eased the strong contractions of his insides.

Hunger . . . and thirst . . . How wonderful those lentils had tasted, said Mazen to his comrade Nazmi. Then he fell silent. Small insects which stung heavily squirmed continually beneath their clothes. They remained there for sixteen hours, unable to move in their places. They had hidden inside a mountain crack surrounded by prickly cedars and wild olive trees. The rock gnawed away at their bodies, the protrusions dug into their sides, and numbness overcame them because there was no space to turn or change their positions inside the rocky holes that offered them shelter. Mazen touched the piece of paper with the faded colours, sticky with perspiration in his breast pocket. He sighed, and choked back a moan. Nazmi stared at his bearded superior, with his big nose and small eyes, and wondered how he could reassure himself about his well-being. Since the beginning of the journey, Mazen was like a blind man lurching in all directions. It seemed that the smells of the corpses everywhere had caused him to lose his bearing, and he seemed lost and without any strength. When they came out of the rocky crack that had sheltered them, blood trickled down Mazen's shoulder and leg because the rocks had scratched him. It seemed as though the man who had broken through the siege while it had been at its height to get to the camp had become a wreck of a man, without the slightest connection to life. He stared raptly at unseen shadows, his invisible losses which meant he would never resume life as he had known it. Everything that had happened; the martyrdom of most of his friends, Hassan and others, then George of whom he knew nothing since he had dropped out of sight, and first and foremost the death of his wife and child due to his own negligence. He pressed on, propelled by a mechanical force drawn from the group's movement. If they were to leave him, or if he were to get separated from them, he would not find it in him to continue walking, even a few more steps. They had now reached the beginning of the next mountain range. They were surrounded by thick trees. Suddenly something shone in their eyes. A huge, tremulous, silvery-green flowing body. A churning noise rose from it. Something buried deep within their forgotten memories compelled them towards it. Right there. Without words or questions. But! One of them murmered something about the exposed position they were in, vulnerable to snipers from this side, from which they had nearly escaped now. They all turned back, trying to make their way to the river, although whoever sought it might be asking for death before reaching it. They kept looking behind them as they walked, until they found a hillside covered with trees. They came down it, unable to believe their eyes. Now, the water. They had reached the water at last. For sixty days, their bodies had not seen or touched water, or been blessed by its grace. Oh, how the tiredness broke down within their bodies, melting away into the wonderfully cold, divine stream without which no person could have come into being. The men waded in with all the aches and wounds they had been trying to ignore, and they splashed water and more water at each other until their limbs almost went numb and froze.

Mazen did not remember that the paper had become wet until he came out of the water, and with his comrades threw himself down on the warm ground so that their bodies and clothes would dry. He left it where it was instead of pulling it out, in case it came apart in his fingers and he would be unable to put it back together. Water! A man might be hounded to death, but not before being immersed in such grace. Blessed was life and all its rivers. If he were to close his eyes for ever after today, he would not grieve or regret a thing.

༄༅༅

Amidst the clamour and shouting, the families, or those of them whose members had found one another, fidgetted nervously. Zeinab stood behind the truck which people surged towards as though it were doomsday. She was carrying her children so they could climb into the truck amidst the infinite chaos, the blows, the pulling and pushing and colliding. Samira boarded holding the hand of her sister, Nisreen. Samir climbed into the back of the huge truck, and his mother handed him the four-year old Abir. As Zeinab was about to climb in, surrounded by the wailing and moaning of children and the calls of their mothers, hands stretched out and pulled down the bars, closing the back of the truck and preventing anyone else from boarding. Zeinab ran to the driver sitting in the front cabin, and panted, "Brother, for God's sake. Open it. I must go with my children."

The round-faced driver, dripping with coldness and lack of concern, answered: "That's it. There's no more room. Board another truck and meet us at the museum."

The museum! The end of the dividing line between the East and West sides. A sharp knife cut the vocal chords. The museum! My God! Zeinab ran to the next truck to hurry and meet them there. Stories spread that the trucks being filled with people were paraded through the other side of the city, where crowds spat at them and threw garbage and dirt. Was there any guarantee that the truck that had just left with the children on board had not gone over there? Slapping her own cheeks, Amneh urged Zeinab, "Hurry up, get in, you miserable thing. Let's see if they get to the museum or they're taken to Ashrafieh!"

When he tripped over in that barren field, over which the morning star had risen, he became aware of dark lumps on the ground. He stretched out his trembling palm and touched them. He found a thick hairy trunk winding like a snake. He felt along it to its tip to find out if it carried anything edible. His fingers found green leaves with fingers like a palm. It was a vine that carried bunches of grapes. George sat cross-legged in the large field, wolfing down one bunch after another. He began to see the rays of sun that had ripened the grapes and filled them with honey-tasting juice. The watery drops shone on his lips, quenching the burning thirst which had almost consumed him. The night was no more. He was able to deal with the darkness after the razor blades cutting up his insides had disappeared. The golden taste poured into his cells, carrying with it the glow of desires which had gone out when he was a lone wolf in the wilderness. If he remained alive, he would see things with a new perspective, in a new way.

He who had given up everything personal. No, next time, he would not allow Hana to leave him, to depart with her mother out of a sense of duty. He would keep her always by his side and not give her the chance to drift away and become preoccupied with other things. His appetite for love awakened with the sugary grape drops as never before. What a cold lover he had been! What a miserable, careless love it was that had lived within him! He wonders how he spent the previous years, driven by the idea of changing human life in its entirety, without doing anything to change his own life. Since the defeat of 1967, he had left university and joined the Resistance to atone for a defeat for which he had not been responsible. To pay the price for the degeneration of the regimes that had deprived him and his people of defending their country, so that the remainder of it had fallen in a farcical war in which not one shot had been fired. He and thousands of other young men, who had rebelled against the entire establishment, and disturbed the peace of their lives to join the armed resistance that would establish the dream state. My God! Where was the dream now! We were driven out of the West Bank, thrown out into Jordan. We left Jordan humbled and humiliated after the forest battles and went to Lebanon. Now, here we are in Lebanon, leaving the Tal Ezz'atar camp. Where to? I don't know. Will this great Arab World in its length and breadth have room for us? Will it accept us with our burden? Or will it always throw us out whenever we hold on to an ember of hope?

Hope! How can we know it and where will we find it with all of these losses within us, burning us from the skin to the eyeballs. George straightened up as he noticed the opposite mountainside and the stream shining below it. No. The river. It was the river again. His mother must have given birth to him on the night the Quran was revealed for him to have been able to reach this spot, the dividing line between the two sides. There must have been many colleagues and loved ones who had not been helped to safety by the very same circumstances. If he were able to heighten his senses and concentrate his attention very accurately, perhaps he could avoid the traps waiting to catch those coming out of the stream. From now on, he would always associate water with his memories of danger. As at the front line of Ali Samer, Mazen's brother, who had withdrawn with other groups via the mountain route. And Mazen? Where was he? No. He would think about all of them when he had arrived. He would think of those of them who were alive and those who were dead the moment he had crossed the line of safety onto the other bank. The image of his friend Hassan flashed before him, and his heart froze. For the first time, he felt that he was bidding farewell to the dearest friend in his life, which had been spent in wars and clashes. The girl appeared like a fleeting flash of lightning. Aisha. He would have to ask after her at her mother-in-law's, Um Hassan. In his thoughts, he remembered all of them and he saw Hana. He had not stopped seeing her all the way. He had seen her in every stone, pebble and passing cloud. He had spoken to her a lot, promising to teach her the meaning of life. Life was not merely victories and small pranks. Not something which made you joke or curse or gossip. Life is finding a drop of sugar allowing you to live with a lover or friend. Only then could hope be fulfilled. The collective dream was certainly not enough for life. He had to love her well, pay attention to her problems and help her more clearly than before. It was not enough to accept her jokes about being an "idiot" or the daughter of a kidnapped person. He would sense her feelings carefully, thank her for the gift of love she had given him, and protect her more closely than his own eyes. He was sure he would find her somehow. She was intelligent and capable and would manage to overcome any obstacles to come and meet him. He had been created to make her happy. Who else but him could understand her? Who else but him could speak to her and understand her feelings?

When he arrived at the edge of the bluff that ran parallel to the river, he saw a group of armed men on the other side, waiting for those who were arriving, beneath an olive tree to which they had tied a mule. They had not seen him yet. They might point their guns at him rather than welcome him. He must think of how to acquaint himself with them. But he! Arrived. When he threw himself into the ice-cold water, he wept aloud as he turned towards the camp. He had not had a home or a family there. But it felt as though he were leaving his family home, the home of his father and mother, and the West Bank where he had been raised. Images danced before his eyes, and he saw everyone he had known in one flash. They all passed, heavy and light through his tears. He sobbed as he swam towards the opposite bank, thinking of the one fighter who was still firing at the invaders with his Doshka cannon on the Al-Meer hill to cover the withdrawal of his comrades. But his hot tears quickly melted in the roaring, pouring water, which his body crossed with great strength. It could not have been good health, but the strength of holding on to life.

When Um Hassan arrived at the Museum gate, she climbed down from the truck, which was almost keeling over because it was so crowded. The shouting of those on board mingled with the crying of children and the wailing of women. She supported the old man, whose body had become so fragile and light that it shook like a feather. She turned around and gestured with her hand, chanting. "Oh. Oh, I leave you behind, Yamma, but I promise to come back and meet you. I'm going now! Yamma, may the angels guard your sleep, Hassan. Don't be upset, my son. I shall take you to the Martyrs' Soil like your brother, Fayez. We are destined to meet again, Yamma. Wait for me, and do not let your sleep be disturbed."

Abu Hassan understood what his wife meant as she addressed her son. He knew that she would never rest until she had moved him to the Martyr's Soil on the West side. His tears flowed over his white beard. He said quietly, "Come, come."

Um Mazen was driving a column of women, who walked behind her. She was scolding her daughter-in-law, Mazen's wife, for falling behind so that she could search for her mother and father. She said to her, "Come on now, walk on, my child. Let's get out of here before they remember us and take us back there all over again. Help me, my dear. No one has been through what we have! Look at me, I haven't been able to search for your uncle, Abu Mazen, either, because I'm worried that they'll see us and remember us if we waste time. Walk on, my dear, walk. You'll find them in the end."

14

⚜

At the gate which divided the city, Aisha turns round hoping to find some of her family. She misses them for the first time in her life. Dryness tears at her insides. Clouds of dust and sweat cover her face, and searing rods of heat burn her nostrils. She stands amongst the people, but does not see them. She sees torn fragments of the remains of crowds of humans who had once been normal people, but were no longer so. And she, as well, like them. Loud voices mingle with anguished cries and screams of grief and loss. Doomsday? The wailing, weeping, moaning, sobbing, screams, sighs and tears. They were not real tears, but bits of mud mixed with salts. Intermittent wailing. Continuous crying. Lost children. Dazed women passing by with expressions of tragedy and ruin. Blood flowing or clotting over open wounds, or others which have been badly bandaged. Everyone fleeing like prey. Everyone? No. Only the women. The only men left were a few old men. The only boys left are a few children. Out of each family, only half or less is left.

Aisha stood as waves of people crashed around her. It was like the day of judgment. Palestine came into her thoughts. Is this happening to us because we want to return to Palestine, as Um Hassan said? No. Aisha remembered the golden pictures which she had drawn in the shadows of her maddening loneliness after Hassan's death and Georgette's disappearance. She mulled over all that had happened and spoke to herself, saying that it had all happened because they were no longer in her mother's town or her father's city. If death were death, why had her parents not accepted dying there, and why had they not committed suicide where they were? Why had they been driven by their fear to what they had imagined would be life outside? Why had they not known that they would face what they were facing now, at the end of the bitter, wearying journey. They had destroyed their lives to build the lives of their children. And now it had caught up with them! If they had possessed an ounce of wisdom, they would have realized that everything they had striven for was an illusion, and that it would have been better to remain there, living or dying, and at least not giving birth to the likes of herself, or Hassan or Khazneh. She imagines Khazneh as she had last seen her a month before on her last visit home. Something twinged in her heart. She must be dead by now. She had heard that most of those working at the medical centre had been killed at the church road-block, and Khazneh must have been amongst them, because she would not have agreed to be separated from the team to which she belonged. Poor Khazneh; she had been unlucky in life and in death. No, all of us. Every one of us also. Who amongst us has had a proper life to merit death? Georgette? Hassan? Or George? My God. He also, if he had not perished with them. He had become a stranger to her, as though he had never existed. She, the naïve one, who had one day thought it possible. Also. But where was Um Jalal? The boy? The injured Ibtissam, and Husam! She felt as though she had been teetering over the brink of an abyss without realizing it, and was just beginning to wake up to it. If they were to disappear . . . and not show up as she surveyed the crowds around her, what would happen to her then? She closed her eyes to a new despair. No, she only needed them because she loved them. She would not need them after today because she would look for a job, any job. It was merely the yearning that she had never felt all of her life, assailing her now, planting fears and suspicions in her heart. She looks at the clear deep blue sky. Not a single cloud. She looks at the rows of trees along the road running from the East side to the

West side. They seem extremely elegant and luxurious, in contrast with the waves of crying, wailing people beneath them. She looks at the other side of the city, but does not notice any change that indicates that something unusual has happened. A normal gas station taking in cars and filling up their tanks. The numbers of juice and cake vendors are increasing as they come from the West side, as though there were some feast or celebration. The sound of crying is all around her like a covey of departing birds in the sky. But there is no one to see, hear, feel and shout, or tear their clothes in grief over what has happened to them. Just the newspaper photographers and those carrying open notebooks and tape recorders. All that death, and they pounce on those coming out as though they were booty from outer space to get a picture that will embellish their newspapers. Aisha heard women rising out of their grief, forgetting it for a few moments, and cursing the journalists and those in power with all their might, using obscenities. Aisha studied the faces of those arriving closely looking for her family, or some of them. Husam might come first, racing ahead in his usual way. Or the tired Assayed might appear, dragging the rest of them behind him. Carrying Ibtissam, who could not walk, must have exhausted him, causing him to totter with the old age that had so quickly overtaken him and destroyed what remained of his strength and health. Assayed had turned into a tired old man, had even lost most of his front teeth. But those who had known him in the days when he had been healthy and strong were not surprised. He was a father in any case, although her emotions had not acknowledged this until she had seen how grieved he had been over Hassan's death. And she? What was left to her?

Rancid smells were still rising from the piles of corpses she had passed on the road behind her. The stifling heat filled the bodies with a thick, damp rot. The small lump turned inside her. No more than a piece of flesh, it would become a human being who had experienced what happened without seeing it . . . She owned nothing any more, except for what was within her. A longing for all those she had known assailed her. All of that had been her life. She would never again drink morning coffee with Um Hassan. And Hassan would never again stroke her growing hair, and she would never again see Georgette, whose return she had never given up on. She would never again wear the pink dress alone in her room to avoid Amneh's butts about dressing like a little girl after being a bride. She looked around with a new anxiety. She pushed her hand into the pocket of her skirt and brought out the hard, sharp shining glass, rubbing it against her cheek and wiping her skin with it. It was the small mirror she had pulled out from the pile of rubbish on her trip with Husam and Ibtissam to the church and the forgotten factories. She still remembered its flashing light as it suddenly shone beside her. She surveyed the most important events of her life. The journey and discovery, even if it had been accompanied by exploding shells and the sounds of battle. The shelter meant nothing more to her than Georgette's friendship. The battles, the shells, the wars, the fortifications, the sandbags and continued tragedies only meant loss to her. The only thing that worried her now was understanding why all that had happened. Why are we here? Why death? Why don't we live normally like other people? Why won't they leave us alone? Why did they kick us out of our country and become angry when we work to return to it, then refuse to accept us where we are! Where, then, shall we go? There, in the middle of the road that divided the city into two parts, Aisha recalled what Um Hassan had told her about their country. Vast fields full of golden wheat and green olives. Pastures as far as the eye could see. And women singing and chanting at the weddings which the girls awaited eagerly because they were held in special places that had captured their imaginations. Not one of them had known homelessness or eviction or the killing of loved ones and children. Their concerns focused on good produce and rain falling and wetting the earth. In the evenings, they would sit in the doorways holding embroidery needles and coloured threads. A golden moon would rise behind them to see the patterns they had embroidered on their fabrics and it would smile. Aisha forced her heavy breath out of her chest. The heat! And the smell of rotten bodies and blood. Living human beings could not possibly turn into such a bitter, murderous smell. Impossible! Was this possible, to quote Um Hassan, who had already gone ahead of her to the other side of the city. She recollected what the old lady had said to her, "My child, we shall all become strong women. Have they left us any other choice? They take everything from us. Marriage, children, homes, stories, old people . . . everything. So, all of the time, we defend ourselves as though we were not women, but standing in the trenches."

Zeinab waited with Amneh for the truck that was carrying her children. They had left before her, but almost an hour later, they had still not arrived at the museum gate. She was jumping up and down, the blood almost exploding in her veins. Where had they gone, and why had they not yet shown up? She closed off her senses from the outside world and tried to follow Amneh's advice and remain courageous. Amneh stood beside her rubbing her hands so hard that they almost bled. They would arrive, they would . . . without any doubt. They would, said Amneh, whose face had become long and lost its skin's lustre through weight-loss. She was the closest member of her husband's family. Now, no one was closer to her than her fatherless children. The siege had destroyed her confidence in everyone around her except for herself. She did not want help from anyone, or tenderness, or domination. And then! The vehicle the children had boarded arrived. Zeinab recognized it by the careless round face of the driver. The truck stopped and the shrieking that accompanied those climbing down from it began. The children came down one by one, except for Abir. First Samir, holding the hand of Nisreen. Then Samira. All the children were crying. Abir had disappeared amongst the feet as the truck had stopped at one of the enemy checkpoints on the way. There had been tremendous over-crowding on the truck, and when it had stopped to be searched, some of the young men who had managed to slip on board would duck down and hide amongst people's feet. Abir had fallen to the floor amongst the feet, and no one had been able to save her for fear that the whole thing would be uncovered, causing the armed men to take revenge on everyone in the truck. Zeinab climbed over the edge of the truck, which seemed more like a vehicle used for transporting cattle, and she let out a long scream.

"Our dear one is gone," she cried as she tugged her children to her. Their faces were blotched with blue bruises that stood out beneath the tears on their faces. She trembled as she searched for her mother-in-law to share the catastrophe with. Amneh gathered the children, and walked quickly away with them. The pretty Abir lay on her mother's arms, her head hanging down like a chick's. Her face bore purple bruises and her skin was tinged with blue. A thick thread of yellowish saliva hung on her lips. The mother walked towards the Barbir hospital, which stood between the two sides, in disbelief saying: "My beautiful daughter. I shall always carry her smell with me. How shall I bring her back, now that she has gone to join her father?"

༄

On the line dividing the two cities, where a huge building called the museum crouches, Aisha stood like a small insect at its gate awaiting the arrival of her family, or whoever was left of it. The building rose imposingly and imaginatively with its Roman, perhaps even Phoenician, columns, as she could recall from the names she had studied at school. She stared at the hard stone and spoke to herself: Why do they do this to us? If it is because they are yearning for Roman glories, are we the Christians to be savaged by lions in the arena? Have we returned to Phoenician times that they should be killing us like this? Those days ended thousands of years ago. Why are they annihilating and killing us?

What have we done to them? The question rang out before her like the buzzing of a giant fly that was bothering her and trying to sting. Suddenly, Aisha raised her head and noticed they were drawing near and speaking to her. Um Jalal came up panting, with Ibtissam hanging onto her back. Husam jumped around her. Aisha did not ask them about her father. She was too apprehensive to ask. She waited for them to tell her. Um Jalal said, as she put Ibtissam's arm on her shoulder and fixed the other arm on Aisha's shoulder: "Khawajah Yacoub, may God strike him down, is the one who finished off your father. How many times did I tell him: Sayyed avoid evil, and don't tell him you're here. But he wouldn't listen to me. He said Abu Nimr was his lifelong friend!"

Aisha was surprised by the matter-of-fact tone in which her mother was relating the circumstances of the death, but thought it must be because of the overwhelming grief that had engulfed everyone.

They walked. Husam began to chatter to his sister about what he had seen on the way. He told her about the Phalangist woman who was dressed in black and carried a big stone. She had tried to throw it at him, but he had run too fast for it to hit him. She had shouted at him: "You killed my son, you bastards, you boys of Ezz'atar. Die like our children."

The noise which filled Aisha's head suddenly turned to a terrible silence that hovered above the world she was leaving behind. Despite the wails of the victims and the women, everything around her entered a horrible, ominous silence. Um Jalal shattered the daze that was consuming Aisha. She stopped, tilted her head backwards and tried to tear the fabric of her dress from her breast with the hand which she was not using to carry Ibtissam. Her voice was loud, hoarse and stretched out like an ululation: "Stop, I want to open my clothes and bare my breast to God and call for revenge.

'In the name of God and the glory of all the prophets

Do not bless them because of what they have done to us

I, the obedient servant who entered their homes and worked for them.

My God, you are my honour, do not forget injustice.' "

Then she took her hand from her bosom, as though she had changed her mind. Aisha said with embarrassment, "Yamma, the day will come. Let's go now."

Um Jalal was relieved as though she were sure that her words had arrived at the gates of heaven and been recorded there. She continued like someone suddenly remembering something: "I hid a piece of lentil dough in my bosom so that Jalal would see it and know how we lived."

The silence of a vast desert spread around their heavy steps and tired breaths. All that had taken place was happening, and no one asked after them or received them. A gas station, a few trucks and soldiers from the Arab Deterrent Forces; that was all that greeted Aisha's eyes at the beginning of the other side of the city. She became aware of her free hand pressing a hard object with a pointed edge inside her pocket. Aisha pulled out her free hand, which was not supporting her sister, and a red thread of blood trickled down her finger. It flowed and spread out. The wound had been caused by the small mirror, which she would never part with from now on.

✿

The four of them walked, this time.

Um Jalal did not have a chance to ask why she had found her daughter standing alone by the roadside until after they had checked

Ibtissam into the temporary hospital which had been set up at the Arab University of Beirut. Then she turned to her daughter Aisha and asked, "Yamma, where are your in-laws?"

To her great amazement, the girl answered: "Yamma, I've come back to live with you. I asked permission from my aunt Um Hassan to stay with you."

Um Jalal was dumbfounded. She was completely taken by surprise at her daughter's decision to forgo her link with her husband's family. The man? But! And she stared at Aisha's emaciated abdomen.

Aisha answered with firm determination, "You mean, because of the child. That's still a long way off. And then I'll visit them every day and spend the night . . . but I want to live with you."

She continued, now that something had destroyed her customary silence. "If it's for the sake of the child, don't worry Um Jalal. Once the child is here, we'll take care of it."

Her hand touched her belly in a movement of spontaneous recognition. Staring at her mother with an unaccustomed boldness, she said: "That is my responsibility . . . I don't want anyone else to take it instead of me."

Liana Badr
✿

Palestinian novelist and film-maker Liana Badr was born in Jerusalem and was forced to leave Palestine in 1967 after the Six-Day War. Since then she has lived in Lebanon, Damascus, Tunis and Jordan, and returned to Palestine in 1994 after the Oslo Agreement. She is married and currently lives in Ramallah. Her works have been translated into a number of languages, and mainly focus on themes of women and war, and exile.

Fadia Faqir
✿

Fadia Faqir was born in Jordan in 1956. She gained her BA in English Literature, MA in creative writing, and doctorate in critical and creative writing at Jordan University, Lancaster University and East Anglia University respectively. Her first novel, *Nisanit*, was published by Penguin in 1988 and her second novel, *Pillars of Salt*, by Quartet Books in 1996.

Samira Kawar
✿

Samira Kawar is a Jerusalem-born Palestinian who grew up in Amman, Jordan. She read English Literature at the University of Jordan before becoming a journalist. Basing herself in Amman, she worked as a newspaper and news agency correspondent, then took up radio and television journalism, covering Jordan, Syria, Lebanon, Iraq and the Gulf. In 1988, she moved to London, working as a television journalist and literary translator.